Also by BB Easton

Sex/Life: 44 Chapters About 4 Men (A Memoir)

The Sex/Life Novels

Speed

Star

Suit

BB Easton

FOREVER

NEW YORK   BOSTON

Copyright © 2016 by BB Easton
Cover images © Shutterstock. Cover copyright © 2021 by Hachette Book Group, Inc.

Forever
Hachette Book Group
1290 Avenue of the Americas, New York, NY 10104
read-forever.com
twitter.com/readforeverpub

First trade paperback edition: July 2021

Forever is an imprint of Grand Central Publishing. The Forever name and logo are trademarks of Hachette Book Group, Inc.

The publisher is not responsible for websites (or their content) that are not owned by the publisher.

The Hachette Speakers Bureau provides a wide range of authors for speaking events. To find out more, go to www.hachettespeakersbureau.com or call (866) 376-6591.

Library of Congress Cataloging-in-Publication Data
Names: Easton, BB, author.
Title: Skin / BB Easton.
Description: First trade paperback edition. | New York : Forever, 2021. |
    Summary: "In 1997, Ronald "Knight" McKnight was the meanest, most
    misunderstood boy at Peach State High School…perhaps on the entire planet.
    Knight hated everyone, except for BB—the perky, quirky punk chick with the
    locker next to his. BB on the other hand, liked everybody…except for Knight.
    She was scared to death of him, actually. All she wanted was to marry Prince
    Eric-lookalike and king of the Peach State High punk scene Lance Hightower and
    have a million of his babies. Unfortunately for BB, Knight was even better at
    getting his way than she was, and once he got under her skin, her life would never
    be the same"—Provided by publisher.
Identifiers: LCCN 2020030163 | ISBN 9781538718346 (trade paperback)
Subjects: GSAFD: Autobiographical fiction.
Classification: LCC PS3605.A8555 S55 2021 | DDC 813/.6—dc23
LC record available at https://lccn.loc.gov/2020030163

ISBNs: 978-1-5387-1834-6 (trade paperback), 978-1-5387-1835-3 (ebook)

Printed in the United States of America

LSC-C

Printing 1, 2021

This book is dedicated to the first boy I ever loved. The one who knew that I deserved better. The one who saved me by setting me free. The one who inspired me to become a school psychologist. I'm sorry I couldn't fix you.

I tried.

AUTHOR'S NOTE

Skin is a work of fiction based on characters and events introduced in my memoir, *Sex/Life: 44 Chapters About 4 Men*. While many of the situations portrayed in this book are true to life, many others were added, exaggerated, or altered to enhance the story. I also changed the names and identifying characteristics of every character (and most locations) to protect the identities of everyone involved.

Due to excessive profanity, violence, graphic sexual content, and themes of juvenile delinquency, this book is not intended for—and should probably be completely hidden from—anyone under the age of eighteen.

INTRODUCTION

If you've read *Sex/Life: 44 Chapters About 4 Men*, then you're familiar with my style. It's sarcastic and profane. It's sexy and fun. It's embarrassingly honest, and it is nothing to be taken too seriously. Thirty-two words in that book aren't even in the dictionary, for Christ's sake. I just made them up.

When I sat down to write Knight's story—this story—I wanted to be honest. I wanted to write about what it was really, truly like to be a fifteen-year-old girl from a working-class family attending an overcrowded, underfunded public high school in the late 1990s. And in order to do that, I knew I would have to bring up a lot of touchy subjects—underage sex being a big one, but also racism, homophobia, suicide, drugs, alcohol, gangs, guns, body modification, bullying, domestic violence, teen pregnancy, eating disorders, mental illness, first loves, first losses, and just plain feeling lost. That was *my* high school experience—and even though I knew the subject matter would be heavy—I wanted to write about it *my* way. In my quirky, lighthearted style.

But *they* didn't give a shit what I wanted to do.

Knight and BB weren't exactly known for following directions in real life, and their characters were no exception. I realized early on that this was *not* going to be another memoir. These characters simply wouldn't allow it. If I told them, "You're supposed to go left here," they would give me the middle finger and say, "But we *wanted* to go right, so we're going right this time." Eventually I tossed my historian hat out the window—it never fit right anyway—and just tried to keep up as Knight and BB ran circles around me. I would put them in familiar settings, try to re-create exact scenarios, and they would do what they did best—whatever the fuck they wanted.

So, for those of you left-brained types who are going to want to know which parts of this book are true and which parts are fictitious, all I can tell you is that most of what you are about to read actually happened, and the parts that didn't actually happen were so true to the characters that they very easily *could* have happened.

It's important to note that all of the secondary characters are amalgams of people I knew in high school—Frankenteens assembled from the assorted physical characteristics and personality traits of at least two of my closest friends each. Any resemblance to a single living person is purely coincidental. All names have been changed as well—including the name of my school and Knight's tattoo parlor—and I compressed the timeline of events to fit into a single school year. The story just flowed better that way.

I learned through this process that by letting go of reality a little bit, I gave my characters freedom to express themselves more fully than they ever were in real life. In that way, this story is even more honest than a rigid recounting of events would have been. It gets to the heart and soul of who Knight and BB really were, what my high school was really like, and all the terrible and beautiful things that really happened when the grown-ups weren't looking.

This book is *my* truth. It's just not one hundred percent *the* truth.

SKIN

Part I

Chapter 1

Positive, positive, positive.

It was my first day of tenth grade, and I was *not* going to be nervous. I was going to think deliriously happy, positive thoughts. I was going to skip down the familiar halls of Peach State High School with a bounce in my steel-toed step and a self-confident smirk on my face because *this* was going to be the year that Lance Hightower finally proclaimed his undying love for me. It just *had* to be.

I wasn't going to beat myself up about the fact that I had been trying and failing to make out with that boy since middle school, *nor* was I going to focus on the fact that I still had zero breasts at the age of fifteen. No, I was going to fantasize about all the wildly spontaneous, highly public ways Lance might choose to propose. After all, I'd just learned—thanks to my dad's unhealthy obsession with watching CNN—that it was totally legal for teenagers to get married in Georgia as long as they had written permission from one of their parents. That wouldn't be a problem for me, seeing as how I'd perfected my mom's signature by the age of twelve.

I was also feeling pretty damn good because I knew I'd picked out the *perfect* back-to-school outfit. My trademark black combat boots and wingtip eyeliner were firmly in place; I was rocking some kickass black spiderweb fishnets under my favorite pair of too-short-for-school cut-off jeans; my gray midriff T-shirt boasted the logo of an indie band I was absolutely *certain* no one had heard of; and my arms were practically pinned to my sides with the weight of a thousand metal, beaded, and leather bracelets. Also, I'd started smoking over the summer (for real this time), and my shorter, edgier, more angled haircut got tons of compliments, even from Lance (which was the whole point).

Of course, all my positivity went to shit as soon as I made it to the church parking lot for a smoke between classes.

It was no secret at Peach State High School that if you wanted to do something bad, all you had to do was walk out past the rust buckets in the student parking lot, step over a guardrail, and clear the tree line. That was it. On the other side you would find yourself in a magical wooded wonderland called *the church parking lot*, a place where kids could escape the oppression of our overcrowded, underfunded public learning institution to laugh, smoke, and be merry (if only for seven minutes at a time). The church was a long abandoned one-room chapel that was in the process of being reclaimed by the forest, and its parking lot was nothing more than a patch of gravel, but to a band of misfit teenagers it was heaven.

Or so I'd heard. I'd never actually ventured out to the church parking lot during school hours before, but this was my year. I just knew that on the other side of those woods I'd find *my people*. Artsy, quirky free spirits who shared my appreciation for alternative rock, avant garde art, and experimental photography. The group that would embrace me with open arms, invite me to sit with them at lunch, and host raging keggers like the ones I saw on TV.

Instead, what I found was the most intimidating group of human beings I'd ever seen in one place. *Fuck me.* Those kids were cool with a capital *C* and twenty-seven *O*s. They had *multi-colored* hair. They had *piercings*. They had expertly painted red lips that I could never pull off with my redheaded complexion. And the accessories—more chokers and studded belts than you could shake a flannel shirt at. One girl was even wearing denim overalls with the legs cut off and one shoulder strap undone. I wasn't punk rock—I was Punky fucking Brewster.

At least my combat boots were vintage and my eyeliner was flawless. That I knew for sure. I'd been perfecting that goddamn cat eye since the age of ten. As long as I kept my grades up my hippie parents never really gave a shit how much makeup I wore, or what I dressed like, or how many F-bombs I dropped at the dinner table. (And by dinner table, I mean my TV tray in the living room.) So I stood on the periphery and tried not to stare, clinging to both my Camel Light and the hope that someone would at least admire my eyeliner art.

I watched the guys all squeezing and kneading and nuzzling their girlfriends, and I watched their girlfriends' giant boobs bounce with every giggle.

I bet they have sex, I thought. *Every one of them.*

My face and neck suddenly felt itchy and hot.

Annnnd, now I'm blushing. Fantastic.

I dropped my head and stared down at my boots, which I could see with no problem at all thanks to my complete and total lack of breasts.

Why can't the heroin chic look still be in? Maybe it'll make a comeback. Please let it make a comeback.

Everyone out there looked like Drew Barrymore and I looked like somebody drew a smiley face and freckles on one of Drew Barrymore's pinky fingers.

My BFF, Juliet Iha, was supposed to be meeting me out there, but after a few minutes it became pretty clear that she'd flaked out on me yet again.

She's probably out here somewhere fogging up Tony's car windows.

Juliet was dating a grown-ass man who'd dropped out of high school at least a decade prior and never seemed to have anywhere pressing to be. Without fail, that creepy fucker always seemed to be lurking around wherever we were, leaning up against his busted-ass old Corvette like an actor cast to play the part of "Potential Child Molester" in a P.S.A. from 1985. Tony definitely gave me the "no feeling," but Juliet really liked him and he was old enough to buy us cigarettes, so I kept my mouth shut.

Just as I was about to stamp out my Camel Light and drag my sad ass back inside, I felt two solid arms wrap around my body from behind. One snaked around my ribcage and the other hoisted me up from behind my knees. Before I could scream "Rape!" I was flipped completely upside down and plopped, ass up, on the shoulder of a giant. It wasn't until he swatted my backside and laughed in that glorious, soft tone that made my body go all warm and bubbly that I realized I'd been captured by my immortal beloved, Lance Hightower.

Lance Motherfucking Hightower. God, he was perfection. Lance was in my grade, but he was easily half a foot taller than most of the upperclassmen and already filled out like a man. Dude had a permanent five o'clock shadow at the age of fifteen. Despite having the dark, chiseled features of a Disney prince, Lance was a punk rock icon. Every day he sported the same effortlessly badass look: faded black Converse, faded black jeans, and a faded black hoodie covered in patches advertising obscure European underground punk bands and anarchist political statements that he painted on with Wite-Out during class. That hoodie was so well known it probably had its own fanzine.

Topping off all that faded black packaging was an equally faded, slightly grown-out, green Mohawk. It probably would have added another three inches to Lance's already six-foot-three-inch frame if he ever bothered to style it, and the color totally brought out the green flecks in his coppery hazel eyes.

Oh, Lance. I had been obsessing over him since the sixth grade. I admired him from afar until last year when we fatefully wound up sharing a pottery wheel in art class. The flirting that ensued was incendiary. Atomic. The only problem was that I was technically "dating" his best friend, Colton, at the time, so things never really got off the ground.

Then a goddamn miracle happened. Colton up and moved to Las Vegas to live with his dad right in the middle of the spring semester. I pretended to be sad for a few hours, out of respect, then immediately resumed my campaign to become the mother of Lance's children. The only problem was that Lance and I didn't have any classes together, so all of my flirting had to be done in seven-minute increments between periods. But in tenth grade, what I was sure would be the best year ever, Lance and I had been assigned to the same motherfucking lunch period. I was going to be sporting his last name by May. I just knew it.

"Lance! What are you doing?" I giggled. "Put me down! I can't breathe with your shoulder in my stomach!"

Lance chuckled. "That's so sweet. You take my breath away too, girl."

God, his voice. Like fucking angel bells. For such a big dude with such an in-your-face look, Lance's voice was surprisingly soft and flirty. It was a total mindfuck the first few times I heard that sweet sound come out of that ruggedly handsome face. And the pick-up lines. I swear to Jesus he had a new one every time I saw him. I fucking loved Lance Hightower.

I giggled harder, which made my stomach hurt even worse, and swatted at his perfect, patch-covered ass. "Put me down, asshole!"

Before he could comply, we heard a sickening smack from across the parking lot followed by a deep voice shouting, "Say it again, motherfucker!"

Lance held on tight to the backs of my thighs and swung around to face the commotion, making me even dizzier as I grabbed his waist and peeked around his side to see what was going on.

Although I couldn't make out exactly what was happening due to the blood rushing into my eyeballs, I recognized the assailant immediately. I'd never met him, but I'd heard stories. Everybody had. He was "the skinhead," the only one at our entire four-thousand-student suburban high school.

I'd noticed him in ninth grade because he was literally the only person I'd ever seen wear suspenders (skinny ones, called braces) to school. In a world full of studded belts and chain wallets, that motherfucker wore suspenders—the epitome of dorkiness—and made them look as scary as the stripes on a venomous snake.

A snake who was standing about thirty feet away, looming over a little skater boy who was clutching his rapidly swelling jaw and trying not to cry.

When the kid didn't say whatever it was the skinhead wanted to hear, he buried his fist deep in Skater Boy's stomach, causing him to lurch forward and release a noise so guttural I assumed something important must have ruptured. With his left hand, the skinhead yanked the guy's head back by his chin-length brown hair and screamed into his terrified face, "Say that shit again!"

I felt like I might throw up. My heart was racing and my head was pounding from being upside down, but all I could register was a sickening sense of helplessness and humiliation for that poor kid. I'd been raised in a house with pacifist parents and no siblings. I'd never seen anyone get hit before, at least not in real life, and I felt that punch as if it had been dealt directly to me.

In a way, it had. That punch shook me to my core. It showed me that senseless violence and cruelty really do exist, and they come wearing boots and braces.

When Skater Boy remained silent, the skinhead responded by shoving his head so hard that he flew sideways and landed, hands and face first, in the gravel. His body slid a few feet before finally coming to a stop. The kid scrambled to pull himself into a ball and made little screeching sounds as if struggling to suppress a scream.

Instead of attacking again, his assailant began to circle him slowly, like a hawk. I held my breath and gripped Lance's waist tighter, ignoring the throbbing in my eyeballs, and watched upside down as he assessed his victim. I was horrified by how calm he was. He wasn't angry or upset, just...calculating. Cold and calculating.

The skinhead approached the kid, who was now trembling and sobbing quietly, and slowly rolled him onto his side with one very heavy-looking combat boot. Still curled up tightly, Skater Boy choked out what sounded like a muffled, garbled apology. Unimpressed, his attacker bent down toward the kid's face and placed a meaty hand firmly on the side of his head. I didn't know what he was doing at first, but when the brown-haired kid started screaming in pain I realized that the skinhead was pressing his face into the gravel.

"What was that?" he asked calmly, tilting his head to one side as if genuinely interested, the veins in his muscular arm beginning to bulge as he applied more pressure.

"I'm sorry! I'm sorry! I didn't mean it! Please stop! Please!" The scream at the end of his apology got increasingly louder as that heartless, hairless demon crushed his face further into the jagged rocks.

The skinhead released Skater Boy's head and stood up. I exhaled and felt my body relax into Lance's shoulder, then watched in disbelief as he kicked the kid directly in the lower back one, two, three times. By the time my eyes registered the strikes and my ears registered the resulting scream it was over, but my spirit was forever changed.

It said, *These people fuck and they fight and you'd better get used to it, little girl.*

Lance set me down, slowly, and I wrapped myself around him like a tree trunk for stability.

I stared, partially hidden behind Lance's sturdy frame, as the skinhead idly spit on the ground next to his victim, lit a cigarette, and walked with long confident strides…directly toward me. The gravel crunched under the weight of his steel-toed boots, which emerged from the bottom of a tightly rolled pair of blue jeans. Bright red laces wound themselves up the front of his boots, and bright red braces slashed across his muscular chest—a chest which was wrapped in a tight black T-shirt emblazoned with the word *Lonsdale.*

Steeling myself behind Lance's comforting presence, I mustered the courage to peek up at the skinhead's face. It was like looking at a ghost. He resembled a person, but there was no color to help differentiate his features. His skin was white. His hair and eyelashes were virtually transparent, and his eyes…His eyes were a ghostly, icy gray-blue. Like a zombie's. And when they landed on mine, my hair stood up on end so violently it felt like a million tiny needles were stabbing me at once.

Those zombie eyes flicked from mine to Lance's with a look of irritation as he approached. I could feel a buzzing electric current of malice radiating off of him well before he reached us, and I winced as he passed, as if bracing myself for his wrath. When nothing happened I carefully opened my eyes, relieved by the change in the atmosphere. The static charge was gone. *He* was gone. But he left a broken boy, a still-burning Marlboro Red, and my scattered wits on the ground in his wake.

As traumatizing as my first smoke break had been, that wasn't the reason I was having trouble concentrating in my honors economics class. It was because as soon as the bell rang I knew I was going to have lunch with Lance Motherfucking Hightower—and my best friends, Juliet and August—but mostly *Lance Motherfucking Hightower*.

I saw the teacher's mouth moving, but all I could hear were my own racing thoughts. *I'm totally going to sit next to him. But what if I get there first? Will he sit next to me? Maybe I should hide and wait for Lance to sit down and then run over and sit next to him before anyone else has a chance. Yes. Totally. Then I'll find an excuse to touch him. And I'll laugh at all his jokes. Not that it'll be hard. He's so funny. And beautiful. And tall. And edgy. And fucking dreamy.*

When the bell finally rang, I jumped up as if my ass were on fire and sprinted to the bathroom to touch up my makeup. Then I high-tailed it to the cafeteria to scope out the cool kid table. Every punk, goth, druggie, drama nerd, vegan, hippie, skater, and metal head at our high school wanted a spot at that table, and even though he was only in tenth grade, Lance was the reigning king of them all. Getting a spot next to him was going to be tricky.

When I ran up I realized that not only had Lance already taken his seat—right in the middle of the fifteen-foot-long table—but goddamn Colton Hart was sitting right next to him.

Shit.

Shit fuck damn.

When the hell did he get back?

Colton was going to be a major fucking obstacle in my quest to become Mrs. Hightower. He was the world's biggest cockblocker—that's actually how I wound up dating him in the first place—he just kept inserting himself between Lance and me until I gave in and let him kiss me. Which he did. A lot. Don't get me wrong, making out with Colton Hart was a spectacular way to spend an afternoon. He was super fucking cute. And cocky. And sarcastic. And *bad*. But he just wasn't Lance.

But technically, he *was* still my boyfriend.

Oh my God. What if he thinks we're still a couple? No. There's no way. He never even called me after he left. He probably screwed all kinds of future strippers while he was living with his dad and brother in Las Vegas, and now I'm small potatoes. I'm just the girl he left back in Georgia who wouldn't let him touch her boobs. It's totally fine. No. Big. Deal.

As I walked up, I couldn't help but admit to myself that he did look damn good. Better than I'd remembered. He was like a wicked Peter Pan. Spiky brown hair with blond tips, pointy ears, perfect male model smile. When he left, he had a definite punk rock style, like a mini-Lance, but I guess his skateboarding older brother had worn off on him while he was in Vegas. Colton had traded in his boots for a pair of shell-toed Adidas, his bondage pants for a pair of black cargo shorts, and his studded belt for a chain wallet.

There was a spot open next to both of them, but I made sure to sit next to Lance just to establish whose girl I was. Or at least, whose girl I wanted to be.

As soon as I walked up and set down my backpack Colton cried, "Kitten! Get your ass over here!" I glanced down at Lance, who made no attempt to rescue me, and sighed. Getting up and walking around him I embraced Colton, who had stood up and was waiting for me with open arms.

Feigning excitement, I said, "Hey Colton! Oh my God! When did you get back?" as he squeezed the shit out of me.

"Last week," he said, rocking me from side to side. "My moms got lonely. What can I say? Living without me is hard." He pulled away and gave me a wink. "Isn't it?"

I rolled my eyes in response, but I couldn't help my traitorous smile. He really was cute. And he smelled squeaky clean. Like a girl. Colton had a thing for products—hair products, skin products— he was vain as hell and proud of it.

After giving me the once-over Colton whistled. "Look at you. You're making me wonder why I left in the first place." I blushed and looked at the ground. "You wanna ride the bus home with me this afternoon? Just like old times? My mom just stocked the fridge with PBR…"

Yes. No. Kinda?

Before I could say something stupid, Juliet swooped in and rescued me. "She's riding home with me, Colton. BB is *my* bitch now."

Juliet set her tray down across from my backpack and glared at Colton. She never liked him. For starters, I kind of forgot she existed after he and I started dating. I just started riding the bus home with him every day instead of her—a dick move, I know, but I was fourteen and he was my first real boyfriend. I'm pretty sure "first real boyfriend" would be accepted as just cause for a temporary insanity plea in a court of law. But Juliet also hated him because I kind of blabbed to her about how hard he'd been pressuring me to do *stuff* with him. I would have given in too, if he hadn't told me he was moving. I was *not* giving it up to somebody who was just going to leave in a few weeks. Besides, I was saving myself for Lance Hightower.

Colton glared back at her for a minute, then smiled and asked, "Can I watch?"

We all laughed, even Lance, who was watching the show with piqued interest. When I sat back down next to him (and away from the pheromone cloud that was Colton Hart) I let out a shaky breath and stared straight ahead at Juliet, thanking her silently. Lance, who had resumed his conversation with Colton, reached under the table and gave my thigh a reassuring squeeze. He left his hand there, and I prayed to every deity I'd ever learned the names of that he would slide it up a little farther. He didn't, but he did absentmindedly lace his fingers through the holes in my fishnets as he spoke, causing me to stop breathing long enough to almost actually fucking die.

My mind was sufficiently scrambled when August, whom I hadn't even noticed, spoke to me from the spot next to Juliet.

I had been friends with August Embry since first grade, when we wound up in the same first grade class. Back then he was a shy, pudgy little thing with no friends, and I was a bossy, talkative little thing with no friends, so we just clicked. I loved him like a brother.

August was still a shy, round little thing. He hid his warm, chocolate brown eyes behind a curtain of dyed black hair, and every night he painted his fingernails black to match. Of course, every day he would pick them clean again—leaving little black flecks behind, like a trail of breadcrumbs everywhere he went. August was the sweetest, most sensitive person I'd ever met.

I could tell from his body language that August wasn't exactly happy to see Colton, either. He and Lance had become kind of close since Colton left. They both liked the same terrible music and competed over who had the best, rarest punk records in their collections, so Lance getting his best friend back didn't bode well for August.

"Hey, A!" I cheered, trying way too hard to sound like a girl who *didn't* have a boy's fingers stroking her inner thigh at that exact moment. "I didn't know you had this lunch period too! Are you growing your hair out? I love it!" August just smiled and looked down at the food on his tray, which he suddenly decided needed rearranging.

I turned to ask Juliet if I could ride home with her and Tony, but she was gone. Her stuff was still on the table though, and I thought I could hear the sound of her voice. As much as it killed me, I moved Lance's hand so that I could peek under the table. There she was, sitting cross-legged on the floor talking on her cell phone, which was strictly forbidden at school. There was only one person she could possibly be talking to.

"Juliet," I whispered.

She looked up, annoyed. "What?"

"Ask Tony if he minds giving me a ride this afternoon."

She winked at me and whispered into her brick-sized Nokia, "Hey. BB's gonna ride home with us this afternoon, okay?" She gave me a thumbs-up after hearing his response.

Cool.

Just then, I felt Lance's hand press down on the back of my head and saw his crotch rise up to meet the side of my face. I screamed and tried to sit up, causing my head to smash Lance's hand into the underside of the table. Laughter erupted from the cafeteria as I emerged, red-faced, looking like a girl who'd just eaten a punk rocker's cock for lunch.

I glared at Lance, trying my best to look angry, but his eyes were shut and he was laughing so hard he wasn't even making noise. Just the sight of that giant, Mohawked motherfucker smiling ear to ear had me reduced to a puddle of swoon juice in an instant. I burst out laughing right along with him, and anxiously glanced over at Colton.

He was laughing too, but his smile didn't quite reach his eyes. Guess he didn't appreciate the entire lunchroom thinking *his* girl-friend was giving his best friend a BJ under the table.

In that moment, I knew that Colton wasn't going to be a prob-lem. Lance had just established, with dramatic flair and in front of everyone, that I was his girl.

All the hope and hormones had my insides on the verge of spon-taneous combustion, so I barely noticed the loud *slam* that came from somewhere behind me. I hardly felt the resulting shudder that rippled down the length of the lunch table. And I didn't turn to look for the source until the faces of all my friends fell and glanced anxiously over my shoulder. Swiveling around on my stool, I followed everyone's gaze to an empty seat at the end of the table.

Um, anyway. Where was I? Oh, right. Planning my spring wedding…

That afternoon I fought against the current of teenagers fleeing the building, dragging my swollen backpack behind me by one strap, in search of my new locker. According to my homeroom teacher my old one had to be torn out over the summer to make room for the new science lab. She had given me a little slip of paper with my new locker number and combination on it, saying only that it was "somewhere over on C Hall." I couldn't wait to find that shit so that I could finally offload a few of the ten-pound textbooks I'd been given that day.

Clutching the piece of paper with my new digits on it, I scanned dozens of identical metal doors until I found the one I'd been assigned. It was almost at the end of the hallway, of course, near the exit doors that led out to the student parking lot. I felt relief wash over me immediately.

My first day of tenth grade was a wrap, and overall it had been a smashing success. I'd smoked with the coolest of the cool kids; wound up with the same lunch period as Lance, Juliet, and August; got a bunch of compliments on my fishnets and new haircut; and now I had a new locker on the same hall as all the seniors. Okay, so maybe it took me a few attempts to get my code to work, but once that shit was open it was glorious.

As I bent over to take the last load of books out of my straining backpack, I stopped short, paralyzed by the sight of two black steel-toed boots with blood-red laces planted just inches away from my face…and pointing directly at me.

Fuck.

Fuck, fuck, fuck.

Not him. Anyone but him.

I took my time gathering my stuff, hoping that ignoring him would make him magically disappear. When I finally stood up, arms full of books, I mustered all the courage I had and looked him in the eye.

Zombie eyes. God, his irises were such a pale, pale gray-blue that his pupils looked like two endless black holes in contrast. Two black holes that were sucking me in.

Speak, dumbass!

"Um, hey," I said in a voice that didn't sound like it belonged to me.

He didn't reply. He simply cocked his head to the side and studied me with those cold, dead eyes. It was the same way he looked at the kid in the parking lot, right before he smashed his face into the ground.

Swallowing hard, I forced myself to break the silence.

"I'm sorry, do you need something?" I squeaked out, trying to sound cute and tiny. I blinked and opened my eyes a little wider, feeling like a woodland creature in danger of being squished by a massive black boot.

"Your shit is in front of my locker," he said. His voice was deep and clear and humorless.

"Oh my God! I'm so sorry!" Tripping over myself, I slid my lightened backpack behind me with my foot. The skinhead immediately grasped the metal latch on the locker beside mine and gave the lower left corner of the door a swift kick, causing the fucker to pop right open, no code necessary. I shuddered involuntarily as my mind conjured images of that same boot landing square in the back of a scared little skater boy just a few hours earlier.

Afraid that he could smell my fear, I quickly hid my face behind the metal door of my own locker, busying myself by arranging my books and notebooks by size, color, the Dewey fucking decimal system, *anything*. Then something occurred to me. Before I knew it, my stupid mouth was moving.

"Shouldn't you be suspended?"

I felt my face blush crimson as the blond with the buzzcut slammed his locker shut and asked, point blank, "Why?"

Was he teasing me? We both knew what the fuck he did.

"That, that fight. Today. In the church parking lot," I said, into my locker.

Thinking about that…*attack* had my blood pumping into my extremities and my mind screaming for me to run. I turned and went back to my organizing, hoping to conceal the terror and embarrassment that I'm sure my big, dumb doe eyes were doing a shit job of concealing. My face always snitched on me, broadcasting my every thought. My every feeling.

My thin metal makeshift shield vibrated as he spoke. "I didn't get suspended for the same reason you're not sitting in detention right now for smoking. That shit happened off-campus."

"Is he okay?"

God! My fucking mouth! Filter, BB. Filter!

"Who? That little pussy wipe from the parking lot? He'll be pissing blood for a week, but he'll live."

Slowly, the door I had been cowering behind began to close. Moving out of the way so that the metal wouldn't graze my face, I reluctantly turned toward the boy with the cadaverous eyes, who was deliberately pushing my locker shut. Once the door was firmly closed and I had nowhere left to hide, Zombie Eyes leaned toward me and reached around my body with his left hand. I squeezed my eyelids shut and braced myself for something violent and potentially bloody to happen.

With his voice lowered so that only I could hear, he said, "If you hit a fucker in the kidney hard enough...right here..." I suddenly felt a thick finger jam directly into one side of my lower back. "He'll piss blood."

My eyes shot open, and I immediately wished that they hadn't. That gray-blue gaze was way too close, too intense. His finger lingered way too long, and there was a crackle in the air that had my senses on high alert.

Danger! Danger! Skinhead Boy is fucking touching you! He could kill you with that finger, BB! Kill you and eat your brains!

But those zombie eyes wouldn't let me move. Up close they were so clear. Like two crystal balls that I wished would give me a glimpse into this twisted creature's soul. In my curious state of hypnosis, again, words tumbled unbidden from my mouth.

"Why'd you hit him?"

After a pause long enough to let me hope that maybe I hadn't actually asked my question out loud, he answered, "Because he called your little boyfriend a faggot."

About three million follow-up questions slammed into my throat at once:

A) Why would a Neo-Nazi–looking motherfucker beat someone up that he doesn't even know for calling some other dude he doesn't know a faggot?

B) Shouldn't he have given the kid a high five instead?

C) Why would he call Lance my boyfriend? Lance is NOT my boyfriend. I mean, I want him to be my boyfriend. Jesus, I want to ride him like a pony everywhere I go and have all of his babies, but he's not my boyfriend.

D) Why would anyone think Lance was gay in the first place? He's sooo dreamy.

But the only thing I could squeak out was, "You were defending Lance?"

I never knew an eye roll could be so terrifying. *Shit.* I'd done it. I'd finally pissed him off with all my stupid fucking questions. Why did I always have to talk to the scary ones? My mom still loves to tell people about the time I picked up my Happy Meal and sat down with a group of leather-clad bikers at McDonald's when I was three just so that I could ask the gnarliest-looking one why he had a ponytail. According to her my exact words were, "Only girls are 'apposed to have ponytails."

My curiosity was going to get me straight murdered one day.

The skinhead, who now looked positively murderous himself, removed his hand from my back and placed it on my locker, just above my head. Cocking his head to the side again he watched me, as if mulling over the best way to skin me alive, and of course I just stood there blinking up at him like a fucking dumbass.

Basic bodily functions like speaking, breathing, and running were completely out of my grasp. It was as if I'd been cornered by a coiled rattlesnake. A rattlesnake that just so happened to smell like dryer sheets, cigarettes, and a sweet hint of cologne.

"No," he said. "I was defending *you.*"

Too much. It was too intense. I broke eye contact and took a step backward, landing on the backpack I forgot was behind me and almost losing my balance. Turning around to pick it up, I took a deep breath and tried to regroup before facing him again. When I did, his ghostly eyes were crinkled at the corners and his mouth was tipped up just slightly on one side. *Fucker.* He was actually enjoying watching me squirm.

Smirk still in place, he said, "When I was outside I heard that little shit telling his buddy about the hard-on he had for 'the little redhead in the fishnets'. Couldn't argue with him there, Punk. I think you gave every guy in that parking lot a semi."

My face was suddenly on fire. *Oh, God. I'm blushing! Is this really happening?*

He continued, but his smirk had been replaced by something that made my blood run cold. "When he saw that giant motherfucker's hands on you, he turned into a pissy little bitch." He spat the last word out through gritted teeth. "Told his buddy you must love taking it up the ass to be wasting your time with that queer."

Gulp. Breathe. What??

"S-so, so you punched him?"

The zombie-eyed skinhead leaned down toward my ear and didn't stop until I could feel his hot, venomous breath on my neck. "I. Beat. His. Fucking. Ass."

My limbs were moving of their own accord. Legs stumbling backward. Hands fumbling with backpack straps. "Um, thanks?" I mumbled, eyes darting everywhere but his. "I, uh, have to go... I'm gonna miss my... Thanks again..."

"Knight," he announced, as I turned and sprinted for the double doors. "Thanks, *Knight*."

Fuck me.

Chapter 2

"We should sleep out here sometime," I said, gazing up at the August sky through a tangle of hundred-foot-tall Georgia pines. Juliet and I were lying on our backs in the middle of my most prized possession—my trampoline.

I had begun begging my parents for a trampoline when I was ten years old. My mom initially said "no" because she thought I would break my neck. My dad said "no" because he thought somebody else's kid might come in our yard and break *their* neck and then we'd get sued and lose our house and die penniless in the gutter. But if I've learned anything from being an only child, it's that all "no" really means is, "You haven't sufficiently annoyed or inconvenienced me yet," so I jumped on their bed every night until it broke.

It took *months*, but in the end my parents had to buy both a trampoline *and* a new bed. I think they learned a very valuable lesson about telling me "no" that year.

Because my parents were still kind of bitter about the bed incident, they referred to my precious as "an eyesore" and set it up way the hell out in the woods behind our house. Which I couldn't have been happier about.

It was perfect—my own private little patch of bouncy freedom.

When I first got it I used to go out there and jump for hours, but by my sophomore year that weathered old rust bucket just served as a place where I could go to write angsty poetry, smoke cigarettes, and talk to Juliet about boys. (And by *boys* I mean Lance Mother-fucking Hightower.)

"Are you crazy? The mosquitoes would eat us alive."

Juliet did not share my appreciation for nature. She definitely shared my appreciation for cigarettes and boys though, seeing as how she had a solid year head start on me in both subjects.

"I have to sit up. My neck is fucking killing me," I said, wincing as I changed positions.

"Are you still avoiding your locker?" Juliet asked in her naturally bitchy tone.

"Maybe," I said, while trying to massage two massive divots out of my shoulders. They were trenches, really, forged from carrying every textbook I owned around on my back for two weeks straight.

"You are such a pussy! Skeletor isn't going to eat you. Just grow a pair and go to your fucking locker before you get scoliosis."

"Oh my God! He *does* look like Skeletor!" I squealed. "He has the creepiest eyes, Jules. I *can't* go back there. I just can't. I mean, he closed my locker while I was still putting stuff in there. Who *does* that? And then he touched me! *And* he beat the shit out of some guy he didn't even know over nothing! Knight is off, Juliet. Like, he's gonna murder somebody one day, and it damn sure isn't gonna be me."

Juliet held her hands up. "I'm not saying he isn't scary. Dude, the way he just sits by himself at the end of our lunch table, staring at you...I'm not gonna lie. He might be an actual, real-life canni-bal. I'm just saying you *have to* go to your locker. Your backpack literally weighs more than you do."

"Maybe I can share your locker?" I asked, batting my eyelashes.

Juliet sat up and looked me square in the eye. "No fucking way.

I've seen *Romper Stomper*. If your little Nazi friend finds out where you're hiding he'll probably curb stomp my ass."

"Maybe not," I said. "Weren't the Nazis and the Japanese on the same side in the war?"

"Yeah, but I'm also half-Black, dumbass." Juliet shoved my shoulder, causing me to flop backward onto the black nylon. We both giggled like maniacs as I bounced back up into a seated position.

God, I loved Juliet. She was so genuine and bold and unapologetic. She was the person I always channeled when I wanted to be stronger. Braver. Tougher.

Once our hysterics died down Juliet lay back down on her side and asked, "What about Lance? Maybe he could go to your locker with you. He'd protect you from Skeletor."

"Maybe if he had on an Iron Man suit."

Juliet grinned and said, "He carries you to second period every day like some kind of caveman. I'm pretty sure he'd stand up to Skeletor for you. It's pretty obvious he wants to fuck your brains out."

"Shut up!" I could feel what had to be the goofiest fucking grin take over my face, along with a four-alarm flush. "If he wanted to . . . do *that*, wouldn't he have at least kissed me by now? I'm starting to think I'm just not his type. He probably wants a girl with hot pink hair and a nose ring."

And boobs.

"You're so fucking stupid! Look at you! And if Lance hasn't figured out that you want his giant cock by now then he's just as stupid as you are."

"Ewww!" I screeched, shoving Juliet's shoulder just like she had done to me. She screamed and caught my arm mid-flail, pulling me down with her.

We flopped and giggled and bounced and snorted like wild

things until Juliet suddenly yelled out, "Oh my God! I know what his problem is! BB! What if Lance has a girlfriend??"

My laughter cut off mid-chortle and Juliet grew quiet too, waiting for my reaction. The only sound that remained from our ruckus was the squeaking of the springs as we slowed to a halt. My mind flew through every interaction I'd ever had with Lance, searching for any missed signs of a girlfriend.

Why would a guy that hot not *have a girlfriend?* It made perfect sense. *I'm sure she's probably a tattoo model or an exotic dancer or a contortionist/sword swallower at the county fair.*

"I could ask him for you." Juliet looked at me with concern in her black, almond-shaped eyes, which were rimmed in jet black eyeliner to hide the fact that she'd pulled out most of her eyelashes. She'd pulled out most of her eyebrows too, which she drew in with the same black pencil, and she had a few hidden bald patches on the back of her head. Nobody knew about that but me.

"No! Oh my God, don't you dare!"

"Are you sure?" Juliet sat up, looking dead serious, long black hair swishing around her shoulders. "What if he does have a girlfriend?" she continued. "Wouldn't you want to know?"

"Yes…No…Ugh! I don't know." I impulsively reached out and plucked a small leaf from her dark mane. I always wanted long straight hair. Like my Barbie dolls. Barbie was the standard of beauty I was raised with, and I looked nothing like that bitch. My hair was reddish and wavy and poofy and wouldn't grow past my shoulders. My skin was covered in brown freckles and scars from falling down all the goddamned time and getting bitten by random stray dogs that I just *had* to pet. And my body definitely didn't curve like Barbie's. It didn't fucking curve at all.

A sinister smirk played on her tiny mouth. "I'll ask him tomorrow."

"No!" I screamed. "I'll do it! I'll do it! Please don't say anything!"

"*You're* going to ask Lance Hightower if he has a girlfriend. Bullshit."

"I will! I swear!"

As Juliet rolled her eyes at me we heard the unmistakable sound of an antique Chevy backfiring in the distance.

"I guess you're not staying for dinner."

Juliet beamed as if the vehicle pulling into my driveway was a white limo with a rose-toting Richard Gere hanging out of the sunroof. In actuality it was a faded red 1980 Corvette with flip-up headlights, the one classic sports car that screamed "child molester" instead of "badass motherfucker."

And I should know. My dad had devoted his life to drinking, playing guitar, being paranoid, obsessing over the news, polishing his guns, and teaching his only child everything he knew about American muscle cars. By the age of twelve I could tell you the make, model, and year of any American sports car ever made, and more importantly, I could also tell you that 1980 was a shit year for the Corvette. After the gas crisis in the '70s they introduced a new small-block engine that year that couldn't make it up a hill unless somebody got out and pushed.

The car was old, but not as old as the grown-ass man driving it. I understood that Juliet was entitled to her fair share of daddy issues, but *Jesus*.

Although he made me cringe with his patchy goatee and his baggy jeans, Tony wasn't *that* bad. I mean, he always seemed super happy to see Juliet, which was sweet, I guess, and he was always willing to give us a ride somewhere, which was pretty clutch seeing as how I lived so far outside of our school district that there wasn't even a bus I could ride to and from school.

The only reason I was allowed to go to Peach State High School at all, considering my address, was because my mom was the art teacher at the elementary school. When I was a kid, my mom thought it would be super convenient to bring me to work with her instead of sending me to our neighborhood elementary school—a decision I'm sure she regrets to this day. I was always getting in trouble for sneaking around in the other teachers' classrooms and stealing their art supplies—which was ridiculous because my mom was the art teacher—and I insisted on coloring my hair with markers so that I would look like Rainbow Brite.

Flash forward ten years and I was still going to school in that district, only now I was at the high school, which dismissed over two hours before the elementary school. With no bus to take me home, my only after-school options were to (a) spend all afternoon sitting on the curb waiting for my mom to come pick me up, (b) forge a note and ride the bus to someone else's house, or (c) ride home with Juliet in Tony's molestation mobile.

Walking to my mom's school was out of the question. I'd tried it *once*. I arrived about an hour later drenched in sweat, feet covered in blisters, and sunburned to a crisp. Two and a half miles is a lot farther than it seems when it's mostly uphill and you're carrying your own bodyweight in books.

Juliet and I made our way out of the woods and said our goodbyes. I hugged her tight and gave Tony an obligatory wave before heading inside.

My parents' place was more of a box than a house. It was four walls and a simple A-frame roof—no porch, no awnings, no frills. And most importantly to them, no neighbors.

My parents loved their pot, even grew some on the back porch, so the fewer eyes and noses around, the better. I didn't get it, personally. I tried smoking weed a few times with Juliet and it just made me feel sleepy and stupid. Diet pills, on the other hand, now *those* were my jam.

"Beee Beeeeee!" my mom cooed from the kitchen. She had the oldies radio station cranked up and was stirring something on the stove. "I made dinner! You hungry?"

I walked over to the kitchen entryway and leaned my shoulder on the wall. "Not really," I lied. "I'm just gonna go take a shower and do my homework."

My mom turned toward me with a guilty grin on her freckled face. "That's probably for the best. We were out of regular milk," she giggled, "so I used the vanilla almond milk instead." She burst out laughing, but I was still waiting for the punchline.

"Is that bad? What were you making?"

"Tuna Helper!" She laughed so hard tears welled in her eyes. Between gasps for air she managed to choke out, "It tastes...like shit."

My dad took that opportunity to shout at me from the back room, where he was probably *drinking* his dinner, "It tastes like somebody shoved a dead fish into a stale Twinkie and heated it up!"

I choked on an unexpected laugh while my mom doubled over, tears streaming down her freckled cheeks and into her *long, straight* red hair.

Bitch.

As her hiccups subsided my mom wrapped her arm around my shoulders, kissed me on the temple, and said, "Honey, I'll order you a pizza if you want." Then her giggles started back up.

I patted her head as if she were a Golden Retriever and tiptoed off to the upstairs bathroom to begin my nightly routine.

I got the water started in the shower and stepped out of my clothes. Unable to help myself, I pinched the skin on my belly, gauging its thickness, before stepping onto the scale.

Shit! I almost forgot!

I jumped back off as if the wicked machine were on fire and plopped down onto the toilet, pissing out a few last-minute ounces.

Whew! That was close!

Before easing back onto the scale, I exhaled completely, hoping that maybe empty lungs weighed less than full ones.

One hundred and three pounds. Yes! Double digits, here I come!

I leapt off the scale and landed directly in front of the floor-length mirror on the back of the door, which wasn't difficult in that teensy tiny bathroom. Full of hope, I turned sideways to visually assess the situation.

Still there. Goddamn it.

I frowned at the sight of my "pooch"—the potbelly that I had been saddled with since birth—and frowned harder at the fact that it continued to stick out further than my tragically flat chest.

My body looks like ET's, I thought. *All belly and no boobs. If I can just lose five more pounds that should take care of the pooch, and then maybe my boobs will look bigger once they aren't being overshadowed by this fucking gut anymore.*

Always one to end on a positive note, I praised myself for losing another pound and focused on the empowering, empty feeling in my stomach as I stepped into the blistering hot shower.

After washing my hair with the fancy salon shampoo I begged my mom to buy because it was *supposed* to help smooth my frizzy waves, I shaved my entire body. I'd started shaving my legs and armpits in fifth grade because my friends were doing it. Then I started shaving my arms in seventh grade after I found out that Victoria's Secret models did it. Then I started shaving my pubic hair in eighth grade when I discovered soft-core porn late one night while flipping through the channels on the TV in my bedroom.

I was fascinated. Not a single one of those women had more than a light dusting of pubic hair (*or* arm hair, thankyouverymuch), and they were clearly *very* desirable creatures. I wanted to be desired too, especially by one giant fucking punk rocker with the warmest hazel eyes and most adorable dimples I'd ever seen. *Sigh.*

Two years later I was still shaving my entire body and was still no closer to being Lance's fucking girlfriend.

Girlfriend…girlfriend… I thought about what Juliet had said earlier. What if he already had a girlfriend? I conjured an image of Lance wrapping his arms around the waist of a tiny manic pixie dream girl. Her super-short fuchsia hair would be effortlessly mussed and would match the pink metal gauges in her ears. Her nose ring would be delicate but her eye makeup heavy, and her clothing style would be something in between Bettie Page and Betty Boop.

I pictured him leaning in for a kiss, but manic pixie dream girl bites his lip at the last second and smiles up at him wickedly. Her eyes say, "You don't scare me, giant. I own your ass."

Slowly, the face of Lance's imaginary girlfriend began to morph into my own as I switched the water from the showerhead to bath faucet. I sat down in the tub facing the faucet and scooted forward until my legs had nowhere else to go, then I lifted them up onto the wall on either side of the faucet. The water crashed down on the most sensitive parts of me like a hot, liquid freight train. And like every night, I leaned back onto my elbows and thought of *him*.

I show up at school with a hot pink pixie haircut and a brand-new nose ring. As soon as I enter the building everybody stops and stares at me. Everybody. Including Lance. Our eyes lock and something changes in him. His usually playful expression turns hard, and he stalks toward me as if I've done something wrong.

Grabbing me by the hand, Lance drags me off down a side hallway and yanks me into the first faculty restroom he can find. My ears barely register the sound of the door locking before I feel a wall against my back, Lance's lips and tongue against my own, and Lance's hands seeking an entrance into my dress. Impatient, he rips the tiny garment off me and shoves it to the floor, leaving me in nothing more than my black lace bra, matching panties, and black mid-calf combat boots.

Lance stops his attack just long enough to appraise me with his eyes, then mutters, "Fuck, BB," as one hand finds its way into my new super-short hair and the other cups my ass. He pulls my head back just enough to expose my neck, then proceeds to kiss and bite and suck a savage trail from my collarbone to my breasts. He's so tall he has to kneel before me to continue his journey.

Grabbing both cups of my bra with his massive hands he yanks down, exposing two tender, aching nipples. Lance looks up at me through impossibly dark eyelashes and flashes me a fiendish smile before gently capturing one with his perfect white teeth. His tongue is warm and wet and slides easily back and forth across the surface of my virginal nipple. Before he can make his way any farther down my body I'm assaulted by a torrent of spasms between my legs that bring me careening back into the present moment.

I immediately slid backward, out from under that unrelenting cascade, and flopped onto my back in the inch-deep water. Pressing my fingertips into my clit, I tried to prolong the last few contractions of my orgasm and the last fleeting images I had of Lance's head between my breasts. When it was over I opened my eyes and stared at the popcorn ceiling above me, awash with a renewed sense of determination.

When I was ten I wanted a trampoline. Now I wanted Lance, and I *always* got what I wanted.

Chapter 3

After my little fantasy I hadn't been able to sleep for shit. I stayed up well past midnight watching soft-core porn, masturbating, smoking cigarettes, and drawing pictures of anime-style girls with big green eyes and short, spiky hair. The last one I drew spoke to me.

She said, "Get your scissors, BB."

So, I did.

At one o'clock in the morning I crept into my bathroom, closed the door, and cut off almost all of my reddish-blonde waves. I gave myself blunt bangs bracketed by two chin-length pieces on either side of my face, then hacked the rest of it off. I left maybe an inch of length all over, but made sure to cut it at odd angles to keep it from looking too much like a helmet.

The next morning I wet it and gelled it into spikes, colored a few pieces pink and purple with some markers I had lying around, painted on my wingtip eyeliner, took a deep breath, and walked downstairs to face my mother. When she saw me her face lit up, much to my surprise, and her hands were immediately in my hair.

She brushed my bangs to one side and squealed, "Oh my God, BB! You look just like Twiggy! You should get some false eye-lashes... Twiggy had big eyes like you, and she used to wear these

long false eyelashes to make them look even bigger..." Holding me
at arm's length, my mom looked me over from top to bottom. "She
was super skinny like you too. God, you're so lucky. I would have
killed to look like Twiggy!"

Um...cool. I guess I'm not grounded.

My mom handed me a muffin wrapped in a paper towel, which
I shoved into the hand-sewn fuzzy tiger-striped purse she taught
me how to make over the summer, and we walked outside into the
humid, still-black morning. On the way to school my mom drove
five miles under the speed limit, never once used her blinker, and
sang along to the oldies station at the top of her lungs. (Okay, I'll
admit it. I sang along too.)

But when she dropped me off at the front door everything
shifted into slow motion. My hand reaching for the door handle.
The air conditioning blasting me in the face as I crossed the threshold. And Lance Hightower, leaning against the wall at the end of
the front hallway, watching me walk toward him as if he'd been
waiting on me.

Before I could reach him, Lance pushed off the wall—all six
feet three inches of him—and stalked toward me with a dimpled
smile on his beautiful face.

When he was close enough for me to hear him, Lance said,
"Holy shit, B! Your hair is fucking sick!" and once our boots were
almost toe to toe Lance reached out with both hands and tugged
gently on the ends of my two chin-length locks.

I beamed up at him—silently praying that he didn't get marker
on his fingers—and asked him to say it again. "Really? You like it?"

Lance leaned down so that I could see every copper fleck in
his hazel eyes and said, "Hell yeah, I like it. You look like a little
badass."

The hot pink streaks in my bangs probably blended in with my
cheeks as I blinked up at him with a *kiss me now* pucker on my

face. The butterflies in my stomach were doing gymnastics, and all I wanted to do was…well, everything. I wanted to tear those sexy black patch-covered clothes off his big, tall body, weave my fingers into his faded green Mohawk, and let him do every single naughty thing to me that the hunky repairman had done to the bored housewife on Skinemax the night before.

Everything would have to wait though, because just then the bell rang, turning the hallway into a riot of scattering teenagers.

Lance gave me a quick hug and said, "See you outside," before letting the current pull him away from me.

I turned around and started to head to my first-period class, drunk on lust, when suddenly I heard the voice of an angel yelling, "Hey girl!" from somewhere behind me.

I beamed and spun back around. Lance was easy to spot, given that he was almost a full head taller than most of the kids struggling to get around him in the hallway. Standing up on my tiptoes, I cupped my hands around my mouth and shouted my rehearsed reply back to him.

"What's up?"

Lance flashed me both dimples and shouted back, the noise and crowd swelling between us, "You must be a parking ticket because you've got *fine* written all over you!"

I grinned and shook my head as the crowd dragged me away.

God, I fucking loved him.

I was smiling so big I thought my face might split open when I walked into my honors chemistry class and noticed that it was empty. The words LAB DAY were written on the dry erase board. *Fuck.* I'd forgotten that Tuesday was lab day, which meant that I would need my lab notebook, which was literally the only thing I didn't have crammed inside of my backpack.

I turned around and fought my way back through the crush of bodies toward my locker. I could see C hall approaching and prepared myself to make the jump. Exiting one of the main hall-ways during rush hour was a lot like trying to get out of a lazy river at a water park—only I would have to do it against the current and with fifty pounds of books strapped to my back.

But before I could get there the tardy bell rang, causing the students pressing against me to scatter, leaving me alone and unsteady on my feet.

So, I was late for class. Whatever. Lance Hightower had said my haircut was badass, and I was going to have all of his babies. Nothing could bring me down from that high.

I turned onto C hall—trying to figure out a name for the little girl with strawberry blonde hair and hazel eyes that I would bear for him (Or would she be a green-eyed brunette?)—and immediately careened into something hard.

Then *something hard* gripped my arms and slammed me backward into the nearest wall. Thankfully, my backpack was so large that it was the only thing that made contact with the cinderblock wall behind me, but my biceps felt like they were being crushed in matching vises.

"What the fuck?"

I heard his voice before I dared to open my eyes. Deep. Clear. No accent.

Oh no. No, no, no.

I forced myself to lift one eyelid, expecting to find a rabid skinhead looming over me, foaming at the mouth and ready to pulverize me for getting in his way. Instead I found a surprised skinhead, bent at the waist, staring at me with his blond eyebrows pulled together.

"Punk? Shit. Are you okay?" His tone was gentle enough that I risked opening the other eye too. Just a little.

"Shit, I'm sorry. I didn't realize it was you. Your hair…" Knight released the death grip he had on my left arm and brought his hand up toward my face. I instinctively winced and turned my head away, then felt a tiny tug on one of my longer side pieces of hair, just like Lance had done.

I opened one eye to peek at Knight's face again, surprised by his suddenly tender behavior, but Knight's face looked anything but tender. His jaw was clenched shut, his zombie eyes blazed almost white-hot, and his grip on my right bicep tightened, almost to the point of pain.

Help! Help! Rape! Mayday, motherfuckers! Mayday!

My eyes darted left and right hoping to find a familiar face, but we were so late to class that the halls were completely empty. I couldn't breathe, but I'm pretty sure Knight was breathing heavily enough for the both of us. His nostrils flared as my right hand began to tingle from lack of blood flow.

The words, "I can't feel my hand," tumbled from my fucking filterless mouth.

Knight released me and stepped back, blinking as if he'd just been woken from a spell. He opened his mouth to speak, then shut it again.

"Well, I'm late, so…" I stuck my thumb in the direction of my locker and took one exaggerated step sideways, toward it. When he didn't come after me, I took another.

"I…like your hair," Knight muttered. It came out sounding like a question, as if he didn't know how compliments worked.

I managed to squeak out the word, "Thanks," without releasing the breath I was holding, then turned and sprinted the rest of the way down C hall.

Once I reached my locker I flew through the combination, pulled open the door, shoved my head inside, and hyperventilated.

Maybe Juliet was right, I thought between gasps of stale, dust-thickened air. *Maybe Knight is an actual fucking cannibal.*

Chapter 4

"No way! You never take that thing off!" My squeals echoed off the rafters of our cavernous two-story cafeteria.

"I just did," Lance said, flashing me his best Prince-Eric-from-*The-Little-Mermaid* smile as he wrapped his iconic black hoodie around my shoulders.

God, he was gorgeous. I had to bite the insides of my cheeks to keep from swooning like a fangirl. I also had to squeeze my legs together to dull the ache induced by that smile. That guy had the most kissable dimples.

"Oh my God! Thank you, boo! I'm fucking freeeeeezing!" I pushed my arms through the sleeves and hugged the warm, soft cotton to my body. It smelled just like him. Earthy. Manly. Divine.

I let my eyes roam over the patches and white logos, but I didn't bother to read them. I had them all committed to memory. I'd joined every radical political group's mailing list (which my dad was positive had put us on some kind of FBI watch list). I'd researched every band, bought all their albums, and could have recited the lyrics to Lance's favorite songs in at least three different languages if anyone had bothered to ask. With the knowledge I'd amassed from that one piece of outerwear, I could have taught a college-level course on punk subculture.

Too bad I didn't particularly like most of it. I secretly preferred listening to the alternative radio station over head-banging to independently recorded vinyl punk records. If we're being honest, it all just sounded like people screaming and breaking things to me. And politically, I was much more of a live-and-let-live hippie-type like my parents than an anarchist. But boy, did I love the fashion. And that jacket was the pièce de résistance of punk fashion.

I glanced around our lunch table and noticed that everyone was staring at me, mouths slightly agape. I blushed and curled a little deeper into the heavenly fabric, singing, *Nanny-nanny-boo-boo, I'm wearing Lance's jaaaacket and yooooou aren't,* in my head.

Lance nudged my hoodie-covered arm with his and said, "Hey girl."

I beamed up at him. "What's up?"

Lance furrowed his brow and tilted his head to the side as if something was really puzzling him. "If I get cold, can I use your thighs as ear muffs?"

"Lance!" I screamed and slapped him on the chest, smiling like a lunatic.

Colton and August were doing their best to ignore the flirt fest going on in front of them, or at least pretend to ignore it. They were sitting across from us discussing the movie *The Fifth Element.* Colton was talking loudly about how he wanted to fuck Milla Jovovich, probably for my benefit, while August picked at the food on his tray and mumbled something about liking the cinematography.

When he saw me looking at him August gave me a little half-smile and said, "I like your hair."

I knew that August wanted to be a filmmaker when he grew up. When we were kids he and I used to stomp around in the woods behind his trailer making little movies with a camcorder he stole from the thrift store. His story lines always seemed to end in everyone being eaten by zombies or ravaged by a flesh-eating plague though.

August was *really* in touch with his own mortality. His mother told me once that he was born a full trimester early and spent his first two years of life in and out of the hospital. Maybe that's why he turned out so little and morbid.

I wished Juliet could have seen me with my new pixie cut, wearing *the* jacket—it was basically the best day of my entire life up to that point—but she was MIA, as usual. She'd been skipping lunch almost every day to make out with Tony in the parking lot, and sometimes she skipped school altogether. Last year she had been in all honors classes with me—that's when we became such good friends—but now she was taking regular old college prep classes and half the time she didn't even go.

Fucking Tony.

A slam reverberated down the length of the table announcing that Knight had just arrived. He always set his tray down with an unnecessary amount of force. The sound completely burst my hoodie-induced bubble of bliss.

"Take that fucking thing off."

Knight's deep voice carried over the white noise of the cafeteria like a record scratch. In my typical fashion, I responded like a woodland creature who'd just heard a twig snap and stared straight ahead, frozen in fear.

Oh, shit. Is he talking to me? Maybe he isn't talking to me. Maybe he's talking to someone else. Maybe if I stay very, very still he won't be able to see me . . .

August was all I could see, since my panic had temporarily deactivated my peripheral vision, and the one dark eye that wasn't hiding behind his hair was full of pity.

"Is your nose fucking broken? That thing smells like shit, Punk."

Fuck. He is definitely talking to me.

I heard Lance's breathing quicken next to me and saw him begin to curl his fingers into his palm, one by one, pushing on each knuckle with his thumb until it cracked.

Knight continued, pressing for a reaction. "You know that motherfucker never washes it. He's too afraid all his little jewels will fall off."

Everyone had stopped talking to watch the spectacle, so there was nothing to drown out the deep timbre of Knight's voice. It echoed through the cavernous cafeteria like a hunter's steps through the forest. And I was Bambi. And Lance was Bambi. And everyone was looking at us.

Lance shifted suddenly in his seat so that his body was facing Knight and puffed up his chest. Unfortunately, he was sitting on the side of me *opposite* from Knight, so I had inadvertently become his human shield.

"What the *fuck* did you just say?" Lance snapped.

Knight snorted. "I said your jacket smells worse than the cum leaking out of your asshole."

Lance moved like he was going to try to get up. I turned and pushed down on his shoulders with both hands, trying to keep him seated, as he shouted over my shoulder, "You should know. You put it there!"

As if that wasn't bad enough Lance had to go and punctuate his little retort with a wink and an air kiss.

Jesus, Lance! Do you want to die??

Nervous laughter percolated around us. I clamped a hand over Lance's mouth and chanced a peek over my shoulder at Knight. His eerily calm eyes were trained directly on me. He wasn't even looking at Lance—the six-foot-three-inch-tall Mohawked punk rocker whom he was goading into a fight—he was simply waiting for me to turn around.

Motherfucker.

If it was my attention he wanted, fine. I'd give it to him. But I was going to do it *away* from my boys. Lance may have been acting cool, but the way he was working those jaw muscles told me he was more than ready to throw down.

Grabbing Lance's face, I looked into his warm hazel eyes and whisper-yelled, "Stop it, okay? I got this. Don't do anything stupid."

Lance glanced over my shoulder again before returning his hard gaze to mine. Forcing a smile, he said, "Who, me? Never."

I leaned closer to his ear and whispered, "Just stay here, okay?"

Lance's hand found my hip under his hoodie as he whispered back, "You sure, B?"

"Sure as shit," I lied.

Then I did the only thing I could think of to defuse the situation.

I jumped on the grenade.

Still wrapped in Lance's massive patchwork sweatshirt, I stood up, becoming immediately aware that there were at least a thousand people staring at me as I walked for what felt like days over to the empty seat beside Knight.

I wanted to make eye contact. I wanted to appear strong and self-confident and annoyed as shit with him, but instead I picked at Lance's sleeve, cleared my throat and whispered, "What are you doing, Knight?"

"Saving your life. You know that fucker probably has AIDS." His tone was harsh, but he had at least lowered his voice enough that I don't think Lance was able to hear him.

Before I could think better of it, I quipped, "I'd rather get AIDS than freeze to death. At least with AIDS I'd have a few more good years."

And that's when I heard it: a chuckle. A chuckle that was quickly masked by a fake cough, but I knew better. I heard that shit. I had made Skeletor the Skinhead laugh.

A warm feeling began to bubble inside me. I felt…special. Proud. I had faced my fear and now, thanks to me, no one was going to get their kidneys kicked in. Nope, not on my watch.

Swiftly recovering his signature scowl, Knight's zombie eyes found mine. He cocked his head to one side, studying me. I felt a molten heat rush into my cheeks and looked back down at my hands, trying not to think about how red my face must be turning under his scrutiny.

"If you need a jacket, I'll get you a fucking jacket, Punk."

What? Is Skeletor trying to be nice?

Looking up through my lashes I could see that his features had softened, just a bit. His mouth was still set in a hard line, but his ghost eyes looked more crystalline than Crypt Keeper. Clear and pale and blue, like shallow water falling into an endless black hole.

"I have a jacket," I lied.

"Then where is it?"

"Um…" I couldn't tell him that it got stolen by Veronica Beazly last spring, lest she be found in a shallow grave, so instead I answered his question with one of my own. "Where's yours?"

Oh my God. I'm such an idiot.

"I don't need one because I'm not a skinny little bitch who gets cold in the middle of August."

Skinny? Knight thinks I'm skinny? I wonder if Lance thinks I'm skinny…

Before I could come up with another lame deflection, the bell rang. I jumped to my feet and Knight followed suit, reaching for his tray, which had remained untouched.

"Oh shit, you didn't get to eat," I said, impulsively grabbing his arm as if he were Lance or August or Colton. "Sorry."

Knight's eyes darted to where my tiny hand was perched on his forearm, the same forearm I saw bulge and erupt into dozens of thick veins as it slowly smashed Skater Boy's head into the gravel a few weeks ago. The image caused me to snatch my hand back as if I'd touched an open flame.

Knight turned to face me, assaulting me with the full force of his attention.

"You don't eat—I don't eat."

And with that he disappeared into the crowd.

Jesus Christ, I needed a cigarette. I grabbed my shit and sprinted down the hallway toward the student parking lot, dying for some nicotine to calm my nerves. I didn't get very far, though. As soon as I neared the boys' restroom somebody grabbed me from behind and shoved me in.

I screamed, but with the noise level in the hallway it didn't matter. The person behind me pushed me all the way into the handicap stall at the far end of the restroom and shut the door behind us. I spun around—which wasn't easy to do with my massive backpack on—to find Lance smirking at me with his index finger raised to his mouth.

"Shhhh," he whispered.

I smacked his arm and mouthed, "What the fuck?" smiling so big it hurt. Lance gasped and clutched his bicep where I'd hit him, acting like I'd injured him.

Oh my God. It's really happening! I cut my hair and now I'm in a bathroom stall with Lance! Dreams really do come true!

Lance reached into the pocket of his jeans, only instead of producing a diamond ring, or a condom, he pulled out a little vintage-looking Lemonheads tin.

Oh, so that's *where he keeps his diamond rings and condoms.*

Lance opened the tin and pulled out a little pale yellow piece of candy, then popped it into his mouth. I just stared at him, confused as fuck about why he'd dragged me into a bathroom stall just to watch him eat dessert, but whatever. We were alone—if you didn't count the dozens of teenage boys pissing and flushing and laughing and cursing on the other side of those particle board walls. Lance could have been reading to me from the phone book for all I cared.

I heard a muffled crunch, then Lanced smiled at me again—this time with half of the Lemonhead captured between his front teeth. He leaned forward, and I prayed for something magical to happen. I opened my mouth the tiniest bit, wanting to believe that he was about to kiss me but not wanting to look stupid in case he wasn't. Lance closed his gorgeous hazel eyes at the last minute, one hundred thousand inky black eyelashes fanning out against his cheek, and tilted his head to the side. Then it happened.

Lance.

Put his lips.

On my lips.

I didn't move, terrified that anything I did would be wrong. I felt Lance's tongue enter my mouth, warm and soft, but along with it came a bitter aspirin taste and a jagged crystal-like object. While I was busy trying to figure out what the fuck was in my mouth, Lance slowly withdrew. It was the sound of crunching that broke my spell. I looked up to see Lance chewing his half of what I now knew was definitely *not* a Lemonhead. His smile was sideways, showing only one of his adorable dimples, but his eyes were dark. Wicked.

I followed his lead and crushed the sour, chemical-tasting rock with my teeth. Lance leaned back against the stall and stared at me while I chewed, looking me up and down in his jacket, then grabbed the pockets of his hoodie and pulled me toward him.

I braced myself with my forearms and landed against his chest, his thigh coming to rest between my legs. A wave of pleasure surged through my body as a tinny, metallic aftertaste hit the back of my throat. My eyes rolled and my heart raced even faster than when Lance's tongue had been in my mouth. I fisted his T-shirt, using him as a lifeline as I rode the crest of this unknown sensation.

I felt Lance's breath on my ear as he whispered, "I don't know what's hotter—you in my hoodie, or you with that fucking haircut."

God, I wanted to fuck him. I'd never gone further with Colton than kissing—never wanted to—but with Lance I wanted it all. I pressed up onto my tiptoes with the intention of kissing his neck, just as the goddamn bell rang.

Noooo!

Lance and I grabbed our bags and sprinted out of there. In the chaos no one noticed which restroom I'd come out of. Lance gave me a quick squeeze and took off down the hall. Luckily, my fourth-period class was right around the corner. I made it to my desk milliseconds before the final chime.

I didn't know if it was from the kiss (Was that even a kiss?), or the not-candy thing I ate, or the excitement of almost being late, but as Mr. Fisher droned on about some shit a bunch of rich white guys did hundreds of years ago, I slowly began to realize that I was *definitely* on something.

My knee bounced under my desk at the speed of light, I couldn't stop sucking on my tongue and cheeks trying to get another taste of that aspirin flavor, and I had to practically clamp my hands over my mouth to stifle the squeals and giggles trying to claw their way out of my throat.

Now, I was no stranger to drugs. I'd smoked my fair share of pot and tried other stuff here and there, but I always ended up feeling like shit. Pot took all my intelligence and flushed it down the fucking crapper. I hated that drug. It made me feel like I was in slow motion, when all I wanted to do was go fast. Cocaine and LSD—which you could buy in the girls' restroom about as easily as a tampon from the vending machine—made me go fast, even faster than my usual hyper self, but the coke wore off in like fifteen minutes and the acid always seemed to take more like fifteen hours.

So, drugs weren't really something I ever took to feel good. To feel different? Sure. I was unhealthily curious about everything. To feel like I fit in? Absolutely. But that Lemonhead thing… that shit made me feel *amazing*. All I wanted to do was dance and laugh and draw and talk and draw *while* I talked and hump something (Lance)—but I couldn't because I was stuck in Mr. Fisher's advanced placement world history class. So instead I flipped the hood on Lance's jacket over my head, pulled my legs up inside of it, and buried my face in the fabric stretched over my knees.

It smelled like him. It was as if Lance and I were one. I'd had his tongue in my mouth and now his skin was on my skin.

My blood felt carbonated. I was effervescence personified. And I just had to hide it for T-minus forty-nine more minutes.

When the dismissal bell rang, I sprang from my turtle shell and bounded out the door. I was on my way to find Lance and give his jacket back (and try to touch him some more) when Angel Alvarez, a new girl I'd seen talking to Juliet a couple of times, called my name from the end of the hall.

Angel had the body of a grown-ass woman but hid her curves under the wardrobe of an L.A. gangster. She was all baggy jeans and basketball jerseys… with an attitude to match.

Practically jogging in place, I stopped in front of her and asked, "What's up?"

Angel snickered and said, "Rough day?"

I quirked my head to one side, wondering why she would ask me that, when she pointed at the hood covering my head.

Oh, that.

I flipped my hood down and said, way too cheerily, "Actually, I'm having an awesome day!"

Actually, it's taking all my self-control to keep from tap dancing right now.

Angel sucked her teeth, making a clicking sound, and said, "Damn, B! Your hair looks dope!"

I had almost forgotten about it. Just one more reason to be ridiculously exuberant—my new pixie cut! "Thanks!" I chirped. "So does yours!"

Angel's long, dark hair had been bleached blonde at some point in the distant past, gauging by her four-inch-long black roots, and she had it pulled up into a messy bun. It looked like somebody had plopped a pale-yellow pouf on her otherwise dark head of hair. I'm sure most people would have thought it looked trashy, but I thought the two-tone effect was pretty rad.

"Pssh. Whatever. My hair looks like ass." Angel rolled her eyes and touched her bun, but I could see a little smile there. She'd appreciated the compliment.

"Yo, I wanted to tell you that I been seeing that Nazi motherfucker hanging around your locker lately."

Yeah, no shit.

"Listen, I know it ain't none of my business, but if that dude's messing wit' you, you just let me know. My brother and his boys'd love to fuck up a white power piece of shit like that. No charge."

No charge? Jesus. Remind me to stay on Angel's good side.

"Thanks for the warning, hun, but I've already pretty much stopped going to my locker because of him." I turned around and smiled at her over my shoulder, showing off the black ball and chain strapped to my back.

Facing her again I said, far too cheerily, "So far he's just been... intense." *If you call the hand-shaped bruise on my right arm intense.* "But if he ever needs a good ass whuppin' I'll let you know."

We both laughed and walked together toward the parking lot. Well, Angel walked, but that afternoon, in that hoodie, with the lingering tingle of *those* lips on my mouth, and whatever those lips delivered oozing through my veins, *I floated.*

When I saw Juliet leaning up against Tony's car in the parking lot I broke into a full-on sprint. I couldn't wait to show her my hair and show her Lance's jacket and tell her about what happened in the bathroom and show her the bruise on my arm and tell her about Knight acting all crazy at lunch and tell her that I was on something and I didn't know what it was but I fucking loved it! She saw me coming and gave me a confused look with her too-cool black-rimmed eyes...just before I tackled her ass.

Wrapping her up in a hug, I swung her back and forth, chanting, "Ohmigod, ohmigod, ohmigod, ohmigod!"

Juliet pushed me off of her and held me at arm's length, immediately noticing that I was wearing Lance's jacket. Suddenly too cool for school Jules was jumping up and down right along with me. "He let you wear his jacket?!?! Holy shit, B!"

"I know!" I screamed. "I cut my hair and he loves it and he loves me and he kissed me in the bathroom, or at least I think he kissed me, it was hard to tell because he stuck this yellow candy thing in my mouth and now I'm super fucked up!"

I couldn't stop jumping up and down, or smiling. At least, I thought I was smiling. I couldn't really tell because I couldn't really feel my face.

Juliet wasn't jumping anymore. She looked around to see who heard my big fucking mouth and opened the passenger door, shoving me and my monstrous bag into Tony's tiny backseat. "Jesus, BB. Tell the fucking world, why don'tcha."

"Sorry," I said in my loudest whisper. "Hi, Tony."

Tony nodded at me in the rearview mirror as Juliet shut her door. The window rattled in the doorframe. Turning around backward in the cracked leather passenger seat, Juliet said, "You don't have to whisper in here, dumbass."

We both laughed as Tony pulled out of the parking lot, the old 'Vette backfiring in protest.

Juliet said, "So, let me get this straight. Lance loves your haircut, he may or may not have kissed you in a bathroom, and he slipped you something but you don't know what it is?"

"And he loves me. You forgot that part. And I'm wearing his jacket."

"Which you were probably supposed to give back." Juliet was teasing me, but I could tell she was genuinely happy for me. Or maybe she was just happy for herself. She'd been listening to me whine and pine over Lance Motherfucking Hightower since she got stuck sitting next to me in honors algebra in eighth grade.

"I would have!" I cried. "But I got stopped by Angel—that new girl in your English class—and by the time I got outside I figured he was already gone."

"Yeah, right," Juliet teased. "You and I both know you're never giving that hoodie back. You're probably gonna be buried in that thing."

"Shut up, whore!" I said and swatted at her face, missing on purpose. We both started giggling and slapping at each other like a couple of immature schoolgirls, which we were.

"Yo, B." Tony interrupted our fake bitch fight, glancing at me in the rearview mirror with his beady little eyes. "I didn't know you liked to party, girl. Anytime you want more of that yellow just let me know. I'll hook you up."

I looked at Juliet, who simply raised her painted-on eyebrows and gave me a guilty little shrug.

So, Tony is the friendly neighborhood drug dealer. Awesome. You picked a real winner, Jules.

I rolled my eyes at her and snuggled down into my stud- and patch-covered cocoon of love. Even though it was ninety degrees outside—and about a hundred and ninety in the backseat of Tony's car—I didn't care. I was a human disco ball, and disco balls don't sweat. They twirl.

Chapter 5

I slept in Lance's jacket that night. *Of course.* I could smell him in my dreams. I could smell him on my sheets the next morning, and on the shirt I had worn the day before. The idea of that smell disappearing from my room was so depressing that I stashed the shirt I'd been wearing that day in a Ziploc bag, hoping the absence of fresh air would make Lance's scent last longer.

My mom liked the jacket. She said it was very "avant garde." When she dropped me off at school I half expected a swarm of paparazzi to come shove cameras and microphones in my face and ask, "What does it feel like to wear Lance Hightower's jacket? Tell us, does it really give you superpowers?"

There was no red carpet, but I did get a few super-satisfying looks from some cheerleaders when I walked in. I don't know if they were looks of judgment or jealousy, but they felt fantastic all the same.

Lance was in his usual spot, leaning up against the wall at the far end of the main hall, a gaggle of punk wannabes hanging on his every word. When I walked up he kept talking, but pulled me to him and tucked me up under his arm like it was the most natural thing in the world.

Oh my God. We're a couple, I thought. *Look at us! I'm wear-ing his jacket and he has his arm around me and yesterday he may or may not have kissed me and NOW WE'RE BOYFRIEND AND GIRLFRIEND.*

I didn't hear a word he or anyone else said until the bell rang, interrupting my ecstatic inner monologue. I looked up at Lance, probably with hearts in my eyes, and said, "Sorry I took your hoodie home yesterday. I couldn't find you after school."

Not that I looked.

"It's cool," Lance said with a one-dimpled smile, staring at me expectantly.

What is he waiting for? Why isn't he going to class? Oh my God. Is he going to kiss me again?

When I didn't read his mind, Lance gestured toward my body. "Can I have it back?"

"Oh my God! Yes! Sorry! Jesus!" Mortified, I shrugged off the boulder on my back and fumbled with the zipper on Lance's hoodie.

"Jesus? You can just call me Lance. Or Your Imperial Highness."

I shoved the wad of cotton and metal into his stomach a little too hard and said, "Thanks, Your Imperial Highness," with an eye roll.

Lance gave me a quick hug and headed off to class. Just like that. He left me with no kiss, no jacket, and definitely no boyfriend.

Bereft.

I didn't see Lance again until lunch. I was freezing in my Misfits T-shirt and cut-off shorts, and even made a show of rubbing the goosebumps on my arms and legs, but Lance was too busy argu-ing with Colton about whether or not Björk's new album was any good to notice. (Colton thought it was amazing. Lance, of course, insisted that it was corporate sell-out trash. I tended to agree with Colton—that entire *Homogenic* album was goddamn brilliant. Of course, I didn't say that out loud.)

Juliet's head suddenly popped up from somewhere under the table, where she had no doubt been sitting cross-legged on the filthy cafeteria floor talking to her drug-dealing boyfriend on her contraband cell phone.

"BB, Tony says he can't give you a ride this afternoon." She spoke loud enough to interrupt Lance and Colton's conversation, and there was a mischievous gleam in her eye. "Hey Lance, do you think BB could ride the bus home with you?"

God, I loved that girl.

"Nope." Lance looked at me and smirked. "I have detention for being late to fourth period yesterday." His fingers found mine under the table and laced through them. "I got held up in the bathroom by a hoodie thief."

Now he's flirting with me again? What the fuck, Lance?

Juliet and I traded glances just as August cleared his throat. "You can ride home with me, BB."

I accepted immediately, before Colton had a chance to offer. I really didn't want to ride home with Colton alone. Not only would he probably try to fool around with me, just like old times, but I was so scrambled and sexually frustrated over Lance that I probably would have let him do it. Again. And then I'd fuck up whatever chance I had with his best friend. Again.

In fourth period, I forged a note from my mom saying that I had permission to ride bus number eleven home with August Embry that afternoon.

We rode the bus with our knees pulled up, pressed into the foamy seatback in front of us just like little kids. There was probably a thumb war at some point. That's what I loved about August. He wasn't like other boys. With him I could just be myself—a fifteen-year-old girl who liked to curse and be silly and draw pictures and smoke cigarettes and watch daytime talk shows.

I loved August—he was the first friend I made when my family moved to Georgia from Oklahoma in the middle of my first-grade year—but there was a sadness about him that I couldn't help but get all over me whenever we were together. There are some people whose feelings are so intense that I can *feel* them, like they're my own. August was one of those people. And whenever I stepped inside his house, I felt shame.

I'd been to August's place tons of times over the years. It definitely wasn't as fun as Colton's house, with his absentee mom and fridge full of Pabst Blue Ribbon, but August had a PlayStation in his room, so there was that. He also had a mean old mama who I'd never seen step foot outside of their singlewide trailer, possibly because—and I say this without a shred of sarcasm—she might not have been able to fit through the door.

August's older sister, named—you guessed it—April, lived there too. She had gotten knocked up with twins as soon as she finished beauty school. With no money for childcare, April left the kids at home with her mama all day while she worked, and from the looks of things, it wasn't going well.

As soon as August and I stepped off the bus we could hear the smoke detector blaring from inside the trailer. As soon as we got the door open we could hear the sound of babies screaming too. Beverly, August's mom, was in the kitchen fanning the blaring, blinking alarm above her head with a magazine, when she should have been fanning the pan on the stove that was in the process of making the kitchen look like an Alice Cooper concert.

The place was so small that in four strides I was able to wriggle around her, dump the pan into the sink, and douse it with water. Two black bricks—which I assumed had once been grilled cheese sandwiches—appeared to be the culprit.

I opened the tiny window above the sink and within a few seconds the smoke detector stopped shrieking. The babies, who were standing in a playpen in the living area, however, did not.

Beverly collapsed onto a maroon faux-leather loveseat—which fit her like an armchair—in the living room area just next to the kitchen. She clutched her chest, hyperventilating, and reached for a leather pouch on the end table that looked like a long coin purse. Opening it, she pulled out a lighter and a long cigarette, which she lit with shaking fingers.

"Thanks, honey," she said to me, between gasps of air. "I got so caught up in my stories that I forgot I was makin' the little 'uns lunch."

The babies were still crying. Was I the only one who cared that the babies were still crying? Even August was just standing there—one eye wide in shock, one eye hidden, like always.

"You okay, Bev?" I asked, genuinely concerned. She looked like she might have an actual heart attack. "You want me to bring you some water or something?"

Waaaaaaaa!

"Oh no, sweetheart. I'm fine." Bev blew out a big puff of smoke, still clutching her chest with the other hand.

Waaaaaaaa!

"Do you, um, mind if I take the babies outside for some fresh air?" I asked. "It's kinda...smoky in here."

Beverly just nodded and waved her long, skinny cigarette in the direction of the door, then began fishing around in the couch for the remote control.

"August," I said. "Will you grab a blanket or something to put them on?"

I didn't know what the fuck babies needed, but I knew it wasn't to be sitting in a bed of ants and chiggers.

August disappeared down the hall while I scooped up one of the kids. They were identical, at least to me. Both boys with fuzzy reddish hair and a strong set of lungs. Poor fucking Bev. She really had her hands full.

Once we got the boys outside I discovered, much to my horror, that the little fuckers could walk already. Luckily, August's yard was a graveyard for old rusty lawn chairs, so I laid a bunch of them down on their sides and August helped me arrange them to make a little tetanus-infested playpen.

When we were done and the babies were happily picking apart the shredded, woven nylon on one particularly weathered specimen of outdoor seating, I lit a cigarette and admired my work.

Evidently, August had been admiring my work too, because he cleared his throat and said, "You're going to be a great mom, BB."

"Pssh." I rolled my eyes and made sure to blow my smoke downwind from the boys. "Not if I wind up with twins. If I have two of these little bastards at once I'm giving one of them to you."

August looked down and kicked at the gravel under his feet. "Maybe I can give them to you."

The fuck?

August didn't look up, and his cheek was turning bright pink, so I knew he meant what I thought he meant. What was I supposed to say to that? I didn't want to have babies with August. What in the hell gave him that idea?

My mind raced—desperately trying to come up with something sensitive to say—until I finally gave up and settled on nothing. We simply stood there, in an awkward silence, in the knee-high grass, in the brutal summer sun, next to a miserable excuse for a mobile home, supervising a couple of half-naked babies in a cage we'd made out of rusty lawn chairs, while smoking cigarettes we weren't old enough to buy yet. And in that moment I realized something. Something that made me sad.

I wouldn't be riding the bus home with August Embry ever again.

Chapter 6

With both August *and* Colton crossed off my list of potential after-school rides (and Lance always coming up with some lame excuse as to why I couldn't come home with him), that made Tony my only source of after-school transportation. Which was fine. He gave me the creeps, but most of the time he just dropped Juliet and me off at her house while he ran around town doing drug-dealer stuff, so I didn't have to interact with him too much.

On Fridays I usually spent the night at Juliet's house, unless I was working. I had a part-time job at Pier 1 Imports, a house-wares store that left me reeking of patchouli and eucalyptus at the end of every shift. I liked it though. (The job, not the smell.) They accepted early on that I was just going to show up wearing what-ever garish, inappropriate outfit I'd worn to school, rearrange all of the candles, glassware, and pillows to my liking (regardless of what the example pictures looked like that corporate had sent), ring peo-ple up when I felt like it, and go home. We had an understanding, Pier 1 Imports and I. And the money I made went straight into a savings account that I was trying to pad enough to buy a car when I turned sixteen.

Juliet stayed at my house occasionally, but we both preferred her place. She liked it there because her mom let Tony spend the night too, which kind of blew my mind. And I liked it because her mom didn't care how late we stayed out or what the fuck we were doing. Her dad might have cared, if he'd been around.

Juliet's parents were technically still married. Her mom was a beautiful African-American woman with hair like Diana Ross. She always had her nails done and her false eyelashes on, which seemed silly to me because she worked in a doctor's office and wore scrubs all day. Her dad was a small Japanese man with a drinking problem and a temper from hell. They were the oddest odd couple I'd ever seen. I'd met her dad a few times when we first started hanging out, but by tenth grade he was just…gone. Not dead. Not in jail. Not divorced. Just not…there.

The Friday after August dropped the baby bomb on me, I rode home with Juliet and Tony, all geared up for our usual Friday night activities. We'd order pizza, drink some of Mrs. Iha's vodka, and maybe go to a pool hall where Juliet and I would sit in the corner smoking cigarettes while Tony networked with all the gangbangers and druggies who hung out there. It was a nice little routine. But on that particular Friday Tony announced that we were going out. Like *out* out, and we needed to get ready.

Juliet caked a fresh layer of kohl on top of her already blacked-out eyes and sat me down for a full-on makeover. She swooped my bangs over to the side and pinned them in place with a barrette, mussed my pixie cut with some product she found in her mom's bathroom, drew an even more dramatic cat eye on me, and swiped sparkly silver eyeshadow practically from my eyebrows to my cheekbones.

Juliet vetoed my Black Flag T-shirt and made me change into a silvery tube top. Of course, I refused to take my padded bra off, so to offset the color of my red bra straps Juliet tried to get me to wear her mom's shiny red patent leather heels. I hated them, and thankfully they were so big that my foot just slid right out whenever I tried to take a step. Juliet finally agreed to just let me keep my boots and ripped-up jeans on. Knowing Tony, we weren't going anywhere fancy anyway.

Tony pulled up around nine p.m. wearing the same baggy jeans, Nike T-shirt, and sneakers that he'd been wearing earlier. I suddenly felt super overdressed. I tossed my purse into the backseat and climbed in after it. Juliet slipped into the front seat looking sexy as hell with her waist-length black hair and actual boobs filling out her much classier black tube top.

"Hey baby," she cooed, giving Tony a peck on the cheek. "Where are we going?"

Tony put his hand on Juliet's thigh as he pulled out of her driveway and toward the entrance of her modest, aging neighborhood. "We're going to a club, baby. I got some business with the owner of this place downtown. It's in Lil' Five, so I thought you and B might wanna come. I know you guys like all that freaky punk shit."

A club?! In Little Five Points?! No fucking way!

"Tony!" I screamed and wrapped my arms around the driver's seat, giving him the best hug I could manage from where I was sitting. Juliet leaned over from the passenger seat and piled on. We both squealed and kicked our feet like...well...like fifteen-year-old girls who were about to go to their first dance club.

Then something occurred to me. "Wait. Tony, I don't have a fake ID. How am I going to get in?"

"Pssh. I got you, girl. Don't even worry about it." Tony looked at me in the rearview mirror and smirked through his goatee. He may have been kind of creepy, and a total fucking loser compared to other grown-ups, but that night, to a couple of high school sophomores, Tony was a goddamn rock star.

And he knew it.

Downtown Atlanta was about fifteen miles due west from our

sprawling suburban hellhole, and Little Five Points was a neighbor-hood right on the outskirts of it. A funky little cluster of bars and shops nestled in front of, next to, and behind the ghetto.

I'd been to Little Five Points plenty of times to go shopping with my mom. There was a store we loved called Trash that sold every kind of counterculture clothing you could imagine. While I perused the racks for animal print stretch pants and boots and obscure band T-shirts my mom would sneak off behind the beaded curtain in back to peruse the goods in the head shop. Then we'd grab lunch at a dive bar around the corner that let people carve their initials into the table. There are so many goddamn *BB*s in that place now.

My mom and I never parked in the parking lot Tony pulled into though. It was poorly lit and sat behind a couple of squat, square brick buildings. They were separated by a skinny alleyway that was so long and dark I could barely see the light from the street on the other side. The building on the left was smaller and flanked by an undeveloped patch of woods. The building on the right was bigger and sat right on the corner of the main five-way intersection that gave Little Five Points its name.

Juliet helped extract me from Tony's cramped backseat, and we followed him toward the building on the right. With every step I became more and more nervous. We were six years younger than the legal age to get into a nightclub. There was no way in hell they were going to let us in.

Tony walked up to the back door and knocked on the metal surface three times. It opened and was immediately filled with a burly dude wearing a shiny black vinyl mask that covered his whole head, a mesh shirt, and what looked like a black Speedo with a metal crotch.

The fuck?

The mouth hole on the behemoth's mask was unzipped,

allowing his deep voice to boom out of it. "Name?" he asked. The word echoed across the parking lot.

"Tony. I got business with Mitch." Tony sounded surprisingly calm to be talking to a giant sadomasochist.

"These two with you?" The giant turned his shiny black head in our direction.

Tony stayed cool while my hands shook in my pockets. "Yeah. Mitch wanted to meet them. Couple a hotties, huh?"

The giant eyed us for a second, then stepped aside and let us through. "Mitch's office is upstairs. Knock three times."

Tony nodded as he passed. Juliet and I held hands and scooted in right behind him before the giant had an opportunity to change his mind.

The inside of the club was nothing like I expected. For starters, it was darker. *Much* darker. And louder. And instead of having one big dance floor with a deejay spinning Top Forty hits, the building had been divided into a million tiny little rooms—each blaring a different, yet similar kind of techno music. Each dripping in red and black crushed velvet. Each adorned with Victorian era chaise lounges. And each filled with undulating bodies swathed in rubber and vinyl, stopping and starting with every flash of the strobes. The effect made me feel like I was watching a Charlie Chaplin–era porno.

We followed Tony into the bowels of the building where a circular wrought iron staircase sat in the corner of the largest room. On his way over to it Tony had to hop over a man on all fours to avoid stepping on him. He was being walked on a leash like a dog by a woman in a fishnet bodysuit. I tried so hard not to stare at her, but she was glorious. In her spiked-heel thigh-high boots she was at least a foot taller than me, and under her bodysuit—instead of a bra—her enviably full breasts bore two black *X*s where her nipples should have been.

I was in fucking Wonderland. No, *Fetishland*. That should have been the name of the club. *Fetishland, where nothing is as it seems.*

At the bottom of the staircase Tony turned around and mouthed to us, "Stay down here. I'll be back," before hiking up his baggy jeans and taking the metal platforms two at a time to the top.

Um, okay. What now?

Juliet was able to blend in just fine with her black outfit, black hair, and black eye makeup to hide behind. She could have been twenty-two for all anyone knew. I, on the other hand, was seriously regretting my disco ball look. Especially considering that my top literally cast sparkles on the wall every time the light hit it. I might as well have been wearing a neon sign that read PLEASE CALL CHILD PROTECTIVE SERVICES IMMEDIATELY. But as I looked around, no one seemed to notice. Everyone had turned to face a raised platform on the opposite side of the room.

Just then the doorman who'd let us in appeared on the stage with a microphone in his hand. Through his zippered mouth he growled something undecipherable, and the crowd, which began flooding into the back room upon his announcement, went wild.

I pressed my mouth to Juliet's ear and yelled, "What did he say?"

Juliet shrugged and yelled back, "I don't know. It sounded like *Grinder Girl.*"

A second wave of cheers erupted as a heavy metal song began pumping through the speakers and a woman in lingerie, chunky knee-high platform boots, and a metal breastplate stomped onto the platform. She was holding what looked like a spinning electric sander in a rock fist above her head, and when the first chorus of the song kicked in she held the implement to her steel covered tits and showered the audience in hot orange sparks. They loved it, holding their hands out to catch the embers like children playing in the snow. Grinder Girl danced like a stripper to the music, doing back bends and hip thrusts, casting sparks everywhere she went.

My glittery tube top suddenly felt a *lot* less ostentatious.

For the grand finale, Grinder Girl pulled the doorman back on stage, chained him to the wall, zipped the mouth hole on his mask shut, blasted him with searing hot embers at pointblank range, then sparked the crowd one last time off the metal plate covering the poor bastard's naughty bits.

It was like nothing I'd ever seen before. The whole place was brimming with sexy, dangerous, creative energy. It felt like anything was possible. Juliet and I just walked around and gawked for what felt like hours. There were people suspended by hooks through their skin in one room, people swallowing fire in another. The best part was that everyone there was so wrapped up in the show, or the music (that they were dancing to like hippies with heads full of acid), or defiling one another, that they never stopped to wonder where their half-empty cocktails had gone.

When the pulsing electronica and blinking strobe lights started to make my brain throb and the floor tilt, Juliet and I plopped onto an elegant chaise in yet another room. We giggled and watched in amazement as a skinny man in a studded G-string was vacuum sealed into what looked like a black rubber sleeping bag on the other side of the room. He was completely blind and immobilized in that thing, and only had one hole to breath out of.

"What the fuck is that?" I yelled into Juliet's ear between drunken hiccups. "How is that sexy?"

Just then no fewer than six bondage enthusiasts swarmed the shrink-wrapped human and began fondling and tonguing his erogenous zones through the thin rubber.

Juliet threw her head back in laughter and squeezed me closer. "You are such a virgin!"

"What? It's not like you and Tony are doing this shit in your bedroom!" I thrust my thumb in the direction of the almost-orgy across from us.

"How do you know?" She flashed me a challenging look that lasted all of two seconds before she erupted into a fit of laughter again.

Smiling, I put my head on Juliet's shoulder and yawned. I almost rubbed my eyes before I remembered how much makeup I was wearing.

Just then Tony peeked his head into the room and looked around, recognition registering on his face as his eyes landed on the two giggling schoolgirls in the corner.

He stumbled toward us and slurred loudly, "Whasss so funny?"

Even in the dark I could see that his eyes were red as hell. *Somebody* had been having a good time upstairs.

"Your sex life," I said, gesturing with my chin to the human petting zoo.

Tony laughed and pulled Juliet up by the hand. I closed my heavy eyelids and snuggled into the plush, velvety chair—that I finally had all to myself—while they groped each other.

Before I even realized I'd fallen asleep I was jarred awake by someone tugging on my arm.

"C'mon, BB!" Juliet whined. "Let's go dance! Get up!"

I waved her off and curled up tighter. Pretending to still be asleep while they discussed what to do with me.

"Tony, we better go. Look at her."

"Nah, fuck that. I wanna party with these kinky fuckers! You think I'd fit in that thing, baby?"

"We can't jusss leave her here." Juliet's voice was almost as slurred as Tony's.

I waved them off again, eyes still closed. "You guys have fun. I'll be fine."

I didn't feel dizzy anymore, just super sleepy. An unfortunate side effect of getting up at five thirty every morning, going to school, and working part-time at night.

Now Tony was the one whining. "C'mon, B. My girl wants to dance. Sit your ass up. I got something to help you stay awake."

I opened one eye and looked at Juliet, who was now bouncing up and down with her hand out squealing, "I want some! I want some!"

I sat up and asked, "What is it?"

Juliet turned to me and said, "Um...It's just like those caffeine pills you like! You'll be able to dance all night!" I loved caffeine pills. Diet pills. Anything that killed my appetite and gave me energy. And I was so fucking tired. I didn't trust Tony as far as I could throw him, but I trusted Juliet.

"C'mon, BB! It'll be sooo fun!"

Oh, fuck it.

I held out my hand, into which a little white pill magically appeared. It looked like a Tylenol with a lightning bolt stamped on it.

No skull and crossbones, I thought. *That's a good sign.*

I popped it into my mouth and washed it down with the last gulp of my latest stolen beverage. Seconds later my empty hand was filled again with Juliet's as she dragged me to the dance floor in the back room. I was so tired I kept my eyes shut as I sleep-danced to the booming techno beat. At some point, though, my dreamlike state began to change.

I could feel the bass in my chest, the notes on my skin, and the heat of the strobe lights warming my closed eyelids twenty-eight times per second. Juliet's hand was still holding mine, but it felt different too. We were like one of those trees that appears to be lots of trees above the surface, but down in the dirt they're all connected. Juliet and I had merged. We were just one big tree, swaying, pulling, pulsing. Black. White. Black. White. Black. White. The flashing lights across our skin reminded me of a blinking Christmas tree. That's what we were. One big Christmas tree.

I love Christmas. It's too hot to be Christmas. So fucking hot. Am I sweating? I feel dizzy.

My stomach churned. I didn't dare open my eyes. It was better with them closed. Less black-white-black-white. I felt so good and so bad all at the same time. If I just kept dancing my Christmas tree girl would keep me grounded. She was me and I was her and we were one.

Until we weren't.

Juliet whispered something in my ear, but I couldn't make out what she said. It was too loud in there. Too black-white. I opened my eyes to ask her to say it again, but she was gone. I looked down at my hand. It was empty. I turned and turned again. Everyone was blinking on and off too fast. I couldn't see her. I couldn't see anything but strangers frozen twenty-eight times per second in different sexual positions. Mouths sneering. Teeth bared. Eyes black. Eyes white.

Unseen hands molded to my hips from behind. They guided my movements, side to side. I didn't like them there. They felt mean. They held me tighter as a hard bulge pushed against my body.

No! I screamed in my mind, but the word was trapped in my throat. Choking me. I clawed at the hands on my hips, pulling fingers in directions they didn't want to go until all ten of them were gone and I was running. Keeping low. Burrowing through tall bodies like a child. Which I was.

I could feel sweat dripping down my back and bile rising up my throat, past my trapped words, as I tunneled.

Where is Juliet?

I made it to a wall and followed it until I found a black-white-black-white door. I opened it and tumbled from the rabbit hole onto a fire escape, but the hot, damp air gave me no relief. It was thick in my mouth and tasted like garbage. Reaching for the thin metal railing in front of me, I pulled my head over the side of the fire escape and puked. My body trying to rid itself of the lightning bolt poison inside of me.

"Punk?!"

I turned my head and saw the silhouette of a bald, hulking creature jump off the neighboring building's fire escape in one graceful swoop. He was coming toward me so fast. Too close. Almost there. I tried so hard to focus on him, to process this new threat, but my gaze drifted to the ground without my permission as my eyelids gave up the fight.

Chapter 7

From some faraway place my mind realized that my body was being carried. The ride was bumpy.

Where is my body going? I wondered, from the safety of my mind. *I hope someplace with air conditioning. And a bed. A bed sounds nice. And a toilet, because...*

"I think I'm gonna puke!"

"Not yet, goddamn it."

I know that voice. That sounds like Knight's voice. He's such a grumpy bastard, I thought, just before my stomach muscles tensed and filled my throat with acid.

My eyelids were suddenly assaulted with brightness and my body was set down on some kind of hard floor. Callused fingers touched my face, causing my eyes to jolt open and take in what looked like a scene from the inner circle of hell.

The walls were covered in flames and bats and naked women with pitchfork tails smiling at me with their giant tits hanging out. Oh, and there was a fucking SKINHEAD TOUCHING MY FACE!

My stomach lurched again, so I threw myself in the direction of the toilet. Nothing came up except more stinging bile, but I crossed my arms over the bowl and hung my head there anyway, too afraid to face the sinister world around me.

"Jesus, Punk. You're fucking wasted."

Is that what I am? Wasted? That means drunk, right? Am I drunk?

I'd never been drunk before, but I imagined it would feel about as shitty. So I nodded into my arms and continued to hide. In the toilet. From the devil.

"Who the fuck brought you here?"

He sounds angry.

"You did."

Really, B?? Now you decide to be a smartass?

Satan let out a quick exhalation that sounded almost like a laugh. I risked a peek out of my right eye to assess the situation and found him squatting on the floor not even two feet away from me, smirking. The overhead light cast deep shadows under his eyes and nose, and even though he was sort of smiling, that motherfucker looked wicked to the core.

I snapped my eye shut again and fought back another wave of bile.

"Goddamn. We've gotta get some bread into you. When was the last time you ate?"

I tried to think, but my brain wasn't cooperating.

Did I eat dinner? Umm… Lunch? No. Breakfast?

"I think, maybe… yesterday?"

"Get up."

"What?"

"Get the fuck up!"

The anger in his voice had my body moving before I could even register his words. I stood, eyes opened wide. I was in a small bathroom with one toilet, one small sink, and one giant skinhead. The walls were covered—floor-to-ceiling—in a collage of tattoo-style pin-up girl she-devils. Those curvaceous red ladies were so cruel—pointing and laughing at my complete lack of tits. And hips. And experience. Mocking me.

"Look at the cute little girl," they sneered with teeth and breasts bared.

"Aren't you up past your bedtime, little girl?" asked the one by the door with the pitchfork tail.

"Maybe she's here to sell us some cookies!" the one behind the toilet teased, her nipples bursting from her corset.

"I think it might be a little boy," the blonde one above the mirror mused. "It's so hard to tell with that body."

"And that haircut," the vixen closest to me giggled.

Did the lightning bolt poison kill me? Is this actual Hell? Are these sexy demons going to make fun of me for the rest of eternity? Is Skeletor the Skinhead the devil for real? Because if so, I called that shit.

"Am I dead?"

Shit. Did I say that out loud?

"You will be if you don't fucking eat something." Knight grabbed me by the arm and led me out into a dimly lit open room lined with black dentist-style chairs. Dragging me over to the chair in the back corner of the room, Knight sat me down rather roughly, then disappeared into the hallway we had just come from. He reappeared seconds later holding a small white to-go box.

Knight thrust the box into my lap then sat on the armrest of the seat next to mine, arms folded over his chest, glaring at me. His almost colorless eyes glowed in the darkness.

"You're going to eat every fucking bit of that," he said.

"What is it?" I asked, trying to make my swimming eyes focus on the Styrofoam container in my lap.

"It's Bobby's chicken parm."

"Who's Bobby?" I asked without looking up.

"The owner of the shop."

"What shop?" I wondered out loud.

"This fucking shop."

I looked around and tried to figure that one out on my own so that I wouldn't have to keep asking *why* questions like a four-year-old. The room was dark, and kind of spinning, but there was enough light from the hallway and exit signs that I could make out the basics.

Let's see... We've got dentist-style chairs, but a dentist office wouldn't decorate their bathroom like Hell's brothel. Could be a barbershop. No, their chairs don't lie back like this.

Finally, my eyes adjusted to the dark just enough to make out some of the framed art peppering the walls.

"This is a tattoo parlor."

"No shit. Eat."

Yes, sir. Damn.

I took a bite of the cold, hours-old breaded chicken sandwich and my mouth instantly exploded with happiness. I couldn't chew fast enough. Before one bite was sufficiently pulverized and swallowed I'd already taken another. Or three.

Knight didn't move. I could feel him watching me with those fucking zombie eyes, but I didn't care. I was having an out-of-body experience with that fucking sandwich.

I didn't realize how hungry I was. Hunger was just something I lived with. Honestly, I liked the way it felt. That empty rumble in my belly made me feel pretty. Powerful. Proud of myself. If I could overcome my hunger, I could overcome anything. I could slay a fucking dragon.

Fuck you, hunger! You don't tell me what to do! I call the shots around here, and I'm choosing to look like Kate Moss!

But sometimes, when I went too long without eating, shit like this would happen. I'd lose all control and eat everything I could get my hands on like a ravenous beast in a fit of carbohydrate-fueled mania. Sometimes I'd stick my finger down my throat afterward and throw up all my mistakes. Sometimes I'd just run up and down the stairs in my house four hundred times. But on that particular night, I didn't give a single, solitary fuck. Whatever drug I was on made that sandwich taste like rainbows and fireworks and I just wanted to crawl inside of it and live there forever.

When I finally forced myself to slow down long enough to chew, something occurred to me. "What are you doing by yourself in a tattoo parlor in the middle of the night?" I asked before I could think better of it.

"I think the question should be what were *you* doing by *yourself* in a fucking alleyway in Little Five in the middle of the night?"

"I asked you first."

Oh my God, BB. Just shut your mouth.

"I work here."

"Really? How old are you?"

Stop it, BB. Seriously.

"How about you tell me what the fuck you were doing at Sin."

"Sin? Is that the name of the place next door?"

"You didn't even know the name of the place you were at?" Knight's nostrils flared as he stood up abruptly and ran his thick fingers over his buzzed head.

Emboldened by the shot of glucose coursing through my veins, I said in an almost convincingly assertive tone, "No, I didn't. My friend's boyfriend brought us there."

"And they let you in? That's a twenty-one-and-up fetish club, and you don't look a day over sixteen."

"I'm fifteen."

"Exactly."

Exasperated, Knight walked to the front of my chair and sat down, legs spread wide, on a tall black stool on wheels. He gave the chest of drawers it was next to a shove with his boot and rolled over a few feet so that he was next to me.

Now that he was sitting again he seemed less scary. Or at least, less angry.

"What about you? Don't you have to be eighteen to work in a tattoo parlor?" I asked.

"Only if you're getting paid." Knight was becoming less resistant to my incessant questioning, which was good because I didn't seem to be slowing down.

"You're not?"

"Bobby pays me in ink, for now. And lets me crash here on the weekends."

"Pays you in ink? You mean, like tattoos?"

Knight swiveled around on his stool so that his back was to me and pulled up his T-shirt, exposing the black outline of a coat of arms that covered his entire back. At the bottom of the shield the word MCKNIGHT had been written inside a tattered banner in Old English.

"Yeah. Like tattoos."

"Oh my God!" I leaned forward and studied the lines. The shading. "It's...It's really beautiful."

Knight chuckled, which sounded more like a cough, and dropped his shirt. "Beautiful, huh?"

I had been sitting sideways on the tattoo chair, practically leaning out of it to get a closer look at his back, when he turned around. Suddenly his face was a mere foot from mine, and...and damn. That tattoo wasn't the only beautiful thing about Knight. He was smiling, kind of, and his pointy nose and sharp cheekbones were covered in freckles that made him look, well...cute. I'd never noticed how fucking cute he was before. Whatever Tony had given me must have been some strong shit.

Swallowing hard and sitting upright, I said, "Your tattoo says *McKnight*. Is that your last name? Is that why you go by Knight?"

"Yes." Knight sat more upright in response and resumed his death stare.

"What's your first name?" I asked.

"Don't have one."

"Bullshit. Are you really not going to tell me?"

"No."

Ugh! This fucking guy!

"I'll tell you *my* name," I taunted.

"I know your name."

"Oh yeah, what is it?"

Knight cocked his head to one side, irritated, and said, "Brooke. Bradley."

Wha?

"How did you know that?"

"Everybody who went to Peach State Elementary knows who you are. Your mom was my fucking art teacher."

I burst out laughing, imagining a tiny little skinhead stabbing pencils through the eyes of his classmates' drawings.

"Holy shit!" I cackled.

"Yeah." His tone softened. "Your mom is actually the one who got me to start drawing. I used to come into her room all pissed off about…" He looked at me, obviously censoring what he was about to say. "…about whatever, and instead of making me sit with the rest of the class she gave me my own little desk in the back corner where she had a basket full of…"

"Oh my God!" I shouted, clamping my hands over my mouth as memories from helping my mom after school flooded my mind. "It was you!"

Knight locked eyes with me in surprise.

"I'm the one who filled that basket for you! My mom said there was a 'special little boy' in one of her classes who was really artistic but didn't get along with the other kids, so she got an extra desk from one of the other classrooms and had me fill a basket with art supplies to keep next to it. That was me!"

The corner of Knight's mouth pulled up slightly. "Well that explains all the glitter glue and heart stickers."

We both laughed. Well, I laughed and Knight did his smoker's cough thing. It was like he hadn't laughed in so long he had to knock the dust off first.

"And now you're going to be a tattoo artist. That's fucking awesome. I can't wait to tell my mom. She's gonna be so proud of you. And she'll totally tell me your first name too," I teased.

Knight cough-laughed, harder this time, and said, "Fuck you, *Brooke*." I kicked his shin in response, making him laugh for real. The sound caused a wave of warmth to slosh over me.

It felt strangely intimate, talking to Knight about my mom. She had liked him. I remembered her talking about how talented he was. She even saved some of his drawings. Disturbing shit, full of blood and weapons and really elaborate dragons, but she hung them up on the bulletin board behind her desk anyway. Right next to mine.

Maybe he's not so bad, my stupid drug-soaked brain thought. *He's just a tortured artist. A tortured artist who can give me a tattoo!*

"I want one!" I blurted out.

"One what?" Knight was still smiling as he took a step backward and sat on the armrest of the vinyl tattoo chair next to mine. God, he really was cute. And his arms looked huge when he folded them against his chest like that. And I liked his suspender things. Nobody else wore those.

"Oh, sorry." *Focus, BB!* "A tattoo. Can you give me one?" I gestured around the room, indicating that yes, we were in a tattoo shop. "Right now?"

And, *poof*, there went his smile.

"Fuck no. I'm not tattooing a drunk-as-fuck fifteen-year-old."

No? Did he just tell me no?

"What about a piercing? If I don't like it in the morning I can just take it out." I could hear the whine in my voice that I used on my parents whenever they told me no, but I didn't care.

"No."

"When are you going to be eighteen? I'll just come in here then and pay for it like a regular customer and you'll have to do it."

"Next month, but I still won't do it because you're…only… fifteen."

"Oh yeah," I giggled. Then I had an idea. "What if I have a note from my mom? I heard that you can get married at fifteen in Georgia as long as you have a note from one of your parents."

Knight huffed out an exasperated breath and rolled his evil ghost eyes. "Goddamn it."

"Ha!" I yelled and slammed my hands down on the vinyl seat. "I knew it! I fucking love Georgia!"

"But that shit only works for piercings."

"Whatever. I'll see you next month, sucker." I folded my arms over my chest in victory, but the silence made me realize just how fucked up I actually was.

Shut up, BB. Shut. Up. Knight was right. You are so wasted.

The room felt like it was beginning to tilt to the right as my stomach threatened to heave again. And this time it was fully loaded.

Oh, God. Please don't let me throw up right here!

"I have to go!" I tried to slide off the chair gracefully, but my denim-covered thighs were stuck to the vinyl upholstery. Knight stood up as if he were going to help me up, but stopped short when I held my hand up in his direction and peeled myself off.

"Juliet is going to wonder where I am. I have to go!" I grabbed my bag off the floor and sprinted down the hall and out the door that I assumed led to the fire escape. I held my breath before the night air hit my face, not wanting to barf again. Knowing that I wouldn't be able to get back inside the club without Tony, I ran through the alley that separated the two buildings and out into the parking lot. Thankfully, Tony's car was still there.

I collapsed onto the hood, welcoming the cool metal against my cheek, and gripped the sides for dear life as the world spun out from under me.

What the fuck did Tony give me? I hope I puke in his car on the way home. He deserves it.

I reached into my purse and fished around for my cell phone, but when I went to dial Juliet's number it didn't beep or light up or anything.

Awesome. Guess I'll just wait here.

I had just turned my face to give the other cheek a ride on the cool metal when I felt a shadow fall over me.

Tony.

"Thank fucking God," I said, rolling over and squinting into the streetlight. "I thought you guys were never…"

Shit. Not Tony.

"Get the fuck up. You are not riding home with that piece of shit."

I curled myself up into a sitting position on the hood, but was too dizzy to stand. I tried to look at Knight's face, but the street-light behind him was too bright. I stared at his boots instead. The ones that had kicked Skater Boy in the kidney not even three weeks ago.

Pull yourself together, girl, my mind warned. *You are in danger.*

"Jesus, you're fucked up. I know drunk, and drunk bitches don't grind their teeth like that."

Was I grinding my teeth?

"You're fucking rolling."

Rolling. The word took a minute to sink in. *Rolling. That meant I was on ecstasy, right?*

I held my head in my hands and spoke to Knight's knees because his boots were too scary. "Hypothetically, if I *were* rolling," I said, "would that make me feel like I want to throw up and knit the world's longest scarf and give somebody a back massage all at the same time?"

"You don't even know what you took?!" Knight slammed his palms down on either side of my thighs, making me jump and cover my face with my hands. Peeking through my fingers, all I could see were his spectral eyes, glowing in the dark. His face was a mere three inches away from mine. I slammed my fingers back together, both to protect myself and to hide the tears that always came whenever someone yelled at me.

"I, I just took a pill that Tony gave me to help me stay awake."

"That motherfucker. *Tony's* gonna fucking die tonight, Punk. Stay here."

Knight pushed off the car and stalked toward the building.

Oh, fuck. Oh fuck, oh fuck, oh fuck.

I pulled my hands away from my face and called after him, "Knight! Stop! Please! I'm fine! It's fine! I just need to wait here because I'm supposed to be staying with Juliet tonight and she's going to be looking for me and my phone is dead and..."

Knight turned around and stomped back toward me, pulling something long and black out of his pocket. He whipped it back and forth through the air with a flourish of flips and twists. I should have run away, but my curiosity wouldn't let me move until I figured out what the fuck Knight was doing. With one last flick of his wrist, the streetlight glinted off something silver extending out of Knight's hand—a six-inch-long blade.

I froze, blinking and swallowing (and probably grinding my teeth), trying to clear the drug-induced fog from my head so that I could respond to the fact that there was a fucking skinhead standing over me with a knife.

Think, BB. Think! Move! Speak! Fucking run!

I watched from deep inside my immobilized body as Knight brought the knife up over his head and jammed it down into the hood of Tony's car, right next to my thigh. That got me moving. I jumped up and tried to run, but Knight reached out and grabbed my hand before I could get away.

Fuck!

I yanked against Knight's grip, which was about as productive as trying to budge a Buick, as I frantically scanned the parking lot for any sign of Tony. I glanced back at Knight over my shoulder. His left arm was stretched out behind him holding on to my hand like a vise, while he lifted and pulled and dragged his blade across the hood of Tony's car with his right.

No!

The word must not have come out, because Knight didn't seem to hear me. Or maybe he was just too focused on whatever the fuck he was carving into Tony's hood to respond. I pulled on Knight's hand again, and noticed the way the muscles bulged in his arm and upper back when he tightened his grip.

I must be on ecstasy, I thought. *Tony gave me fucking ecstasy. There is no other reason why I would be thinking about Knight's back muscles right now. Or the tattoo covering them. Or the fact that he is holding my hand. Tattooed skinhead = scary. Dark parking lot = scary. Knife = scary. So why does scary + scary + scary + back muscles + hand holding = ten thousand fuzzy tingly goosebumpy thingies all over my body?*

When he was done, Knight flipped and twirled the knife again, shoving it back into his pocket before turning the full force of his attention back to me. The expression on his face reminded me *exactly* why I shouldn't be thinking about those things. He looked positively possessed.

"There. Now *everybody* will know where the fuck you are. Let's go." As he dragged me away by the hand, I walked backward so that I could get a look at what Knight had been working on. There, on Tony's hood, scrawled in giant, pointy, capital letters, were the words,

BB IS WITH KNIGHT
MOTHERFUCKER

Chapter 8

Away from the car, back into the alley, up the fire escape stairs, and back into the tattoo parlor I was pulled. Knight slammed the door behind me and paced back and forth in the dimly lit shop hallway, running both hands over his almost bald head. I liked it better when he was holding my hand. This standing in the doorway watching him pace thing was freaking me out.

I should have been freaked out about the fact that my best friend's boyfriend's car had just been carved up like a prize fucking turkey, but...my brain was broken. I was too busy grinding my teeth and fighting the urge to give Knight's uber-tense body a massage to worry about silly things like vintage Corvettes.

I guess Knight figured out whatever he'd been working on because he suddenly stopped pacing, fished his keys out of his pocket and said, "C'mon. I'm taking you home."

"I can't go home," I said, surprising myself with how calm I sounded. How resolute. I guess because it was a fact. I couldn't go home. It was the middle of the night and evidently, I was rolling my balls off. Ixnay on the oinghomegay.

I thought he was going to argue with me, but Knight simply

shoved his keys back in his pocket and said, "I guess that makes two of us."

Neither of us asked any follow-up questions. We just stared at each other. I remember thinking that his eyelashes were pretty. With the little bit of light provided by the emergency exit signs I could tell that—even though they were blond—they were really long and full. I wanted to touch them.

"So, I guess you're staying here then," he said. I couldn't help but pick up on a tiny bit of hopefulness at the end of that sentence. Like his voice went up when it usually would have gone down. But maybe not. I was pretty fucked up.

I shrugged and said, "I guess so."

Knight's whole body visibly relaxed. "Wanna smoke?"

"Yeah. I do."

We went back out onto the fire escape where I sat on the top step with my head against the building just to keep the world right side up. Knight sat down next to me and lit one of his Marlboro Reds. He offered it to me, but I made a face at him, so he popped it in his mouth and dug around in my purse until he found my box of Camel Lights. He lit one of those and handed it to me. That time I accepted.

"Why don't *you* want to go home?" I asked, no longer giving any fucks about what came out of my mouth. My filter, as well as my depth perception and inner gyroscope, were completely shot to hell.

"Another time," he said, exhaling in the direction of the parking lot, directly in front of us.

Another time, I thought, happy little floaty bubbles dancing through my veins. *That would be fun. We should do this another time. Only without the whole scratching up Tony's hood thing. Like a slumber party.*

Despite having the spins, I was starting to feel pretty damn good. The nausea was gone, and it took everything I had not to grind my teeth and let my eyeballs roll up inside my head in sheer bliss. My cigarette tasted *amazing*, and all I wanted to do was hold this boy's hand and look into his pretty eyes and ask him a million and one questions about his childhood.

I felt like I knew him somehow.

And I guess, in a way, I did. I knew something that other people didn't know. I knew that he liked to draw.

"Will you show me some of your tattoo designs?" I asked, turning to face him but not quite ready to pick my head up off the wall.

Knight tilted his head to the side as he looked back at me, then nodded once. There was a vulnerability about him that was really sweet. I made a mental note to ask him about his art more often.

We flicked our cigarettes into the alley and Knight helped me stand up. Once we were inside he flipped on some of the lights in the main room, and they helped to ease my dizziness. Knight walked up to the front desk and pulled a three-inch-thick binder out from one of the drawers. I followed and stood next to him behind the counter as he set the binder down on the desk. For a moment we both just stared at it, wordless.

There was an electric charge in the air between us that caused my hairless arms to erupt in gooseflesh. Skeletor the Skinhead was shrugging off his armor. He was going to let me gaze upon his soft, pink underbelly, and he was trusting me not to gut him.

I slowly opened the notebook and began to flip. With each passing page I felt more and more insecure about my skills as an artist, and more and more honored to have been allowed a glimpse into Knight's mind. His drawings were intricate, dark, and detailed. His themes revolved mostly around old English and medieval iconography. Dragons, castles, coats of arms, shields, swords, and my favorite, knights.

One particular knight drawing caught my eye. It was a solid black silhouette of a jousting knight on a galloping horse.

"This," I said, pointing to it. "This is your next tattoo."

Knight's face paled, if that was even possible, and he asked quietly, "How the fuck did you know that?"

"It's a knight. You're a Knight. It just makes sense," I said, beaming with pride over my Nancy Drew skills.

"I'm actually getting that one done as soon as my back piece is finished. I just have to figure out where to put it."

"You should put it on the side of your neck!" I exclaimed. "That would look fucking badass!"

"I thought about that," Knight said, "but if I put it there I won't ever be able to join the military. They don't allow visible tattoos."

"Pssh! You? Join the military?" I burst out laughing. I couldn't help it. "You might as well stick that tattoo on your forehead, honey, because you're more likely to end up in prison than the fucking military."

The next morning was kind of a blur. I don't really remember falling asleep or waking up, but I do remember Knight giving me a ride back to Juliet's house in a very large, very loud truck. I remember worrying about whether or not Tony's car would be there, and I remember sighing in relief when we pulled up and it wasn't. I also remember giving Knight the most awkward wave goodbye as I leapt out of his monster truck and stumbled, still wasted, up the stairs to Juliet's porch.

Once Knight's truck was out of sight and the coast was clear I stumbled right back down the stairs, through Juliet's neighbor's backyard, and into the shopping center on the other side of the woods. I wandered into the grocery store in my silver tube top and smeared eye makeup, looking like more a cracked mirror than a disco ball, and took two hundred dollars out of the ATM inside.

It was almost all the money I had. I just hoped it was enough.

When I got back to Juliet's house I let myself in using the key her mom kept hidden under a dead fern. I tiptoed through the living room and down the hall to Juliet's bedroom unseen. Her mom was probably still in bed, and the sounds coming from the basement suggested that her unsupervised little brother was indulging in a little *Ren & Stimpy* downstairs.

I left the cash on Juliet's pillow, along with a note.

Dear Juliet,

I'm soooooooo sorry about Tony's car. It's a long, fucked-up story. Call me and I'll tell you about it later. Here's some money to fix the damage. Tell Tony if it's not enough I'll pay him the rest later. And tell him I'm really, really sorry.

Love,

BB

I washed my face, changed back into my T-shirt from the day before, and dashed outside at ten a.m. on the dot when my mom showed up in her Band-Aid–colored Ford Taurus station wagon.

I pretty much spent the entire half hour car ride home lying to my mom about how much fun Juliet and I'd had watching scary movies and eating pizza the night before. Then, during the last five minutes or so, I finally mustered the balls to ask my mom if she remembered the boy we made that basket of art supplies for when I was a kid.

"Of course I do!" she said. "Ronald McKnight. I'll never forget *that* name. That boy was psychotic. He stabbed a kid with a pair of scissors on his first day in my class."

Well, he was liquefying a kid's spleen with his boot the first time I met him, so I guess some things never change.

"Thank God they were just those little kid scissors with the rounded ends," my mom continued, "but he still managed to break the skin. After that I let him sit in the back by himself and just draw whatever the hell he wanted." She laughed. "I didn't teach that boy a damn thing, but at least nobody else got stabbed."

"Well, you must have made some kind of an impression," I said, "because I saw him at school yesterday and he said you inspired him to become a tattoo artist."

"Really?" my mom asked, sounding genuinely surprised. "I just assumed he'd be in prison by now. A tattoo artist, huh?" She thought about it for a minute and then laughed. "Well, he was artistic and he did like to stab people, so that sounds about right."

I laughed nervously.

Ronald McKnight. No wonder he didn't want to tell me his first name. Poor bastard. I'd be pissed off too.

Once we got home I said a quick, "Hey," to my dad, avoided the whole "Have you eaten?" conversation entirely, and ran upstairs to my room where I tore off my boots, plugged in my phone, and passed the fuck out.

When I woke up, disoriented as hell, I glanced at my phone to see what time it was and noticed that I had about a hundred missed calls. They were all from Juliet, and all from that morning and the night before. I listened to most of them. Or tried to. It was hard to understand what she was saying over the sound of Tony yelling in the background.

Shit.

I called Juliet back while I was getting ready for work and apologized profusely. She said Tony calmed down once he got the money I left. He was already at his buddy's shop getting his hood fixed, but she was pretty sure that he still wanted to kill Knight.

Juliet then unloaded a million and one questions about what happened the night before and if Knight had hurt me and why he was at the club and was he stalking me, but all I said was that I didn't really remember. I gave her a few details, but said the rest was really hazy.

I left out the part about where Knight worked.

And about me spending the night with him there.

I left out the part about what kind of vehicle he drove.

And how he had a tattoo that covered his whole muscular back.

I left out what an incredibly talented artist he was.

And how he held my hand while he carved up her boyfriend's hood.

I'd never kept anything from Juliet before, but something deep down told me to keep this one a secret. Maybe it was because I was afraid Juliet would tell Tony and somebody would get hurt. Or *maybe* it was because I didn't want to admit to my half-Black, half-Japanese best friend that I'd spent the night with a skinhead.

Who I kind of, sort of, might be friends with now.

Chapter 9

On Monday morning I chewed my fingernails to the quick as I stared out the passenger window of my mom's car. I was going to see Knight again. How should I act? Should I just keep avoiding him? Even if I never went to my locker again, I'd still have to see him in the church parking lot and at lunch.

What if he thinks we're, like, friends now? I know he took care of me when I was super fucking wasted and all, but I can't be friends with a skinhead. With the skinhead. That's basically like being bros with Hitler. Everybody will think I'm down with the fucking KKK or whatever, when I am the least racist person in this whole goddamn redneck state.

To distract myself, I started doing that weird thing I used to do in the car where I would tap a beat with my thumb and try to time it just perfectly so that it missed every telephone pole and street sign that passed by my window.

It didn't work.

Maybe if I go by my locker this morning and talk to him there, then he won't feel the need to talk to me out in the parking lot where everybody will hear us. Or at lunch. Oh, God! Lunch! Juliet will be there and he fucking carved up her boyfriend's car! I hope she doesn't say anything. She's pretty scared of him, so maybe she won't. And I paid to fix it, so . . .

I was so lost in thought that I barely realized that I had gotten out of my mom's car, entered the building, and was rounding the corner to my locker when I saw him. Standing there. Waiting for me.

Pale blue zombie eyes locked onto mine, and a series of still images from Friday night came rushing to the forefront of my mind. Freckles. Drawings. A knight on horseback. A smile.

But this Knight wasn't smiling.

Instead of walking past him to get to my locker I stopped just a few feet in front of him, deciding that I was close enough. I tried to make my face contort into something resembling relaxed indifference, but I couldn't tell if I was pulling it off or not. From the way Knight was studying me, I guessed not. Was he waiting for me to do something?

Oh! I know!

I pulled the muffin my mom gave me that morning out of my purse, still wrapped neatly in its paper towel.

"Hey. I brought you something, just to say, you know . . . thank you."

Knight looked at the muffin like it disgusted him, then turned those undead eyes on me like I disgusted him too.

"Y-you don't like muffins?" I asked.

Knight let my question hang in the air, giving me a look that made me feel like a piece of shit for not already knowing the answer. What the hell? How was I supposed to know he didn't like muffins?

"Are you fucking kidding me?" Knight practically spat the words at my doughy offering.

"Um . . . no?" I just stood there, blinking my big confused eyes at him, the soft hunk of carbs still outstretched in my hand.

"I have food, Punk. I eat. *You're* the one who's fucking starving. That's *your* breakfast, isn't it? You probably told your mommy some bullshit little story about how you were gonna take it to school and eat it with your friends, *didn't you?*"

I knew his stare was powerful. I knew it hurt when he turned it on me. But until then I didn't realize it could slice me open and expose my insides like a laser. I didn't know it had the power to gut me.

"Well, *we're* friends now—aren't we, Punk?"

I slowly nodded my head, embarrassment and anger probably screaming back at him now that my mask of cuteness had been cut to ribbons.

"Good. Then you can eat that fucking muffin. Now."

When I hesitated Knight narrowed his spectral eyes at me. Then he slammed his palm against the locker just above my head. I ducked and pulled my hands up around my ears automatically, the tingle of unshed tears building behind my eyes.

Staring down at me as I cowered, Knight said, "Punk, either you take a bite of that muffin or I'm gonna shove it down your fucking throat."

I went to turn away from him—both to shield myself from his stare and to keep him from seeing the angry tears that were welling up in my eyes—but in doing so I accidentally smashed my huge backpack into the lockers next to me. My clumsiness only added to my embarrassment.

I took a bitter bite of the baked good in my hand, and it was so surprisingly delicious that I almost forgot why I was so upset. I closed my eyes and savored the sweet, fruity fluffiness, floating away on a flesh-colored cloud of calories.

"Give me that." Knight's clipped tone cut off my moment of pleasure, reminding me that I was supposed to hate food, and hate him even more.

Knight extended his hand toward my back and flicked his

fingers up twice, gesturing that he wanted my backpack. I gave him my best sideways *eat shit and die* look, but when his nostrils flared and the muscles in his jaw contracted, I shrugged that shit off and handed it over.

"Jesus, Punk. What the fuck do you have in here? A dead body?"

Now it was my turn to let the question hang in the air. I took another spiteful bite of muffin, leaned back against the lockers, and crossed my arms over my chest.

Knight glared at me for a second before turning around and kicking the bottom left corner of my locker door. The metallic sound clanged and echoed down the hallway as Knight swung the door open and stared into my completely empty locker.

"Where's all your shit?"

I flicked my gaze from his face to the bag in his hand and then resumed my staring contest with the wall across from me, taking another exaggerated bite of muffin that no longer tasted like anything other than contempt.

"You carry *all* of it?" Knight's tone was significantly softer, and I heard something in it that made me feel even worse than I already did. I wanted to explain, but I couldn't. I couldn't even look at him. I simply stared straight ahead while he put two and two together, and continued my mechanical cycle of biting, chewing, and swallowing.

"Why don't you use your locker, Punk?"

Bite.

"Why the fuck don't you use your locker, Punk?"

Chew.

"Are you fucking crying?"

Swallow.

"You know what? Fuck this."

Slam.

Knight dropped my bag of books on the floor where he stood

and stormed off. Once he was gone twin black tears slid down my face, as I slid down the locker I'd been leaning against. My backpack and I sat side by side—two lumps of similar weight but one was far too heavy for its size.

And one was far too light.

I felt exposed. And humiliated. And attacked. But that wasn't why I was crying. I was crying because of what I heard in Knight's voice when he asked me *why*.

Evidently, the boy who hated everybody had feelings, and I'd just crushed them without saying a word. By standing there trying to look tough, I'd allowed him to believe that the girl he took care of Friday night—the one he'd shown his drawings to—would rather suffer day in and day out than risk standing next to him for a single minute. I could have easily come up with some lie to spare his feelings, but I hadn't. Because I'd wanted to hurt him.

And now I just wanted to take it back.

The first bell rang, indicating that I had seven minutes to get my ass to first period. I looked at my backpack, but for some reason I couldn't make myself pick it up. I couldn't shoulder the burden of my own cruelty.

So I stood up, smoothed the wrinkles out of my Ramones T-shirt, adjusted my studded belt, and kicked open my locker with one tiny black combat boot—nailing it on the first try. In they went. All of them. Book after book after book. With every pound that I unloaded my conscience felt lighter, but not light enough.

I never felt light enough.

Chapter 10

I went back to my locker after first period to switch out books—and to hopefully apologize to Knight—but he wasn't there. My locker was just a few feet away from the exit that led out into the student parking lot, so if I hurried I'd still have enough time to get out there and suck down a cigarette before second period. Which my nerves desperately needed.

I emerged from the woods into the church parking lot and saw him immediately. He was standing on the opposite side of the parking lot, away from everyone, smoking and staring at me. Like he'd been waiting to see if I'd show. From that distance he looked even more intimidating somehow. His stance, his glare, his Neo-Nazi boots and braces, the word *Oi!* splashed like blood across his T-shirt, which barely fit around his chest and arms. It was no wonder he always stood off by himself. Knight's presence alone filled half the parking lot.

I lit a cigarette and took a step toward him. I didn't know exactly what I was going to say—or if I would even make it all the way over there without having a panic attack—but I had managed to piss off Skeletor the Skinhead and I had to make it right. Both for my conscience and for my safety.

I made it about three steps closer before the world spun out from under me. Literally. Lance scooped me up from behind and spun me around at least a half dozen times before setting me back down on my feet and rotating my floppy body around to face him. I laughed and clung to his biceps to steady myself, still clutching my Camel Light between two fingers.

At nine o'clock in the morning it was already well over eighty degrees outside, but Lance had that goddamn hoodie on anyway. The one that made me weak in the knees. The one that made me homesick for a bathroom stall. I looked up at his Prince Eric face, with that stripe of brown and green hair, and smiled.

"You're so pretty."

Shit! Did I just say that out loud?

I wanted to cringe and clamp my hand over my mouth, but when I saw the megawatt, Disney-caliber smile it earned me from Lance, I relaxed. At least on the outside. On the inside my brain was screaming, *Kiss me! Kiss me! Kiss me!*

Right on cue, Lance began to lean toward me. I closed my eyes and waited to feel his lips on my lips again.

Oh my God! He loves me! We're sooo getting married! It's all happening!

But nothing happened. When I opened my eyes again, confused and disappointed, Lance wasn't even in front of me anymore. He was bent over picking something up off the ground. I blew out an exasperated huff just as Lance stood back up...holding a dandelion.

With his panty-searing dimple-cheeked grin still firmly in place, Lance stuck the yellow flower behind my ear and said, "So are you."

All of the chemicals in my fifteen-year-old brain fired at once, making me feel almost as high as whatever the fuck that yellow thing was that he gave me the week before.

I squealed and wrapped my arms around Lance's waist, pressing my cheek into his chest. He pulled me closer, and I inhaled him without shame. His hoodie smelled like cigarettes, sweat, and some kind of earthy vegan deodorant that was having trouble keeping up with a six-foot-three-inch teenage boy who insisted on wearing a black sweatshirt in the summertime. My favorite combination.

When I opened my eyes they landed on Knight, who I'd forgotten was out there, and who was also walking directly toward us. The Magnolia and pine tree branches that crisscrossed overhead slashed war paint-like shadows across Knight's hard face. As he advanced he exhaled a slow stream of smoke through his nostrils, which danced in and out of the pockets of sunlight breaking through, further obscuring his features behind an ominous, iridescent shroud.

Knight tore his eyes away from mine just long enough to flick his still-lit cigarette directly into a broken window on the side of the abandoned church. Then he passed us by without a word.

My stomach churned with fresh guilt. And fear. I'd come outside to apologize but instead I'd just twisted the fucking knife. That motherfucker was the last person on planet earth I wanted to piss off, and somehow I'd managed to do it twice in one day.

Oblivious to what was going on, Lance tapped my shoulder and said, "Hey, girl," in his silky-smooth voice.

I painted my smile back on, looked up at Lance's gorgeous face, and asked, "What's up?"

"Is it hot out here, or is it just you?" he asked with a one-dimpled smirk.

I giggled and slapped him on the arm. "Come on, we're going to be late."

As Lance and I walked back down the trail I turned around to make sure there wasn't any smoke coming out of the church window.

Maybe I shouldn't go out of my way to apologize to Knight, I thought. *Maybe I was right to avoid him. I mean, who the fuck flicks a lit cigarette into a wooden building? A fucking psycho, that's who. The same fucking psycho who bullied me into eating a muffin and stabbed some kid in art class and ruptured Skater Boy's kidney and carved up Tony's hood with a six-inch blade and cost me two hundred dollars this weekend.*

I took one last puff off my Camel Light and smashed what was left of it into the trail until I was completely sure it was out. Then I walked arm in arm with my beloved across the student parking lot, resolute.

You know what? Fuck that racist asshole.

Of course, my attitude was a little different once I no longer had a six-foot-three-inch punk rocker on my arm. Before lunch I sprinted to my locker, darting in and out of classrooms with the *Mission Impossible* theme song playing on a loop in my head. Once I'd swapped out my books, I darted out the exit doors and ran around to the front of the building just so that I wouldn't have to walk back down C hall and risk passing Knight.

Popping into the restroom, I touched up my makeup then headed into the cafeteria, praying that Juliet wouldn't be there. I loved her, but being at a table with Knight was going to be uncomfortable enough. I didn't need the girlfriend of the guy whose car he fucked up there too.

I took my usual spot next to Lance but really wished I had someone on my left as an added buffer between me and Knight, whenever he finally arrived. Spotting August walking up I waved at him and patted the seat next to me. It was a shitty thing to do, using him as a human shield, but I'd been wanting to talk to him anyway. I didn't like how we'd left things the week before.

Within a few minutes, August and I had fallen into an easy banter about our favorite *Beavis and Butthead* episodes, and thankfully, Juliet was nowhere to be found. So far so good. I hadn't even chanced a glance at the end of the table, but I hadn't heard him slamming shit around down there so I figured Knight was a no-show too.

Colton leaned forward so that he could see August and me from the other side of Lance's big body and shouted, "Hey! You guys want to come over after school? My mom just stocked the fridge with PBR." His voice got all sing-songy on the "R," trying to entice us with the world's best shitty beer.

With Juliet being MIA I *was* in need of a place to go. And if other people were going to Colton's house with me then I probably wasn't in any danger of being dry humped, either.

"How are we all going to get there?" I asked. "I can forge a note, but I don't think all three of us can do it and get away with it."

"I'll take you."

Huh?

I spun to my left and peeked around August to see Knight sitting at the end of the table, just as still as a jungle cat. How long had he been there? He usually made such a fucking ruckus whenever he sat down.

Knight's newer calmer disposition gave me the creeps even more than the older angrier one did. I didn't trust it. Something was up. And why didn't he have a tray?

All four of us looked at one another, then Colton shrugged. "Okay, but you're not going to like, curb stomp us or anything, right? I mean, you can curb stomp them all you want," he gestured to us, "but I'm way too handsome to get my teeth knocked out."

Everyone laughed nervously at Colton, except for Knight, who just raised an annoyed eyebrow at him in warning.

"Cool, cool. I guess we'll just meet you in the parking lot," Colton said, then leaned back and whispered under his breath, "Oh my God! I've always wanted to ride on the Battle Ram Chariot!"

I snorted and bit my tongue to keep from giggling. Evidently, I was the only one who got Colton's Skeletor reference.

When the dismissal bell rang, I headed straight to the student parking lot with a bundle of nerves sparking and short circuiting inside my empty stomach. But Knight had beaten me out there. He was leaning against the flagpole with his arms crossed, waiting.

In the bright summer sun, Knight's skin, hair, eyebrows, and irises appeared to be almost colorless. He looked like somebody from another planet. Peach State High School was an incredibly diverse place, with over four thousand students of every race and nationality, but *nobody* looked like him.

Nobody dressed like him, either.

I remember wondering where he bought his clothes. Everybody else wore colorful Doc Martens that they purchased with their mommies' credit cards at the mall, while Knight wore jet black kidney kickers that looked like they'd been issued to him by the military. Everybody else wore baggy jeans, all tattered at the bottom, but Knight wore his tight and rolled up to show off his bright red bootlaces. Everybody else wore studded belts, but not Knight. Nope. Red braces. His entire look was both iconic and foreign. And I hated how much it interested me.

What made a person raised in the same town as the rest of us so...different? What happened to him that didn't happen to everyone else? What had he been exposed to that we hadn't? I wanted to open up his shaved head and peek inside. I suspected that his insides were probably just as dark as his outsides were light.

Without a word Knight pushed off the flagpole and walked toward me. I felt a sliver of fear before I assessed his body language and realized that he didn't seem angry. He wasn't happy, he was just...*not* angry.

I stopped walking once I was a couple of feet away from him, but Knight kept approaching. He didn't stop until we were toe to toe, at which point he reached up and grabbed both straps of my backpack and slid them off my shoulders.

"It's lighter," he said, surprised.

I blushed and looked down as he tossed my bag over his shoulder like it weighed nothing. "Um, yeah. I...I put my stuff in my locker. Sorry."

Thick fingers clasped my chin and tilted it up. Knight's face blocked out the sun, but I had to squint to look at him anyway.

"The next time some motherfucker makes you cry, you don't say you're sorry. Do you understand me?" His voice was quiet, but firm.

I nodded and blinked rapidly.

"You don't get to be sorry."

I nodded again, looking at his mouth. His eyes were too intense.

"Next time, you kick him in the fucking balls."

An unexpected laugh escaped me just as Lance, August, and Colton walked up. Horror radiated from their faces at the sight of Knight looming over me, clutching my face. Lance's eyes narrowed to slits.

Oh my God! Is he jealous?

Knight dropped his hand, and within milliseconds Lance smoothed his features back into their usual flawless, charming positions. Smiling like nothing was wrong, Lance gestured toward me with his chin and said, "Hey, girl."

I swallowed hard, regained my composure, and delivered my line. "What's up?"

"You must be tired"—he glanced very obviously at my backpack on Knight's shoulder—"because you've been running through my mind all day."

"Pssh." I giggled, uncomfortable with our audience for once. "You're so cheesy."

Lance smiled back, but it quickly faded as I felt Knight's shadow disappear from my side.

He's leaving??

I turned and hustled after him, the guys following behind, as Knight took long, graceful strides across the parking lot. He finally came to a stop in front of a fucking monster truck, parked in the grass with one of its front tires lurched up onto a boulder. *Holy. Shit.* It rose up over us like a white tidal wave cresting a rocky shoreline, threatening to kill us all.

I vaguely remembered Knight driving me to Juliet's house in a big truck, but I didn't remember it being *that* big.

"Get in." Knight had to reach up to almost eye level to open the passenger side door. He tossed my backpack onto the floorboard then turned around with an expectant look on his face.

The cab only had one long bench seat with a few pieces of duct tape stuck on it here and there. There was no way we were all going to fit.

As if reading my mind Knight said, "Not them. *You.* They're riding in the back."

The back? Like, the back back? *Like in the back of the fucking truck?*

Before I could protest Colton said, "Fuck yeah!" and scaled one of the knobby, four-foot-tall tires, and hopped over the side of the truck bed. Pretending to look around, he said, "Hey, Knight? You got any rebel flags back here we can fly on the way home? I wanna play *Dukes of Hazzard!*"

Lance just smirked and climbed in behind his best friend.

Once he was up there, Lance turned around and held out his hand to help August up, but August just waved him off and climbed up on his own—albeit a little more slowly than the other two.

Satisfied that everybody was okay, I turned back toward Knight, who was still standing in front of the open passenger side door. How the hell had I gotten in there before? The floorboard was chest-high and there wasn't a step or handle or anything I could see that would help my ascent. Just as I was beginning to consider simply climbing into the back with the rest of my friends, Knight wrapped his thick fingers around my waist and hoisted me into the air, setting me down gently on the worn, gray leather.

I didn't know shit about trucks, but I could tell that that baby was *old*. And it looked like it had been pieced together from a few different vehicles. The dashboard was faded black, but the glovebox was gray. The original radio had been replaced with a CD player, but there was an old-fashioned CB radio below it that looked like something from the '70s. The shifter knob was shiny and new, but the cracked leather on the steering wheel was clearly original. I couldn't even tell if it was a Ford or a Chevy. Maybe both?

I have no idea how Knight managed to climb into the driver's seat with the front tire up on that rock, but his door opened and he appeared, easy as pie.

I was about to ask him if he'd built the Frankentruck himself when he cranked the engine, rendering me momentarily deaf. The truck's lift kit bounced us up and down violently as Knight backed off the boulder and over the curb onto the pavement. I held onto the dashboard as my ass bounced off the seat, Colton shouting, "Woo hoo!" from somewhere behind us.

Knight pulled out of the parking lot and gunned it. The engine sounded like diesel-fueled hellfire and spewed a cloud of black exhaust behind us, temporarily shrouding my friends in toxic fumes.

"Where to?"

It had been months since I'd been to Colton's house, but I remembered it like it was yesterday. The peeling paint. The cracked driveway. The sagging front porch where Colton gave me my first real kiss. The itchy mustard brown—colored wool couch where he gave me a lot more kisses, and did some over-the-clothes stuff too.

I also remembered that his mom probably wouldn't be there since she worked like forty-seven jobs just to pay the rent on that piece of shit. Colton was too much of a spoiled brat to get a job and help her out, and his older brother, Jesse, was still living in Las Vegas with their dad—who I'm pretty sure was one of the founding members of White Snake. Colton's mom, Peggy, had *former '80s hair band groupie* written all over her.

"Um, just go right on seventy-eight and turn right again after the Waffle House. Colton lives in the neighborhood behind it."

"Cool."

Knight lit a cigarette, prompting me to light one of my own, and we rode in silence for a few minutes as I looked around, trying to remember more from Saturday morning. It was such a blur and it seemed so long ago, but it had only been two days. Two days. And there I was again.

And my friends in the back had no idea.

"Thanks for the ride," I said, trying to break the tension. "I didn't think you'd want to come."

"I don't." Knight exhaled a puff of smoke toward the cracked driver's side window, never taking his eyes off the road.

"Oh. Then why—"

"Because you needed a ride."

Knight flicked his icy eyes to mine for just a moment. Just long enough to make my breath catch.

Thankfully Colton's street came into view just then, giving me an excuse to change the subject. I pointed and told Knight which turns to take.

When Knight pulled into Colton's driveway, it was so much worse than I'd remembered. The bushes and grass were at least a foot taller, and the places that needed painting before now looked like they needed to be replaced altogether.

Knight hopped out and came around to my side of the truck. I opened my door, prepared to jump out of the ten-foot-tall cab like I'd done at Juliet's house, but before I could, Knight reached in and pulled me out. Just grabbed me around the waist and yanked me out. I didn't appreciate that he thought he could just touch me whenever he wanted, but I did kind of like how little it made me feel when he did. How light.

From the back of the truck I heard a loud groan followed by hysterical laughter. I spun around, my cheeks flushing, thinking the guys were reacting to Knight's hands on my waist, but they weren't even looking at us. They were gathered around Lance, who was rolling around on the driveway holding his crotch.

I ran over and asked what happened, feeling Knight's shadow following right behind. Colton said, through his giggle fit, that when Lance jumped out of the back of the truck his pointy-ass bullet belt stabbed him in the groin when he landed. Now we were all laughing, including Lance, who was still curled into the fetal position on the driveway. I turned around to see if Knight was laughing too. He wasn't, but there was definitely a smug little smirk playing on his lips.

Once Lance had recovered enough to stand, Colton led everybody up the rickety front porch and into Peg's 1970s time capsule of a home. Surprisingly, Peg *was* home, and she was running around in a tizzy.

"Colton, baby! Have you seen my keys? I'm gon' be late for work! And you have *got* to cut the grass *to-day* or the county's gon' fine us again! And poor Shep ain't been fed since—" Noticing that she had company, Peg turned toward us, hopping on one leg while trying to smash a tiny white waitress's sneaker onto her foot. Her stringy dishwater blonde hair was so long it almost touched the ground when she bent over to grab the other shoe.

"BB! Oh, my goodness, look at you with that sassy hair! I love it, girlfriend!" Peg came over and gave me a quick little hug, then snatched her keys off Colton's outstretched finger and kissed him on the cheek. "Y'all be good, and Colton—I mean it about the grass."

As Peg tried to pass through the small crowd of teenagers

gathered on the parquet square she called a "foi-yay," she suddenly stopped short and looked directly at Knight.

"Ronnie? Ronnie McKnight? Is that you?" Knight clenched his jaw and looked at me, then nodded slightly at Peg. "Oh, my goodness! I ain't seen you since you was on Jesse's baseball team!"

Recognition lit Knight's face as he braced himself for Peg's hug.

"Oh honey, look at you! All grown up! And so handsome! I can't wait to tell Jesse. You know, his daddy got him some fancy sports agent out in Las Vegas and now he's a professional skateboarder. Those tricks he does scare the shit outta me, but ain't nothin' I can do about it. You boys always was rowdy as hell."

Peg smiled as Knight just blinked at her, then said, "You tell your mama I said hey, okay?" then opened the door, turning around one last time to yell at her son, who had already taken a seat on the couch and flipped on *The Jerry Springer Show*. "Colton! Cut the grass and feed the damn dog! I mean it. Now!"

Slam.

Knight played baseball? I couldn't imagine him doing anything so...normal. I wondered if he had hair back then. Had he been happy? Or was he just an angry kid with a buzzcut who liked hitting shit with a bat?

Knowing that Colton was a terrible host, I went and grabbed five cans of PBR out of the fridge and brought them back into the wood-paneled living room. August and Lance were sitting next to Colton on the world's itchiest brown sectional, but Knight was nowhere to be seen. I assumed that when he got back he'd want to sit by himself, so I left the equally itchy plaid armchair open and squeezed into the space between August and Lance on the couch.

We drank and laughed as Colton announced the blow-by-blow for every fight that broke out on *Jerry Springer*, just like a boxing emcee. "Ladies and gentlemen, I do believe Tanya-Lynn just got her wig split. Yes, folks, that is a third-degree split wig right there.

Jessica is going in for the kill. But wait! Here comes Jasmine, and she's taking off her earrings. I repeat, Jasmine is taking off her earrings. This is a game changer, folks."

Realizing it was after three thirty, I walked through the tiny dining room and into the kitchen so that I could call my mom's school. I had a cell phone, but my minutes weren't exactly free until after seven o'clock. My mom didn't even have a phone, so every day I had to leave a message with the secretary letting her know where to pick me up when she got off of work.

After I hung up I grabbed a glass out of the cabinet and walked over to the kitchen sink. No more beer for me. My mom would be there in less than an hour.

I looked out the dirty window as I filled my cup, and noticed that Knight was outside in the backyard. He was carrying two metal bowls over to a skinny, gray-faced German Shepherd who was lying in the shade and panting like a son of a bitch. Shep was old and mean and mangy as hell, but Peg liked him because he was a "good guard dog." (That's Southern for "a biter.")

I was about to bang on the window and tell Knight to get the fuck out of there, but something about their interaction made me stop. Knight was approaching Shep so slowly it almost looked like he was doing tai chi, and Shep was letting him.

Knight crouched down and set the bowls aside, then held out both hands, palms up. Instead of growling or snapping or gnawing them off, Shep simply sniffed them. Then Knight turned his hands over and let Shep sniff the backs of them too. I'd never seen anybody do that before. It was like some weird *Crocodile Dundee* shit.

Unable to peel my eyes away from the lion taming going on in the backyard, I called over my shoulder, "Colton, you gotta see this! Knight is out back feeding Shep! And he isn't even dead yet!"

"Cool," Colton yelled back. "Hey, why don't you be a doll and go show him where the lawnmower is too?"

Chapter 11

The rest of the week went pretty much the same way, only I made sure to throw my muffin away *before* I got to my locker in the morning. Knight kept his calmer, quieter demeanor going, which I appreciated, but it made me feel uneasy at the same time—like I was standing next to a dormant volcano. It wasn't natural for him, I could tell.

He waited for me every morning at his locker, but when I got there he never said much. At lunch I never even noticed him sit down anymore—he did that quietly too—but Colton noticed.

Every day he would lean around Lance and call down to the end of the table, "Yo, Knight. You wanna hang out today?" (Which we all knew was code for, *You wanna give my friends a ride to my house and do my chores?*) And every day Knight would cast his icy eyes over to me and raise one scowling eyebrow, asking silently if I was going to come too.

Knight never really interacted with anyone at Colton's—just busied himself outside, but I usually made a point to at least bring him a beer and say thanks for the ride.

By Friday I was actually kind of looking forward to my new routine when a familiar face plopped down across from me at the lunch table. It was Juliet. And she looked like a completely different person. The eye makeup she usually caked on to hide her lack of eyelashes and eyebrows was shockingly absent, and the hair she usually killed herself to straighten had been braided back into cornrows.

It reminded me of how Tyra Banks looked whenever the tabloids posted a picture of her on vacation—no makeup and cornrows. I guess Juliet had been on a little vacation of her own. And she seemed pretty happy about it.

"BB! I missed you so much! You should spend the night tonight!" The confusion on my face must have come across as suspicion, because she lowered her voice and said, "No clubs. Okay? I promise."

With that she flashed a death stare at Knight but quickly brought her gaze back to mine, looking a little shaken. Ha! She should have known better than to try to compete with the Skeletor Scowl.

All I really wanted to do that afternoon was sit on Lance's lap, drinking beer and willing him to kiss me, but I knew I needed to go with Juliet. I felt bad about the weekend before, and she looked like she could use some girl time. And a shower.

I told the guys they were on their own and tried my best to ignore the fact that the side of my face was being seared off by Knight's disapproving stare.

When I found Tony and Juliet in the parking lot that afternoon I was pleased to see that Tony's hood actually looked better than before. Of course, the new glossy red finish clashed completely with the rest of his faded, rust-encrusted paint job, but at least it didn't say BB IS WITH KNIGHT MOTHERFUCKER on it anymore.

Tony and I exchanged glances, but neither one of us spoke. I tossed my lightened backpack into the backseat and climbed in after it.

As we exited the parking lot Tony turned left instead of right, muttering something about needing to make a "quick stop" on the way home. I assumed he meant he needed to get gas or something, but a few minutes later he pulled into the parking lot of a shitty apartment complex right off the main highway. I'd seen it a million times, but I'd never known anyone who actually lived there.

I wanted to volunteer to just wait in the car, but early September in Georgia still feels like mid-July, so I decided I'd take my chances inside.

Juliet walked beside Tony like she knew where she was going, absentmindedly plucking at the few eyelashes she had left. She reminded me of August that way. They were both pickers. August picked because he was anxious and afraid of everything, but not Juliet. Juliet wasn't scared of nothin'. She just liked the pain.

Tony knocked three times, which I was beginning to think was the universal code for *Ding-dong. The drug dealer's here.*

The guy who opened the sliding glass door wasn't wearing a shirt. And he was ripped. And his beefed-up chest had a huge tattoo on it that said *No Regrets*, which was partially obscured by several thick gold chains. And his boxer shorts stuck a good eighteen inches out of the top of his impossibly low-hanging jeans. Oh, and he had a purple bandana on his head.

Awesome.

"Yo! Cholo!" The guy cupped Tony around the neck and pulled him in for a violent-looking hug. Turning to whoever else was in the house, he said, "Heeey! T-bag's here!"

The masculine-sounding cheers that erupted from inside let me know that (a) Tony was popular with whatever gang wore purple bandanas, and (b) the entire purple bandana gang was inside that apartment.

I flashed a nervous glance at Juliet, then followed Tony through the open sliding glass door. Sure as shit, there were at least twelve dudes in there who looked like they could get walk-on parts in any prison movie they wanted. It was just a sea of tan skin, gold jewelry, and purple squares of fabric. Every flat surface was covered in half-rolled blunts and forty-ounce beer bottles, and every seat in the living room and small eat-in kitchen had a thug in it.

And all twenty-four of their eyes were on Juliet and me.

"Yo, T-bag, you brought some party favors for us?" The guy who opened the back door said, gesturing to Juliet and me with a sneer.

Before Tony could respond a female voice said, "What up, bitches!" We looked over by the fridge and saw Angel Alvarez, the new girl who told me her brother and his friends would fuck Knight up for me. She smiled at us with heavy eyelids as she made her way over.

Evidently, Angel's brother and his "friends" were the east Atlanta chapter of the Bloods or Crips or some other shit I didn't want to have any part of. I had assumed that Tony was their dealer, but considering the amount of weed just within my view, I suspected that they might be his supplier instead.

Angel was wearing a purple LA Lakers jersey and baggy jeans, but all the thuggish clothes in the world couldn't hide that body. I was so jealous. She had tits for days, her messy bleach-blonde bun looked effortless, and she didn't even bother to wear makeup.

Angel walked over and gave us both a half-assed hug. "What's uuuup, chicas?" Her voice sounded a little scratchy. Even that was sexy.

Tony got pulled into the living room by the guy who answered the door—Angel's brother, I assumed—while the three of us stayed back in the kitchen.

Angel handed Juliet a small glass bowl and a lighter, which she accepted graciously, and slurred something about it being crazy that I was at her house. Weed wasn't my thing, and neither was being on gang turf, so I just kind of smiled and stood there, letting my rigid posture broadcast my discomfort.

The music that I hadn't even realized was playing in the living room suddenly got louder, and somebody yelled to Angel that her jam was on. It was "1st of tha Month" by Bone Thugs-N-Harmony, and Angel grabbed Juliet's hand and ran into the living room.

I peeked around the half-wall that divided the two rooms to see Angel's ass damn near on the ground as she humped the air to the beat of the song. As she came back up, Juliet went down, gyrating the same way Angel had.

When the fuck did the two of them find the time to choreograph an entire twerk routine to "1st of tha Month"? I didn't even know they'd been hanging out. I guess when you only go to school on Fridays it gives you time for all kinds of new hobbies. And friends.

Not wanting to get stoned and/or freak dance for grown-ass men who'd probably all been to prison for murder, I tiptoed out the back door and lit a cigarette on the patio. I was considering calling my mom and telling her to just come get me—fuck spending the night with Juliet—when I heard the door behind me slide open.

I snapped to attention, then relaxed when I saw that it was just Tony. He bumped his shoulder on the doorframe as he stumbled out and lit a cigarette of his own. He leaned up against the side of the building, probably trying to look cool, which was impossible with that patchy-ass goatee, and said, "Yo, B."

"Hey, Tony," I said, trying not to roll my eyes.

"I bet you're pretty strapped for cash after payin' to fix my ride, huh?"

Awesome. We're having this conversation now.

"Yeah. That was almost everything I had. I'm glad it was enough. Sorry you had to deal with that. I don't even remember what happened."

End of story. Let's move on.

Tony took a long drag off his smoke and gave me a phony smile.

"You know, if you ever need some extra cash my bros in there would hook you up real nice. Gi' you whatever you want."

"What do you mean, 'hook me up'?"

Tony flicked his only half-smoked cigarette into the parking lot behind me. "You know, get you paid, girl."

"For what?" The whole twenty questions routine was getting old, but my curiosity demanded that I find out what the fuck he was talking about.

"For doin' what you do. What you like to do. You like to dance, right? You like to party."

I just stared at him with my brow furrowed. Was he saying that guys would pay me to dance? Like Angel and Juliet? Is that why they were dancing in there? Was someone going to give them money? It didn't make sense. Nobody would pay for that.

Tony pushed off the wall and took a few unsteady steps toward me. I backed up until my ass was against the wobbly metal patio railing and gripped it tight.

"I could get you some more of that yellow you like, too." His heavy-lidded eyes traveled over my body. "Girl, you could be rollin' in green and yell—"

One second Tony was advancing toward me, and the next second he was flying away. I blinked and blinked again trying to figure out why Tony was now on the other side of the patio. And why his back was to me. And why he suddenly looked like Knight.

"You gonna drug her again, you fucking rapist? I heard what you said! You didn't get what you wanted last Friday, so now you're back?"

Fuck. That was definitely Knight. From where I stood he appeared to be talking to the wall, until I saw arms that weren't his flailing out from his sides.

I slid sideways down the length of the railing until I could see that Knight had Tony in a chokehold up against the apartment wall, which just so happened to be the only thing separating us from a dozen drunk and high OGs inside.

Shit. Shit. Shit.

Tony fought back—or tried to—swinging wildly and kicking at leather-covered shins that blocked his every strike. Never taking his left forearm off Tony's throat, Knight stomped on his Nikes with his left foot, pinning them both down with one heavy boot, then punched him with his right fist in the ribs. And stomach. Again. And again.

My instinct was to cover my head with my hands and curl up in a little ball until it was over. The last time Knight went off like this I had Lance to hide behind. This time I was by myself, and so close I could practically see the blood vessels bursting in Tony's eyes. It was so awful—the sound of bones cracking against bones. The scuffling of feet trying to wriggle free. The grunts and gasps for air. But as afraid as I was of the vicious skinhead trying to kill my best friend's boyfriend with his bare hands, I was even more terrified of the gangbangers inside.

I had to do something.

"Knight," I whispered as loudly as I could. "Knight!"

But he didn't hear me. Tony's eyes were bugging out of his beet-red face, and when Knight punched him low on his left side he made a guttural noise just like Skater Boy had made. I guess that sound was some kind of submission cue, because as soon as he heard it Knight stopped punching. He took his right hand, which was already beginning to swell, and wrapped it around Tony's face, smooshing it between his fingers and shoving his head against the building.

"Knight, you have to go." I took a step toward him. "There's a whole gang inside. If they see you out here—"

But Knight ignored me. Leaning forward, pressing harder on his victim's throat, Knight spoke to Tony's purple face through gritted teeth. "Is this why you sent Juliet to school today? So you could snatch my girl and bring her here?"

Whoa. His girl?

Tony tried to say something but his voice was muffled in the palm of Knight's hand and his throat had all but caved in under the weight of his forearm. Knight pulled his face forward and smashed it against the wall again. Tony's eyes slammed shut in pain.

"What was that? Speak up, motherfucker!"

I took another step closer. "Knight," I whispered, trying to make my voice sound as soothing as possible. "Knight. Let him go. Okay? Just let him go. If the guys inside hear you..."

Knight didn't look at me, but I thought he heard me because his shoulders seemed to relax a little bit.

Then he smashed Tony's head into the bricks again.

Digging his index and middle fingers into the skin just under Tony's eyes, Knight pulled his bottom eyelids down, exposing the fleshy pinks and bloodshot reds inside. "She is *never* going anywhere with you again. Do you understand me? If I find out you've given her drugs again, or even given her a fucking ride, I will gouge your shit-colored eyeballs out." Tony's whimper let me know that Knight must have increased his pressure. "And I will shove them down your fucking throat."

Knight looked like he might just go ahead and do it right then and there, so I took one final step closer and tugged lightly on his bulging arm. "Knight, stop. Please. We have to go. *Now.*"

I don't know why I said "we." *I* didn't have to go anywhere. I could have gone back inside, where my best friend was, and told the boys in purple that some skinhead had just jumped her boyfriend. I probably should have. I'd been friends with Juliet for years, and I'd only known Knight for a month (and from what I could tell, he was batshit crazy), but I couldn't make myself do it. I couldn't go back into the place where grown men paid teenaged girls to "do what they like to do."

Knight gave Tony's face one last shove before releasing it and stepping off of his feet. Knight didn't even bring his fists up to block in case Tony tried to hit him. He knew he'd won.

Knight spat on the ground—his signature victory move, I was coming to find out—grabbed my hand, and walked toward the parking lot.

What started as me being pulled turned into me doing the pulling as I sprinted for Knight's massive white monster truck, dragging him behind me. Knight had no idea the shit storm he'd just unleashed. Tony was probably inside right now telling the entire cartel what had happened.

Knight hoisted me into the passenger seat of his truck, and the second he appeared in the driver's seat I screamed, "Fucking go! Now!"

Knight threw the truck into drive and flew out of there as I tried to explain through my hysterics, and over the roar of the engine, what was coming for him.

For *us*.

Knight's truck tore down the highway, made a couple of quick turns through a car dealership parking lot and the loading area behind a shopping center, then jumped the curb and headed directly into the woods through a tiny opening in the tree line.

The dirt trail led straight up a steep hill, and Knight's massive, screaming Frankentruck was practically vertical as it bounced and bounded up the embankment. All I could see was the white-hot September sky and a few tree tops letting me know that we were still somewhat attached to the earth. I gripped the dashboard and prayed to any deity available to please, please, *please* keep the damn thing from flipping over.

When we got to the top I tapped both shoulders, my forehead, and then my belly button with my fingertips—crossing myself just like my Irish Catholic mother did whenever she had some kind of near miss.

Knight killed the engine and studied me with those unnaturally pale eyes. "Are you okay?"

I looked straight ahead at a wide blue-green tower rising up out of the trees directly in front of us. "We are so fucked," I said. "We are soooo fucked."

Turning toward the bloody-knuckled skinhead next to me, I spoke to his T-shirt when I said, "Knight, those guys are probably looking for us right now, and they probably have fucking guns."

"Oh, I'm sure they do." Knight wasn't being sarcastic. And he didn't sound afraid. His voice was calm and even.

Fucking psycho.

"What are we going to do?!" I could hear the panic in my voice, and the anger. Why was I the only one taking this seriously?

"*We* aren't going to do shit, because *they* aren't going to do shit."

"How do you know that?!" My voice was getting all shrill, and I hated it. It's amazing that even while fearing for my life some small part of my brain still had the capacity to feel self-conscious.

"Because I didn't fuck with their members, their money, or their *mota*," he said. "Those cholos probably hate Tony. They just use him to push their product and bring them girls who are willing to suck cock for cocaine."

Jesus. Was that true? Is that why Tony brought me there? No. Angel and Juliet were having a good time. They weren't... doing that. And those guys seemed like they really liked Tony. Why wouldn't they go after somebody who'd just beaten him up?

I didn't know what to believe. I had so many questions swimming around in my scattered mind, but one in particular rose to the surface, demanding to be asked.

Forcing myself to look Knight in the eye, I asked, "How did you know where I was?"

... you fucking stalker.

Knight pursed his lips in annoyance and said, "Since you didn't need a ride this afternoon," his voice dripping with disdain, "I went to weight training in the gym after school. The douchebag who was spotting for me got a call from Carlos Alvarez saying that Tony had just shown up at his place with a couple of bitches who were DTF."

"What's DTF?" I asked.

"Down to fuck." Knight cocked his head to the side and glared at me like I'd done something wrong.

"Don't look at me like that!" I yelled, crossing my arms over my chest with a huff. "I didn't even know where I was! Tony just brought me there. What was I supposed to do, wait in the car and die of heat stroke?"

"Give me your phone."

"No!"

"Give me your fucking phone." Knight's tone had me digging in my purse immediately.

I fished the glittery plastic brick out and shoved it into his hand like an obstinate child. Knight jammed at the buttons with his thick thumbs, and within seconds I heard a buzzing sound coming from his pocket. He hung up my phone and handed it back to me.

"Next time, you call me."

Without waiting for my reply, Knight opened his door and jumped out.

I glanced at my contacts list and sure as hell there was a new entry under the K section.

Knight.

When I got out of the truck I looked up and realized that the blue-green thing jutting out of the ground in front of us was the city's water tower. I'd never been up there before. I'd only seen it from the highway, poking up out of the trees, and I just assumed it was a really tall tower. I didn't realize it was also up on top of a giant, steep-ass hill.

I turned around and walked to the back of the truck, where

Knight was putting down his tailgate. He had parked in front of a clearing in the trees, and from that vantage point you could almost see the whole town.

I looked at the tailgate, which was about shoulder-high, and wondered how I was going to get up. For all of two seconds. Before Knight lifted me up by the waist and set me down on it with minimal effort.

He didn't join me though. Instead he walked back around to the driver's side door and got back into the truck. I heard the back window of the cab slide open, and some old country song came pouring out of it. I didn't really know shit about country music. I didn't mind it, but I definitely didn't peg Knight for a cryin' in your beer kinda guy.

"You listen to country?" I yelled to him while he dug around in the glove box. "I thought you'd be more into punk or death metal."

Knight slammed his door and rounded the corner of his truck, holding a silver flask in his hand. His knuckles were definitely swollen and beginning to scab.

Hopping up onto the tailgate next to me, Knight said, "I like that shit too, but right now I just want to calm the fuck down so that I don't drive back to Carlos's house and finish what I started with your little friend Tony."

Funny, he seemed pretty damn calm to me.

Knight unscrewed the cap on the flask with one flick of his thumb, took a swig, and handed it to me.

I sniffed the opening and winced from the fumes. Taking the vessel, I examined the engraving on the side. It looked like an etching of the earth with an anchor behind it and an eagle perched on top. "What does this mean?" I asked, turning the flask slightly so that Knight could see.

"That's the Marine Corps symbol. My grandfather was in World War II. That used to be his."

"Oh, I'm sorry," I said.

"Don't be. I never met the guy. He just left me all his shit."

I was just about to take a swig when something occurred to me. "Hey, is this, like, some kind of a test?" I asked. "I mean, you get all pissed off whenever somebody offers me dope, but now you're trying to give me alcohol?"

Knight snatched the flask out of my hand. "Yeah, Punk. That's all this is. It's just one big fucking test, and you passed. Let's go." He hopped off the tailgate and extended his mangled right hand to me. Jaw clenched. Eyes narrowed.

Oh, shit. He's pissed. I pissed off the skinhead. Again. Shit, shit, shit.

Without thinking I leaned over and snatched the flask out of Knight's left hand and took a big swallow. Immediately, I felt the liquid eat away at everything in its path like battery acid. I coughed and hacked and handed the vile poison back to its owner. Knight laughed—well, cough-laughed—and hopped back onto the truck bed.

Thank God.

Taking another swig, Knight slapped me on the back. "You know, for a bitch in combat boots you're kind of a pussy."

I smacked him on the arm in retaliation, then asked, "What is that stuff? Moonshine?" as flames licked the roof of my mouth.

"Nah. It's just Southern Comfort—poor man's Jack Daniels."

A warm, fuzzy feeling enveloped my stomach. "It burns like hell," I said, reaching for the flask again.

Knight handed it over with a chuckle. "You get used to it."

I took another swig and Knight pulled the flask away from me. "Don't drink too much. Your tiny ass'll get fucked up in no time." I noticed the fuzzy feeling had already spread to my extremities, so I didn't argue. Instead I relaxed a little and took in the view.

From up there our town looked like a lush, hilly forest with channels carved out for roads and patches scooped out for apartment complexes and strip malls. It was actually really beautiful. Even though my parents didn't have much money, we had managed to do some traveling. I'd been to the desert, the beach, the plains, the mountains, but the hilly woods and winding roads of home were always my favorite.

I also noticed that there were a ton of crosses sticking up out of the trees. I'd never realized how many churches there were in our town before. The green canopy was dotted with so many white crosses it almost looked like a grassy cemetery. One of them caught my eye, not because it was particularly grand or tall, but because it looked like utter shit compared to the rest. It was weathered and stained and even tilted to one side.

"Holy shit! Is that the abandoned church?"

"Yeah." Knight pointed just next to it and said, "See that big rectangle next to it? That's the new scoreboard they just installed on the football field."

"Where's your house?" I asked.

Knight didn't answer me at first. He didn't even point. He simply stared at a patch of green that I suspected contained some very bad memories, then said, without looking away from it, "It's not my house. It's my stepdad's."

"Oh. It's like that, huh?"

"Yeah." Knight took a long pull from his flask, screwed the cap back on, then set it aside. "It's like *that.*"

"That sucks," I said, not really knowing how to salvage the conversation. "What about your mom? Is she still there?" My mom was my favorite person in the world, so I thought maybe Knight's mom would be his favorite person too.

But Knight didn't respond.

"Shit. I'm sorry." I backpedaled. "That was like, really personal—"

"She's there," he said, cutting me off. "She's always there."

Knight turned his hateful gaze on me, and I couldn't tell if he was warning me not to push him on the subject or begging me to. My brain churned, trying to come up with the most sensitive thing to say, but my mouth was way ahead of it, as usual.

"Drugs?"

I don't know what made me say that. It just fell out of my mouth. It wasn't even the most logical assumption. She could have been home on disability. She could have been mentally ill. Maybe she was just a bitter, bored housewife who started happy hour at noon. But something in my psyche said *drugs*, and I was right.

Knight nodded—his jaw clenched too tight to speak.

"You don't want me to end up like her," I said, not really expecting him to respond.

But Knight nodded again. "Yeah. Something like that."

"Knight, you don't even know me."

He looked at me with pupils like pinpricks, and I suddenly felt nauseous. Whatever I had done to attract the undivided attention of this irrationally violent, racist motherfucker, I wanted to undo it. STAT.

We sat in an uncomfortable silence for a few minutes, staring at the topography of our working-class city. God, I needed a cigarette. I considered hopping off the tailgate to go get one, but then decided that I'd rather *not* break an ankle, so I turned around and crawled down the length of the truck bed and over to the open cab window instead. I had to snake the entire top half of my body through the opening so that I could reach my shoulder bag over by the passenger door.

Bag. Singular. As in one. As in I had my purse but not my backpack. Because my backpack was still in Tony's car.

Goddamn it!

I grabbed my purse and made a mental note to call Juliet later and ask her to bring it to school (and apologize for what happened... again). But just as I was about to extract myself, I noticed

Knight's wallet sitting in the unused ashtray. Making a split-second decision, I snatched the hunk of black leather and took a quick peek inside at his driver's license.

Ronald McKnight. No middle name. Born on September seventeenth.

His birthday was in two weeks.

"Everything okay back there?" Knight called, as I put everything back exactly the way I'd found it.

"Yeah," I said, sliding back out the window and down to the tailgate. "I was just grabbing my bag."

I sat back down next to him and began rooting around in my bottomless pit of a purse for a smoke. I fished out my pack of Camel Lights, popped one in my mouth, and extended the pack to Knight while I continued searching for a lighter. I was so focused on my mission that I didn't notice his hand reach out until it had already clasped my chin.

My heart completely stopped pumping—my life literally suspended in Knight's thick, callused hand—while he slowly lifted and turned my face toward his. I had no choice but to make eye contact, and when I did I felt something stir in my chest. It felt unwelcome and unfamiliar. Like it didn't belong to me. It felt like…sorrow.

I searched Knight's face and noticed the crease in his brow, the downward pull at the corners of his mouth.

This is Knight's loneliness, I thought. *It's so big I can feel it through his hand.*

Just then an orange flame appeared in the space between our faces, causing me to blink and recoil. Knight steered my face back toward the fire and said, "You should never let a beautiful woman light her own cigarette."

I smiled in relief—which was difficult with his meaty hand wrapped around my jaw and a cigarette between my lips—and accepted his offer. Once my cigarette was lit, Knight lit his own, then shoved an old fashioned–looking Zippo back into his pocket.

"Is that another gift from your grandfather?" I asked.

Knight exhaled a puff of smoke without taking the Camel out of his mouth and said, "You're pretty fucking smart, Punk."

I thought he was pretty fucking smart too. In a scary way. In a cold, calculating, all-too-observant way.

A strong breeze whipped through the shady clearing, making me shiver even though the air was hot.

"Are you seriously fucking cold right now?" Right on cue, observant as hell. "Jesus. Look at your arm."

I didn't have to look. I knew it was covered in goosebumps.

"Punk, I'm gonna ask you again, and this time I want the truth. Where the fuck is your jacket?"

I took a drag and exhaled away from him as I lied. "I lost it. Last spring. But I'm gonna get a new one."

"Oh yeah? When?"

"As soon as I save up some money and convince my mom to drive me to Little Five."

Knight jumped off the tailgate and disappeared around the side of the truck. I heard his door open and shut, then he reappeared holding a black hooded sweatshirt.

"Here. Put this on." He tossed the pullover to me and I held it up for inspection as he hopped back onto the tailgate.

"What does this mean?" I asked, staring at the letters on the front.

"It means nobody can fuck with you."

"No, the logo. *Lonsdale*. What's that?"

"It's a British boxing company," Knight replied. "Like Everlast."

"Oh." That wasn't so bad. I had expected him to tell me it meant *Long live Hitler* in German or something.

Satisfied that it wasn't the written equivalent of a swastika, I set my cigarette on the edge of the tailgate and pulled the hoodie on over my head, careful not to disturb the effortlessly spiky look I had put a shit ton of effort into that morning.

The sleeves hung six inches past my hands, but the cotton was deliciously warm, having been in the hot truck all afternoon. I pressed my hands to my face and inhaled. It smelled like dryer sheets and cigarette smoke and some kind of sweet, cinnamony cologne. I liked it.

Knight noticed what I was doing and said, "It smells a hell of a lot better than that giant homo's hoodie, doesn't it?"

I suddenly liked it a hell of a lot less.

"Would you stop saying shit like that?" I turned to face him, emboldened by my sudden need to defend my love. "Lance is not fucking gay. And even if he were gay, what would you care? Do you *have* to hate gay people? Is that like, one of your skinhead rules?"

Knight seemed amused by my little outburst. His mouth curled up on one side as he said, "I make my *own* rules, and I hate fucking everybody."

"Yeah, well, you seem to hate him a little extra," I snapped, crossing my hoodie-covered arms over my chest.

"Maybe that's because he has something I want," Knight said, tilting his head to the side.

"Oh, really. What's that? Hair?"

Knight laughed. "Yeah, Punk. I'm jealous of his puke-green Mohawk."

Eager to change the subject, I glanced at my watch and saw that it was almost four o'clock and I hadn't called my mom to tell her where to get me. She would be leaving work any minute. Knight agreed to drive me to her school, which was only a few minutes away. When I offered to give him gas money he told me to shut the fuck up.

I had him drop me off in the back of the building so that none of my mom's coworkers would see me getting out of a skinhead-piloted monster truck. Before hopping out, I carefully pulled his hoodie off over my head.

"Thanks," I said, handing the black sweatshirt back to him.

Knight made no move to accept it. "Keep it," he said.

"I can't."

"Why not?" he asked.

"Because everybody knows it's yours."

"So?"

So, it's a skinhead hoodie, dumbass! I can't wear that shit to school!

"So . . . it's way too big for me."

Knight just glared at me. He knew why I wouldn't take it, but he still left me sitting there with my arm outstretched.

"Um, well, thanks again," I stammered, setting the hoodie down on the seat between us. "And thanks for the ride. I guess I'll see you on Monday? 'Kay, bye!"

I grabbed my purse and leapt from the truck with a surprising amount of grace. I landed like a bitch who had experience jumping out of monster trucks. The thought was unsettling. I didn't even really like Knight, yet somehow I'd managed to wind up in his truck on six out of the last seven days. How was that even possible?

Chapter 12

As soon as I saw Juliet's number on my caller ID that night I immediately hit the send button and launched into my rehearsed apology.

"Juliet! I'm so—"

"Shut the fuck up."

Tony.

Shit.

Shit, shit, shit.

Act concerned, BB.

"Oh my God! Tony, are you okay? I was so scare—"

"Listen to me, you fuckin' cunt." His voice sounded like Knight might have actually crushed his windpipe. It was so strained and gravelly I could barely understand him. "My boys are out looking for your little Nazi friend right now. He done fucked wit' the wrong crew."

It was Friday, so Knight was probably at work. They wouldn't know to look for him there, but they'd know where to find him come Monday morning.

"Tony, I'm so, so sorry. He was just trying to protect me, I swear. He thought—"

"I don't give a fuck what he thought!" Tony screamed into my ear, his voice almost giving out completely at the end. "You tell that peckerwood motherfucker that the East Side Kings is comin' and they gon' pop a cap in his white ass when they find him."

Even though I was sitting in the middle of my bed, I felt like I was in a free fall. My mind went completely blank, and my stomach floated up into my mouth. I looked around my room, blinking and waiting for my brain to begin working again. Thoughts would have been fucking awesome. Words? Rad. Solutions? Totally welcome.

"Oh, now you got nothin' to say?"

"Um…" I reached over and grabbed my purse off the end of the bed with trembling hands and began digging through it, looking for a cigarette to calm my nerves. I tossed my wallet onto the mattress to make more room, and it fell open, giving me an idea.

"Do you want money?" He let me pay him off before, right? It was worth a shot.

"Errybody want money, bitch. You got some?"

Well…shit.

"Um, not right now. I'm still wiped out from fixing your car, but I get paid again on the fifteenth." I finally dug my cigarettes out and lit one with shaky fingers.

"You on that first and fifteenth, huh?"

I wondered how Tony knew my pay schedule, but then I vaguely remembered the song Juliet and Angel were dancing to earlier said something about getting paid on the first and the fifteenth, so maybe that was a common thing.

Without waiting for me to respond Tony said, "From now on, the fifteenth's gon' be *my* payday. You get paid on the first, Tony get paid on the fifteenth. You gimme a bill erry month, and I'ma make sure yo little white-power friend don't get plugged. You forget about good ol' Tony when you cash that check, and I'ma forget we had this conversation. Ya heard?"

Fuck! A hundred bucks? Every month?! To keep somebody alive that I don't even like?

"Tony, I . . . I need that money. I can give you another hundred, but every month? I'm trying to save up for a car."

"You a cute girl, B. You ain't gon' have no problems findin' a ride. Just look how long my ass been doin' it . . . Erry month, or the Nazi get capped. Period."

Tears welled up in my eyes and a silent scream built inside of my head as I realized that my lifelong dream of four-wheeled freedom was being snatched away from me as if it were nothing. As if it were candy, and I was the baby.

"When you get that check you gon' cash that shit on the spot and leave a bill under a brick behind your work. No handoff. You got me?"

I nodded, not caring that he couldn't hear my devastated consent.

"You say one muthafuckin' word about this to Jules, you miss one muthafuckin' payment, and our little *arrangement* gon' go poof. Don't test me, bitch."

Click.

I stared at my phone, which was wet with my old tears and blurry through my new ones, and wondered how something so small could ruin my whole fucking life.

If it weren't for that phone, my ever-optimistic inner voice chimed in, *then Knight might still have a target on his back. Did you stop to think about that? You may have just saved a life, BB. You should be proud of yourself.*

Oh, yeah? Fuck you, brain.

Chapter 13

I woke up Monday morning, took a piss, and weighed myself. Ninety-nine pounds. Double digits. I fucking did it, but I was too busy being upset about the loss of a different goal to enjoy achieving this one.

Maybe I would feel less heartbroken about not being able to buy a car if the life I was saving in return had been August's. Or Lance's. Or my mom's or Juliet's. But no. It had to belong to fucking Skeletor the Skinhead—a violent, impulsive, hateful, homophobic racist with no friends and creepy zombie eyes. I wanted to stamp my feet and scream, "It's not fair!" but it wouldn't have done any good. I was being extorted by a gang-affiliated drug dealer and that was that.

Into my purse went my muffin. Into the still-dark morning went my mother and I. Into her Taurus station wagon went my body. And into outer space went my mind as I warred with myself about whether to be angry at Tony, angry at Knight, mournful over the loss of my future car, or stoically resigned to my fate. I was leaning toward plain old depression when my mom's voice pulled my racing mind back into the car.

"Baby, I've got the heat turned all the way up and you're still shivering. We have got to get you a new jacket. Maybe this week-end we can go to that store you like downtown. You know I'd take you tonight if it wasn't so damn far away."

"I know, Mom. It's fine. I have to work tonight anyway," I said, staring out the window at nothing in particular.

At the next red light my mom reached into the backseat and handed me an oversized green cardigan with the words PEACH STATE ELEMENTARY embroidered on the breast pocket. It was the teacheriest garment I'd ever seen, but it was warm and soft and smelled like crayons and I burrowed down inside of it as if it were an Egyptian cotton bathrobe.

When my mom pulled up in front of the school I gave her a peck on the cheek, grabbed my purse, and exited the car. My inner battle picked up right where it had left off as I mechanically made my way to my locker. I was shooting for resignation, really concentrating on it, but I kept landing somewhere between sorrow and self-pity.

When I turned onto C hall Knight was standing at the end, waiting for me like I knew he would be. Alive and breathing and shit. I told myself to be happy about that, but I couldn't pull off happy either.

I couldn't even muster a smile.

I mumbled a greeting at Knight as I walked up, then stopped in front of my locker. Just as I was about to open it I realized that I didn't need to.

Because I didn't have my backpack.

Because I'd left it in Tony's car.

Because of the motherfucker standing next to me.

Awesome.

"Punk?" Knight's voice was the softest I'd ever heard it. "Aren't you gonna open it?"

I guess I could at least get my physics book out of there. And maybe some paper. And I could probably borrow somebody's pencil.

Goddamn it.

Sighing, I grabbed the latch and kicked the corner of my door, popping it open with ease. I didn't even remember my combination anymore. Knight's method was so much more efficient.

And then my heart stopped.

Inside—hanging from a hook that I'd never noticed before—was a black canvas backpack covered in safety pins and punk rock buttons. *My* backpack.

I turned and looked at Knight in utter disbelief. "I...How did you...?"

Knight pulled up one side of his mouth in an almost-smile and said, "When I dropped you off on Friday I noticed that you didn't have it. So, I went and got it."

My stomach dropped. "You *went and got it*? What does that mean?"

"It means that old cars are easy as shit to break into," he said, shrugging like it was no big deal.

I wanted to hug him and hit him at the same time. Sure, it was sweet, but it was also suicidal. What made him think he could just show up on gang turf, beat the shit out of an affiliated drug dealer after carving up the hood of his car, and then *break into* said car hours later without any repercussions. There *were* fucking repercussions, and *I* was the one paying them.

"They want to kill you, you know." That was all I said. What was done was done. I had my backpack and Knight had his life and yelling at him wasn't going to change a goddamn thing.

Turning away from him, I unzipped my bag and wondered why—instead of books—there was a bundle of shiny green fabric spilling out the top of it.

I looked at Knight, who gave nothing away, and pulled the

material out. The heap unraveled in my hands, revealing itself to be a military-style bomber jacket. It had bright orange lining and a little pocket on the sleeve. And it appeared to be just my size.

Clutching the coat, I turned to face Knight.

"Turn around," he commanded, his liquid smoke stare rendering me temporarily unable to argue.

I did as he said and let my mom's sweater—which I was mortified to realize I was still wearing—slide off my shoulders to the floor. I watched our reflection in the window of the exit doors as Knight slid the slick, cool nylon over my dangling hands and up my arms. With our size difference, I looked like a child being dressed for school. By a skinhead. It was a regular fucking Norman Rockwell painting of an image.

The sight was jarring, but for some reason it also made me smile. I looked beyond our reflection to the neon pinks and oranges streaking up and across the morning sky and finally felt the resignation I'd been seeking settle into my bones.

I was glad Knight wasn't dead.

Even if it did cost me a hundred bucks a month.

Heavy hands landed on my shoulders. "I can't believe it fucking fits. I knew you were tiny, but shit, Punk. I got this thing when I was in middle school." Then he laughed. It was quiet and deep and didn't sound like a cough at all.

I turned back around and didn't recognize the young man standing before me. His teeth were straight and white and *dazzling*. His nose, just slightly upturned at the tip, was actually kind of cute. And his eyes—crystalline blue, rimmed in miles of feathery blond lashes and narrowed in laughter—reminded me of the stained-glass window at my grandparents' church that depicted the archangel Gabriel.

Clearly no one had seen this boy smile before, because if they had, they'd be spending the rest of their lives trying to make him do it again.

I could feel my face beaming back, big and bright. I didn't want it to, but I couldn't help it.

"This is for me?" I asked.

Knight's smile faded to a smirk. "Can't have you getting AIDS on me, now can I?"

Oh my God. Is he flirting with me?

Fuck, what do I do?

I can't wear this. What will Lance think? What will Juliet think??

But I don't want to piss Knight off and get murdered over a jacket.

UGH!

I took a deep breath and met his fading smile. "I don't know what to say, Knight. This is really, really thoughtful, but I... I can't wear it."

"Why the fuck not?" And there he went. The beautiful golden boy was gone. Knight shoved his hands into his pockets and furrowed his brow. Skeletor was back.

"Knight... my best friend is Black."

"So?"

Gulp. "So... it's a skinhead jacket."

"No. It's a flight jacket."

"But it belongs to a skinhead."

"Now it belongs to a punk."

Running my eyes over his outfit, I tried to look for some evidence of his racism to help my argument. A swastika or an Iron Cross, anything, but Knight was clean as a whistle. He had on a fitted red polo-style shirt that stretched across his defined chest and was tucked into a pair of tight Levi's. His jeans were held up at the top by a pair of thin white braces and were rolled up at the bottom, showing off his signature black combat boots and red laces. No symbols. No logos. Nothin'.

I swallowed hard and asked the million-dollar question, bracing myself in case his response happened to be a fist to my face. "Knight, you're a Neo-Nazi, right? I mean, I don't know all the terms, but aren't you, like, into white power and the KKK and all that?"

Because if you are we can't be friends. And if we can't be friends then I need to change lockers. And schools. And identities.

Knight looked over my shoulder as a few kids trickled in from the double doors behind me. Not wanting them to hear whatever he was about to say next, Knight leaned down and placed his mouth, the same mouth that was capable of producing *that* smile, within millimeters of my ear.

I waited for him to bite it off, or scream into it, or do something equally unpleasant to punish me for the ball-busting question I'd just asked, but instead he whispered, "I'm *not* a Nazi, okay? I don't hate people because of their race. I hate people because I just fucking hate people."

After his confession Knight pulled away and locked eyes with me. His features were sharp, but his impossibly pale blue eyes were soft and searching. There was an intimacy there I'd never felt with a boy before.

Skeletor the Skinhead had just told me a secret.

Chapter 14

It was September seventeenth.

Knight's birthday.

What the fuck do you get for the guy who hates everything?

I guess, technically, his birthday gift from me was the fact that he got to see another birthday—a privilege that I'd left most of my paycheck under a cinder block behind Pier 1 Imports for him to have—but he didn't know about that.

He didn't even know that I knew it was his birthday. I contemplated just keeping that information to myself. After all, my new post-extortion budget was pretty tight, thanks to him, so I didn't say anything that morning at our lockers. I stayed mum in the church parking lot, as well. But by lunch it dawned on me that if I didn't tell him happy birthday, it was possible that no one would, and that seemed like a fate worse than the death I was trying to save him from.

I only had about a buck forty-two in my wallet, but I knew one thing I could get pretty easily and for free—cafeteria food.

I'd noticed that Knight hadn't been eating lunch lately—which seemed weird, especially for a dude his size—so I decided to grab him a chicken sandwich on my way to the table. Literally. As in I just walked by and grabbed it.

I never felt bad about stealing back then. When you and every-body you knew were hugging the poverty line, stealing wasn't something kids did to impress each other or rebel against their par-ents. It was just something kids did.

At lunch I always sat sideways—facing Lance and Colton, but more importantly, facing *away* from Knight. At first it was because Knight scared me, but after the whole jacket thing I think I kept my back turned because seeing him down there all by himself made me feel like shit.

I was beginning to realize that I only spoke to Knight when we were one-on-one—at our lockers or in the cab of his truck on the way to Colton's house (which was now an everyday thing)—but whenever someone else was around I ignored him.

Sure, I was afraid of his violent tendencies—terrified actually. And the fact that he put his hands on me whenever he wanted defi-nitely made me nervous. But if I was being honest with myself, the main reason why I ignored Knight in public was because I didn't want the stigma of being friends with Skeletor the Skinhead.

Knight was already at the table when I walked up, but instead of ducking my head and scooting past him like I typically would have done, I sat down in one of the permanently empty seats next to him, thrust out my little gift, and chirped, "Happy birthday!"

I expected Knight to at least take the damn sandwich. Maybe say thank you. I thought there might even be a chance that I'd get to see that big stained-glass-window smile again.

I thought wrong.

Knight's brow, which had been tightly furrowed, smoothed and lifted in surprise. His glacial eyes widened, and his lips parted in a soul-baring silent gasp. It was a heartbreaking expression of grati-tude and disbelief.

It was worse than I'd thought. It was as if Skeletor the Skinhead had never received a gift in his life. I could almost hear his armor clatter to the floor as I peered into the face of someone vulnerable, aching, and alone.

Of course, he snatched his scowl back up off the ground within milliseconds and shot me a glare that had me questioning my sanity.

Wait. Now he's mad at me? What did I do this time?

"Are you fucking kidding me?" Knight said as he flicked his eyes from mine to the sandwich and back again. "You want to do this again?"

Do wha—Oh, right. The muffin thing.

I stammered, "I just, I noticed that you haven't gotten lunch in a while, so, I...I just thought..."

"You don't eat, I don't eat. *Remember?*" Knight's words were clipped and his jaw was clenched like he was holding something back. Something that would probably make me cry again.

"Is that why you haven't been eating lunch?" I asked, my eyes welling up even without him screaming at me.

Knight stared at me with pure venom in his undead irises and nodded. Once.

Oh. My. God.

For weeks Knight had been sitting down there, all alone, trying to prove a point to a girl who wouldn't so much as look in his direction.

"Knight, I...I'm sorry. I had no idea."

I realized as his nostrils flared that Knight was very much like a pit bull. Vicious. Loyal. Misunderstood. And once he clamped that jaw of his shut, it was very hard for him to open it again.

It appeared to be taking all of Knight's strength not to go psycho on me. The least I could do was meet him halfway.

"Do you...want to split it with me?"

Knight didn't even nod. He just watched me as if I were trying to lure him into some kind of trap, jaw muscles tensed, suspicious.

I unwrapped his lukewarm gift and pinched and pulled the sandwich apart until it was two jagged semicircles. Handing one to him, I took a bite of the other and closed my eyes. It tasted fucking amazing. Then again, everything tasted fucking amazing when you never ate anything.

I was almost done with my half before Knight had relaxed enough to open his mouth and take a bite of his. Of course, he finished it about four seconds later. Evidently, eighteen-year-old weightlifting skinheads can fucking *eat*.

To break the tension, I nudged his knee under the table with mine and said, "Hey. Happy birthday."

Knight nudged my knee back and gave me a gift in return.

That fucking smile.

Chapter 15

I needed to focus.

All this drama with Knight and Tony had pulled me away from my ultimate goal, which was to get Lance Hightower to ask me to marry him by the end of the school year. It had been almost a month since he'd kissed me in the bathroom, and the most I'd gotten out of him since then was holding hands at school and sitting on his lap at Colton's house.

I was doing something wrong. Or not doing something enough.

Maybe my stomach still poked out too much. Or maybe I was too flat-chested. There wasn't much I could do about those things though—other than starve and wear the most heavily padded bras I could get my hands on, which I was already doing—so I decided that my only course of action was to go edgier with my style.

After all, the one kiss I had gotten out of him came the day after I cut most of my hair off, so maybe if I cut *more* of my hair off, I'd get *more* than a kiss. Right? I mean, that's just basic logic.

So, I shaved my head.

Well, not all of it. Just most of it.

I left my bangs.

And the two long pieces on either side of my face.

And guess who told me it looked "rad" the next morning but then put exactly zero of his body parts into zero of my orifices?

Yeah. Lance Motherfucking Hightower. That's who.

Back to the fucking drawing board.

Chapter 16

You know who did love my haircut? The only other person I knew with a shaved head. Yeah.

So, that plan backfired catastrophically. And it only made my reluctance to be seen with Knight at school stronger. You can't just shave off most of your hair and then publicly befriend the town's only skinhead. Everyone would assume we were some kind of white-power power couple. The image I was going for was *cute little NON-RACIST punk girl who is betrothed to Lance Hightower*, not *bride of Skeletor*.

Just to make sure nobody got it twisted, at lunch I sat even closer to Lance than ever. I sat about as close to him as you can get to another person without getting pregnant, but I did at least start stealing a sandwich for myself every day so that the skinhead at the end of the table would fucking eat something. I mostly just picked at it and gave Lance the rest, but it was enough to keep Knight off my back.

The Friday after Knight's birthday he was in a surprisingly non-homicidal mood when I walked up to him at our lockers. I thought maybe his lack of scowling was because I was wearing his jacket. The mornings had started to cool off, and I'd finally decided that

I'd rather wear Knight's admittedly kickass flight jacket than a frumpy old Peach State Elementary School cardigan with tempera paint stains on it.

"You're in a good mood," I said as I approached. "Who died?"

Knight shoved his hands in his pockets and smiled a little. Like he didn't want to, but couldn't help it.

"I...Can I show you something?" he asked.

"It's not a severed head, is it?" I replied, enjoying the ounce of vulnerability he was showing me a little too much.

Knight set his plain black backpack on the ground, unzipped it, and handed me a piece of paper. He stood back up and looked at me expectantly as I read it. The first three lines were typed in bold and told me all I needed to know.

GEORGIA DEPARTMENT OF PUBLIC HEALTH

FULTON COUNTY

BODY ARTIST LICENSE

"Knight!" I screamed. "You fucking did it! You passed the exam!"

He couldn't hold back anymore. Knight smiled, for the third time in a week, as I jumped up and down clutching his certificate— his future—in my hands.

"Can I be your first customer?" I asked with a grin.

"No," Knight said, snatching the piece of paper back. "You're only fifteen, remember?"

"And I have a note from my mom, *remember*?"

Knight eyed me suspiciously. "What do you want done? You know I can't tattoo you with a note. It can only be a piercing."

"Um...*gulp*...what about two piercings?" I blushed instantly. Hard. I could feel the prickly pink spread all the way to my fucking toes.

Knight's eyebrow quirked up as he considered my request.

I can't believe I just asked this psycho to touch my tits. Not that I have any. All I have are nipples, which is exactly why I need to get them pierced. Because when Lance finally sees them—and he will, goddamn it—I need him to be so distracted by how badass they are that he doesn't notice how not there they are.

"How about tonight?" Knight asked in a surprisingly professional tone for a dude who'd just been propositioned to touch somebody's boobies. It put me at ease, a little. "But it has to be after-hours," he added.

I was suddenly feeling a lot less at ease.

"Why does the shop need to be empty if I have a note?"

So that you can hack me to little pieces and eat my brains?

Knight leveled me with a no-bullshit glare and said, "Because if I bring a minor into the shop the day after I get licensed Bobby will beat my fucking ass, note or no note."

Did I want my nipples pierced badly enough to risk being alone in the shop with Knight again?

Does a bear shit in the woods?

"I get off work at nine thirty," I said.

"I'll pick you up."

That afternoon Knight gave me a ride from Colton's house to work and it was *awkward*. I was nervous as shit and Knight was... Knight. He pretty much just smoked and scowled at the road the whole way there.

My five-hour shift felt more like five days as I struggled to keep myself distracted. Thank God we'd just gotten a new candle fragrance in that day. I took the entire project over, shoving my well-meaning coworkers out of the way, and made the display for Autumn Splendor my bitch. I really liked the scent too. It smelled like cinnamon, and for some reason I found that comforting.

At nine thirty sharp I heard it—the screaming bat-out-of-hell roar of Knight's monster truck pulling into the employee parking lot. I gave my manager a little salute, grabbed my stuff, and dashed out the back door.

I expected Knight to do what a normal person would do when they pick someone up from work—park with the engine running and wait for you to hop in. Instead Knight had lurched one tire up on the curb, walked around to the passenger side door, opened it, and was standing there waiting for me. He was wearing the Lonsdale hoodie he'd tried to give me, and I had to resist the urge to sniff it when he gave me a boost into the truck.

Not that I would have been able to smell it over the mouth-watering fragrance of hot food that was wafting out of the truck. When Knight climbed into the driver's seat he tossed me a paper sack with CHICK-FIL-A stamped on the side of it.

"Eat," he said. I pulled out the aluminum pouch inside and it was still warm. "Can't have you passing out on me."

"You got me a chicken sandwich?" I asked, trying to sound more appreciative than I felt. The whole force feeding me thing was really getting old.

"You need to eat something before getting a piercing, and that's one of the only things I've ever seen you eat, so...eat."

I did as he instructed, welcoming the excuse not to talk, and Knight shoved a CD into the stereo to fill the silence. It wasn't country this time. It was some kind of punk-ska hybrid, and I fucking loved it.

I bounced in my seat, enjoying the music and—as much as I hated to admit it—my dinner.

"Who is this?" I asked after swallowing my last bite.

"Operation Ivy," Knight yelled over the growl of his engine. He took his eyes off the road just long enough to cast me a smug look. "I knew you'd like it."

"Well, I hope you like it too, because from now on this shit is all we're listening to."

Knight smiled as I reached over and turned it up.

The song "Sound System" was my favorite, and I made him play it at least four times in a row until I knew it word for word. I'm sure he wanted to punch me in the face, but he hid it well because every time I said, "Again! Again!" Knight just chuckled and hit the back button. The music was so fast and upbeat that by the time the suburbs melted into the city and the lights of Little Five Points were in view my anxiety had morphed into full-blown mania.

I was fucking amped. As soon as Knight parked, I hopped out of the truck and practically shadowboxed my way up the fire escape in the alley where Knight let us into the shop through the back door.

As I waited for him to get the door unlocked I noticed a few tiny bowls on the stoop filled with cat food and water.

This Bobby guy must really like taking in strays, I thought. *Like Knight.*

When we crossed the threshold, Knight flipped a few switches, illuminating the shop. It was weird seeing it sober. It was almost like I had only been there in a dream.

The back door opened into a skinny hallway, lined with doors on the interior wall that led all the way to the main studio. I assumed one of them belonged to the bathroom with the traumatizing wallpaper. I *did* remember that.

Knight opened the second door and flipped a switch inside. I peeked my head in behind him and saw a small room that resembled the break room at Pier 1—only this one was painted black. It had the same black and white tile floor as the rest of the shop. A simple white counter ran the length of the left wall, supporting a sink, coffee maker, microwave, and minifridge, and white cabinets hung above and below. A worn but comfortable-looking black leather couch took up the back wall, and in the center of the room was a cheap aluminum table that looked like patio furniture with a few matching chairs shoved underneath—tattoo magazines fanned out across the glass top.

Knight walked in and opened one of the cabinets, pulling out a bottle of Southern Comfort and two shot glasses. I moved out of the way as he exited the room with them and continued down the hall into the main area of the shop. Knight flipped up at least four light switches, then made his way over to his station in the back corner.

I hadn't seen the shop fully lit before (or while fully conscious). It was the coolest fucking place I'd ever seen. Framed flash art adorned almost every square inch of the blood-red walls. There were eight stations, each with its own black leather dentist-style chair, rolling black leather stool, rolling tray table, and shiny red tool chest—like the ones mechanics used. Knight's tool chest had a partially deflated *Congratulations* balloon tied to it.

"Is that for passing your licensing exam? That's so sweet!" My voice echoed off the walls it was so loud.

Goddamn, I need to rein it in.

"Yeah. Bobby likes to bust my balls," Knight said, setting the bottle and glasses down at his station.

As I took my assigned seat in his cold leather reclining chair my excitement began morphing back into its original form—anxiety. Knight turned around and handed me a shot glass filled to the brim with sweet smelling liquor. Upon further inspection, I noticed a logo etched into the glass that read TERMINUS CITY TATTOO.

"This will help with the pain," he said. "Cheers." Knight clinked his matching glass into mine, and downed his drink in one swift swallow.

I took a little sip of mine and quickly lost all feeling in my lips, tongue, teeth, and throat.

Jesus, this shit works. Maybe I should just dip my nipples into it.

As Knight turned back around, his mood turned serious. He was laser focused on whatever he was doing, which appeared to be sanitizing and arranging half a dozen torture implements on a little metal rolling tray. There was no small talk, no music, just me and my drink and my erratic fucking heartbeat thrumming in my ears.

I felt a drip of sweat slide from my armpit into my bra.

Shit! I'm so nervous I'm sweating. Oh my God. What if I stink? I'm going to have to take my bra off in a minute and I have no tits and now I fucking stink!

I had been clutching the shot glass in my lap like a security blanket, but when I brought it to my lips, nothing came out.

No!

"Um, Knight?" I asked.

"Mm-hm." He didn't turn around.

"If you're going to take much longer, I'm gonna need another shot."

Knight laughed and looked at me over his shoulder.

"You nervous, Punk?"

"Honestly, I'm more nervous about you seeing my boobs than I am about you shoving a needle through them." I cringed after my accidental admission, thankful that Knight couldn't see my face. Evidently that whiskey was more of a truth serum than a painkiller.

Knight turned around and leaned against the tool chest, staring at me with eyes that were the same color and temperature as the cold, hard implements he was arranging on his little tray.

"Why?"

"Because nobody's ever seen them before." Okay, so maybe the whiskey was equal parts truth serum and painkiller, because I couldn't feel my blush at all, and I knew that one had to be a doozy.

Knight raised an eyebrow and asked, "Not even Colton?"

Goddamn, don't you ever blink? Stop looking at me like that!

"He tried, but…" I threw my hands over my face, still clutching my empty shot glass. "Ugh! This is so embarrassing! Turn back around! You're freaking me out!"

I felt the shot glass leave my hand and heard the welcome clink of glass on glass.

"Here." I peeked through my fingers and saw Knight turned around, his back to me, holding my refilled glass out behind him.

Okay. That was sweet.

"Thanks." I took another tiny sip. The weight of the glass in my hand and the tingly, numbing sensation on my lips immediately brought my anxiety down a few notches.

This shit really is comforting.

"Why are you getting them pierced if you don't want anyone to see them?" Knight still had his back to me and his voice was quiet. Curious.

"I do want someone to see them! I just need them to, I don't know, look better first." I cringed at my honesty and took another sip of my truth-serum-slash-painkiller. "And this is cheaper than a boob job."

Knight coughed out a laugh. "Yeah, a surgeon probably wouldn't accept a forged permission letter from your parents either."

I giggled and said, "I don't know, man. I forge a *mean* permission letter."

Knight turned around and rolled his tray over next to me. "All right," he said. "Let me see these fugly-ass tits you've been warning me about."

I laughed and downed the last of my whiskey. Slamming the shot glass on the armrest of the chair, I said, "Fuck it. You ready?"

"I don't know. They sound like a freak show." Knight smiled at me—full-on—and in that moment I had to fight the overwhelming urge to kiss him. To just grab his face and kiss the shit out of him for doing this for me and for making me laugh and for giving me alcohol and buying me dinner. He tricked me when he smiled like that. He made me see someone else—a cute boy with perfect teeth, a hard body, and a smattering of light brown freckles across the bridge of his nose. A boy I might not mind showing my boobs to—after a few shots of cheap whiskey.

Before I could change my mind, I pulled my Misfits T-shirt off over my head—being careful not to snag one of my earrings or smudge my eyeliner—took a deep breath, and unclasped my red, lacy Wonderbra. It was the heavy-duty model—the one with the squishy cups filled with liquid. It was basically like wearing breast implants on the outside. And back then, I wouldn't have fled a burning building unless I had that thing on.

Exhaling, and really wishing the lights were off, I squeezed my eyes shut and let the five-pound undergarment slide down my arms and form a puddle in my lap.

Thank God for whiskey.

"Hey…Look at me," Knight said, his tone barely above a whisper.

What I saw when I opened my eyes made me want to kiss him even more. He was still smiling. At my face. He wasn't staring at my tits in horror or disgust or pity. He was smiling, at *me*.

"You're beautiful."

I blinked away his compliment and crossed my arms over my chest defensively, suddenly feeling every bit as naked as I was.

"Thanks," I said, a bit too breathily.

Graciously changing the subject, Knight reached behind him and presented me with a plastic tub filled with dozens of tiny baggies containing jewelry. "Pick your poison."

They were all so pretty. There were straight barbells, curved barbells, circular barbells, hoops with different colored captive beads, and these curved pieces that ended in points like devil horns.

After a minute or two I gave up. "You better pick something for me or we'll be here all night. I want them all."

"Are you sure?" Knight eyed me suspiciously as if it were some kind of test.

"Yes, just hurry up! I'm dying!"

Knight chuckled and hunted around in the tub, as if he knew exactly what he was looking for. He selected them quickly, and set them on the tool chest behind him before I could see what he'd chosen.

I lay down on the chair and covered my eyes with my right elbow, using my left arm to shield my tiny virgin titties from the harsh outside world.

I could hear Knight's voice from some faraway place saying something about a pinch and a...I don't know. I blocked him out, filling my head instead with pleasant thoughts of Lance's face the first time he saw my beautifully adorned boobies. I felt latex-covered fingers gently move my arm to my side. I felt a metal contraption clamp down firmly, but not painfully, onto my right nipple. Then I heard Knight's deep voice say, "Three...two..." just before a white-hot pain slashed through my soul.

Fuuuuuuuck it hurt. I bit my lip and squeezed my face harder with the crook of my arm, fighting back the urge to whimper and gripping the edge of the chair with my free hand as hard as I could.

"Take a deep breath, and then blow it out slowly."

Words. Knight said words. Focus, BB. Focus. He said, um, to breathe? Right. I should do that.

I took a deep breath through my nose, and as I exhaled Knight pushed the needle out and pulled the jewelry through. The blinding pain was immediately replaced by a dull throb.

"You did it, Punk." I went to look down, but Knight shielded my nipple with his gloved hand and scolded me. "Uh, uh, uh. Not 'til we're done."

"I have to do it again??" I whined, throwing my elbow back over my eyes.

Five minutes (and one more brutal impalement) later I was standing in front of the mirror mounted above Knight's tool chest, staring at myself in sheer amazement.

"Oh my God, Knight. I fucking love them. Are those little... wings?"

Knight stayed on his stool, letting me have my moment, but I could feel his eyes on me. "Yeah. They're just straight barbells with little silver angel wings that screw on instead of beads. We just got them in a few days ago, and for some reason I stashed them at my station."

"Because they're fucking awesome."

Knight hesitated for a moment. "Yeah. They are." His voice sounded throaty and I got the sense that he wasn't talking about the jewelry.

Okay, peep show's over.

I wanted to ask Knight to hand me my bra and T-shirt, but then he'd realize it was full of water and weighed eight hundred pounds and I'd had enough embarrassment for one night. I covered myself with one arm and shimmied behind him to grab my clothes. I got dressed with my back turned, then plopped back down sideways on his chair.

"How much do I owe you?" I was totally bluffing. I didn't have any fucking money. Twenty bucks, maybe.

"On the house. Consider it a birthday present."

"But it's *your* birthday. I'm supposed to give *you* something."

"Oh, you did," Knight said, leaning against his tool chest. Gripping the edge with both hands, he stared at me as if he were assessing whether or not I could handle what he was about to say. "You showed me the cutest pair of tits I've ever seen, *and* you let me make them bleed. That's the best fucking present anyone's ever given me."

"Jesus, Knight." I covered my tender chest with my arm again, feeling so vulnerable I forgot I had clothes on. "That's fucked up."

Knight's jaw did that thing where it clamped shut, and I could instantly tell I'd said the wrong thing.

Shit. Cigarettes. I need cigarettes. And air. And darkness, so that I won't be able to see the look Knight is giving me right now.

Trying to mask my abhorrence over his last comment, I hopped off the chair and grabbed my purse. "Well, you can at least let me give you a cigarette. C'mon."

As we walked to the back door I thought, *Well done, BB. You're alone, downtown, at night, with a violent skinhead, who has a thing for blood play, and you have no way to defend yourself or get home on your own. Super duper.*

Knight pushed open the door into the alleyway and propped it ajar with a chunk of concrete that probably came from the crumbling stairs we were standing on. The air outside was humid, but cool. Summer was starting to release its chokehold on the city, much to my dismay.

Reaching into my cavernous, button-and-stud-covered, fuzzy tiger-striped shoulder bag, I pulled out a pack of Camel Lights and a lighter—which were immediately plucked from my fingers by Knight. He pulled two cigarettes out, stuck one in each of our mouths, and lit mine first.

After a long drag, Knight broke the silence. "When do you need to be home?"

"I told my mom I was spending the night at Juliet's tonight, so I don't have a curfew. You can just drop me off at Juliet's...um..."

"What?" Knight could tell I was keeping something from him. His tone of voice was accusing, and his undead eyes were boring into me, searching for more information.

"It's just...I just remembered that Juliet usually stays at Tony's place on Fridays, so...she probably won't even be home."

That was a lie. I had actually just remembered that *Tony* usually spent the night at *Juliet's* house on Fridays—and practically every other day for that matter—and I didn't want Knight to pull up and see his car there. I didn't know if he'd cause a scene, but... actually yes. Yes, I did know. Knight would totally cause a fucking scene.

Knight took another drag off of his cigarette and eyed me suspiciously while he exhaled smoke through his nostrils. "So, you have nowhere to go?"

Shit. Is he pissed? I'm such an idiot. Why didn't I think this through better?

"Not...until noon when my shift starts?" It came out sounding like a question. "But...you know what? You can just take me home. I'll just tell my dad that...I don't know. I'll figure something out on the way. It'll be fine."

It would *not* have been fine. My dad was a paranoid insomniac. Not only would he have been wide awake when I got there, but he'd probably be standing on the front porch with a shotgun by the time Knight's loud-ass truck made it to the top of the driveway.

"You can stay here again, Punk."

Oh, thank God.

Before I could think better of it I attempted to hug him, then screamed and let go because my nipples had just been impaled with steel barbells less than thirty minutes prior to that and ramming them into someone's hard chest was a terrible fucking idea.

Knight laughed and said, "This actually works out a lot better for me, because if I don't have to drive you anywhere tonight, I can polish off that bottle of SoCo."

"Can I help?" I definitely needed another drink if I was going to spend the night there...again. *Jesus.*

"What do you weigh? Like ninety pounds?"

Pssh. I wish.

"No more for you until you eat something else. You're not getting wasted on me again."

Oh, God! The last time I spent the night here I fucking puked and fainted in the alley!

I pouted to mask my embarrassment, then huffed and said, "Okay, fine. Whaddya got?"

"Nothing, but there's a gas station on the corner." Knight pushed off the railing he was leaning on and grabbed my hand, tugging me down the stairs behind him.

I thought he'd let go when we got to the bottom, but he didn't.

I thought he'd let go when we exited the alley and got to the crosswalk, but he didn't.

I thought he'd let go when he opened the door to the convenience store for me, and he did.

But I kind of wished that he hadn't.

Inside, Knight stood with his arms folded while he waited for me to choose something. I made my way up and down the aisles of junk food slowly, trying to pick something that would be filling, but with as few calories as possible. I settled on a giant Rice Krispies treat. Knight simply shook his head at me. Next, I picked up a bag of Doritos. Knight shook his head again.

"Real food," he said.

"Look around, man." I did a little twirl with my arms out. "There's no real food here."

Knight walked past me toward the back wall where the freezer section was and jammed a thick finger into the glass. Inside the case were all kinds of frozen food-wrapped-inside-of-other-food type things. Burritos and empanadas and corn dogs and sausages wrapped in pancakes wrapped in waffles dipped in grits. One glance at Knight's expression told me he was not going to budge on this, so I sighed and opened the freezer door.

The cold air instantly made my nipples contract, causing me to wince and suck in a pained breath through my teeth. Knight chuckled and pushed me out of the way. He reached in, grabbed a box, and walked back toward the register without even showing me what he'd selected.

I called out, "Wait! What is that?" and hustled after him. Without turning around Knight held the box up over his shoulder. Ham and cheese Hot Pockets.

Damn. Those are *good.*

The cashier was a Southeast Asian man who greeted Knight with a look that suggested he'd rather reach across the counter and strangle him than ring him up.

Oh, right. Skinhead.

I stood there and watched their wordless interaction. So much animosity between two people who had probably never met before. I didn't understand why Knight would choose to move through the world dressed in a way that made perfect strangers—even nice ones—hate him. He wasn't even a racist, which was actually kind of rare where we lived, so why? Why let people form an assumption about you that isn't even true? Was it because he wanted to be feared? Or left alone? Did he think he deserved to be loathed?

I was staring at the back of Knight's head—hoping I would spontaneously develop x-ray vision so that I could figure out what the fuck made him tick—when he turned around, a scowl on his face and a flimsy white plastic bag in his fist. As I followed him out the door I could feel the cashier's eyes on the back of my head, the way mine had been on Knight's. He was probably trying to figure out whether or not to call the cops and report a kidnapping.

Knight held the door open for me again, but this time his energy seemed a little pissy. I guess the staring contest with the cashier had his dander up.

The crosswalk light said WALK, so we stepped into the street without pausing. Unable to shake my curiosity, I blurted out, "Why do you dress like that if you know it will make people treat you like shit?"

Evidently the truth serum was still in full effect.

Without looking at me Knight replied, "I don't know, Punk. Why do you dress like *that* if you don't want to put out?"

I stopped in the middle of the street and heard somebody say, "Fuck you." Somebody who sounded a lot like me.

Shit. Did I just say that out loud?

Knight turned around, his body completely illuminated by the headlights of a car waiting at the intersection. "Am I wrong?" he asked, raising his voice. "You want everyone's attention, but once you get it you don't know what the fuck to do with it."

His words felt like a slap in the face. "I don't want everyone's attention!" I snapped back.

Just Lance Hightower's!

The light turned green and the car that Knight was standing in front of honked its horn. The sound startled the shit out of me, causing my already racing heart to practically burst from my chest. I sprinted to the other side of the road like a frightened squirrel, but Knight turned and stalked directly toward the little Honda.

No, no, no, no, no!

I ran back into the street and grabbed his arm, but Knight shook me off and slammed his palms down on the hood, screaming at the terrified Rastafarian in the driver's seat.

"Honk again, motherfucker! Honk one more fucking time!" I tugged on his arm, but he didn't budge. Leaning over the hood, Knight pointed directly at the driver and screamed, "Get the fuck out of the car! Right now! Let's go, motherfucker!"

The poor guy looked like he was about to shit himself. Or already had. I pulled as hard as I could, digging my nails into the soft flesh of Knight's inner arm until I felt the skin give beneath them. What the fuck was wrong with him? He was like a rabid animal and nothing had even happened.

I squeezed and pulled until my fingers were buried almost to the knuckle between his bicep and tricep muscles. I stabbed into his big hard arm even harder until the rest of his big hard body came with it. I twisted my nails in deeper just to make sure he kept moving, and I didn't let up until we were back in the alleyway. Then, I shoved him away from me and stomped off in the direction of the stairs.

I didn't know why I was so angry. I never got angry. Ever. Normally someone raising their voice and causing a scene would have me rocking myself in tears, but for some reason Knight's outburst made me want to attack him right back. It's like his aggression was so big and so toxic that it seeped into my pores and made me crazy too.

I pointed at him and yelled, "What the fuck is wrong with you? You're going to get yourself fucking killed!"

Knight didn't look at me. He just paced back and forth between the buildings, rubbing his hands over his buzzed head.

"What if that guy had had a gun, Knight?" I threw my hands in the air for emphasis. "Look at yourself! You can't just attack random cars in the middle of the night dressed like a motherfucking Neo-Nazi!"

More pacing. More head rubbing. Was he even listening?

"Do you *want* someone to kill you?" I yelled. "Is that why you dress like that? Because I know for a fact that it has nothing to do with what you believe in. You don't fucking believe in anything!"

Knight continued ignoring me. *Ugh!* Needing something to do with my hands, I lit a cigarette and sat on the stairs that led up to Terminus City Tattoo. I filled my lungs with smoke and held it for a few seconds before exhaling. It was something I'd seen my dad do whenever he was stressed out—which wasn't often now that he was unemployed—and it actually seemed to work.

Feeling calmer once I had some nicotine in my blood and physical distance from the noxious anger cloud surrounding Knight, I looked into the alley and saw my words hanging heavy in the air between us. It felt like I might be able to just reach out and take them back. Just scoop them up in my arms and drop them into the dumpster behind the nightclub. But instead I stared at them—my ugly words—while Knight paced and pretended like he couldn't see them too.

"I'm sorry," I said in a more soothing tone. "Knight, I'm sorry, okay? I just...I don't want you to get hurt. Will you sit down? Please?"

Knight didn't reply, but he at least stopped pacing and sat next to me on the stairs. Reaching into his pocket, he pulled out his pack of Marlboro Reds and stuck one into his mouth. I extended my lighter to him before he could find his own, and the flame made his face look monstrous.

I was sitting next to a ticking time bomb and had no idea which wire to clip.

Keeping my voice low and even, I said, "Knight?"

No response.

"Did something...bad...happen to you?"

Knight stared straight ahead and exhaled a puff of smoke through his nose. His jaw muscles flexed and his eyes narrowed.

Shit. Okay, don't clip the red wire.

"You don't have to tell me. It's okay," I said, trying to figure out a different approach.

Keep it light this time. Try the yellow one.

"I'm sorry I asked about your clothes," I said. "I didn't realize it was such a sore subject. I...I just want to understand you better."

Knight flicked his gaze to me in warning, but I pressed on.

"Where do you shop?"

Bingo.

Knight laughed—he fucking laughed—and in my head I pictured a little digital countdown timer stopping with only *00:03* left on the clock.

We're going to live! I silently cheered. *WE'RE ALL GOING TO LIVE!*

"Where do I shop?" He coughed out another laugh. "What are we, fucking girlfriends now?"

I pictured Knight with little blond pigtails and laughed too. "Well, we *are* having a sleepover, and you *did* pick out some killer accessories for me earlier."

"Well, goddamn." Knight flicked his cigarette ash into the abyss. "I guess I am your girlfriend."

I nudged his arm with my shoulder. "So spill it. Where do you shop? I know those boots didn't come from Trash. That's *my* store."

"How about I show you in the morning."

"Really?" My voice was an octave higher than usual.

Knight's features had softened so much it was hard to believe he was about to pummel a Rastafarian in the middle of the street just a few minutes before that.

"Yeah," he said. "You don't have to be at work until noon, so we could swing by there after breakfast. The shop opens at ten, and if I'm still here when Bobby shows up she'll put my ass to work."

"She?"

Bobby's a chick?

Knight chuckled. "You wouldn't know it to look at her—I still think she might have a dick under there somewhere—but according to her she was born without."

"Is she the one feeding the entire Atlanta stray cat population?" I gestured behind us at the bowls and saucers lining the landing at the top of the fire escape.

"No. That would be me." Knight's voice lowered, and something unspoken passed between us.

Oh.

"So, am I like, one of your strays now? Is that why you're always trying to feed me?" I smiled, but the thought that Knight might see me as some sort of charity case stung more than I wanted to admit.

"Pssh. You're a hell of a lot harder to feed than a cat."

I laughed at his gracious deflection, but then my face fell when realization struck me. "Oh shit! The food!"

Knight and I both ran out of the alley and over to the intersection where we'd just been. A dirty, crumpled white bag lay on the side of the road closest to us. Knight picked it up and looked inside. His face said it all. The Hot Pockets hadn't survived the altercation with the Honda.

"Are they...dead?" I asked, unsure how he would respond to the bad news. I mean, we could easily just go buy more, but Knight's reactions tended to be...erratic.

As Knight pulled one very unharmed box out of the bag, his frown morphed into a sinister sneer. That motherfucker.

"Looks like we're getting drunk tonight after all, Punk."

Greeeat.

Chapter 17

Somewhere between getting up at five thirty a.m., going to school, going to work, getting my nipples pierced, being put through the emotional wringer by Knight, and generally being awake for twenty hours straight, my ass must have gotten worn out because the second that hammy, cheesy goodness hit my belly I curled up on the leather couch next to the microwave and passed the fuck out.

When I woke up it was pitch black, except for an illuminated exit sign in the hallway, and for a few terrifying seconds I had no idea where I was. I was freezing, I knew that. And my face was stuck to a leather...armrest? Yes. I was on a couch.

I glanced above my head, looking for the microwave I'd used just a few hours ago, and there it was. Red digital numbers informed me that it was 7:22 a.m. I tried to process that information.

Was I late for something?

No.

Was that early?

Fuck yes. Too early.

I went to curl my arms and legs up to my chest in an attempt to get warm enough to go back to sleep and immediately regretted it. Slicing pain ripped through my chest, as the events of the night before came back in one big rush.

Shit! My nipples!

I sat up and felt my way over to the door, flipping on the light switch so that I could assess the damage. I lifted the bottom of my T-shirt up to my neck and pulled one heavy bra cup away from my chest. Inside my nipple looked...crusty, but so fucking rad. I guess some blood had dried around the jewelry overnight, so when I changed positions on the couch the jewelry must have shifted and broken the scab. I would have to remember to ask Knight what I needed to do to take better care of them.

Knight.

I wondered where he was. I assumed the couch was probably his bed, unless the shop had some secret dungeon I didn't know about. Leaving the break room light on, I poked my head into the hallway and looked both ways. On the floor, next to the fire escape door, were two pairs of black combat boots, lined up neatly and facing the wall. Knight must have taken my boots off after I'd fallen asleep. Why had he put them there? Next to his? It was such a domestic thing to do.

I guess he does kind of live here.

There was a door on either side of the doorway I was standing in. One that contained the restroom from hell, and one that was shut with a heavy duty–looking deadbolt above the knob. I tiptoed past the restroom, which I desperately needed to visit, and peered into the shop. Light streamed in through the front windows, illuminating a heap of a human on the chair in the far back corner.

I tiptoed back into the hallway, my striped tube socks silent against the matching black-and-white tile floor, and paused outside the restroom door. If I flushed, it might wake up the sleeping skinhead, but if I didn't flush I ran the risk of Knight having to deal with a toilet full of my piss first thing in the morning.

Fuck that. I'll just pee at the gas station. I need to buy a toothbrush anyway.

I grabbed my purse out of the break room and slipped my feet into my boots. I noticed, as I bent over to lace them up, that Knight's boots were filled with all of his personal effects. I could see his wallet, his keys, his cigarettes, and what I assumed was his knife.

Before I could think better of it I'd already pulled the metal handle out of his boot. I examined it like a magic wand that I didn't know how to activate. It wasn't like a switchblade—there was no button or anything—just two long, black pieces of metal, side by side, that were attached at the bottom with a hinge.

A hinge! That's how it works!

Grasping the two pieces of metal in each hand, I slowly spread them apart, exposing a shiny blade tucked away inside. The two black pieces rotated all the way down and met again beneath the blade, forming a handle. I remembered the way Knight had flipped and twirled it in the parking lot that night. Almost like it was a pair of nunchucks. Holding the knife in my right hand, I attempted to flip the handle shut, but ended up flipping the blade over with it, right onto my knuckles.

Fuck!

Luckily, it was the dull side of the blade, but it was enough of a shock for me to remember why we're not supposed to play with knives.

When I dropped the knife back into Knight's boot it clinked against his keys.

Keys! Truck! My jacket! Fuck yeah!

I snatched the key ring—which contained at least twenty-seven keys and one bottle opener—and headed out the back door, making sure to prop it open with a chunk of cement like Knight had done. A black cat eyed me wearily from the bottom of the stairs as

I headed out into the parking lot to retrieve my, I mean, *Knight's* jacket.

Luckily, one of the keys had a Ford logo on it, otherwise I would have been out there trying to unlock his passenger door all morning. I guess when you live in three different places you end up with a lot of keys. My coat was freezing from being left outside all night, but as soon as I shrugged it on and zipped it up I could feel my bones begin to thaw. I slammed Knight's passenger door shut and lit a cigarette as I walked over to the main intersection.

The whole neighborhood looked so pretty in the daylight. It was like an outdoor art gallery. All the shops and bars in Little Five Points were (and still are) covered in murals and multi-textured mosaics and laughing skulls and dancing bears. On one corner of the central five-way intersection is a large patio area, dotted with an eclectic collection of benches shaded by potted trees with branches dripping in crystal mobiles and tinkling wind chimes.

One of the benches caught my eye. It was tucked up under a purple crepe myrtle, made from heavy wrought iron that had been painted bright turquoise and lit by an errant streak of sunlight. I still had half a cigarette left, so—for possibly the first time in my short little life—I decided to stop and smell the roses.

I was hyper. I was busy. I was always running late. But that morning I…wasn't. Too tired from lack of sleep to rush and nowhere to be anyway, I sat on that fucking bench and snuggled into Knight's downy jacket and watched pink clouds race like snails across the tree line.

When the pink changed to white and my cigarette joined the hundreds of other discarded butts on the sidewalk, I made my way across the street to the gas station convenience store. There was a new cashier working the morning shift. I bought a toothbrush, a travel size stick of deodorant, and a box of frozen sausage biscuits from the man, then made my way straight to the door marked RESTROOM.

I usually weighed myself after I peed every morning, but with no scale around I was forced to do a visual and tactile belly check instead. I lifted my shirt and looked in the mirror sideways, then pinched my fat, in the exact same spot I always did. The Chick-fil-A and Hot Pocket Knight had forced me to eat the night before didn't appear to have done any immediate damage, but I'd have to rein it in for the next few days to make up for it.

Thank God I'd decided to shave most of my head the week before. My naturally fluffy, wavy hair would only stay spiked or straightened for so long before it reverted back to its clown wig ways. With it shaved I only had my bangs to worry about. I washed my hands and wet my bangs quickly in the grimy sink, then blow dried them straight while kneeling under the hand drier. I found enough makeup in my purse to undo the damage that five hours of couch surfing had done to my face, so once I brushed my teeth and slapped on some deodorant, I was almost presentable again.

When I slinked back into the tattoo shop Knight was still passed out, so I tiptoed into the break room to make him some coffee and a biscuit. I didn't exactly know how to make coffee, but I'd seen my mom do it a few thousand times so I just winged it and hoped for the best.

While it brewed, I hunted through the cabinets for a mug and some creamer. I found them, but I also found a little cardboard box that I assumed belonged to Knight. It contained a bottle of cologne—Obsession for Men, *fitting*—a razor, shaving cream, toothpaste, dental floss, a toothbrush...and condoms.

Condoms.

I'd never thought about Knight having sex before, but he *was* eighteen. Most of the people I knew lost their virginity in middle school. I probably would have too if Lance hadn't been playing so damn hard to get.

That made me wonder if Lance was still a virgin. Surely not.

He was so gorgeous, and funny, and *tall*. So who was he fucking? Maybe Juliet was right. Maybe he did have a girlfriend. Maybe I was just his plaything.

I ripped my new toothbrush out of the packaging, slathered on some of Knight's minty toothpaste, and angrily brushed my teeth as the image of Lance's phantom big-tittied, pink-haired girlfriend taunted me.

A shadow fell over the wall in front of me and I screamed, dropping my toothbrush into the sink as I brought my hand up to cover my foaming mouth. Knight leaned into the doorframe and chuckled. "Jesus. Do I look that bad in the morning?"

Actually, Knight didn't look bad at all. He looked...cute. He was all squinty-eyed and barefoot, and his jeans were still rolled up at the bottom. His braces hung from his waist—instead of being up over his shoulders—and his T-shirt was half untucked. He kind of reminded me of a grown-up, hard-bodied Huckleberry Finn. He just needed a straw hat and a fishing pole. I giggled at the thought and quickly rinsed my mouth out in the sink.

"You actually look *less* scary in the morning," I said, as I tossed everything back into the box.

"Don't tell anybody, okay." Knight half-smiled and then said, "You look fucking hot in the morning, especially with that jacket on." I hid my blush as I turned and tried to shove the box back into the cabinet where I'd found it.

"You can just leave that out," he said. "I need to brush my teeth too."

"Sorry, I just kind of helped myself to your toothpaste." I handed Knight the box and felt the prickly heat in my cheeks intensify.

Here, have some condoms, buddy.

Thankfully, he just set the box on the counter and sniffed the air. "Goddamn, Punk. Are you making breakfast?"

The microwave dinged right on cue. I pulled out a steaming

biscuit wrapped in a paper towel and handed it to him with pride. Knight scowled at my outstretched hand, then gave me *the look*. The look that said, "*You and I both know I'm going to make you eat that, so let's just skip the theatrics, shall we?*"

I fucking hated that look.

Without a word Knight walked around me, took another biscuit out of the mini fridge, and popped it into the microwave. Grabbing his box off the counter Knight left the room, and left *me* standing there holding the biscuit.

I could smell him coming before he re-entered the room, and it made my newly pierced nipples ache. Something about the unique combination of shaving cream, toothpaste, deodorant, and the cologne he wore was like fucking catnip. I wanted to stick my head under his T-shirt as soon as he crested the doorway and just breathe for a while.

I'd set his biscuit next to mine on the small glass table in the center of the room and poured him a cup of coffee. When Knight walked in and saw the little table—all set for breakfast like we were fucking grown-ups—he smiled. Really smiled. And it made me feel like the queen of the fucking universe.

"Damn, Punk. I think I'm gonna like being your girlfriend. We should have a slumber party every weekend." Knight sat down while I concentrated on trying not to blush. And failed. Miserably.

"Only if you promise to get some better bedding," I said as I took my seat next to him. "I froze my ass off last night."

"That's because you're a pussy," Knight said with a mouthful of biscuit.

I reached over and smacked him on the arm. "Oh really? Would a pussy get her nipples pierced?"

"Shit!" Knight said, suddenly serious. "I didn't give you any Bactine to put on them last night. Have you looked at them today?"

"Uh, yeah, dude. It's not pretty."

"Let me see."

My face flushed for real that time. "I . . . uh . . . okay."

Knight was a professional, right? It was just like going to the doctor's office. Not weird. At all. Nope. *Totally* normal.

I reached up under the back of my shirt and unclasped my bra, then lifted my shirt and both five-pound liquid-filled cups up at the same time. Knight's lips parted and he leaned forward in his chair, fascinated, like I had a pair of two-headed frogs under my shirt.

"Welcome to the freak show, everybody! Step right up and see the Tit-less Wonder! What she lacks in breasts she makes up for in nipple crust!"

Holding my shirt and bra up with one hand, I covered my tomato-red face with the other. *One Mississippi, two Mississippi . . .*

"Oh my God! Are you done yet? This is so humiliating!"

Knight said, "Stay right there," then hopped up and left the room.

He's probably going to barf.

When he came back he was wearing a pair of latex gloves and had a plastic baggie full of gel packets and cotton swabs in one hand. I stayed frozen in mortification while he sat back down and went to work methodically cleaning my piercings. When he was done he explained that I would need to apply that goo every morning and night and then slide the jewelry side to side to work the antiseptic all the way through.

"Like this," Knight said, as I peeked out from between my fingers. He cupped my tiny breasts in his gloved hands and gently slid both barbells back and forth between his thumbs and forefingers at the same time. The sensation was unlike anything I'd ever felt. My panties were suddenly soaked, and I had to bite my tongue to keep from moaning out loud.

I guess I didn't hide my arousal as well as I thought, because Knight said with a smirk, "Or I can just do it for you."

I slammed my bra and shirt back down and jumped up from my seat. Turning and opening random cabinets behind me I rambled, "Do you need, like, cream or sugar or something for your coffee? I fucking hate coffee, so I don't really know how the whole thing works, but I know most people—"

"Nah. I'm good," Knight said as he slipped off his gloves. "I usually just take it black."

"You would," I muttered under my breath.

Knight and I finished our breakfast and cleaned up like a couple of domesticated little bitches. He made sure his tattoo station was tidy while I straightened up the breakroom. Then we sat on the fire escape and laced up our boots together before setting out on our little field trip to Boots & Braces—or as I called it, in my head, The Skinhead Store.

Since it was still early, Knight suggested that we walk there to kill time.

I had assumed it would be in Little Five Points somewhere.

I was wrong.

Boots & Braces was located at least a mile outside of Little Five, in a goddamn metal warehouse that looked like a high school gymnasium, inside a barbed wire fence, inside an industrial park, on the wrong side of the tracks, with absolutely no signage.

When Knight opened the gate and walked up to the door I seriously expected to be asked for ID or a password or a secret handshake or something.

What the fuck, Knight? All this for a pair of skinny suspenders?

He opened the door for me, but I just stared at him. There was no fucking way I was going in there first. I may have been naïve, but I wasn't stupid. That place had *rape shack* written all over it.

Knight laughed and said, "I thought we were girlfriends. Do you want to see where I shop or not?"

I peeked my head in and, sure as shit, the place was filled with racks of clothes, just like any other clothing store. The back wall supported shelf after shelf full of combat boots, and the far side of the warehouse was walled off with a ten-foot-high chain-link fence that guarded what appeared to be the surplus inventory.

I wandered in like Alice after she'd hit the bottom of the rabbit hole. What was this place? Was I dreaming? Were those band T-shirts *really* only $8.99? An entire wall of Grinders and Doc Martens in every size and color?

A voice from behind us broke my reverie. "You little bitch. Get over here and give me some sugar."

I turned and saw a big dude, dressed just like Knight, standing behind a makeshift checkout counter. He must have been in his late twenties, maybe thirty, and he was obviously no stranger to the gym. His neck was as big around as a tree trunk, but his face was kinder than Knight's.

When Knight walked up to do the whole handshake-slap-on-the-back thing that guys do, the beefcake pulled him into a headlock and gave him a noogie just like an older brother would have done. It made me smile to see somebody treat Knight like family.

Knight shoved him off and jerked a thumb in my direction. "Leo, this is Punk. Punk, meet Leonard. He owns the place. And he's a fucking dick."

Leonard raised an eyebrow at me and said, "Punk?"

"BB," I corrected, walking over to…I don't know…shake his hand? That's what grown-ups did, right?

But Leonard decided to make it less cordial and way more awkward by shoving Knight's shoulder and saying, "Damn, son! Where the fuck did you wrestle up this piece of ass? I guess you gotta grab 'em while they're young, huh? How old *are* you, Punkin'?"

Knight shoved Leonard back a few steps and yelled, "Her name isn't fucking Pumpkin, old man. It's Punk. Does she look like a fucking vegetable to you?" His deep voice echoed off the sheet metal walls.

Leo grinned like the Cheshire cat and clapped a hand down on Knight's shoulder. "Oooooh! He likes you, Punkin' Pie! I've never been able to rile this motherfucker up. He's usually Stone Cold Steve Austin up in here."

I didn't want to like Leonard, but his smile was infectious.

"Any shirt you want is on me, Punkin' Spice." He gestured to the $8.99 rack I noticed earlier. "I think I got some punk shit over there. Mostly for profiling purposes, but have at it."

Eager to get the fuck away from their pissing contest, I squeaked out a "Thank you," and made a beeline for the T-shirt rack. Knight and Leonard kept talking and laughing and smacking each other like a couple of old war veterans while I dug up a Dead Kennedys tank top, size extra-small.

Score!

When Knight was done shooting the shit with Leo he walked me around and explained to me where every brand and label originated. I felt like I was peering through the looking glass into a whole different lifestyle. Most of the clothing companies were based out of the UK, and evidently there were two different styles of skinhead. "Working-class skins" wore jeans and T-shirts, while "smart skins" wore nicer clothes—Fred Perry polo shirts and Ben Sherman button-ups—but they *all* wore boots and braces. Hence the name of the shop.

I'd seen Knight wear both styles. In fact, I think I'd seen Knight wear every single thing in that store. Except for one rack. It was completely devoted to T-shirts with various logos on them that all said SHARP in capital letters. Knight explained that SHARP stood for Skinheads Against Racial Prejudice. I think I laughed out loud when he told me what the acronym stood for, but he claimed that it wasn't a joke.

He said the whole skinhead culture originated in Europe as this working-class pride movement. It had nothing to do with white supremacy. They even listened to Jamaican ska and reggae music instead of the European music that was popular back then. The modern day SHARP skins wanted to take the subculture back from the Neo-Nazis, who they felt had hijacked their style to give their fascist cause a more distinctive look.

"So, does that make *you* a SHARP skin?" I asked, hopeful.

"Nah. I don't give a shit if people think I fucking jerk off to a picture of Hitler every night. Fuck 'em."

Oh, right. Of course he wasn't out there trying to convince people he was a good guy. He *wanted* them to think he was a Neo-Nazi. He *wanted* them to hate him. Because Knight had a motherfucking death wish.

I left with my prized tank top, no bag or anything, and a half-assed apology from Leonard for "being a dick." The noon sun had me tying Knight's flight jacket around my waist as we hiked past the dilapidated bungalows and overgrown lots back to his truck. A pang of sadness struck me as he hoisted me up into the cab. I didn't want to leave.

Knight made me choose a fast food restaurant to stop at on the way to work, so I chose McDonald's because I'd heard that their plain hamburgers only had like a hundred and fifty calories. Of course, Knight ordered a whole Happy Meal and made me eat it in front of him right there in the Pier 1 Imports parking lot.

Fucker.

While I chewed, Knight said, "The next time I have you in my chair, I think I'm going to pierce your clit."

I choked and gasped for air. "What the fuck, Knight? Why can't

I just get my belly button pierced like a normal girl? Why does it have to be my clit?! Jesus!"

"Because you're not a normal girl. And also because it needs to be in a place where your parents won't see. Mrs. Bradley would beat my ass if she found out I'd pierced her precious daughter."

I laughed at the thought. "She would, too! When I was little she used to spank me with a fucking meter stick. Not just a regular ruler. A three-foot-long strip of wood." I spread my hands apart to illustrate the length. "That shit stung like hell."

Knight laughed and said, "Any time you wanna play house you just let me know. I'll spank you with whatever you want."

"So you want to play the mommy?" I teased back. "Damn, Knight, you really *are* fucked up."

Suddenly, the atmosphere changed. Our jovial banter died, and Knight's jaw clenched shut.

Note to self: Do not call Knight "fucked up."

"I...I'm sorry," I said. "You don't like it when I say that, do you?"

Knight didn't respond. He just stared at me with those glacial eyes—pupils like pinpricks from the afternoon sun, jaw muscles working overtime.

"Hey," I said, placing my hand on top of his in the seat between us. Knight glanced down at the place where we touched and I could almost feel the skin on the back of my hand get colder under his stare.

Fuck. Okay...what now?

"Thanks for last night," I stuttered. "For the piercings, and for letting me stay. I..."

...wish I didn't have to go to work...wish we could hang out all day...wish I hadn't ruined the mood...wish I could make you smile again...

Knight squeezed my hand, *hard*, and looked back up at me with the intensity of a laser beam.

"I don't want you to go," he said.

It was direct and honest and not at all what I was expecting.

And neither was my reaction, which was to smile like a fucking idiot and smash my lips into his cheek.

Then leap from the cab of the truck as if it were on fire.

Chapter 18

I wish I could say that after that weekend I began talking to Knight in front of other people. That I finally accepted him as a friend and didn't care what people thought of me. But I didn't. Because I was an asshole teenager with a crush on someone else.

So, we resumed our routine like nothing had happened. Like Knight hadn't touched my tits. Like I hadn't kissed him on the cheek. Like the jacket I was wearing didn't belong to him. And like we hadn't spent the night together *twice*. For the next month we talked in the morning. We gave each other tiny nods in the church parking lot and at lunch, and we spoke in the truck on the way to Colton's. Meanwhile, I was all but throwing myself at Lance.

Okay, I was *full-on* throwing myself at Lance.

One afternoon in late October, Lance, Colton, August, and I were all watching *Jerry Springer* on Colton's woolen couch, shooting the shit and ignoring Knight, who had just come in from feeding the dog. Colton was telling us a riveting story about how he'd just tried to get a job at a haunted house.

"And then the owner said, 'I can't hire you. You're too pretty to be a zombie!' I told him I could just wear a mask, but he said he wouldn't feel right asking me to cover up a face this handsome."

Fucking Colton. That boy couldn't pretend to be humble if his sack depended on it.

"So that got me thinking," he continued. "What kind of a job *could* I get with a face like this? And then it hit me—male model!"

We all died laughing and Lance shoved Colton's *oh so* beautiful face with his open palm.

"I'm serious, you guys! I called my dad and he got me an agent, just like he did for my brother! I'm moving back to Vegas! Tomorrow!"

Lance crossed his arms over his chest and looked pissed. "What the fuck, dude. You just got back."

I pressed my hand to Lance's mouth to shush him, then leaned around his body and squealed, "That's awesome, Colton!"

Okay, I maaaay have been excited about Colton leaving for selfish reasons, but I was genuinely happy for him too.

"Maybe we can be roommates one day," I said. "I've always wanted to be a showgirl in Las Vegas. You know, the kind with the giant feathered head—"

"Fuck that," Knight interrupted me from his spot over on the recliner.

"What?" I asked, turning toward the man whom I had honestly forgotten was even in the room.

Knight leaned forward with his elbows on his knees and pointed a finger directly toward my chest. "Fuck. That. You need to get a new fucking career goal, Punk."

I looked at his finger, shining an invisible spotlight on my non-existent breasts, and an angry pink shame exploded in my neck and cheeks.

"Oh, you don't think I can be a showgirl?" I asked. "Because I have no tits? Well, fuck you, Knight! They make these magical things called breast implants now—"

Knight leapt out of his seat and crossed the room in milliseconds, grabbing my face in his right hand, and smooshing my cheeks until I made an involuntary kissy face. He planted his knee on the couch next to my hip and shoved my head back into the cushion behind me. Looming over me, Knight brought his face within inches of mine. My eyes went wide in shock, partly because Knight just attacked me and partly because none of the other boys made a move to stop him.

"You're not gonna be a *fucking* showgirl," he hissed through gritted teeth, "because I will *fucking* follow you to Las Vegas, and I will *fucking* kill every single mother*fucker* who thinks he has the right to look at your perfect *fucking* tits."

Bathroom. Space. Air. Now.

I pushed Knight off of me and ran to the "powder room," as Peg called it, before anyone could tell how flattered I was by Knight's twisted complimentary threat.

Perfect? Did he really just say "perfect tits" about me? In front of everyone?

I glanced in the mirror to see if I could see what he could see, but all I noticed was that my face and neck were covered in dark pink blotches.

Shit. I better wait a few minutes.

I sat on the toilet to pee and kill time until my skin returned to its normal color, realizing quickly that the thin bathroom walls did little to muffle the words being exchanged in the living room.

One of the voices belonged to Colton. I pressed my ear to the wall to hear him better, which was only about a foot away from the toilet in that tiny half-bath.

"Well, technically," Colton said, "she's still *my* girlfriend."

Oh no. Colton, shut up! I screamed to him telepathically. *Don't be a hero! What are you doing?*

"Well, *technically*," I heard Knight answer back in a voice deep and laced with malice, "I'm gonna fuck your girlfriend before you do."

Now, I'm not a religious person—never have been—but upon

hearing those words I crossed myself, just like my Irish Catholic mother did whenever she drove through a yellow traffic light—and whispered the only prayer she'd ever taught me.

Our Father who art in heaven, hallowed by thy name.
Thy kingdom come. Thy will be done on Earth as it is in heaven.
Give us this day our daily bread, and forgive us our trespasses
As we forgive those who trespass against us.
Lead us not into temptation, but deliver us from evil fucking skinheads.
Amen.

Chapter 19

I needed a friend. And not another confusing guy friend. I needed Juliet.

That afternoon, as soon as I got home, I ran upstairs and called my girl. I knew things were probably irreparably fucked between us—thanks to her gang-affiliated, drug-dealing, money-extorting boyfriend and my...whatever he was—but I missed her.

Juliet answered on the first ring and said, "BB?" on a broken sob.

"Oh my God! Juliet, what's wrong?"

Crying.

More crying.

"Sweetie, where are you?"

"At hoooome," she wailed.

"Did something bad happen? Do you want my mom to come get you?"

Sniffle. "I just...I just—"

"Juliet! Tell me what the fuck is going on!"

"I'm pregnant!" she screamed. "I just took a test, and I'm fucking pregnant, okay?!"

Pregnant?

My mind immediately filled with images of Juliet with a big belly, Juliet holding a little baby, me holding the little baby...Tony holding the little baby (shudder).

"BB, say something!" she screamed.

"You are going to be the cutest pregnant lady ever," I blurted out.

"I'm not a lady! I'm only f-f-fucking fifteeeeeeen!" she sobbed.

"Yeah, but by the time you have the baby you'll be sixteen, and that's practically an adult. And your mom will totally help you out. And I'll help too. I fucking love babies. And you can go to that alternative high school that has a daycare on site." I was rambling, vomiting out every positive scenario I could think of, hoping that one of them might cheer her up.

I had no idea what she was going through. I'd never even had sex. Babies were the furthest thing from my mind, and here Juliet was growing one inside her body.

"BB, please don't tell anybody. I haven't even told Tony. I...I might not tell him," she sniffled.

"Sweetie, I think he's gonna figure it out sooner or later."

"No, I mean...I might not..." Juliet couldn't even say it. Her hysterics started all over again and I had to hold the phone away from my ear until she calmed down.

She might not have it. Jesus. I hadn't even thought of that.

"Shhh...It's okay. You don't have to decide right now."

Juliet didn't say anything, but I could feel her nodding on the other end.

"Hey, Jules?" I asked. "Will you do me a favor?"

"What?" she whimpered.

"Will you *please* come to school tomorrow? I'm getting really fucking sick of listening to Lance and August talk about Eurotrash punk bands all lunch period."

Chapter 20

Not only did Juliet and her swollen, puffy eyes make it to school the next day, but she even came out to the church parking lot after second period with me. I knew she shouldn't have been smoking, but hey, at least she wasn't smoking *and* skipping school. Baby steps.

Juliet and I didn't talk about what had happened at Carlos and Angel's apartment. I wondered how much Tony had even told her. There was no way he would have been able to hide his cracked ribs, bruised throat, strained voice, or the busted blood vessels in his eyes, but knowing Tony, Juliet didn't get the full story. I knew for a fact that he hadn't told her about our little "arrangement" either.

Fucker.

The thought that a piece of shit like him could impregnate someone so smart and beautiful and badass made me sick. It wasn't fair. But maybe this was what she needed to get back on track. To stop skipping school and acting like she didn't care. Maybe a baby would get her to focus on her future a little more.

If she kept it, that is.

We didn't really talk about that either.

Just about the only thing Juliet did say during our little seven-minute reunion was "Is that Knight and Lance?" as we walked back down the trail to the student parking lot.

Sure as shit, there they were, cutting across the far side of the parking lot a few feet apart from each other. I guess I'd been so happy to have Juliet back—even if it was a gang-affiliated, hopelessly depressed, almost mute version of her—that I hadn't really noticed they were missing.

Even if I had noticed, never in a million years would I have assumed that they'd be *together*. Knight and Lance despised each other. Even after hanging out at Colton's every day for over a month they still weren't exactly on speaking terms. I couldn't begin to guess what the hell they'd been doing, or where they were coming from. There was nothing in that direction but cars, and beyond that, more woods.

Cars.

Maybe that was it. Knight's truck was usually parked in that direction. Maybe Lance had left something in it the day before. That was the only thing that made sense. Hopefully Knight hadn't been too big of an asshole to him about it. Guessing from their body language and the fact that they were walking so far apart, whatever had happened hadn't gone too well.

Even though Juliet was back, I didn't dare ask for a ride home.

And she didn't offer.

I rode to Colton's with Knight as usual, but that afternoon there were only two boys in the back of his truck instead of three. Colton was already on a plane headed back to Las Vegas. I wanted to miss him, but... *meh*. Mostly I would just miss hanging out at his house and drinking his mom's beer.

Oh, shit.

I yelled over the roar of the engine to Knight, "Hey, if Colton's gone, where are we gonna hang out?"

Knight glanced at me then flicked the impressive collection of keys hanging from his ignition with two fingers. "Peg said she wants me to keep coming by every day to feed the dog and shit."

His tone told me all I needed to know about his mood. I mean, Knight was pretty much always in a shitty mood, but he seemed even more irritable than usual. I wondered if it had something to do with his interaction with Lance earlier. I never did ask about it.

Walking on eggshells, I asked as sweetly as possible, "Are you sure it's okay for the rest of us to come too?" Even I had to admit that hanging out at a forty-something-year-old lady's house and drinking her beer while she worked forty-something odd jobs just to keep the lights on seemed like a shitty thing to do.

"Yeah, I guess."

I'd have to remember to leave her some beer money after I got paid on the first. Poor Peg.

As soon as we stepped inside Peg's house Lance grabbed me by the hips and pulled me down onto his lap in the middle of the couch. I squealed and giggled as he tickled me and buried his face in my neck.

August awkwardly took a seat next to us.

I sat on Lance's lap all the time, but he'd never made such a spectacle of it before. It was like he was trying to make Knight jealous or something. Why the fuck anyone would want to piss Knight off was beyond me, but in that moment, I didn't care. Lance's hands were on my body and his breath was on my clavicle and I let my blissful ignorance swallow me whole.

Knight growled something about Lance getting his AIDS all over me as he headed out of the living room toward the back door. Lance pulled his head up to make a kissy face at him in response, but Knight was already gone. I appreciated Lance's confidence—in fact, I thought it was sexy as hell—but he had no idea who he was fucking with.

Just then August cleared his throat, reminding us that somebody was still in the room, and that somebody was uncomfortable as shit.

I hopped off of Lance's lap—he seemed to be done playing with me anyway—and announced that I was going to grab some beers. On my way to the kitchen I stopped by the "powder room" to pee and make sure I didn't have mascara under my eyes from my little giggle fest. I could already hear Lance and August talking about record labels. Those guys talked indie music the way most dudes talked sports. It was like a never-ending stream of bullshit they could tap into whenever they wanted.

I grabbed some beers from the fridge and headed back through the tiny dining room that connected the linoleum-lined kitchen to the wood-paneled living room, but got distracted on the way by a loud banging noise coming from outside. I peered through the window on the back door and saw Knight hammering the shit out of the weather-beaten wooden stairs that led from the deck to the yard. Veins bulged from his forearm as he worked, and I began to wonder if he was fixing the deck or just fucking it up more.

Note to self: Do NOT piss Knight off while he's holding a hammer.

I wanted to watch him until I figured out what the hell he was doing, but the freezing cold beers in my hands demanded to be put down more than my curiosity demanded to be fed.

Lance and August were so far gone in their conversation that they barely even acknowledged me when I returned with their beverages. As annoyed as I was that August was cock-blocking me, a part of me was still really happy that he'd at least made a friend—a real friend—who wasn't me.

I popped the tab on my can and flopped onto the open spot on the couch over by the end table—the home of the ashtray and the remote.

I was bored. No one was entertaining me, including the hillbilly family having a painfully contrived food fight on *The Jerry Springer Show*. I rolled my eyes at the TV and stamped out my third cigarette just as a familiar metallic jingle sounded from somewhere next to me. I looked over and saw that Lance had pulled out his Lemonheads tin and was shaking it back and forth gently.

"Anybody wanna party?" he asked with a playful smile.

August and I traded glances. I could tell he wanted me to take the lead on this one, but I stayed mum. I totally wanted to "party" if that meant Lance and I would get to pick up where we left off in that bathroom stall two months ago, but with August and Knight there that would be pretty fucking awkward.

Cock blockers. Everywhere.

August finally shrugged and asked, "What is it?"

"Crank," Lance said, as he leaned over and unzipped the front pocket of his backpack. He said it the way someone might say "jelly beans" or "candy corn." Like it was no big deal.

Crank? Crank. I've heard of that. Crank is yellow, right? Yeah, I think it's made from crystal—

"Meth," I whispered, as Lance sat back up holding a lightbulb and a straw. August and Lance both looked at me, but I didn't flinch. I didn't want them to think I was judging them. I wasn't. I'd done drugs, plenty of 'em. I smoked. I drank. But meth? That shit rotted your face.

"Nah, I have to work tonight," I lied. "You two have fun. I'm gonna go see what the fuck Knight is doing. I think he's building a coffin or something. Probably for you, August."

August's eyes went wide and I laughed. That poor kid could not take a joke. Just as I stood up and started heading toward the back door, I heard Lance's velvety soft voice say my two favorite words in the English language.

"Hey, girl…"

My face split into a stupid tipsy grin as I spun around and asked, "What's up?"

Lance smiled back, and his dimples made me weak in the knees. "I hate to see you go, but I loooove to watch you leave."

I wrinkled up my nose in feigned offense and stuck my middle finger in the air. Lance gasped and clutched his heart as I turned and sashayed through the dining room. And away from that yellow shit.

As the sound of Knight's hammering got closer I remembered that he was Lance and August's ride home. If Knight found out that they were both tweaking he'd probably kick their asses out on the side of the highway. If they were lucky he'd slow down first.

As my hand landed on the doorknob, I called out over my shoulder in my too-loud, tipsy voice, "Hey, you guys? Y'all might want to wait to do that until you get home because Knight fucking hates drugs, and—"

Just then the door opened into me. I stumbled backward a few feet but managed to keep a tight grip on what was left of my almost-empty beer.

"I fucking hate *what*?"

Knight's sweaty figure filled the doorway and his nostrils flared from what I hoped was exertion rather than rage.

"Nothing. Shit! Go back outside." I tried to shove him back through the doorframe, but Knight wouldn't budge.

"Did he just fucking try to give you something?!" Knight's eyes were crazed.

Oh, Jesus Christ. Not this again. Not with Lance!

Before I could shout "Run!" Knight had pushed past me and stomped into the living room in three huge strides.

The house was immediately filled with the sounds of furniture hitting walls and skin hitting skin.

Lance!

I ran after Knight, but it was too late. The side table had been knocked over. The carpet had become a bed of cigarette butts and lightbulb shards. August was pressed up against the wall as if he were trying to blend in with the wood paneling. And Knight and Lance were in a full-on brawl on the living room floor.

I didn't know how to break it up, but I knew I had to do something. Knight would fucking kill Lance. The only reason Lance was holding his own at all was because (a) he was three inches taller and at least thirty pounds heavier than Knight, and (b) he'd been fighting his older brother since he was a toddler. In fact, that's exactly how Lance was fighting. Knight looked like he was out for blood, while Lance was just blocking and wrestling like he was sparring with a sibling.

Knight was not his fucking brother though. Lance's brother wouldn't punch him in the fucking face. Lance's brother wouldn't try to break his bones. Lance's brother would stop when someone screamed, "Stop it! Stop it! You're KILLING HIM!"

Knight wouldn't.

Knight would stop when Knight felt like stopping. Which was the second Lance lost consciousness. Satisfied, Knight stood up, spit on the floor next to my future husband's limp body, then stomped past me without so much as a glance and slammed the back door behind him.

What.

The fuck.

Was that?!

I ran over to Lance, who was just coming to, and helped him sit up. His left eye was already starting to swell and turn purple, his nose was bloody, and his jaw looked like it was hanging crooked.

"I had that fucker right where I wanted him," he said, standing up way too quickly for someone who'd just been knocked out. "Did you see that shit, B? I'm a fucking champion!"

Then he winced and clutched his jaw.

I reached out to touch it, but stopped short, not wanting to hurt him. "Shit, Lance. Do you think it's broken?" I asked.

Lance waved his hand at me dismissively and said, "Nah. Probably just bruised," as he bounced on the balls of his feet. He was fucking amped.

"WOO! That shit was awesome! Who's next?" Lance clapped his hands together and glanced back and forth between me and August with his one open eye.

I looked over at August, who was still pressed up against the wall, hiding behind his flop of black hair, and noticed that he was feverishly picking at his fingernails even though his black polish was long gone.

"August, you okay, hun?" August nodded at the speed of light, but kept staring at his fingernails, picked clean and probably bleeding.

Oooooooooh no.

I was too late.

"Lance, I know this is a shitty thing to do while you're fucked up, but you have to go, baby. You and August need to get out of here."

"Boo!" Lance said, and stuck out his bottom lip like a little kid, pulling me toward him. I wanted to climb him like a tree and suck that lip into my mouth. I wanted cute, crazy, hyper, badass, invincible Lance more than I wanted regular Lance, which shouldn't have even been possible. I wanted him to push another one of those yellow crystals into my mouth with his tongue and let me follow him into whatever manic marshmallow-covered magical mystery land he was living in.

But then Knight would kill him.

And that would kill me.

Which, in turn, would kill August.

As much as it pained me to send them away, especially in their condition, and especially with no ride, they had to go. Luckily, August's trailer was only about a mile away. I opened the front door and gestured for them to exit.

August left first, probably eager as fuck to get out of that place, and I gave him a big hug. "Go straight home, okay?"

August nodded, a little too fast and a little too long, then dashed down the rickety wooden stairs and into the yard.

Lance picked me up over his shoulder and spun me around on his way out, swatting my ass before putting me back down.

"Go straight to August's house, okay?" I begged.

Lance smiled like a goofball with his swollen-shut eye and jacked-up jaw.

"Hey, girl!" he shouted in my face.

"What's up, Lance?"

"Are you a beaver?"

"No, Lan—"

"Because daaaaaam!"

I burst out laughing, and Lance—all six feet, three inches of him—jumped off the front porch and landed on his feet on the slab of cement at the bottom of the stairs.

As soon as he landed Lance screamed, "Fuuuck!" and gripped the tops of his thighs, causing August to erupt into a nervous fit of giggles. Motherfucker had stabbed himself with his bullet belt again.

When I shut the door I felt a little bit better. Lance and August were going to be okay, as long as they didn't get hit by a car on their way home.

I never thought I'd say this, but thank God for crank.

Now what?

It was just me and the psycho, who, from the sound of things, was outside hitting shit with a hammer again.

Fuck me.

I looked around the room at the destruction those assholes had left in their wake, and my anger toward Knight returned full-force. I didn't care how many jackets or rides or meals or piercings he had given me—he was a fucking monster. I should have just left with Lance and August. Why hadn't I? Why was I still there?

I grabbed what was left of my beer and peeked out the kitchen window again. Knight had stopped hammering and was standing on the deck with his back to me looking down at the stairs—or what used to be the stairs—*shirtless*. The black lines of his McKnight coat of arms tattoo stood out in stark contrast against his pale skin, which appeared to be glowing in the midafternoon sun. Red braces hung down from the waistband of his jeans, and his muscles were swollen from use and shiny with sweat. I choked on my beer.

I may have been furious with him, and he may have been psychotic, but my feet were fueled by curiosity and pheromones, not logic.

When Knight heard the back door open he turned and practically sliced me in half with his laser-like pupils.

Clutching the doorframe for support, I asked, "Why are you covering up Peg's stairs?"

"It's a ramp," he said. His tone was clipped. Annoyed. "For Shep."

Upon hearing his name, Shep, Peg's geriatric German Shepherd, limped over to Knight from a shady spot on the deck and rested his head against the shirtless skinhead's thigh. Knight reached down and rubbed his head, right behind his ear.

Was this seriously the same person who just beat a six-foot-three-inch-tall Mohawked motherfucker unconscious in the living room?

I looked at Knight—past his tough exterior, through those haunting colorless eyes—and into the soul of a man with the most confusing combination of qualities a human could possess. When it came to animals he was gentle and thoughtful, but when it came to people I got the sense that he genuinely wanted to kill them all.

Except for me.

I hoped.

"That's...really sweet of you," I said.

"It's not fucking sweet. It's what needed to be done." Knight's voice got louder, and he shoved a finger in the direction of the yard. "They can't just leave him out here by himself all day." Louder still. "They think just because he has teeth and claws, just because he was built to kill shit, that he can just take care of himself. Well, he can't!"

Gesturing toward the heap of fur and protruding ribs on the deck next to him, Knight shouted, "Look at him! Fucking look at him! Does he look okay to you?!"

He didn't. Honestly, Shep looked like he was at death's door. I'd never noticed before.

Turning away from me, Knight balled his hands into fists and pressed his bloody knuckles to either side of his head. "You can't just leave somebody alone all day every day and expect them to be okay! It's not fucking okay!"

We weren't talking about Shep anymore. We weren't talking about animals at all.

Without thinking I launched myself at Knight and wrapped my arms around his waist as tightly as I could. His heart was beating wildly against my cheek. His chest was hot and damp with sweat, but still smelled like cinnamon. "I'm sorry," I whispered into it.

Knight raised his arms, as if he didn't know what to do with them. As if my behavior confused him.

As if he'd never been given a hug before.

His reaction made my heart constrict.

"I'm so sorry," I whispered again, a black tear careening down the slick planes of Knight's chest. I didn't need to know what all he'd been through—I knew enough. I knew he'd been neglected, and I knew that what I'd been doing to him was no better. I'd seen his fangs and claws, and I'd left him alone too.

Knight didn't respond, but after a minute he did at least lower his arms. He wrapped them around me, loosely at first. His body stayed rigid for a while, but I could feel his heart rate decreasing beneath my cheek—beneath the black mascara stain on his chest. Eventually the arms around my shoulders squeezed me back, finally brave enough to accept my comfort, and within another few minutes Knight's big hard body relaxed into mine.

He rested his cheek on the top of my head and held me as if I were keeping him afloat. I didn't want it to, but it felt amazing. I'd never been held like that before. By anyone. Like I was necessary for their survival.

After a few minutes Knight asked, "Is he going to be okay?"

Who? Oh... Lance.

"Yeah," I said. "He's fine. Everything is going to be fine."

Lies. All lies.

Chapter 21

The next day Lance and Knight were missing from the church parking lot again. Juliet didn't come either because she said it was "bad for the baby." *The baby*. Maybe she was going to keep it after all.

With no one to talk to, I sat on the railroad ties that lined the parking lot and played with the gravel. I hadn't seen Lance or Knight before first period either, and I was starting to worry. Okay, I was totally worried. Was Lance okay? Was he in the hospital? Did his parents take one look at him and call the cops? Was Knight in jail?

I stamped my cigarette out and buried it under the little mountain of gravel I had amassed. As I walked back across the parking lot, one of my questions was answered. I saw Lance come flying around the side of the building like a bat out of hell. He was headed in the same direction I'd seen him come from the day before, and he was running so fast it was like he was being chased.

Lance didn't run from shit, not even Ronald McKnight, and his pulverized face was proof. The only things I could think of that would have him hauling ass like that were a grizzly bear, a madman with a gun, or maybe the cops.

"Lance!" I shouted, jogging after him. "Lance! Wait up!"

He didn't wait up though. Lance sprinted across the parking lot, bobbing and weaving through the sea of cars, and disappeared into the woods. When I got to the edge of the parking lot, I realized that he'd gone down a trail I didn't even know was there. I followed it and found Lance, waiting for me on the other side, in someone's backyard. We were in a neighborhood.

Breathing hard, I leaned over with my hands on my knees, and said, "What's (gasp) wrong? Where (gasp) are you going?"

Lance was pacing back and forth with his hood pulled over his head. I couldn't see the full extent of the damage Knight had done, but I could tell that his right eye was still definitely swollen shut.

"Somebody fucking narced on me!"

"What?"

Lance stopped pacing and faced me. "The assistant principal pulled me out of first period to tell me that they'd gotten an anonymous tip that I was carrying. I told her she couldn't search me without a warrant, so the bitch left to call the school resource officer. I fucking bailed as soon as she was gone!"

"Shit. Lance, what are you gonna do?"

"I know I'm *not* just gonna sit there and wait to get fucking arrested!" Lance turned and stomped through the yard we were standing in toward the house.

"Who lives here?" I asked as he walked away, confused as shit.

"I fucking live here!" he yelled into the cool mid-morning air.

"Wait. What?"

I forced myself to follow him into the modest ranch house, but my mind was racing.

Lance lives here? Here. Two hundred yards from school. All those times I was scrounging for a place to hang out after school and … and he never said anything. Why? Why didn't he ever invite me over? Why didn't he mention where he lived when we were smoking in the church parking lot? It's right fucking here!

Because he didn't want you to know, a tiny sinister voice in the back of my mind answered back. *Because he doesn't want you.*

When my inner dialogue died down I realized that I was standing in Lance's bedroom. The walls were covered from floor to ceiling with band posters, flags, and stolen street signs. It was every bit as layered and decorated as he was, but unlike him, his room was fucking tiny. Lance could barely move around in there. I assumed he just had to leave his larger-than-life personality at the door.

I watched from the threshold as Lance dumped out the contents of his backpack and began shoving clothes into it. He then threw open his closet, grabbed a duffel bag, tossed it onto his unmade twin bed, and began filling that too. He wasn't just packing for the weekend—he was packing for good.

"Lance," I pried. "Where are you going?"

He didn't even look at me. Just kept shoving shit into bags.

"Lance?"

With a huff, he stopped and glared at me with his one good eye, obviously annoyed with my presence. "I'm not just gonna stay here and go to jail! I'll fucking stay at Colton's dad's place in Vegas—I don't know!"

"How are you going to get—"

"I'll take a fucking cab to the Greyhound station! What the fuck do you care? Your little Nazi boyfriend is probably the one who narced on me in the first place!"

I shouted back, "He is not my fucking boyfriend!" while a million other sentiments became lodged in my throat.

You were supposed to be my fucking boyfriend!

You were supposed to marry me and give me tall, hazel-eyed babies!

I love you!

Don't leave me!

Take me with you!

Why don't you love me back?

Lance pushed past me and ducked into the hall bathroom where he cleared the counter into his duffel bag with one long-armed swoop. I just stood there and watched, one foot in his bedroom and one foot in the hallway, as my reason for living prepared to walk out of my life.

Next Lance hit up his parents' room, probably hunting for whatever cash they had on hand. The kitchen was his last stop. Lance used the cordless phone on the counter to call for a taxi while he walked around filling a grocery bag with all the vegan-friendly food he could find.

When Lance was done packing he headed for the front door, so I followed.

He sat in a wicker rocking chair on the front porch, so I did too.

He smoked, so I smoked.

And when the cab pulled up in his driveway, he left without a word.

So I cried until I threw up.

By the time I dragged myself back to school I had missed second period and lunch. I sat down in third period, balled myself up, and replayed every agonizing second of my last moments with Lance Hightower. I wished I had taken something from his room. A memento, something to remember him by.

Because I knew he was never coming back.

Because he hated me.

And he never even wanted me to begin with.

Someone delivered a note to my third-period teacher while he was lecturing us on buying low and selling high, which was a joke because none of us was ever going to have enough money to invest that shit in anything. He glanced at it, then handed it to me. It said that I had detention due to my unexcused absence from second period.

Awesome.

I willed myself not to cry through fourth period, then schlepped my way over to my locker when the dismissal bell rang.

I didn't want to see Knight. I didn't want to have to explain why I was upset. I didn't want to hear him call Lance a faggot or admit that he was the one who ratted him out. I also didn't want to accidentally blurt out, "Stay the fuck away from me! I hate you! You're ruining my whole fucking life!"

But, of course, there he was.

When I walked up Knight immediately asked, "Where were you during lunch?"

I wanted to ignore him, but after what he'd said at Peg's house the day before, I knew ignoring him was the absolute worst way to go.

"I skipped," I said matter-of-factly. I opened my locker with an angry kick and busied myself inside.

"With Lance?" His tone was accusing, and I didn't fucking appreciate it.

"Yeah, with fucking Lance," I snapped. I wanted to unload on him so badly. I wanted to blame him for everything that was falling apart my life. I wanted to pound on his chest with my fists. But I knew better.

So, instead, I slammed my locker and walked away.

Knight followed, not missing a step. "Where the fuck are you going?" he asked. His tone was still condemning, like he thought I was going to see Lance again. And snort a big line of coke off his cock. Or do something else he didn't fucking approve of.

"Detention," I said, facing straight ahead.

"I'm coming with you." It wasn't an offer. It was a declaration.

"I don't need a fucking babysitter," I spat, walking faster.

"You don't know what the fuck you need."

I threw open the door to the detention room and hoped to find a desk by itself to sit in. No such luck. Evidently, out of four thousand students, only like five of us had gotten detention that day. No matter where I sat, Knight would be able to sit next to me.

Sigh.

I chose a desk in the back and immediately pulled out my homework. Knight sat next to me, like I knew he would, but instead of a book he took a sketchpad out of his backpack.

About ten minutes later I heard a tearing sound, then Knight slapped a small piece of paper on my desk with jagged edges. I glanced at it out of the corner of my eye, and my breath hitched.

It was a drawing of me, hunched over my desk, head in a book, biting the end of my pencil. My bangs hung in front of my face—one of the long pieces tucked behind my ear—and a tiny line on my cheek marked the spot where I'd been bitten by a dog as a child. It was beautiful, and for Knight, effortless. I'd forgotten just how talented he was.

I looked over at him cautiously, but he was already working on something else.

A few minutes later another rip sounded and another square landed on my desk. This one was also a drawing of my face, but I was wearing a clown nose and clown makeup. I smiled involuntarily.

I heard several more rips after that, but no more pieces of paper made their way over to me. Happy to have the rest of detention to mourn my lost love uninterrupted, I finished my homework, packed up my shit, and turned to face Knight once we were dismissed.

His body was angled toward me, and his eyes were waiting for mine to find them. They were usually full to bursting with hate or annoyance or suspicion, but in that moment Knight's gray-blue gaze was…empty. Like two open windows on a cloudless day.

His hands weren't empty though.

Knight was holding a fistful of paper flowers.

He extended them toward me slowly, and only by a few inches, as if he were preparing himself for them to be rejected.

I don't know if it was because of everything that had happened with Lance, or because no one had ever given me a bouquet of flowers before, or if I was sad that Knight was obviously bracing himself for rejection, but as I reached out and accepted Knight's offering, fresh tears puddled in my eyes.

"Those were supposed to cheer you up," Knight said, his brow furrowed. "Did I fuck that up too?"

"No," I said, shaking my head and blinking back my tears. "No, you didn't."

"Good. Let's go get drunk."

Chapter 22

As we walked across the parking lot toward Knight's truck, I clutched my parchment roses in one hand and fought the urge to hold Knight's hand with the other. That was something we had only done downtown, when we were away from prying eyes.

Thinking of all the potential witnesses in the parking lot made me realize that August was missing. Damn. Poor kid. I made him walk home from Colton's house while he was tweaking the day before, and didn't even think to find him and tell him I'd gotten detention that afternoon. I made a mental note to call him later.

Knight lifted me into his truck and asked, before shutting the door, "Do you have to work tonight?"

I shook my head *no*, and he smiled a little. Once Knight was inside the cab he reached under the bench seat and handed me his flask. "Just a little. I know your ass hasn't eaten shit today."

I did as he said, taking tiny sips as we roared through town blasting Operation Ivy with the windows down. Something about the combination of whiskey in my belly, notebook paper roses in my lap, the cool autumn wind on my face, and poppy punk music filling the air had me feeling about eighty-five percent better.

When we got to Colton's house Knight grabbed a Coke out of

Peg's fridge, poured a little bit into the sink, then flicked his fingers at me, gesturing for the flask that I didn't even realize I had carried inside. I handed it to him, and he filled the can the rest of the way up with whiskey. Knight kept the flask, but handed the can to me.

"I have to feed Shep," he said. "Wanna come?"

I nodded and carried my drink outside, sitting by myself on a rusty metal bench on Peg's porch. The spot was sunny, and the drink was good. Sweet and fizzy. The leaves on the trees in Peg's wooded backyard were beginning to turn orange and yellow. The grass was incredibly overgrown, and a rusty swing set on the edge of the yard was in the process of being swallowed by kudzu vines. I tried to imagine Colton and Jesse playing on it when they were little. Was Peg happy back then?

Shep wagged his long skinny tail when he saw Knight, and climbed up the ramp to greet him. Knight squatted down so that he was eye to eye with him and rubbed Shep vigorously behind the ears—really gave him his undivided attention—then he took his bowls inside the house to refill them.

While Knight was gone Shep came over to sniff me. He must have decided I was cool because he licked my hand then went back to the door to wait for Knight. I couldn't believe how afraid I had once been of that dog. He seemed so sweet and harmless now.

I guess I could say the same thing about Knight, as long as no one else was around to set him off.

When Knight was done tending to Shep, he walked over to where I was sitting and plucked the Coke can from my hand. Shaking it from side to side, gauging its fullness, he said, "C'mon. You need another drink."

"No, I don't," I said. "That one is still—"

Before I could finish my sentence Knight brought the almost full can to his lips and chugged the whole thing, letting out a huge belch before handing the empty can back to me. "Not anymore. C'mon."

Knight prepared another whiskey and Coke concoction in the kitchen, handed it to me, then carried the flask of Southern Comfort with him into the living room. He sat on the couch instead of in the recliner, and I sat down next to him, in my usual spot.

Knight lit a cigarette as I studied him. He seemed so…adult-like. So serious and responsible. Having a stiff drink after a hard day.

I wondered why he never went home. I guess Peg's house was kind of his home away from home, but he wasn't even really that close to Peg. Or Colton. In fact, he expressly *dis*liked Colton, yet there he was. Hanging out at his house, taking care of his dog. It was the weirdest shit ever.

I took a few big sips from my can, for courage, then asked the question that had been on the tip of my tongue for months. "Knight, why don't you ever go home?"

Knight took a swig from his flask and stared at the front window as if he could see through the smoke-stained plastic blinds. "My mom's husband has a restraining order against me."

"What happened?" I asked in surprise, then quickly changed my tone. And my question. "What did you do?"

Knight swallowed and faced me. "Cocksucker thought he could put his hands on my mom." He shrugged. "I made him think again."

"Do you love her?" I don't know where those words came from, but I wished I could take them back. Stupid fucking truth serum.

"Everybody loves their mom," Knight snapped back.

"Not everybody," I said gently.

Knight clenched his jaw and was quiet for a minute, then took a deep drag before answering. "I used to."

It was honest, and sad, and incomprehensible.

"What about your dad?"

Knight didn't look at me. He just stared at those fucking closed blinds, like he was trying to see something that wasn't ever going to be there.

"My dad lives in Chicago. He was some big shot businessman with a wife and a couple of kids who knocked up my mom on the side. He was never in the picture—just a shitload of boyfriends that my mom said were my *uncles*."

Knight's words were devoid of emotion, like he'd told that story a thousand times before. But to whom?

I didn't get a chance to ask, because Knight took over the interrogation. "What about you? Why don't you ever go home, Punk?" His gaze bored into me, letting me know he wanted the motherfucking truth. Knight probably assumed my story would be similarly shitty. Everyone's story was shitty where we came from.

"I don't know," I said, taking another sip. "I never really thought about it. I guess I just don't like being alone. I mean, my parents are there, but...they're not *really* there. You know what I mean?"

Now I was the one staring at the dirty blinds, picturing my folks. "My dad is super anxious and paranoid and doesn't ever sleep or leave the house. He just sits on the couch watching CNN and playing guitar all day and night. And you know my mom. She's like, the nicest person ever, but she mostly just smokes pot and reads when she's at home. Plus, we live out in the middle of fucking nowhere."

I looked back at Knight, who was hanging on my every word, and said, "I guess I'd just rather be out here in the real world, living a real life, than stuck in the woods with a couple of middle-aged hippies."

Knight smiled a tiny bit, probably relieved that I wasn't some child abuse victim, and took another swig. Gesturing around the room with his flask he said, "You call this a real life?"

I smiled back. "I'm drinking whiskey at three o'clock in the afternoon with a skinhead, in my ex-boyfriend's house, and there is no one around to hear me scream. That feels like living on the edge to me."

"I'll toast to that." Knight held up his flask, and I held up my Coke can.

"To living on the edge," I said.

We clanked our vessels together and drank in unison. I thought of something as I swallowed, and blurted it out as usual.

"So, if your stepdad has a restraining order out against you and you live with him, how does that work?"

Knight screwed the cap back on with a flick of his thumb and said, "He travels for business during the week, so I just have to find somewhere else to be during the weekends."

"So you stay at the tattoo shop."

"Yeah. Bobby lives nearby, so she usually lets me run over to her house to take a shower in the mornings before the place opens."

"So, you're basically homeless three days a week, but you still manage to stay in school *and* shower daily. That's pretty amazing, Knight. *I* don't even shower daily," I giggled in embarrassment.

Fucking truth serum.

Knight stamped out his cigarette in an overflowing ashtray next to him on the end table and asked, "How else am I supposed to get pussy? Bitches like guys who smell good."

I laughed so hard I spit whiskey and Coke across the room. Thankfully, the shag carpet was basically the same shade of brown as my drink. It burned like hell, so I smacked Knight's arm in retaliation while I coughed and laughed and secretly agreed that he did smell good. *Damn* good. Sweet musky cinnamon and Marlboro Reds good.

Once I calmed down I said, "I can't believe you fucking stay at the shop overnight. That place scares the shit out of me."

"It's not so bad, once you get used to all the ghosts." Knight smirked, then brought the flask back to his lips.

Laughing again, I said, "If there are ghosts, they're probably all afraid of *you*."

Knight set the flask down and turned toward me. Smirk gone. "I'm pretty sure the only thing dumb enough to *not* be afraid of me is you."

"I am not dumb!" I yelled louder than I intended. "I'm in all AP classes *and* I'm going to graduate early! I'm the smartest person you know!"

I took another drink to hide behind my Coke can for a second while I reined in my feistiness. The caffeine and alcohol were giving me way too much energy to sit there having serious conversations any longer.

"In fact," I continued in a less shouty voice, "I'm smart enough to know that I *don't* have to be afraid of you. You're not going to hurt m—"

"Yes I will," Knight interrupted. "That's what I do, Punk. I hurt people."

C'mon, Knight. Lighten up! I'm the one who lost the love of my life today. Why are you so damn serious?

"Prove it," I teased, begging him to play with me.

"You want me to hurt you?" Knight asked.

"Yep." I hiccupped.

"What, like you want me to punch you in the face or something? Jesus, Punk. You're like a damn man when you get drunk, you know that?" Knight sounded annoyed, but I could see a smile creeping into the corners of his mouth.

"Oh yeah?" I slurred, my can almost empty. "Well you're like a little bitch when you get drunk."

Knight chuckled, showing me the gorgeous smile I never got to see anymore. The one that made him look boyish and cute instead of cold and calculating. The one that made me forget who I was dealing with.

"Oh, really?" he said, leaning in closer, all snowy white teeth and icy blue eyes. "Would a bitch do this?"

Then he kissed me.

When Knight's lips first touched mine they were still smiling. I wanted them to stay like that. It felt nice, that part. When we were still just a couple of friends, drinking and smoking and joking around. A split second before everything changed. Before Knight's whiskey-flavored tongue was in my mouth. Before his callused hand was wrapped around the back of my neck.

Before I kissed him back.

I'd kissed Colton at least a hundred times on that very same couch, but this wasn't one of Colton's kisses. This wasn't a kiss from some cocky teenaged boy who didn't care about anything other than getting his hands under my clothes. This was a kiss from a *man* who didn't care about anything other than *me*.

It was intense. Too intense. So I put both hands on Knight's hard chest and pushed him off of me. The alcohol and adrenaline must have given me superstrength because I was actually able to launch him all the way back to his side of the couch. I didn't know if I was more nervous about the kiss, breaking the kiss, or shoving that motherfucker off me, but some combination of those things caused me to erupt into a total hysterical giggle fit.

"I can't believe I pushed you that far!" I said through my hysterics. "You really do turn into a little bitch when you drink!"

Knight's face cracked open into a malicious grin. It wasn't boyish. It was frightening.

Knight sneered, then grabbed my leg and yanked me toward him, causing me to fall sideways onto the couch. Screaming between my giggles, I took my other combat boot–covered foot and pushed off of his hard thigh, clawing my way over to the other side of the scratchy sectional. Before I could get away, though, Knight got a hand around one of my ankles.

"No!" I screamed, kicking again with my free foot, but this time Knight grabbed it as well and slid me backward until my knees were on his lap. I couldn't kick out, so I flipped over onto my back, causing my feet to twist out of his hands.

My whole body was alive. I was wrestling with a skinhead, and I was winning! I'd never had any confidence in my athletic abilities whatsoever. I was weak and uncoordinated, but evidently, I was *fast*. It was exhilarating.

When Knight went to grab my legs again I rolled onto the floor. When his hands came down around my waist I screamed and dug my nails into his skin. When he let go I crawled halfway to the armchair before my legs were pulled out from under me. And just when I thought I was going to be pinned on my stomach, I flipped over onto my back and tickled the shit out of him.

I'd never seen someone react so violently to being tickled. Knight let go and clutched his sides, laughing and yelling, "You fucking bitch!" as I army crawled across the brown shag carpet. Just before I made it to the ancient wood-paneled television set—which I envisioned myself picking up and smashing over his head, WWF style—Knight caught me and slid me at least three feet backward. The friction burned a new hole into the knee of my jeans.

I flipped over and tried to tickle him again, but that time Knight was ready for me. He straddled my thighs and squeezed my legs together between his knees. Then, when I lunged for his sensitive sides again, Knight grabbed my wrists and pinned them to the ground on either side of my head. Knight was suspended above me, eyes crazed, chest heaving, and the reality of the situation hit me like a Mack truck. Being drunk and alone with a violent skinhead in a place where no one could hear my screams—"living on the edge," as I'd called it—suddenly felt like a really, really stupid idea.

This wasn't the same boy who'd just playfully kissed me on the couch. There was something predatory in his movements, his stare. Like he'd finally caught the mouse, and now he was licking his chops.

I blinked up at him with wide, helpless eyes, silently begging him to leave me whole—to not take too much—but Knight's eyes were elsewhere. They lingered at the place I'd already let him touch, shove needles through, adorn with jewelry. He was the only one who'd ever seen me there, and from the way he stared, I could tell he wanted to see it again.

Without releasing me from his grip or gaze, Knight slowly lowered himself onto me. I didn't breathe. I didn't fight. I couldn't flee, so I did what I did best. I froze.

I braced myself to have something taken from me, ripped away, but instead Knight gave. He pressed his sweet, whiskey-flavored lips to mine, and gave me a kiss. One that sent sparks coursing through my cortisol-flooded bloodstream and made my immobilized arms and legs tingle. There was a tension in his body that suggested he was exercising a great deal of self-control, and for a split second, I wished he wouldn't.

Instead of deepening our kiss, like he had before, Knight pulled away and pressed his forehead to mine in yet another unexpectedly tender gesture. He loosened his grip from my wrists and laced his fingers through mine. Our noses touched, barely, and Knight exhaled a long, shaky breath.

He was holding his breath too, I thought.

I don't know whether I tilted my mouth up toward his or whether he brought his down to mine, but somehow our lips found each other's again.

Knight swirled his tongue around mine in controlled, unhurried circles, before capturing my bottom lip between his teeth and sucking it in a way that made me wish my thighs were free so that I could wrap them around his waist.

I immediately took that thought back, however, when Knight lowered his torso the rest of the way down onto my body. Something unnaturally long and hard pressed against me, causing my breath to falter and my eyes to squeeze shut in terror.

It seemed to stretch from my pelvis all the way to my rib cage, and I went as still as if a fucking copperhead had just slithered up onto my chest.

Dear God, if you're listening, it's me, BB.

When I stopped reciprocating Knight's kiss he immediately released me and pushed up on his forearms, removing the threat. His concerned colorless eyes darted all over my face, looking for clues as to why I'd suddenly gone limp on him. Embarrassed by my reaction—but relieved by my sudden freedom—I smiled shyly.

And then I tickled the shit out of Ronald McKnight.

I was pinned again within milliseconds, but this time I welcomed it. Knight and I were laughing and breathing too hard to resume our make-out session, so Knight kissed me chastely and said, "Stay the fuck here," before getting up to grab his cigarettes and flask. I would have gotten up just to fuck with him, but I was exhausted. In the best possible way.

When Knight came back I glanced at his crotch quickly to see if the monster was still there. Oh, it was there all right. And it was every bit as huge as I'd imagined. The bulge extended beyond the waist band of his jeans and up under his T-shirt, ending just below his belly button. I dropped my eyes to the ground and took a few shallow breaths.

Fucking hell.

I had no experience with peni. Zero. But I knew that whatever the fuck *that* thing was, it wasn't normal. It couldn't be. There wasn't an orifice on the human body equipped to take that thing on. I averted my eyes quickly before it sensed my fear and attacked.

Knight and I sat side by side with our backs against the TV stand and smoked in a contented, exhausted silence. Well, he seemed content. I, on the other hand, was drowning in panic-stricken thoughts about what was going to happen next.

Am I, like, Knight's girlfriend now?

I can't be Knight's girlfriend. I can't. Everyone will think I'm a racist and they'll hate me.

Juliet will hate me.

What if I just don't tell anybody?

That might work. Knight doesn't have any friends. I'll just keep the fact that we made out to myself.

I can't fucking believe we made out.

I can't fucking believe he can kiss like that. Colton never kissed me like that.

Knight kissed me like… like…

Like he loves me.

Oh my God.

This is bad.

This is so bad.

What if I reject him? I know what happens to people who piss off Ronald McKnight. He'll fucking chain me up in his mom's basement and make a wedding dress for me out of the skin of his enemies.

What if I don't reject him? Am I going to have to touch his… oh God… his thing??

I grabbed the flask out of Knight's hand and took a swig, grimacing at the burn. Knight snatched it back and said, "No more until you eat."

I pouted, but Knight ignored it. Standing and pulling me to my feet, he said, "C'mon, Punk. Let's go."

"Where are we going?"

"I'm taking you on a date."
Fuck me. We are *dating.*

Knight said he didn't want to drive me anywhere until he sobered up, so we walked (Well, he walked. I stumbled.) to the restaurant with the greasiest food and the strongest coffee that we could get to on foot—Waffle House. (Okay, so it wasn't a fancy date.)

Knight held my hand the whole way there, which sadly reminded me of Lance. I missed him, and felt kind of like a whore for making out with someone else just a few hours after he left. But why? It's not like he was my boyfriend. It's not like he even *wanted* to be my boyfriend. I'd changed my whole wardrobe, studied every underground punk band in the developed world, shaved my head—fuck, I'd even gotten my nipples pierced—and for what? For nothing.

I'd wasted a fifth of my life chasing a boy who didn't want me back.

The realization was sobering. Actually, it was depressing as shit. The sting of a rejection three years in the making seized my chest and squeezed my guts until my vision went blurry. But then I felt the squeeze of something else, and it helped massage away some of the pain.

Knight's hand around mine helped. Knowing that *somebody* wanted me helped. I just wished that somebody didn't have to be Skeletor the motherfucking Skinhead.

Chapter 23

Knight had to go to work that afternoon, so he drove me home after we ate. He offered to let me come to work with him, but I doubted that his boss would appreciate having a fifteen-year-old hanging out in her shop all night. I also doubted that my parents would appreciate their only daughter being dropped off by a skinhead in a monster truck, but I wasn't exactly long on options.

Knight looked pitiful when he pulled up in my parents' driveway. We stared at each other for a while, trying to figure out the most appropriate goodbye. We'd kissed, twice, but did that mean that was, like, what we did now? Were we people who kiss, or were we people who had kissed?

Finally, Knight broke the silence and said, "C'mere," patting the seat next to him.

I smiled and slid over. I wrapped my arms around his torso, deciding a goodbye hug would be the best way to go. Knight's body instantly went rigid in my embrace, just like it had the day before. Evidently, hugs *and* tickles were foreign to him. The thought made me squeeze him tighter.

After a few seconds Knight began to breathe again and pulled my body into his. With my ear pressed against his chest, I could hear his heart fluttering wildly. I wanted to reach between his ribs and pet it like a frightened bird. I wanted to shush it and make it feel safe. I touched the hard, muscular cage protecting all that was vulnerable with my fingertips. Followed by my lips.

Knight tilted my chin back with two fingers and ran his nose down the length of mine. It was a warning. If I didn't move away, Knight was going to kiss me again.

I didn't move.

I let his lips find mine.

Again.

And again.

And again.

When I finally peeled myself off of him, I floated into the house in a confused daze. I was every bit as giddy as I was *what-the-fuck-have-I-done*, and I was probably still a little drunk too.

I curled up on the couch next to my mom, who lazily played with my super-short hair and asked about my day. I told her that Lance had moved. I didn't tell her that he'd actually run away, nor did I mention that Colton had moved too. I might need her to keep picking me up from his house after school, and that was just a weird conversation that I was not prepared to have.

My mom told me she was sorry about Lance. She asked what I'd had for dinner. She probably asked me some other stuff too, but I don't remember because I passed the fuck out.

A few hours later I woke up, disoriented as hell, to the sound of my phone ringing. I rolled off the couch and sprinted into the kitchen, rummaging around in my purse until I found my phone. I jammed my finger into the talk button about a half second before I missed the call and gasped, "Hey," into the plastic brick.

"Hey," a deep voice said. A voice that was not Juliet's. Or August's. A voice that had *never* called me before.

I glanced at the clock on the microwave. It was after ten o'clock.

How long had I been asleep?

I grabbed my purse and backpack and sprinted up the stairs to my bedroom.

"Did I wake you up?" Knight asked.

"Yeah, but I was just asleep on the couch."

Knight did his cough-laugh thing. "Yeah, day drinking will do that to you."

I set my stuff down and carefully lifted Knight's paper flowers out of my backpack. "Were you busy at work tonight?"

I listened to Knight describe his clients as I arranged the delicate pieces of art in a plastic cup on my desk.

I assumed we'd be on the phone for five minutes at the most—Knight wasn't exactly a talker—but it wasn't until the sun peeked in through the slits of my blinds the next morning that we finally said goodbye.

The same thing happened Saturday night, and again on Sunday. Knight managed to avoid talking about anything too heavy during our marathon conversations, but by Monday morning he sure knew everything there was to know about my chatty ass.

Monday morning.

I told myself it would be fine. I told myself, *Knight doesn't have any friends. Your secret is safe. No one has to know that you guys are . . . whatever you are.*

Then Knight kissed me at our lockers when it was time to go to first period. He held my hand on the way to the church parking lot. He seemed to be *completely* over his little aversion to hugging. And he carried my backpack for me everywhere.

Knight even sat *right fucking next to me* at lunch. Right in Lance's old seat. It felt so wrong. Like my lover had died and I'd already replaced him with another. But Lance hadn't been my lover, and by the time he left, I wasn't so sure that he'd ever even really been my friend.

Juliet was *super* freaked out—I could tell—but she graciously ignored Knight and made small talk with August, who looked even sadder than usual.

So maybe Knight didn't need to open his mouth to spill our little secret after all. I had forgotten that Knight was a man of action, and his actions spoke way louder than words. In fact, on that particular day, they were screaming *BB IS MINE!* into a fucking bullhorn.

The jig was up.

Whether I liked it or not, I had become Skeletor the Skinhead's girlfriend.

Chapter 24

That afternoon Knight carried my backpack on one shoulder and held my hand as we walked across the parking lot to his truck. It felt both completely natural and completely mortifying at the same time. We got more stares than usual, but over the next few weeks they died down.

People accepted us as a couple pretty quickly, much to my dismay. Honestly, I couldn't blame them. We both wore black combat boots, tight jeans, band T-shirts, and had shaved heads. To anybody on the outside I'm sure we looked like the perfect fucked-up couple.

By mid-November I was still not really comfortable being affectionate toward Knight at school, but at Peg's house, with no one else around, I discovered the unparalleled bliss of cuddling.

Knight got over his hug aversion pretty damn quickly. After he finished his chores at Peg's house we didn't even flip on the TV anymore. Most days we didn't even crack a beer. Instead we swan dived onto the couch where we would cuddle and kiss and float in and out of consciousness for hours.

The best days were when we both fell asleep and I woke up first. There was no experience more delicious than lying captured under

Knight's heavy body, inhaling the sweet muskiness of his cologne, feeling his baby-soft buzzcut against my cheek, and realizing that his heartbeat—usually so frantic in his chest—had slowed and synchronized with mine. Feeling that easy, steady rhythm pulsing through not just one body, but two, was better than any high, any buzz, any tweak I'd ever experienced.

Nothing could possibly feel better than this, I thought as my fingertips traced the peaks and valleys of Knight's broad back.

But Knight was about to prove me wrong.

Very, *very* wrong.

Part II

Chapter 25

It was the week before Thanksgiving break. Knight had just finished feeding Shep and patching up some molding around Peg's back door, and I had just finished a beer and about two and a half cigarettes while watching him. I loved watching him.

Whenever Knight looked at me I felt like he was memorizing the exact size and placement of every blemish, freckle, and pore on my face, but while he was working I got to watch him for a change. Everything he did he concentrated on fully, completed quickly and thoroughly, and cleaned impeccably afterward.

Not that day, though. That day Knight tossed his tools aside the second he finished the job. As they clattered to the ground he yanked my ass off the bench on Peg's back porch so fast I thought the damn thing must have been strapped with dynamite. Knight led me by the hand through the house and over to the couch without a word, then pulled me down onto his lap so that I was straddling him.

Something was different. We usually laid down and cuddled before making out, but Knight already had his tongue in my mouth, his hands on my thighs, and his rapidly swelling cock filling the space between us. It startled me, but after a minute or two Knight had me worked into a fiery ball of need.

Knight broke our kiss, and looked at me with hard eyes and soft, feathery blond lashes. "It's been six weeks," he said.

"Six weeks since what?" I asked, a little breathless.

"Since I pierced your nipples."

Seeing *that* mouth say *that* word, with that *thing* pressed against my sex had my hormones cranked up to eleven. Unsure what to do about it, I just froze and prayed that Knight would develop mind reading abilities.

"Do you know what that means?" It was the same tone I imagined the Big Bad Wolf must have used when he said to Little Red Riding Hood, *"Come closer, my dear."*

Unblinking, I slowly shook my head from side to side, excited in the most terrifying way. It was taking all my willpower not to grind against the throbbing beast between my legs. I wanted to. I didn't want to. I wanted to.

Knight kneaded my thighs with his hands and narrowed his glacial eyes at me. The corners of his mouth twitched, like he was suppressing a sneer.

"I'll show you," he said.

Not waiting for a response, Knight lifted up my Ramones T-shirt and long-sleeved thermal undershirt at the same time. My arms cooperated and lifted up with them, allowing him to easily slip the garments over my head.

With a deep breath, I reached back and unclasped my five-pound water bra. Even though Knight already knew I was flat-chested, I didn't need him handling the proof of my insecurity. I tossed it onto the floor next to the other half of my outfit and sucked in my stomach.

I felt that old familiar fire crawl up my neck and into my cheeks as Knight stared at my body. The fire had crept into his eyes as well, turning them from arctic blue to white-hot. Knight's hands slid from my hips to my ribs, then came to rest just under the slight swell of each petite breast.

Like he'd done the morning after he pierced them, Knight grasped both of my winged barbells and gently slid them back and forth. That time there was no pain, only a lightning rod of pleasure that coursed through my veins like an actual electrical current. The sensation caused my eyes to roll back, my spine to arch, and my fingers to dig into Knight's denim-covered thighs.

My eyes flew open again when the sensation was replaced with something hot and wet on one side. I looked down and saw that Knight was still teasing my right nipple with his fingers, but his fuzzy blond head was hovering in front of my left, moving subtly as his tongue flicked across the surface of my diamond-hard nipple.

I kept watching, my panties drenched, as he swirled his tongue around and around the perimeter, making sure to press and pull slightly on the barbell with every pass. But when his lips closed around my pebbled pink skin and sucked, I couldn't watch anymore. I squeezed my eyes shut, threw my head back, and humped his enormous cock with abandon.

Knight wrapped his hands around my waist and drove my movements. He slid my body up and down his length, lifting his hips to meet me, as he lavished my right nipple with the same attention he'd given my left. Just as my core began to contract I grabbed his face with both hands, lifted it to mine, and moaned into his mouth as the most powerful orgasm I'd ever had ripped through my body.

I'd been masturbating almost daily since I was eight years old, but nothing I'd ever experienced or seen on TV had prepared me for *that*.

Holy shit.

Once I came down I wrapped my arms around Knight and

buried my face in his neck. I wasn't ready for him to look at me yet. Self-conscious doesn't *begin* to describe what I was feeling.

Knight put his hands on my shoulders and gently pushed me back to my original position. I looked down to avoid having to make eye contact with him, which was a mistake because all I could see was cock. It looked like there was a log of cookie dough under Knight's clothes. And it wasn't going away.

"Look at me."

I peeked up through my lashes at him. His face was severe.

"Do *not* be embarrassed about that," he said, indicating that my prayer for him to suddenly develop telepathy must have come true. "Watching you come was the sexiest fucking thing I've ever seen."

Knight gripped my hips and pressed his denim-covered member into my denim-covered crotch again. The pressure caused my muscles to contract immediately.

"In fact"—Knight's hands slid from my hips to the fly of my jeans and began unbuttoning—"I want to see you do it again."

I lifted up onto my knees to allow him access to my zipper. I wasn't sure if I could handle another orgasm so soon, but I was willing to find out.

I was willing to do anything to feel that again.

In one motion Knight pulled my jeans and ruined panties down over my ass, just far enough to expose my bald pussy. I'd been shaving my whole body for years—in preparation for Lance, of course—but I was suddenly wishing I had at least a little patch of hair to hide behind.

"Fuuuck," Knight whispered as he slid his hands up the insides of my thighs. They came to rest on either side of my sex, and I held my breath and closed my eyes as he spread my naked pussy apart with his thumbs. The cool air reminded me what a slippery, wet mess I must have been, and I flushed harder.

Oh my God! What is he doing? Fucking examining me?

Knight took one thumb and circled it around my virginal entrance, then slid it back through my folds, bathing me in my own moisture. He then did the same thing with his other thumb, and I felt my hips jerk in response. Right thumb, left thumb, over, around, and through. The sensation was amazing, like a slow, slippery massage. Knight wasn't fingering me—much to my surprise—he was spoiling me rotten.

Knight leaned forward and flicked his tongue across my right nipple as his thumbs continued their sensual assault. "Lean back," he breathed against my skin as his tongue danced in unhurried circles down the length of my torso.

Looking behind me, I gauged the distance from the couch to the weathered wooden table, then created a bridge between the two with my body, propping myself up on my forearms. In that position I was completely exposed to him, and completely immobilized.

I took a deep, shuddering breath and peeked down through my lashes just as Knight's mouth reached the crest of my mound. He looked up at me with blue eyes blazing, then dragged his sharp, straight nose down the length of my slit. It was a movement I recognized. Knight was telling me that he was about to put his mouth—

There.

Holy fucking shit.

I watched it happen. One second Knight's nose was grazing my clit, and the next second it was replaced by his tongue.

His tongue!

I couldn't spread my legs any wider with my jeans around my thighs, but I wanted to. I wanted to wrap them around his fucking ears. Knight spread me wide open with his thumbs for better access, and alternated between flicking and swirling his tongue against the most sensitive parts of me.

And I couldn't even move.

I thought I was going to pass out from the pleasure. I clutched the edge of the table and looked down to reorient myself. The sight of Knight's fuzzy blond buzzcut between my thighs, doing *that* with his mouth, made me come instantly. My fingers dug into the table as my insides squeezed and grasped at nothing.

Then Knight gave them something to squeeze. A thick finger suddenly slipped inside of me, and my body greedily clenched around it as it pumped in and out. It took all my strength to stay upright as I came, and came, and came—my spindly arms and legs shaking with effort and exertion.

As my orgasm receded, Knight wrapped his arms around me and pulled me to his chest. I melted into him, turning into a mostly naked, fully sated, practically purring heap of bones. He kissed the top of my head as I snuggled deeper into his embrace. I wasn't in Peg's house anymore. I wasn't in my own body. I was in a sunny meadow picking petals off daisies, asking them if he loved me or loved me not. *He loves me*, the last one always said.

Up to that point I had tried alcohol, caffeine pills, marijuana, LSD, cocaine, crank, prescription painkillers, and ecstasy, but I had *never* felt euphoria like that.

I wondered, from my faraway place, if I could ever make Knight feel as happy as I was right then. He was so angry and hateful all the time. Maybe he just needed... to come.

As I wiggled to get comfortable, which wasn't easy with my jeans still around my thighs, I realized that Knight's erection still hadn't gone away.

Far from it.

I wanted to do something to reciprocate, I really did, but wanting to and knowing how were two totally different things. I'd never even seen a penis in real life. Maybe if it had been a little cute one I would have been more willing to experiment, but that thing? I felt like I needed to take a class or something first. Get certified. Get some shots. Maybe have an ambulance on standby.

I settled on pretending to be asleep while I waited for it to go away. That technique had been working for me so far—why mess with a good thing? Besides, seeing Knight's penis would probably harsh my mellow, and right then I felt way too good to do anything other than cuddle and pretend to snore.

Chapter 26

After that day, Knight went down on me every single day after school.

Let me repeat that.

Every.

Single.

Day.

I was done giving two shits about who saw us together at school or how it made me look. That crazy motherfucker with the colorless hair and the colorless eyes who wore skinhead clothes imported from England even though he wasn't even racist and beat the shit out of people with almost no provocation was the same motherfucker who made me notebook paper flowers because I was sad. The same one who said, "You don't eat, I don't eat." The same one who gave me his jacket, pierced my nipples, drew me pictures, held my hand, lit my cigarettes, told me I was beautiful, and most importantly, gave me mind-blowing orgasms every day with zero pressure to reciprocate.

In four short months, Knight had gone from being the person I feared most on this planet to the center of my whole fucking universe.

Happily, people didn't seem to treat me any differently, as long as Knight wasn't around. Nobody accused me of being a white supremacist. Juliet and I even stayed friends—we just didn't talk about our boyfriends. Ever. August kind of withdrew though— even more than usual—and he looked like he'd lost some weight. I felt bad for the guy. I guess I should have invited him to hang out at Colton's house with us, but then there'd be no cunnilingus, and dammit, that was the best part of my day.

But when Knight was around, it was an entirely different story. His don't-fucking-come-near-me aura eclipsed my friendly-perky-approachable one tenfold. I wished people could see the side of him that I knew. I wished that I knew why he insisted on keeping them away, why he wanted them to hate him.

It felt like Knight was really two people. Ronald—the sweet, chivalrous, artistic, animal-loving boy with the fuzzy blond head who lived to cuddle and eat pussy, and Knight—the heartless, hopeless, hate-fueled, tattooed, bodybuilding inferno of violence and intimidation.

Then, one day in mid-December, Ronald and Knight converged.

That fall had been warmer than usual, so the trees hadn't reached the height of their ruddy spectrum until maybe the week before. Another week or two and they'd be bare. It made me sad. I hated that winter was coming. I hated being cold. I was always fucking cold.

On the way to Peg's house, I asked Knight if he would drive back up to the water tower. I wanted to take in the fall leaves and appreciate the sunshine before they both disappeared. I rolled down my window and actually giggled as Knight's truck bounced and snarled up the hill, more confident that we weren't going to flip over and die that time.

Knight parked in the same spot that he had before, but the vibe was completely different. No one was after us—thanks to three payments to Tony, so far—and I wasn't afraid of being alone in the woods with a skinhead anymore, either.

Oh, and the music drifting out of Knight's back window was *definitely* not country.

Knight gave me a boost into the bed of his truck, and I scrambled over to the open window to get a better listen. Turning back to him, I squealed in utter disbelief, "*You* own a Mazzy Star CD?"

Knight hopped into the truck bed, flask in hand, and sat down with his back against the glass. One leg out straight in front of him and one knee pulled up, pointing toward the bulbous blue-green tower blooming overhead. Shrugging, he said, "You love this song."

"How do you know?" I asked, my mouth hanging open in amazement.

Knight shifted his weight and pulled his knife, lighter, and a hard pack of Camel Lights—he'd switched to my brand—out of his pocket.

"Because when it came on while we were at the Waffle House you got all fuckin' excited and said, 'I love this song.'" Knight reached out and stuck an unlit cigarette into my open mouth and smirked at me.

I went to smack him on the shoulder, but Knight caught my wrist in midair and yanked me down into his lap. I landed with a gasp between his legs, my back to his front.

Sigh.

The view was all crimson and copper and gold, sprinkled with white crosses like confetti. The air was cooler in the shade, but Knight's body kept me warm. I think it was the inferno of hate that burned inside of him. He always seemed to run hot.

Remembering that I still had an unlit cigarette in my mouth, I turned my head sideways so that Knight could see it and wiggled it back and forth with my tongue—the universal sign for *I need a light*. Right on cue, Knight reached for his Zippo. The action brought my attention to the collection of crap he'd pulled out of his pockets. Before I could think better of it, I picked up his knife and began studying it. Knight didn't seem to mind.

"Will you show me how it works?" I asked.

"Sure," Knight said, reaching around me with both arms and plucking the closed knife from my hand. "It's called a butterfly knife, because the handles open like wings." He slowly spread the two hinged metal pieces apart, exposing a nasty-looking six-inch blade inside.

I thought it was funny that somebody so tough walked around with a "butterfly" anything, but once it was in my face that fucker was anything but funny.

Knight closed it and offered it back to me, but I didn't accept.

"Now will you show me how you *really* open it?"

"What? Like this?" Knight's arm slashed back and forth while his wrist made several quick figure-eight-style movements. The silver blade and painted black handles became a spinning blur of glinting metal, then came to rest as a knife. It was the coolest fucking thing I'd ever seen.

"Do it again." I was mesmerized. Knight opened and shut the blade a few more times, slower so I could see what he was doing, then handed the closed weapon to me again.

My first few tries were disastrous. I kept leaving out a spin, causing the sharp side of the blade to bounce off my knuckles when I flicked it open. Knight laughed as I floundered, but once I worked in that last spin I got the hang of it—at least a simplified version of it.

I flipped the knife open and shut while we talked and smoked and drank and breathed in our last gasps of fall.

I noticed that Knight seemed distracted, which wasn't like him. Whenever we were together he usually clung to my every word as if I were about to tell him the next winning lottery numbers, but his eyes kept leaving my face to watch the knife in my hands. Licking his lips and swallowing hard, Knight finally said, "Punk, you gotta stop."

Something in his tone made me stop immediately, mid-flick. The blade kept going though, and the extra momentum from my quick stop caused it to slice across my knuckles far worse than before. It hurt like a bitch. When I looked down I noticed that my knuckles were covered in several tiny little bloody cuts and one large gash that cut across my index and middle fingers and was bleeding freely.

Jesus. I guess that's why Knight wanted me to sto—

The next thing I knew the knife was gone, my wrist was behind my head, and one of my bloody knuckles was in Knight's mouth. As he tongued and sucked my wounds his grip on my wrist tightened and his cock swelled against my back.

Holy shit.

I wanted to be freaked out that my boyfriend was drinking my blood, but the feeling of his tongue on my skin, darting in and out between my knuckles, lapping up every scarlet drop, had me thinking about his mouth on other parts of my body. It also made the cut feel better, so I closed my eyes, leaned my head back against his shoulder, and let him go at it.

I flashed back to the night he pierced my nipples. Knight had said that making me bleed had been the best gift he'd ever gotten. I'd thought he was just being dramatic. Who knew?

So, my boyfriend is a vampire, I thought. *No big deal. Hey, maybe this explains why he's so pale.*

Then I felt teeth.

"Ow!"

I pulled my hand away, and felt Knight's body go completely rigid behind me. I turned around, slowly, and peered into the face of a goddamn madman. Knight's eyes were crazed. His muscles were so tense it was as if he was using all his strength to keep from morphing into a fucking werewolf. His cock was hard. Oh, and he was holding a knife.

"Knight..."

His jaw snapped shut. I knew what that meant. I was about to get the silent treatment.

"Are you okay?" I asked anyway, in my most soothing tone.

Knight was breathing hard. His nostrils flared with every exhalation, and his jaw muscles flexed. Something seriously fucked up was going on inside that head.

I was not safe. Knight knew it, and I knew it.

But what could I do? Where could I go? It was just me and one freaked-out skinhead—who might or might not want to eat me—in the middle of the woods.

I had to figure out how to calm him down. STAT.

"Hey, it's okay," I said. "It didn't even hurt. You just...surprised me. That's all."

Heaving chest. Dilated pupils. No response.

I turned around completely so that I could talk to him more easily, but that forced me to straddle his legs and confront his seriously uncomfortable-looking tight-jeans-massive-bloodlust-boner situation.

"Knight?" I reached up and put my hands on his shoulders. "What's going on with you?"

Knight locked eyes with me so intensely it felt as if he was willing me to look into his soul. Begging me to see his secrets so that he wouldn't have to speak them out loud. So, I tried. I peered into those two expanding black portholes, but all I could see was darkness. Darkness slashed with red.

Blood.

"Blood turns you on," I said, trying to sound as nonjudgmental as possible. His jaws were still clenched shut, so I knew he wouldn't talk, but I thought maybe he would at least nod.

He didn't.

"Do you...want to make me bleed?"

Knight looked so angry, so hateful, the way he was staring at me. Again, he refused to answer, but he didn't have to. His thoughts floated to the surface of the blackness like some kind of fucked-up Magic 8 Ball. One read, *Yes*.

The other, *Run*.

Knight wanted to hurt me.

Knight didn't want to hurt me.

"What if I do it for you?" I blurted.

Fucking whiskey.

Knight's eyes went wide but the rest of his body remained rigid. He was exerting a painful amount of self-control, and I wanted to give him some kind of relief. Some kind of pleasure to counteract the lifetime of pain he was reliving before my very eyes.

Taking my right hand in my left, I spread apart the seam of my wound until it began to bleed again. Thanks to the whiskey, it didn't hurt that bad. I kept my fingers pointing downward as I reopened the gash so that the red rivulets would run down toward the tips. I felt Knight's hands grip my thighs, hard—one of them still holding the knife.

Once the blood began to drip from my fingertips, I pressed them against the tightly closed seam of Knight's mouth. Red smeared across his lips, making him look even more vampiric. Knight's black pupils swallowed his pale irises as they bored into mine, and his jaw flexed beneath his skin.

Open up, baby. You can do it.

Knight's body was practically vibrating with rage and shame and self-restraint, and if I didn't do something to get him to calm the fuck down, there was a good chance he might actually explode and kill us all.

I reached down with my left hand and clumsily unfastened his jeans. Knight's cock instantly spilled out of the opening, the elastic waistband of his boxer shorts unable to restrain it.

Jesus Christ.

It was like one of those gag gifts where you open the lid and a fucking snake pops out. Only this one was a king cobra. And it was real.

I said a silent prayer, reached into his boxers with my left hand, and wrapped it around his venomous appendage. His skin was buttery soft, and it slid like silk as I slowly worked my hand up and down his length.

That was the thing about Knight. He was hell on the eyes, but to the rest of my senses, pure heaven.

I looked back at Knight's face for some kind of, I don't know, encouragement? Validation? But his eyes were closed and his brow was furrowed in pain. It broke my heart. And it fueled me.

I worked Knight's smooth cock until his lips parted in defeat.

"It's okay," I whispered.

Then I slid two bloody fingertips inside.

Knight's eyes rolled up into the back of his head, and he grabbed my wrist with his free hand. An appreciative moan rumbled in his throat as he swirled his tongue around each dripping digit.

The action made my clit throb.

I could do that to him, I thought. *For him.*

Feeling brave, I scooted backward a little, leaned over, and took the scary cobra snake into my mouth. Teeth instantly clamped down on my fingers again, but that time I didn't flinch. I was focused.

I didn't have use of my right hand, and I couldn't take him very far into my mouth without gagging, but I persevered. The way Knight was dragging his tongue along my wound, sucking the blood directly from my body, had me dragging mine up the length of his cock and increasing my suction with every pass.

Soon Knight's hips began to thrust as his already hard shaft stiffened in my hand. I'd seen enough porn to know what was going to happen next, but nothing had prepared me for the actual event. I heard the knife clatter to the bed of the truck just before the first spurt of hot cum exploded into my mouth. Knight's hands found their way into my super-short hair and held my head still as he came. I struggled to swallow it all, between gags, but he just kept coming. His body convulsed. His hips jerked. And I marveled at my power. I wasn't just making Knight come.

I was performing an exorcism.

When I tucked Knight's thoroughly wrung-out cock back into his boxers and sat up it was clear that whatever had been haunting him, holding him captive inside his own body, had been expelled. His muscles were putty. His black, hateful eyes were closed. His chest rose and fell in a slow, sleepy rhythm. And across his face, an easy, contented blood-smeared smile.

I kissed that little smile, and the gesture made it blossom into a full-blown grin. With teeth. Perfect fucking teeth. Figuring out how to get a glimpse of that particular freckle-faced, teenaged boy smile had become my reason for getting up in the morning. That and all the cuddling. And the cunnilingus.

Knight sat up and wrapped his arms around my waist, then rested his sated head on my bony shoulder. "You're still here," he said, squeezing me harder.

His words made my heart constrict. "Of course I am," I said. "Where else would I be?" I squeezed him back and ran my licked-clean fingers over his fuzzy blond head.

"With somebody who's not so fucked up." He spoke the words into my neck. *Fucked up*. The words I'd used to describe him weeks ago. The words he hated.

"Maybe I like fucked up," I said, surprising myself with the amount of truth in that statement.

Knight sat up and scanned my face. His pupils had gone back down to a more natural size, and all traces of hate were gone from his chiseled features. He looked...normal. No, better than normal—he looked fucking cute. As long as you ignored the evidence that he'd just been feasting on human blood, of course.

Deciding that I was not full of shit, Knight leaned forward and kissed me. I could taste my coppery mark on his lips, and I'm sure he could taste himself on mine, but neither one of us cared.

Pressing his forehead against mine, Knight said, "I love you, Punk."

"I love you, too, *Skin*."

Chapter 27

Just like every other milestone in our relationship, Knight took those three little words and fucking ran with them.

The next week he showered me with love notes at school. I was used to him shoving little folded pieces of paper into my hands between classes. They usually contained intricate drawings that I'm sure he thought were romantic—anatomically correct hearts and bloody daggers and little notes about how he missed me, scrawled in his psychotic, all-caps, no-curves handwriting. But these notes were the real deal. They were sweet and honest and more vulnerable than I'd known Knight was even capable of being.

On Monday, Knight presented me with this one:

DEAR BB,

   I KNOW WE'VE SAID IT A FEW TIMES NOW, BUT I DON'T THINK YOU WILL EVER FULLY UNDERSTAND HOW MUCH I FUCKING LOVE YOU.

I'VE NEVER BEEN CLOSE TO ANY-ONE, BUT FOR SOME REASON I CAN'T STAY AWAY FROM YOU. I LET MYSELF GET CLOSE EVEN THOUGH I KNEW YOU WOULD RIP MY HEART OUT AS SOON AS YOU FOUND OUT HOW FUCKED UP I REALLY AM. I DIDN'T EVEN CARE. I THOUGHT IT WOULD BE WORTH IT JUST TO BE WITH YOU FOR A LITTLE WHILE.

BUT I REALIZED ON FRIDAY, WHEN I THOUGHT YOU WERE GOING TO RUN AWAY FROM ME, JUST HOW FUCK-ING STUPID THAT WAS. THERE IS NO WAY I COULD TAKE THAT KIND OF PAIN. IF YOU LEFT IT WOULD FUCK-ING DESTROY ME.

I LOVE YOU MORE THAN I LOVE MYSELF.

KNIGHT

I got this one on Tuesday:

DEAR BB,

I REALIZED SOMETHING LAST NIGHT AFTER I DROPPED YOU OFF AT WORK.

I'M FUCKING HAPPY.

FOR THE FIRST TIME IN MY LIFE I'M FUCKING HAPPY AND IT'S BECAUSE OF YOU. YOU PROBABLY DON'T UNDERSTAND BECAUSE YOU'RE HAPPY ALL THE TIME, BUT I DIDN'T EVEN KNOW WHAT IT FELT LIKE UNTIL YOU KISSED ME IN THE PARKING LOT THE DAY AFTER I PIERCED YOU. I COULDN'T STOP SMILING FOR THE REST OF THE WEEKEND. BOBBY THOUGHT I'D LOST MY MIND.

AND NOW I CAN'T STOP SMILING AGAIN. THESE FUCKERS ARE GOING TO THINK I'VE GONE SOFT.

I LOVE YOU.

KNIGHT

Knight stuck this one in my back pocket on Wednesday:

DEAR BB,

I STILL CAN'T BELIEVE THIS IS REAL.

I KNOW TO YOU THIS PROBABLY SEEMS REALLY FAST, BUT I THINK

I'VE BEEN IN LOVE WITH YOU SINCE WE WERE KIDS. YOUR DRAWINGS HUNG ABOVE MY DESK IN THE BACK OF THE ART ROOM, AND THEY WERE SO FUCKING COLORFUL. EVEN YOUR SUNS AND MOONS HAD LITTLE SMI-LEY FACES ON THEM. I WANTED TO LIVE IN YOUR HAPPY LITTLE WORLD INSTEAD OF MY OWN.

NOW I DO.

I LOVE YOU.

KNIGHT

And Thursday:

DEAR BB,

I CAN'T FUCKING CONCENTRATE. IF I FAIL MY SENIOR YEAR IT'S YOUR FAULT. MAYBE I SHOULD FAIL JUST SO THAT I CAN COME BACK NEXT YEAR. I CAN'T HAVE THESE MOTHER-FUCKERS FORGETTING WHO YOU BELONG TO.

I LOVE YOU.

KNIGHT

When I sat down in my fourth-period class on Friday to read my final note of the week, I was practically giddy. No one had ever written me love notes before. Especially not one every single day. Knight had me feeling like a magical fairy fucking princess.

I was also giddy because it was the last day before winter break. I so needed those two weeks off. Between school, work, my after-school "activities," and staying up late talking to Knight on the phone every night, I was exhausted.

I opened the note—which had been intricately folded into the shape of a heart—slowly, savoring the experience, while my teacher began to drone on about the results of our end-of-semester exams.

DEAR BB,

   I CAN'T FUCKING WAIT UNTIL THIS AFTERNOON. I HAVE SOMETHING PLANNED THAT I'VE BEEN THINK-ING ABOUT SINCE THE DAY WE MET. PLEASE DON'T WORRY. I KNOW YOU PROBABLY THINK I'M JUST USING YOU FOR SEX, BUT I'M NOT.

   I LOVE YOU.

                              KNIGHT

Sex?
Sex.
SEX?!

No matter how many times I read it, the only word my virginal fifteen-year-old brain could comprehend was *sex.*

Knight wanted to have sex with me. In, like, two hours.

Ohmyfuckinggod.

I didn't even notice that the bell had rung until most of my classmates had vacated the room. Shoving the now sweat-drenched piece of paper into the pocket of Knight's jacket, I stumbled out the door. For once, I was thankful to be swept up in the current of exiting teenagers because my impending panic attack had hijacked even the most basic of brain functions. Such as walking. And forming thoughts that required words.

I still had access to images though, because the sight of Knight's massive cock falling out of his jeans the week before was playing on a loop behind my eyes.

The river carried me out the C hall door and practically dumped me at his feet. Knight was leaning up against the flagpole as usual, wearing his Lonsdale hoodie and a sneer. He closed the distance between us and kissed me in a way that was far too intimate for school. I pulled away when I felt his cock begin to thicken against my belly—my face a gorgeous shade of mortified, I'm sure. Without releasing me Knight asked if I'd read his last note.

I nodded.

Please don't make me talk about it. Please don't make me talk about it.

"I meant it."

I know.

Knight stripped me of my backpack and practically dragged me by the hand toward his truck. Although I was used to him carrying my stuff, on that particular day it felt more like he was using it as collateral.

I scanned the parking lot, looking for some kind of distraction, some way to delay the inevitable decimation of my hymen. It came in the form of August Embry. He was up ahead of us, cutting across the parking lot toward the woods. That was weird. August usually rode the bus home.

I should invite him to Colton's house! That's it!

"August," I yelled.

No response.

"August!" I yelled louder, cupping my free hand around my mouth.

He turned around and waved at me that time, but he didn't stop walking. In fact, I think he might have even sped up a little bit.

Maybe he's mad at me. I have kind of ditched him for Knight. Or maybe he's just walking home for exercise. He does look skinnier. That must be it.

Out of ideas, I surrendered and let Knight boost me up into his passenger seat. We didn't speak the whole way to Peg's house. I stared out the window and worried the edges of the note in my pocket as Mazzy Star coached me on the ways of loving someone who lives in shadows.

When we arrived, I followed Knight inside with knocking knees and trembling hands. We'd crossed that splintering, rotten threshold dozens of times before, but on that eerily warm December day, I knew going in that part of me was never coming back out.

It was time to grow up.

Knight disappeared into the kitchen while I loitered on the four-by-four square of parquet just inside the front door—Peg's "foi-yay"—immobilized by indecision.

What should I do? Should I sit? Should I head outside to the back porch? Should I grab a beer?

Before I could formulate a plan, Knight reemerged from the kitchen, looking all too pleased with himself. He stalked toward me in bare feet—*When the fuck did he take his boots off?*—grabbed my hand without saying a word, and led me up the sagging, squeaking stairs to Colton's old bedroom.

I'd only been up there once before, but it was exactly the way I remembered it—sparsely furnished, impersonal, and kind of sad. Colton had never stayed long enough to decorate, and Peg was either too depressed or absent to bother. Colton tried to make out with me up there once, but being on a bed with a boy kind of freaked me out back then.

Still did.

Knight dropped my hand once we reached our destination and turned to face me. I think he could smell my fear, because he cocked his head to one side, the way he did when he was analyzing something, and asked, "Do you trust me?"

I straightened my posture and nodded, trying to seem confident, but looking into Knight's eyes was about as easy as staring down both barrels of a shotgun. When he finally lowered those cobalt crosshairs from my face I breathed a sigh of relief. His hands began to roam over my trembling body, taking with them my jacket, my Siouxsie and the Banshees T-shirt, and the safety pins from my plaid wraparound skirt. I made sure to remove my five-pound water bra myself, but Knight left my panties on.

I was freezing and afraid, but I was still there. Trying to be brave. Part of me wanted to reward Knight for being so sweet to me. Part of me was scared to tell him no. And part of me—the pathologically curious part that got itself into situations like this— just really, really wanted to know what this whole sex thing was all about.

Knight ran his hands up and down the length of my arms to keep me warm as he gazed down at my almost-nakedness. His hands drifted to my breasts, where he grasped both winged barbells and slid them back and forth, gently, while we both watched. The sensation had my panties soaked immediately. Would I ever get used to that? I hoped not.

Sliding one hand between my legs, Knight rubbed me over my panties, making me crazy with need. I wanted them off. I wanted something to fill me, and I wanted it now.

I moaned involuntarily, drawing Knight's attention up to my mouth. He split my lips with his tongue and kissed me deep, still teasing my nipples, teasing my clit. He kissed the cold and the fear and the self-consciousness away. Kissed me until I wanted him to fuck me, right there, on my ex-boyfriend's bed.

Reading my mind, Knight grasped both sides of my purple panties and stretched them to their breaking point. I released a tiny gasp of surprise, which was immediately followed by a much louder one when Knight brought the shredded fabric to his mouth and slowly ran his tongue over an embarrassingly large wet spot.

A large, *red* wet spot.

Ohhhhh shit.

Knight's eyes rolled back the second the taste hit his tongue, and I have to admit, that shit turned me on. When his eyes reopened, they looked like they had the first time he tasted my blood. Wild.

Pushing me backward against the wall, Knight grabbed the back of my head with one hand and plunged a finger into me as deep as it would go. He assaulted my mouth, practically snarled into it, as he slid another finger in. His pace was frenetic. His need palpable. The room heated up at least ten degrees, then Knight withdrew his fingers.

And painted my skin red.

He swiped scarlet swirls around my nipples and twin stripes down the length of my sternum. Knight, the blood fiend, and Knight, the artist, had converged, and I needed for one or both of them to make me come before my head exploded.

As his fingers filled me again, Knight traced the lines of his painting with his tongue, erasing it lick by lick.

It was the most erotic thing I'd ever seen. My legs began to shake and I sank down onto Knight's fingers.

"Knight…please…" I whispered, clawing at his hoodie and T-shirt.

Heeding my plea, Knight stood up and pulled both garments off over his head, revealing the entire head of his extremely hard cock bursting out of the top of his jeans.

Knight tossed his T-shirt onto the center of the bed, tossed me on top of it, then began removing items from his pockets and setting them on the nightstand in rapid succession. In two seconds flat he'd managed to extract a lighter, a pack of cigarettes, his keys, his knife, his wallet, a condom from inside his wallet, not one but two pairs of handcuffs, and a clear plastic bear filled with honey from his jeans.

What in the mother fuck?

While I was busy trying to figure out the logistics and reasoning behind the assorted items of sin arranged on Colton's dusty nightstand, Knight had stepped out of his jeans and Union Jack print boxer shorts. He was naked and beautiful. He was thrilling and frightening. He was sensitive yet bloodthirsty, and I wanted all of him.

Knight smiled my favorite smile as he gazed down at me, lying on my back—all skin and bones and combat boots—and I opened my arms to let him in. Before I could blink, Knight grabbed the wrist closest to him, slapped a handcuff on it, and secured it to Colton's bedpost. I laughed in surprise and watched Knight's smile morph into a mischievous grin. He picked the other set of bracelets up and climbed on top of me.

Knight secured my other hand to the opposite bedpost, then hovered over me in triumph. He looked so . . . happy. Wicked, brutally fucking masculine, and quite possibly insane, but happy.

"You didn't tell me you were on your period," he said, dragging his thick cock through my slippery folds.

"I didn't know," I whispered, trying not to blush.

Lowering himself so that we were skin-to-skin, Knight growled into my ear, "I fucking love it."

"I can tell," I giggled, pulling on my restraints for leverage as I lifted my hips into his slip-sliding shaft.

"Can I lick you...there?"

I nodded, desperate for it.

Knight kissed his way down my body, which had already been licked clean, and I let my knees fall open for him. I wanted to run my hands over his fuzzy blond head while he fucked me with his mouth, but I couldn't. All I could do was tug on my shackles and take it.

The helplessness excited me, as did the low groan Knight let out as he strained to fill me with his tongue. My hips jerked in response to the sound, and my insides fluttered. Sensing that I was close, Knight reached around my thigh and rubbed my clit in small, quick circles until an earthquake of pleasure shook my core and swallowed me whole. My arms involuntarily yanked at my restraints as I fell into an oblivion of moans and curse words and spasms and darkness.

While I concentrated on trying to survive my orgasm, Knight wiped his face clean with the T-shirt he'd laid under me, tore open the condom wrapper, and stretched the latex sheath almost to its breaking point over his swollen, neglected cock.

Positioning himself at the opening of my throbbing orifice, Knight hesitated. His face looked severe, worried even. The trepidation in his eyes told me all I needed to know. My fearless Knight was scared—scared for me, and of himself. He was about to hurt me worse than I'd ever been hurt by another person.

But I was ready.

Or so I thought.

No sooner had I confidently nodded my consent than I could feel my insides being sliced to ribbons. I grasped the handcuffs firmly with both fists and sucked in a pained breath through my clenched teeth as I fought back the tears welling up behind my tightly shut eyelids.

Don't cry out. Don't cry out. Just go to your happy place and wait it out. You can do this, BB. You're a badass.

But I couldn't go to my happy place. Because I was already there. I was skin-to-skin with the man I loved, being worshipped by the devil himself.

I don't remember how long it lasted. I don't remember what Knight did when he came. I don't remember him withdrawing that foot-long chainsaw from my mutilated vagina. But I do remember the way he wrapped himself around my body when it was over. The way he buried his face between the pillow and my cheek.

I didn't know if he was seeking comfort for what he'd done or offering it, but his arms felt like giant bandages putting me back together. I wanted to return his embrace, but my arms were met with immediate resistance and the sound of metal scraping wood.

Knight's head shot up at the sound, and his face immediately contorted into a crumpled mixture of remorse and concern when he registered where it was coming from. "Fuck! The handcuffs!"

He leapt up and grabbed his key ring off the nightstand, pausing only to discard the murder weapon into the trashcan. After freeing my hands, Knight pulled me into his lap sideways and wrapped his arms around me, where he alternated between kissing, rubbing, and apologizing to my abraded red wrists.

"I'm sorry," he said, kissing a particularly nonexistent scratch. "I'm so fucking sorry." Knight's worried eyes scanned me head to toe. Finding another invisible wound, he kissed that one too. "Are you okay? Please tell me you're okay. I tried so hard not to hurt you. You're the only thing I've ever loved, Punk. If I hurt you, it would fucking destroy me."

Although my body had just suffered excruciating pain at the hands of that man, my soul felt brand spanking new. Shinier. More powerful. The pain had scorched away the last, lingering traces of my childlike innocence, weakness, and naiveté—qualities that no longer served me—and allowed a stronger, braver, wiser version of me to rise from the ashes.

I rubbed Knight's fuzzy head, and kissed his downturned mouth at least a dozen times. "Oh, I'm better than okay," I beamed. "I want to do it again."

My boyfriend—my sweet, worried, lovesick psycho—treated me to my favorite smile, and his cock immediately twitched against my hip.

"Knight?" I asked, catching a glimpse of the collection of stuff he left on the nightstand. "What's the honey for?"

Knight captured my bottom lip between his grinning teeth and snarled, "That's for round two."

Chapter 28

Winter break was amazing. With no school and us only working nights and weekends, Knight and I had all day to hang out at Peg's house and find new rooms to christen. And pieces of furniture to christen. Hell, by the end of those two weeks we were having trouble finding a patch of carpet that we hadn't done it on.

And when we weren't fucking, we were cuddling. Oh my God, the cuddling. It was official. I was madly, truly, deeply, stupidly in love.

And I was sore. As hell.

But one day during the break—the day before Christmas—there was a car parked in Peg's driveway when we got there.

"Shit. I guess Peg got Christmas Eve off," I said. "Where should we go?"

I didn't volunteer my house because…skinhead. I mean, it's one thing to get picked up and dropped off by a guy with a shaved head. It's another thing entirely to bring him inside to meet your parents dressed like a Neo-Nazi.

"The shop is closing early today, but it won't be cleared out until about three," Knight said.

"Can we go to your house?" I asked.

"I don't have a house," Knight responded in a clipped tone.

"You know what I mean. Your stepdad's house. Is he there?"

Knight sighed and put the truck in reverse. "He won't be home until this afternoon."

"So, I finally get to see where you live?" I chirped.

"No. You get to see where I stay four nights a week. I don't fucking live there."

Knight drove past our high school and turned into a massive, gated community about a half a mile up the street. I knew the neighborhood, but I'd never been inside. *Those* kids didn't go to our school. They all went to private schools.

Knight had to open his door to type his code into the keypad because his truck was jacked up so high. It was all so ridiculous.

"You live *here*?" I asked as Knight's truck snarled through the opening gate.

"No," Knight corrected me, again. "I don't fucking live here. I keep my shit here. I'm not some little rich boy."

"Okay, okay. Jeez."

I practically licked the glass as we drove past mini-mansion after mini-mansion. The streets were lined with perfectly spaced Bradford pear trees. There were ponds. There were fountains. Every home was a completely different custom style, yet they were all similarly decorated for the holidays.

When Knight finally pulled into a circular driveway and shut off his engine, I had to suppress a giggle. The house...was pink.

The place was gorgeous, don't get me wrong. It looked like a European chateau—three stories tall, Spanish tile roof, an elaborate wrought iron staircase leading up to a set of massive wooden double doors—but the stucco had been painted an unapologetic shade of salmon.

I could see why Knight felt more at home at Peg's place. His stepdad's joint looked like the Barbie Fucking Dream Home.

I followed Knight down a paved path to the right side of the house. Evidently, that entire wing of the home was dedicated to storing aircraft carriers. There were four garage doors, but one of them was easily double or triple the height of the other two.

With one of the forty-seven keys on his keychain, Knight unlocked a nondescript door attached to the garage and held it open for me. Inside I saw why Knight's stepdad needed such a big garage. The man owned a motherfucking sailboat.

"Holy shit!" I blurted out.

Knight just ignored me and walked through the garage, past some little sports car under a tarp, and up a set of stairs. The door at the top made a beeping sound when he opened it, just before we entered into the Barbie Dream Chateau kitchen.

I felt like Alice in Wonderland after she drank the potion that made her shrink. Everything was so big. The ceilings went on forever. The moldings were a foot wide. Even the tiles on the floor were gigantic, and you could have roasted an entire pig in the oven.

A high-pitched voice echoed through the house, "Ronnie?"

Knight rolled his eyes at me and called back, "Yeah," as he opened one of the massive fridge doors and peeked inside.

A tiny, tired-looking woman appeared in the kitchen with waist-length white-blonde hair. She was holding some kind of little frou-frou dog under her arm like a handbag and was wearing a shit ton of makeup—probably to hide the fact that her eyelids didn't appear to want to stay open.

"Oh, my goodness," she squealed as she set the yappy little critter down on the floor and made her way over to me. "You must be BB!" Our two bony bodies would have clanked against one another when she squeezed me if it weren't for her comedically large breast implants.

"Oh, my gosh, you are just as pretty as a picture!" It was like she was doing a bad impersonation of a Southern pageant mom. Nobody's voice actually sounded like that.

"Candi, this is BB. BB, this is my mom, Candi," Knight said as he slammed the fridge shut and began walking out of the room.

I guess that's my cue.

"Nice to meet you," I said, turning to follow Knight, lest I be lost in that labyrinth forever.

"Wait." Candi reached out and touched my arm with her cold little hand.

When I turned back around to face her she kind of glanced left and right to make sure no one was listening, then leaned forward and whispered, "Do you have a cigarette I can borrow, honey?"

I bit back a laugh and whispered, "Sure."

As I dug in my purse, Candi looked around like some kind of paranoid woodland creature who'd just heard a twig snap.

I handed her a Camel Light and asked if she needed a lighter.

"Oh, no, honey. I've got one. Thanks," she whispered. "My old man hates it when I smoke, but what he don't know won't kill 'im, right?"

She forgot to use her pageant mom voice on that last sentence. Her pitch was still high, but she sounded a lot more like a woman who would use the term "my old man" than the vacant trophy wife she was pretending to be. I bet if I'd looked in her closet—past the Burberry trench coats and matching Louis Vuitton luggage—there'd be a vintage motorcycle jacket, size XS, tucked away in the back that I'd just love to "borrow."

I said my goodbyes and rounded the corner that Knight had taken. It led into a foyer that put Peg's four-by-four patch of parquet to shame. The space was two stories tall, contained a grand circular staircase leading up to the second floor, and was practically filled top to bottom with an ornate *Better Homes and Gardens*–looking Christmas tree. When I got upstairs, I found myself in a hallway lined with at least ten closed doors and one open door, way down at the end of the hall.

I tiptoed over to it and peeked inside. The room was spacious, had a large window with a view of one of the neighborhood's many fountained ponds, and looked like an army-navy surplus store swallowed a pet shop. The walls were painted a dark hunter green and were covered in gun racks and knife racks and glass cases containing vintage-looking grenades and land mines and shit. There was a collection of glass aquariums and cages by the window. A tattered POW-MIA flag hung over a wooden twin-size bed. And on the bed sat a skinhead, who was angrily unlacing his boots.

"She bummed a cigarette off you, didn't she?"

"Hell yeah, she did," I laughed as I walked around, inspecting all the weaponry.

Knight chunked a boot into the open walk-in closet next to his bed and started unlacing the other one. "She won't fucking buy 'em herself because she's afraid Chuck will find out, so her rich ass tries to steal 'em from me."

Knight sounded pissed, but I thought it was kind of funny. "Why don't you just have her give you cash and you can buy her some?"

"Because fuck her."

Damn. Okay. New subject.

"Knight," I said, taking a mental inventory.

"What?" Jesus, he was pissy. He really did hate being there.

"Why do you have thirteen rifles, eighteen knives, three swords, and four, no, five hand grenades in your bedroom?"

"My grandfather."

Oh, right. The war hero.

Knight pointed at a glass case standing upright on a desk by the door. "Those are all of his medals. Fucker was hardcore."

I noted, as I pretended to give a shit about his grandfather's medals, that there wasn't a stitch of skinhead propaganda or paraphernalia to be seen. Everybody I knew decorated their bedrooms with the things they loved, things they identified with. Lance's room had been full of punk rock shit. My room was full of punk rock shit, magazine cutouts of eight-pound supermodels, paintings I'd done of eight-pound anime characters, Knight's drawings, and photos of my friends. Knight's room was full of weapons. And animals. And proof that once upon a time, there was a man in his family that he could look up to.

I walked over to the cages by the window. "Who are these guys?"

Knight leaned back on the bed, resting on his elbows, and said, "That's Igor, Banana, and Sweetie."

"Let me guess. Igor is the iguana, Sweetie is the snake, and Banana is the canary."

"Banana is the snake because she's yellow, and I named her when I was like, seven. Sweetie is the parakeet. She was my mom's but I brought her up here because Candi's dumb ass kept leaving her cage open and the fucking cat almost ate her. And yeah, Igor is the iguana. She's a little bitch."

Girls. They were all girls. Little helpless girls that he put in cages and fed and protected from danger.

Wanting to lighten Knight's shitty mood, I turned and said, "Hey, I have your Christmas present! I thought you might want to go ahead and open it since I'm gonna be doing family stuff all day tomorrow."

It worked. Knight smiled and said, "Okay, but you have to open mine first," as he hopped up and disappeared into his closet. A second later he emerged holding a big cardboard box.

We sat on the bed next to each other, and Knight handed me his gift. Of course, instead of wrapping it Knight had drawn a huge, lifelike, tattoo-quality bow on top of it in black marker.

Talented bastard.

I opened the box and pulled out a fuzzy, super-soft leopard print blanket. It was almost as soft as Knight's head. *Almost.*

Knight said, "I found it at Trash. It reminded me of your fuzzy purse. And you're always cold, so it can keep you warm when I'm not around."

Awwww.

I thanked him and gave him an exaggerated kiss, then unfolded the blanket in one big motion and wrapped it around my shoulders. It was heavenly.

Reaching into said purse, I pulled out a much smaller box, which, of course, was decorated to the nines. Pier 1 had put me in charge of holiday gift wrapping—probably because it kept me from rearranging all of their displays—so Knight's present was dripping with stolen wrapping paper, ribbons, and bows.

I'd ordered his gift online the day after I lost my virginity. When Knight finally broke through all the packaging he looked at me with an unreadable expression.

"It's to replace the one I ruined," I squealed, barely containing my excitement. "I ordered it from England!"

Knight held up the white T-shirt with the logo for the band The Last Resort silkscreened across the front and smirked.

"Thanks," he said, "but I like the original one better."

My face fell. "Oh, I thought I got the same one. Sorry."

"You did," Knight said, reaching underneath his pillow. "But I like this one better." With that, Knight produced the blood-stained shirt he'd laid underneath me on Colton's bed the week before.

"Ew! Knight! You fucking sleep with that thing?! That's so gross!"

Knight ignored me as he held a small rust-colored spot up to his nose and inhaled deeply.

I covered my face with my blanket so he wouldn't see me blush. How was it that something so nasty had me feeling so giddy? Knight pulled the plush fabric away from my face and said, "I love the shirt. Thank you."

"I love *you*," I said, wrapping the blanket around us both.

We tumbled to the bed where we cuddled and kissed and kissed and cuddled until my boots ended up on the other side of the room, my jeans ended up around my ankles, and Knight's fuzzy blond head ended up between my legs under my equally fuzzy leopard print blanket.

He asked me if I trusted him before he went down on me. I thought it was weird, because the last time he'd asked me that was when he took my virginity. I didn't regret a second of that—even if it did still hurt to pee and walk up stairs—so I nodded and let my legs fall open to him again.

Of course, by the time I felt my orgasm build I had forgotten all about Knight's little question. I had practically forgotten my own name. Until I heard the unmistakable sound of a butterfly knife being flipped open, that is.

Shit!

I felt the knife bite into my inner thigh, but before I could even register the pain Knight's mouth was there to soothe the sting as his fingers took over the fucking. The bottleneck of opposing sensations—pain, pleasure, desire, fear—competing for the attention of my brain resulted in a full-body short circuit. I convulsed like a live wire and saw sparks behind my eyelids.

As I recovered, Knight rolled on a condom and crawled back up my body. There was blood on his mouth, which I was getting used to, and madness in his icy eyes.

When Knight pushed into me my pleasure-pain index was only heightened. It hurt, but I was getting used to that too. Couldn't get enough of it, actually.

I tore our shirts off, needing to feel his skin on my skin. His bedroom door was wide open, but I didn't care. I didn't care about anything that didn't involve being devoured by Ronald McKnight.

Knight sat up on his knees and pulled me up with him so that

I was straddling him in the middle of the bed. His vampire mouth claimed mine, and the taste of every bad thing on his tongue made me crazy.

Reaching between us, Knight swept a finger along my fresh cut and smeared a dot of blood on the tip of my pert, pink nipple. I watched as he sucked it off, and I came all over again.

Once we'd regained consciousness and were pulling our clothes back on, Knight said, "Promise me that you'll tell me if I hurt you. Okay? Or if I'm freaking you out. You have to fucking promise."

"Honestly," I said, fastening my jeans. "Since you asked, I am a little freaked out that you let the canary watch."

Knight swatted me with his new T-shirt and laughed. "It's a fucking parakeet."

He shrugged the shirt on and walked over to the cage. "She can talk, too." Tapping the wire frame, Knight said to the bird, "Sweetie, say hi to BB."

Squawk. "Go fuck yourself." *Squawk.*

Knight beamed with pride.

I giggled. "Does she not like me, or is that all she can say?"

"Oh, she hates everybody," Knight said, opening the cage and letting her climb onto his finger. "I taught her w—"

It happened so fast I didn't even have time to scream. A flash of white fur and black claws. A cage crashing to the ground. Squawking and screeching. Snarling and hissing. A blur of human motion and rage. Then, a cat darting out the door into the hall, followed by the most terrifying silence I've ever heard.

In a matter of seconds, Knight had gone from smiling at a little bird on his finger, to kneeling in a pile of yellow feathers, clutching its lifeless body to his cheek.

Knight's face crumpled into deep ridges of pain as he pulled his knees to his chest and rocked back and forth. He sobbed and rubbed the bird's motionless body against his face the way

I imagine someone would cuddle a recently deceased child. The sounds coming from him pulled stinging hot tears from my eyes. I wanted to go to him, to comfort him, but I had gotten pretty familiar with that particular time bomb, and I knew it was too late.

As Knight stood up and stormed down the stairs the countdown timer in my mind read *00:00*.

Boom.

We're all dead.

The sounds of Knight shouting and Candi screaming and furniture smashing and glass breaking shook the walls. It echoed up the stairs and bounced down the hallway and filled me with dread. Especially when another clock came to mind. The one on the VCR that said it was almost four.

I had to get him out of there.

I followed Knight's trail of destruction through the house. My heart pounded with closed fists against my ribs as the riotous clamor of things breaking and Candi's screaming got louder. Where was I? How did I get there? When would I wake up?

I stepped into a two-story great room at the back of the house that looked like ground zero. The only things left unbroken in that room—including the two people inside—were the floor-to-ceiling windows that flanked the two-story stone fireplace.

It was a nightmare. A living nightmare. Knight was swinging an iron fireplace poker like a baseball bat, smashing the glass panes out of every single built-in cabinet on the left wall of the room. Candi was screaming and shielding a nearby curio cabinet full of dolls with her body.

"Do you love *this*?" he shouted, smashing another cabinet door. Reaching in and pulling out some porcelain trinket, he yelled, "What about this?" just before chunking it at the wall beside her head. It must have been a music box because when it shattered a few sad, errant notes filled the air.

Candi covered her face and screamed at him to stop in that high-pitched girlie voice of hers. Knight ignored her, shattering another cabinet and pulling out a large wedding photo in a crystal frame. His forearm was bleeding.

Holding the picture out toward his mother, Knight took a few steps closer to her and screamed, "Do you even love *him*? Or do you just love his money?" He smashed the frame on the edge of a bookcase.

Taking two more long strides, Knight stopped directly in front of his mother's face, holding the poker in his right hand as blood trailed down his left. She recoiled and turned her face away, still shielding the little glass cabinet full of bullshit.

"You don't fucking care about anything but your pills and your stuff," he seethed, looming over her. "You're not a mother. You're not even a fucking person. You're a piece of shit gold digger. That's all you've ever been. Pussy for a paycheck."

"Knight!" I screamed. "Stop it!"

Just as Knight turned his head toward me, a figure came barreling through a doorway next to where Candi was standing and tackled him. The two men fell to the ground, but Knight got the upper hand immediately. Candi disappeared through the doorway as Knight pummeled the shit out of a middle-aged man in a business suit.

The two rolled around through the broken glass until Knight managed to coil his left hand around the guy's tie. Using the strip of navy-blue silk as a leash, Knight yanked his head off the ground and clocked him across the face with a bloody right cross. The blow landed so hard I thought the bastard's head was going to spin all the way around.

Then I heard the *click*.

Standing in the doorway was a tiny, shaking woman, holding a tiny little gun, with the tiny little hammer cocked all the way back.

"Get the fuck outta my house," she said, all traces of her pageant mom persona gone.

Knight turned around slowly, breathing hard, his stepfather unconscious beneath him.

"Get out!" she screamed, mascara pouring down her face. "Get out!"

"You're choosing him?!" Knight shouted, still panting. "He fucking beats you! He fucks other women! And you're choosing him?!"

"I *chose* him! I *married* him!" Candi screamed, her heavy diamond rings clinking against the steel in her trembling hands. "You're the one I didn't get to choose!"

I ran to him.

I didn't care about the gun.

I didn't care about the glass.

I didn't care about the moaning, writhing, bloody stranger on the floor.

I ran to my man.

Throwing my arms around his shuddering, adrenaline-fueled body, I formed a human shield against those ugly, hateful words.

I let him know that somebody had chosen him.

I had.

That night, while Candi and Chuck were at the hospital getting his nose reset, I helped Knight move out. I couldn't believe Chuck didn't press charges. Knight mumbled something about having dirt on him. Whatever it was must have been pretty bad for a pompous asshole like him to take a beating like that and keep his mouth shut.

I offered to clean up all the broken glass while Knight packed, but he told me to leave it. He said Candi would just have the maid do it in the morning. Like it was a normal thing.

We filled the back of Knight's truck with his weapons, his clothes, and his two remaining pets and headed over to Peg's house. She smiled when we got there and said she was happy to have him. I believed her. Peg needed a new son almost as badly as Knight needed a new mom.

See Knight? Peg chose you, too.

The next day I invited Knight to spend Christmas with me. In my house. With my parents. He kept his pant legs rolled down and his Lonsdale hoodie on—probably to hide his braces as well as the three-inch gash in his forearm that really needed stitches—but even without his full skinhead costume it was still pretty fucking awkward. My parents warmed up after a few mimosas though, and Knight seemed to relax a little too. I showed my mom some of the drawings he'd done for me, and delighted in watching him squirm as she praised his work.

When I kissed Knight goodbye in the driveway that night, he said it was the best Christmas he'd ever had.

I smiled the whole way up the stairs to my bathroom, where I stuck my finger down my throat and puked the whole day back up.

Chapter 29

January

"But I want a tattoo!" I whined.

"I told you the next time you sat in my chair I was piercing your clit. You're sitting in my chair. I'm piercing your fucking clit."

"Can we do both?" I asked, batting my eyelashes.

"Punk, I'm not tattooing a fifteen-year-old. I don't care how much you beg. You don't know what the fuck you want."

"Yes, I do," I pouted.

"You think that now, but I promise, what you want is going to change. If I had gotten a tat when I was fifteen I'd probably have the word *skinhead* written across my forehead right now."

"But girls mature faster than boys. I'm basically already eighteen in boy years."

"Ask me again when you're eighteen in girl years."

Although I hated being told 'no' more than *anything*, the fact that Knight assumed that we would still be together in two and a half years made my little heart go all pitter-pattery.

Knight handed me a shot of Southern Comfort. Damn, he

was serious about this piercing. He didn't bust out the shot glasses unless he wanted to get me numb.

"Can I at least tell you about the tattoo?" I asked, accepting the whiskey with both hands.

"Uh huh." Knight's back was to me, and he appeared to be sterilizing something pointy.

I took a sip of the fire water, followed by two or three deep breaths, then declared, "I want a knight."

That got his attention. Knight turned around and looked at me with a furrowed brow, as if he wasn't sure that he'd heard me correctly.

"*The* knight," I specified, "the one you said was going to be your next tattoo—I want that one." Taking another gulp for courage, I lifted my left hand and tapped my ring finger with my thumb, right where a wedding ring would go. "Here."

Knight's confused scowl slowly slid off, revealing my favorite smile underneath. Leaning forward he kissed me with that cute, freckle-faced grin and said, "If you still want that tattoo in two and a half years I'll be the luckiest sonofabitch on earth."

He kissed me again, deeper that time, and my insides erupted in anticipation. The burn of the whiskey in my belly, the tray full of clamps and needles and gauze, the boy I loved telling me we had a future. Pleasure and pain. That was our thing. Couldn't have one without the other.

When Knight finally pulled away from me he had a full-fledged erection that I really wanted to attend to.

But Knight had other plans. At least for the moment.

Flashing me an evil grin, he asked, "Do you trust me?"

Those were becoming my four favorite words in the English language.

Before I was done nodding, Knight began removing my ripped

jeans, tiger-striped tights underneath, and one of the new lacy thongs I'd bought with my Christmas money to impress him. I was cold as shit, and colder still once he wiped between my legs with an antiseptic towelette.

Jesus. Was that what he did at work all weekend? Play with other girls' pussies? I'd have to ask him about that later.

Knight tinkered around some more at his station, then laid a square sheet of plastic wrap between my legs. I assumed it was part of the piercing setup until Knight leaned over and licked my clit through the clear material.

The fuck?

I watched in awe as the area I thought was about to be impaled was lavished with pleasure instead. From that angle, with that lighting, I had no choice but to watch. Damn, it was sexy, and Knight wasn't even touching me. His talented tongue flicked and sucked at my polypropylene-covered slit while his latex-wrapped fingers held the sheet in place.

I finished the rest of my shot, let my head fall back, and gritted my teeth in frustration as he teased me. If he was trying to distract me, it was working.

Suddenly, Knight's mouth was gone. Then I heard a zipper. Looking down, I watched in rapt wonder as he stretched a condom over his swollen cock. Placing the head of it at my entrance, underneath the sheet of plastic wrap, Knight flashed me a salacious smirk. But he didn't fill me. Instead he snapped off his gloves and put on a new pair from his station.

I writhed against him, seeking some kind of relief, as he lifted the plastic sheet and clamped a delicate pair of steel tongs onto the left side of my hood. I winced and gripped the edges of the chair, thinking my tender, oversensitized flesh was about to have a needle shoved through it.

But Knight continued his torment, instead. He pushed his

latex-covered cock into me, maybe half an inch, before withdraw-ing, and massaged me through the plastic with his latex-covered fingers. I was agonizingly close to coming, but he just kept me there. Right where he wanted me.

I'd been tortured in that chair before, but it was nothing like that. The anticipation drove me mad. At any given moment, I could be fucked or impaled. Which would come first? The pleasure or the pain?

Just as I was beginning to consider hitting him out of frustra-tion, Knight filled me to the hilt in one swift, hard thrust, and my body gratefully detonated around him on contact. While I was busy cursing and coming, Knight tore off the plastic wrap and pierced me in yet another swift, fluid motion. The sudden pain caused all my muscles to tense, my pussy to squeeze even tighter, and heightened my orgasm to a level I never dreamed was possible.

While I writhed and moaned, two gloved hands grabbed me by the waist and yanked my body down the length of the chair until my ass was hanging off. Then Knight rolled me onto my belly. As soon as my feet touched the tile floor, he slammed into me from behind.

His hands gripped my hips, and I gripped the edges of the chair for support. Knight growled into my neck with every thrust, and my newly pierced clit throbbed with every beat of my racing heart. The moment I felt his teeth sink into my shoulder, his fingers dig into my hips, and his cock stiffen inside me, I was a goner.

When it was over, I watched Knight out of the corner of my eye as he gathered all of the clear plastic things to be thrown away—needle and jewelry packaging, plastic wrap, gloves, the condom—and one skinny metal needle. Just before dropping it all in the trashcan, Knight licked it clean.

"How do you work around so much blood when...you know?" I asked, my cheek pressed into the vinyl, my body wrung out and unable to move.

"I don't know. It's almost like it calms me down when I'm at work. Unless it's you. When I pierced your nipples, I was so hard I thought I might come in my fucking pants. I even licked your blood off my glove when you weren't looking. That shit was torture."

"No fucking way!" I laughed, finally mustering the strength to push myself up. "I thought you were so professional!"

"What about this time?" He smirked.

"I think I was the one getting tortured this time. And, by the way, that better not be standard practice around here or you're gonna be looking for a new job."

Knight laughed and handed me a small mirror so that I could see his handiwork. There it was. A slightly curved barbell, right through the left side of my hood.

Fuck yeah.

As Knight cleaned me up and helped me get dressed he explained all the dos and don'ts of a clit piercing. We couldn't get body fluids on it for four to six weeks. No oral without plastic wrap. No sex without a condom. And when we did have sex, doggie-style was best.

Condoms. That reminded me...

"I think I'm gonna get on birth control."

"Really?" Knight asked, helping me out of the chair.

"Yeah," I said as we walked to the back door for a cigarette. *Slowly.* "Those condoms look like they hurt. And they smell weird. And if I get on the pill soon, then by the time my piercing is healed we shouldn't have to use them anymore."

Knight grabbed my jacket out of the break room and beamed at me as he wrapped it around my shoulders. "I fucking love you," he said, leaning in to kiss me. "I'll go with you to your doctor's appointment, if you want."

Sweet psycho.

Outside the air was freezing. Knight lit my cigarette while I rubbed my hands together and mustered the courage to ask him the question that had been plaguing me for months. "Knight?"

"Yeah?" he asked, flipping the hood of his sweatshirt up to stay warm. Knight had a flight jacket of his own, but he never wore it. The cold didn't seem to bother him like it bothered me.

I swallowed. "I was just wondering, how do you know so much…about sex? I mean, I've never seen you with anybody at school, like a girlfriend."

Who have you been fucking? How old were they? How many were there? May I please have their names and addresses? Did you love them? Were they better than me? Where are they now? Buried in those woods over there?

Knight looked past me into the alley and took a drag from his cigarette. Just when I thought he was going to ignore my question altogether he said, "There's a bar around the corner, called Spirit of Sixty-Nine. It's where all the Atlanta skins hang out. The bartenders are all regulars here, and they used to pay me to come by after-hours to help clean up. Whenever I went it always seemed like there was some drunk as fuck skin chick waiting around to take me home."

It made my stomach turn to think of him with other girls. *Women.* And skinhead bitches at that. I must have seemed so inexperienced compared to them. I could feel my face get hot with self-consciousness and jealousy, but I pressed on.

"Did you date any of them?"

Am I your first girlfriend, Knight? Am I special?

"After the shit I did to them?" Knight snorted and exhaled a puff of smoke through his nose. "Fuck no."

Dread settled into my belly.

"Wh-why? What did you do to them?"

Knight flashed me a look that said he was done with my little line of questioning, but he answered me anyway. "I did what I do," he said, exhaling through his nose. "I made them bleed."

"They didn't like it?" I hated the way I sounded—so young and naïve. Knight had made me bleed plenty of times, and sure, it scared me at first, but the way he did it was just so...sexy. Was I not supposed to like it? If those skin chicks didn't like it, did that make me a freak?

Knight narrowed his eyes and evaluated me. It was as if he were trying to decide whether or not he could trust me with some secret. I felt like I was about to be turned into either an accomplice or a vampire, but I was okay with either one as long as it meant I was special.

"I didn't *want* them to like it," he said.

Oh.

"You hurt them," I whispered.

Knight clenched his jaw and nodded, staring straight ahead.

"Because somebody hurt you."

Knight shot me a severe look. His pupils were huge in the darkness—as black as whatever lurked inside him. He didn't have to tell me what happened. He let me peer in and see it for myself.

"You don't want to hurt me though."

My words were gentle but firm. I phrased it as a statement to let him know that I didn't question it. I knew. Sure, he'd cut me and bitten me and stabbed me with needles, but that was Knight's way. He wasn't *trying* to hurt me. He was trying to make me feel good.

And he was really fucking good at it.

Knight shook his head slightly. It was like he wanted to shut down, but some tiny part inside him was forcing him to answer me. To stay open.

"Because you love me," I said.

Knight's expression softened. His eyebrows lifted a little bit, and he nodded again.

I smiled and took a step forward. Wrapping my hands around

the back of his neck, I said in a sing-songy voice, trying desperately to lighten the mood, "Because you want to *marry* me."

Knight's hands came down around my hips and he pulled me into him, closing the distance between us. His eyes still black, his face sincere, Knight didn't smile when he leaned down to my ear and said, "I do."

His voice was gruff and the texture changed my skin from smooth to rough on contact.

"You...do?" I whispered back.

Knight nodded, burying his face in the bend of my neck. I pushed his hood off and rubbed my cheek against his fuzzy blond head. "You know," I murmured with closed eyes, "fifteen-year-olds can get married in the state of Georgia as long as they have a note from their parents."

I felt Knight smile against my neck as his hands shifted from my hips to my ass. He scooped me up in one fluid motion and I wrapped my legs around his waist in response. The movement caused my tender new piercing to scream in protest, but I didn't listen. I couldn't. I was too busy feeling Knight's tongue slide across mine, tasting his vices, which were the same as mine, delighting in his velveteen softness under my fingers, and admiring the way his pulse synchronized with mine—the way it always did when our hearts were pressed together.

When Knight tilted his head back to look at me his pupils were still huge, but when I peered inside I didn't see darkness anymore. I saw my own reflection smiling back.

"Since you want to marry me and all, does that mean you'll give me that tattoo now?"

Knight chuckled. "Goddamn, you don't give up, do you?"

I beamed and shook my head as he lowered me back down onto my feet.

"Okay, fine—but on one condition. You have to let me put it on the *inside* of your finger."

I nodded and clapped and jumped up and down as Knight led the way back to his tattoo chair.

I guess I was right when I'd assumed that I'd be engaged before the end of tenth grade. I just didn't realize it would be to Skeletor the motherfucking Skinhead.

Chapter 30

DEAR BB,

HAPPY VALENTINE'S DAY.

I HAD THESE SPECIAL ORDERED, BUT I NEVER ACTUALLY THOUGHT YOU'D STICK AROUND LONG ENOUGH FOR ME TO GIVE THEM TO YOU.

EVERY DAY I WAKE UP THINKING I'M EITHER GOING TO FUCK THIS UP OR FIND OUT THAT IT WAS ALL JUST A DREAM. BUT FOR SOME REASON, YOU'RE STILL HERE.

I DON'T KNOW WHY. I'M A FUCK-ING ASSHOLE. I'M POOR. I HAVE NO FRIENDS. AND I HATE MY OWN FAM-ILY. BUT I LOVE YOU. I LOVE YOU SO MUCH IT SCARES ME. I'M SCARED

I'M GOING TO HURT YOU. I'M SCARED
THAT WHEN I DO, YOU WON'T LEAVE.
AND I'M SCARED THAT I'M KEEP-
ING YOU FROM FINDING SOMEONE
BETTER.

BUT I CAN'T LET YOU GO. SO UNTIL
YOU FIGURE OUT WHAT A PIECE OF
SHIT I AM, I'M GOING TO BE THE HAP-
PIEST PIECE OF SHIT ON EARTH.

LOVE,

KNIGHT

I leaned across the barn wood table, almost every square inch covered with people's names and initials, and kissed my boyfriend. My sweet, self-loathing, psychopathic boyfriend. Knight had surprised me for Valentine's Day by taking me to my favorite restaurant in Little Five Points, The Yacht Club. It was a shitty dive bar with a fancy name—the place my mom and I used to go where they let people carve stuff into the tables. I had already found three *BB*s since we'd been there.

After sitting back down, I looked down into my left hand. The tiny Ziploc bag that had fallen out of Knight's note sat in my palm, while the black silhouette of a jousting knight on horseback sat on the inside of my ring finger. Both made me smile like a lunatic.

There were two small surgical steel hearts inside the clear pouch, each with an arrow-shaped barbell jutting through it. Some guys give their girlfriends earrings for Valentine's Day. Mine gave me nipple rings.

"These are cool as shit!" I said, holding up the clear plastic pouch. "I can't wait to put them in! Thank you so fucking much!"

"*I* can't wait to help you put them in," Knight said with a smirk.

"I got you something too," I said. Reaching into my cavernous purse, I pulled out a Pier 1 gift-wrapped special.

Knight eyed me suspiciously, but took the gift. While he was busy tearing through all fifteen curly ribbons I'd tied around it, I quickly slid most of my chicken fingers and fries into the napkin on my lap. Knight wasn't above force-feeding me, so I'd learned to be more covert.

Once Knight had made it past my King Tut–worthy wrapping job, he slid the lid off the box and gently removed a simple black picture frame I'd stolen from work. Inside was a photo of the two of us, taken by my mom, standing in front of an artificial Christmas tree dripping with homemade ornaments.

"I noticed that you don't have any pictures in your room," I said, gesturing toward the frame.

Knight looked at me with wide, ghostly eyes. His lips parted, but he said nothing.

"Knight?"

Looking back down at the picture, Knight sat in silence. *Shit.* I hoped I hadn't triggered something traumatic. Since Knight wouldn't talk about his past, I had no idea what might set him off. Well, I knew that drugs were off limits. And animals dying. And confronting him about the way he dressed. And anything having to do with his parents. I was learning, I guess, but I was learning the hard way.

Eventually Knight swallowed and choked out, "Can I...have more?"

"More what? Pictures?"

Knight nodded and looked back up at me, sincerity shining out of his icy blue irises. "Yeah. I want one for my station at work."

"Sure, baby. I can print another—"

"…and I need one for my wallet, too. And my truck. And my locker," Knight interrupted, completely serious.

Sweet fucking psycho.

I set my fried food–filled napkin on the seat next to me and slid into the booth on the other side of the table, next to Knight. Draping my arms around his neck, I kissed his chiseled mouth at least four times—once for each of the photos he'd requested. Then I squealed as Knight scooped me up off the bench and set my ass down sideways in his lap.

After kissing me back until a bulge began to press against my hip, Knight said, "I love you so fucking much."

"Oh really?" I asked, my lips brushing against his. "Then why don't I see any *Knight loves BB* hearts on this table?"

Before I could blink Knight had flipped and twirled and swished his blade out and set to work.

Some guys carve their initials into trees, mine carved ours into the table of a dive bar named The Yacht Club.

When we left the restaurant and headed back toward Terminus City Tattoo it was already pitch-black outside. All of the assorted potted trees in the square were wrapped in white lights—left over from the holidays—and the effect was stunning. Although the temperature was dropping fast, I was willing to risk frostbite to bask in the romance of it all for just a few more minutes.

"C'mere," I said, pulling Knight by the hand toward a turquoise bench under the skeleton of a once-purple crepe myrtle tree. "Sit with me."

Knight didn't ask any questions. He simply flipped up his hood, lit a cigarette, and held my hand as we walked over to my special place.

I sat as close to him as I could get, soaking up his body heat.

"I sat here and watched the sun rise the morning after you pierced my nipples," I said, blushing at the memory. "You were still sleeping, so I went to get you breakfast. I saw this bench and...it was weird. I just sat here and watched the sun come up. Like I was home or something."

"I wasn't asleep," Knight said in a gruff voice. "I stayed awake all night thinking about what you said...about not wanting to see me get hurt." Knight looked away and took a drag off his cigarette. I knew that pause. He was preparing himself to say something difficult.

Meeting my gaze again, Knight took a deep breath and said, "That was the first time anyone had ever acted like they gave a shit whether I lived or died. And it had come from Brooke Fucking Bradley—the girl I'd been in love with since elementary school."

He talked about me the way I used to talk about Lance. I knew that kind of longing. It broke my heart to think that Knight had felt it for me all those years and I never knew, but I was also overjoyed for him. Knight had succeeded where I had failed. He made me love him. He fucking did it.

"All night I told myself not to get too excited, that I'd probably ruined whatever chance I had with you by being such an asshole the night before. So when I heard you get up and leave the next morning, I just assumed you were sneaking out. I didn't even try to go after you. I just laid there hating myself."

Knight looked away and went to take another drag off his cigarette, but I caught his face in my icy hands and turned it back toward me. After kissing his mouth at least a hundred times I finally pulled back and said, "I'm so sorry, baby. I had no idea."

Knight smiled a little, as much as he could with my hands still on his cheeks, and said, "Don't be sorry. When you came back it was the happiest moment of my pathetic fucking life."

I let go of Knight's face and watched his smile morph from sweet to sinister. "Then you looked so fucking hot making breakfast in my jacket that I had to go jerk off in the bathroom just to be able to function around you for the rest of the morning."

"Eww!" I shrieked and elbowed him in the ribs. "I don't wanna know about that! I thought you were in there brushing your teeth!"

"That too," Knight said with a grin, his features softened by the white lights all around us.

"How much do you think it would cost to rent a place down here?" I asked. "If making you breakfast is that much of a turn-on I want to do it *every* morning."

"A shitload," Knight said. "I'd definitely have to get a roommate. Rent in the city is fucking insane."

"What if I were your roommate?" I asked, hopeful.

"Punk...I would love nothing more than to get a place with you, but we don't have any mon—"

"Shh," I whispered, touching my fingertips to his lips. "Just pretend. Okay? If we weren't so fucking broke, if I weren't so fucking young, where would you want to live?"

Knight exhaled a stream of smoke and looked at me with a playful gleam in his eye. "Honestly?" he asked, as if he needed permission to share his secret desires with me. Looking behind me, Knight took a deep breath and pointed to something over my shoulder. "There."

I turned and looked in the direction of his outstretched finger. The road darkened on the other side of the five-way intersection, but I could vaguely make out the outline of an old Victorian-style two-story house in disrepair.

"Hell yeah," I said. "We could fix it up on the weekends. Paint it gray. That's my favorite color."

"Ugh. Like the Counting Crows song?" Knight asked, feigning disgust.

"You know the Counting Crows?" I laughed.

"Don't tell anybody," Knight said, nudging me.

I giggled. "It would be perfect. You could walk to work and I could take your truck to schoo—"

Before I'd even finished my thought Knight had burst out laughing. "You can't even get into the damn thing by yourself!"

"Shut up. Yes, I can," I snapped. "*Anyway*," I said, pegging him with a watch-your-ass glare, "I'd come home from school, go to work..." I looked around, then pointed a freezing cold finger in the direction of a building with a giant skull for an entrance, "at Trash...so I could get a discount on clothes, and when we both got off work we could meet somewhere for dinner!"

"You're not going to cook for me every night?" Knight asked, pretending to sound surprised.

Now it was my turn to burst out laughing.

"Not if you want to live." I snorted.

"Ooh!" I said, pointing at the MARTA station entrance. "Then, after I graduate, I can just take the train in town and go to Georgia State for college."

"What do you want to be when you grow up?" Knight asked. "And if you say a showgirl in Las Vegas again I will seriously lose my shit."

"I don't know. Maybe a special ed. teacher?" I said. "Or a psychologist? I loooove psychology. Or maybe I could be like an art therapist? Do they have those?"

"And a mom?" Knight asked, his face hardening.

"Yeah," I said. "And a mom. Definitely a mom. Oh! I forgot to tell you! Juliet's having a boy!"

Knight didn't respond. He just stared straight through me.

"Do you not want to have kids?" I asked hesitantly, praying to God that the man whose symbol was tattooed on my ring finger wasn't about to tell me that he didn't want kids.

"I..." Knight's voice trailed off and I could see his mind going somewhere else. "What if they...what if they're...like me?"

"Like what?" I asked. "Smart? Strong? Artistic?"

"You know." Knight flicked his eyes to mine in sudden annoyance. "*Fucked up.*"

"First of all," I said, raising my voice slightly, "anything *fucked up* about you got that way because of your parents. And you won't be anything like your parents. You know why?"

Knight looked through me again. He wasn't hearing me. He was going to his dark place. I laced my fingers between his and squeezed them a little until he made eye contact with me again.

"Because you give a shit," I said.

Knight turned his face away from me again, but gripped my hand tighter. "You don't know what's inside of me, Punk. It goes away when I'm with you, but it's not gone. It's never gone. I have these urges that I fight every day, just to have them play out in my dreams every night."

Knight turned back to me and confessed, "I kill shit, all night long, Punk. People. Zombies. I hack them into little pieces with machetes. I rip their bodies apart with my bare hands. I smear their blood on everything and wake up hard from it. I—"

"So what?" I interrupted, trying to stop his downward spiral of self-loathing. "So you've got a vivid imagination. You're an artist. As long as you're not hacking people up in real life you're good. Plus," I added with a smirk, "our kids would have me as a mom, so *obviously* they'd be perfect."

Knight didn't laugh, though. Instead he tucked one of the longer pieces of my hair behind my ear and said, "You *are* perfect, Punk. You're too fucking perfect. You shouldn't be here with me. You shouldn't be talking about having kids with me. You should be finding a nice, normal guy who will give you nice, normal kids."

"What the fuck, Knight?" I snapped, pulling my hand from his so that I could use it to make big dramatic hand gestures in the air. "Do I look like the kinda girl who wants nice and normal? In case you forgot, most of my head is shaved, I'm pierced, I'm tattooed, and I'm wearing fucking combat boots. Do I look like the kind of girl who's going to end up with an accountant?"

"Not on the outside," Knight said, "but I know you. I know that deep down you want the white picket fence. The two point five kids. You want all of that shit. And you deserve to get it."

"So do you," I said with a huff. "When are you going to get that through your fucking head? You aren't keeping me from something better. You *are* my something better. Look around, Knight," I said, gesturing to the twinkling, eclectic majesty of Little Five Points at night with my frostbitten fingers. "How could anything possibly be better than this?"

Part III

Chapter 31

March

I stuck five twenty-dollar bills under the cinder block behind my work, then sat on top of it to wait for Knight to pick me up. Tony and I hadn't spoken since he made our "little arrangement," but Knight hadn't been turned into Swiss cheese yet, so I kept on paying. Seven hundred dollars so far. It sounded like a lot, but I was sure that being with me had probably cost Knight at least that much between the gas his truck guzzled, the meals he insisted on buying me, and the alcohol and cigarettes that I was more than happy to help him consume. The least I could do was keep him alive.

I could hear Knight's truck coming long before it roared around the corner of the building. The sound made my heart beat faster. Even though I had totally figured out how to climb in by myself, Knight always insisted on coming around to my side of the truck to give me a kiss and a boost. With a little bit of ass grabbing.

He tossed my overnight bag in behind me and shut my door. My mom still assumed I was spending the night at Juliet's house every Friday, and every Saturday afternoon she picked me up at work, none the wiser. In reality, I'd been spending almost every Friday night curled up on a couch in the break room of a tattoo parlor with an eighteen-year-old skinhead on the outskirts of downtown Atlanta.

As much as I loved our time together, there was only so much to do at Terminus City Tattoo. At least Peg's house had cable. I guess we probably could have stayed there and slept in a real bed, but neither of us felt super comfortable being at Peg's house together while she was home. I mean, I was her son's ex-girlfriend. Did she really want to hear me making his bed squeak with some other guy?

I yelled over the snarling engine and blaring stereo, "What did you used to do at night, before I started coming around? You know, for fun?"

Knight turned the stereo down and said, "I used to hang out at Spirit of Sixty-Nine a lot, but I doubt you want to go there."

Oh, right, the bar where he used to pick up skin chicks. Yeah, no thanks.

"But there *was* this other thing I liked to do." Knight took his eyes off the road just long enough to flash me an evil grin. "I'll show you."

When we pulled into the parking lot behind Terminus City, Knight parked in the back like usual and jumped out.

I hopped out too, but before I could grab my bags Knight said, "You can just leave your stuff in the truck." Then he reached behind his seat and pulled out an old school–looking wooden baseball bat.

I shut my door and walked around to his side of the truck, breathing into my hands to keep them warm. "So, what? We're gonna do some batting practice?"

Knight chuckled. "Yeah, Punk. You could call it that."

Instead of walking toward the alley, Knight turned and walked out of the parking lot and away from the main five-way intersection. The street was poorly lit that way, and lined with houses that gave me the creeps. It was the same way we had walked to get to

Boots & Braces, but after dark the neighborhood took on a significantly more sinister vibe.

Knight's arm around my shoulder helped me feel safer, as did
the old weathered baseball bat he had slung over his shoulder. We
had just walked past the industrial park where Boots & Braces was
located when Knight took a sharp left and walked directly into
a patch of woods. I should have been scared, but I wasn't. I was
excited. I was curious. Knight was going to give me a glimpse into
his pre-BB life, and I would have walked through hot coals to see it.

After taking only a few steps into the woods, Knight stopped.
Looking up, I realized that we were standing in front of an eight-
foot-tall chain-link fence, with an additional two feet of barbed
wire on top of that. On the other side a few stray lights illuminated
what appeared to be an undulating sea of derelict automobiles.

"Is this...where we're going?" I asked.

"This is it," Knight said, leaning over and prying the bottom of
the chain-link fence up just high enough to toss in his baseball bat
and ninety-eight-pound girlfriend. "Slide under."

I did as he said. I didn't ask any questions. I didn't even ask
where we were. I just shimmied my waifish body under the fence
and tried not to snag Knight's precious childhood jacket on the
jagged edges.

Once I was through, Knight scaled the fence like it was nothing,
fucking barbed wire and all. I didn't have much time to admire his
athleticism, however, because as soon as his boots hit the ground I
heard barking. A lot of it. And it was coming straight toward us.

Without a word, Knight picked up the bat and handed it to me,
then found a fallen tree branch on the ground and held it across his
lap as he crouched down in front of me.

*Fucking shit. Did he fight junkyard dogs for fun? Is that why we're
here? And why am I the one holding the motherfucking bat?! Is he
going to wrestle it with his bare hands??*

Within seconds the barking beast emerged from the sea of vehicles. It looked like some kind of pit bull–warthog mix and was practically foaming at the mouth. I held my breath and gripped Knight's bat so hard I thought the skin on my knuckles was going to split open. Although my lungs weren't working at all, my heart was putting in overtime, pumping blood to extremities that were too scared to move.

As soon as the demon dog saw Knight it stopped barking, but it continued to approach, slowly and with its teeth bared. Once it was a few inches from Knight's outstretched hands I closed my eyes and fought back a whimper.

When nothing happened, I opened them again to find the hound from hell sniffing Knight's palms. Just as he'd done with Shep, Knight flipped his hands over and allowed the beast to sniff the backs of them as well. The mutt began to wag its gnarly little nub of a tail, then looked at Knight expectantly. Knight offered the dog the stick in his lap, then snatched it away at the last second.

Jesus! Don't fucking tease it! Are you crazy?!

But the little monster loved it. He lunged and snapped playfully at the stick. When Knight finally stood up and threw that fucker as far as he could, Cujo flew away after it like a bat into the night.

As soon as Knight turned around, I shoved his chest with both hands and whisper-screamed, "I THOUGHT I WAS GOING TO FUCKING DIE, YOU ASSHOLE!"

Knight gave me that smile, *that* smile—disarming me just as easily as he had done to Cujo—and said with a shrug, "I told you, I get along with animals way better than people."

I rolled my eyes and leaned over, trying to stave off a heart attack, as Knight turned and gazed out across the automobile graveyard. A dirt road cut through the center of the junkyard leading from the fence all the way to a tiny white building at the bottom of the long hill. At the top of the hill, where we were, an old-ass champagne-colored Cadillac seemed to have caught Knight's attention.

Pointing to it, Knight said, "How do you feel about Cadillacs?"

"Honestly, I'm more of a muscle car girl," I said. "I don't know shit about Cadillacs, but I can tell you that those ones from the eighties with the cloth tops look fucking ridiculous. I mean, who did they think they were fooling? Everybody knows that's not a fucking convertible."

Knight laughed and gestured toward the car with a tilt of his head. "Wanna fuck it up?"

I looked at him and saw pure glee shining out of his shadowed face. Knight's teeth gleamed. His eyes blazed white. His energy made the air feel fizzy. Effervescent. It made me want to clap my hands and jump up and down. Finally, for maybe the first time since we'd met, Knight and I were going to have some actual fucking fun.

"Fuck yeah," I said with a smile, resting the bat on my shoulder like Knight had done on the walk over. He extended an arm toward the doomed vehicle, as if to say, *"Ladies first,"* and I set my sights on the windshield. That thing needed to go.

I got a running start and swung for the fences, smacking the windshield with every ounce of momentum my skeletal body could generate. I turned my head at the last second, expecting to be showered with glass shards, but instead the bat bounced right off the windshield and flew out of my hands.

Knight practically had to bite his fist he was laughing so hard. I'd never seen him crack up like that, and it was the only thing that made my embarrassment bearable. *I* did that. Nobody could make Knight laugh the way I could. Whether I meant to or not.

"I'm glad somebody's having a good time," I said with my hands on my hips, pretending to be insulted.

Knight picked up the bat and walked toward me, still chuckling to himself. "I fucking love you," he said, giving me a peck on my pouting, pursed lips. Then he hopped onto the hood of the Cadillac in one graceful leap.

Knight stomped up onto the roof of the car and raised the bat over his head like some kind of medieval king about to slay a dragon with his mighty sword. I watched in awe as his muscles rippled beneath his hoodie, just before he stabbed the bat directly into the crack I'd made seconds before. Time almost stood still as the windshield exploded into a million tiny cubes of glass. Shards flew like confetti into the black sky, glinting in the light of the full March moon before falling back to earth with a melodic tinkle.

I threw my hands up as if Knight had just kicked a winning field goal and cheered silently. He leapt off the roof, grinning from ear to ear, and pulled his butterfly knife out of his pocket. "Here," he said, handing it to me. "Why don't you go take care of that rag top you love so much?"

Fuck yeah.

I smirked and flipped the knife out on the first try without even cutting my knuckles. It wasn't as impressive as when Knight did it, but I still caught him checking me out as I walked away.

As I stabbed and sliced the fabric from the metal, Knight made the rounds smashing out every window on the vehicle. Once he was done, Knight traded me the bat for the knife.

"I saved you the headlights and taillights," he said with a wink.

What a gentleman.

When I swung at the first taillight it caved in with a satisfying crunch. I looked at Knight in shock. *I did it!* I mouthed. He was smirking at me and clapping, silently.

No wonder Knight loves this shit, I thought, smashing the other three lights out with ease. I felt like a total fucking badass.

Tossing the bat back to Knight, I crawled up onto the hood as he made the rounds, denting every fender, door, and flat surface available. I sat on the cold metal and watched him in awe. The aggression just poured out of him so naturally. I had to muster something foreign and feral from deep inside myself just to break a taillight, but Knight, he had to put forth effort *not* to be violent. Out there, he was free.

When Knight was done smashing shit, he climbed up onto the front bumper and jumped up and down, making the car bounce and squeak underneath me. I giggled and clung to the hood with my cold fingers, trying in vain to keep from sliding off.

Just as I was about to scream for him to stop, the bumper fell off with a thud under the weight of Knight's feet. Both of us erupted into the kind of delicious laughter that doesn't even make a sound when it comes out. Tears streamed down my cheeks as Knight climbed up onto the hood and lay next to me, our bodies shuddering silently.

As I struggled to catch my breath, I stared at the stars above us, gently twinkling, as if they were laughing too. I felt Knight's breath, warm and welcome on my neck, as his heavy, strong arm snaked around my middle and pulled me closer. The weight of him grounded me. I breathed in. I breathed out. And for a brief moment, in the epicenter of all that destruction, I found peace.

Just as Knight's playful teeth found my earlobe, I heard a voice that was not his in the distance.

"Who the fuck is out here?" The voice was garbled and slurred and punctuated by what sounded like a shotgun being pumped.

Before I had time to react Knight had already slid off the side of the Cadillac, pulling my rigid body with him. We both ducked down beside the front tire as fear coursed through my veins, paralyzing every inch of me.

"I'ma shoot yer asses dead. Ya hear me! Yer on private property. I got rights, you sons a bitches."

I looked toward the fence where we'd come in. I might have

been able to shimmy underneath it in time, but there was no way Knight would be able to climb over the top without being seen. And possibly shot.

We were fucking trapped.

I looked at Knight, who had managed to pick up the bat without making a sound, and he looked at me. Playtime was over. Zombie eyes were back.

Neither one of us made a move, silently agreeing to stay hidden until the coast was clear. The sound of cursing and gravel crunching underfoot got closer, and I felt twin beads of sweat drip down my ribs and into my bra.

When the junkyard owner got to the top of the hill he stopped, just on the other side of the Cadillac. His shadow fell across my lap in the moonlight and spittle from his slurring mouth misted the air as he yelled, "Where the fuck are you at, you pieces of shit!"

Knight and I held our breath, waiting for the man to turn and go back down the hill. Just another few seconds and we'd be home free. We just had to wait him out for another few...

Fuck.

Black eyes, shining out from between two cars, met mine. Black beastly eyes, regarding us thoughtfully. Cujo tilted his head slightly, as if he were deciding whether or not to keep our secret. He was designed to be loyal to the bastard who fed him, but it was as if something in him wanted to protect the one who had shown him kindness as well.

Knight held his hands out, offering to give the mutt some affection in return for his silence. Cujo mulled over his offer, his black eyes shifting from Knight to the man behind us, then he crept forward, accepting Knight's offer.

Just before I could breathe out a sigh of relief, the tags on Cujo's collar jingled slightly, causing the shadow man's head—*and gun*—to swivel in our direction. Everything that followed happened in an instant.

Knight disappeared.

A shot was fired.

A man groaned.

A body fell.

The ground shook.

Sounds of struggle, muffled.

Grunts and crunching gravel.

Silenced by a loud crack.

Then another.

And another.

And another.

My hands on the cold earth.

My knees, crawling.

Peeking around the front fender.

Knight, standing over a bloated body.

Dark wetness, like motor oil, everywhere.

Cujo lapping it up.

Black eyes.

Zombie eyes.

The fence.

I shoved myself underneath feet first, pushing with my hands and scraping my back in my haste. Before I could get all the way through Knight cleared the top and pulled me the rest of the way out by my legs. We ran through the woods, the unlit streets, hand in hand. My lungs burned, my legs burned, but they kept pumping, desperate to keep up.

As soon as we made it into the alleyway I collapsed in a heaving, gasping heap onto the fire escape. Knight growled and smashed the bat into the wall at the bottom of the stairs, breaking it in half, then threw the handle at the dumpster at the end of the alley, causing an avalanche of crashes and clanks to echo between the two buildings.

Cut the yellow wire, BB. Quick! Knight's gonna blow!

I sat up, trying to act cool while still trying to catch my breath, and said, "Jesus. You sure know how to show a girl a good time."

Knight didn't laugh though. Instead he gripped his head with both hands and shouted, "Shut up! Shut the fuck up!"

His scream hit me like a fist, knocking me backward.

Knight turned his head and looked at me with pure venom in his eyes. Hatred.

"I killed him."

"What?" I asked, not processing his words.

"Are you fucking deaf? I killed him! I smashed his fucking head in! Look at me!" Knight spread his arms and turned to face me.

I looked. Really looked. Knight's eyes were crazed. His chest heaved under the place where it used to say LONSDALE on his hoodie. The place that was now smeared with something shiny and dark. And new veins bulged in his face, under skin that had been splattered with the same dark substance.

Knight looked exactly like a man who'd just beaten another man to death with a baseball bat. He looked like a monster, ready to feast on human hearts and howl at the moon. I wanted to tell him he was wrong. Tell him he hadn't just killed someone, but one look into his eyes told me to shut the fuck up. The blackness of his soul had overtaken his irises, and he looked more undead than ever.

"He pointed a gun at you." Knight jammed a blood covered finger in my direction. "He pointed a *fucking* gun at you!"

Knight was breathing heavy with rage and shaking from the adrenaline. He looked like he wanted to kill him all over again. Or me.

"Hey. It's over. Okay? Shhhhhh. It's over." I reached out slowly, like he did to that mangy dog, gauging his reaction before I pushed any further.

"Shhhhhh…" I touched my fingertip to the one he was still pointing at me, and watched as his face crumpled and his eyes squeezed shut.

"Shhhhhh…" I laced my fingers between his, and watched his breathing become shallow, as if he were fighting back tears. As if I were hurting him. Then suddenly he crushed my bony fingers between his and I became the one who was breathing through the pain.

Knight spoke just barely above a whisper, grimacing as he struggled to control his emotions. "Eighteen years. I've been fighting what I am for eighteen years, and tonight I fucking lost it." His grip on my fingers tightened even more, to the point that I had to bite the inside of my cheek to keep from whimpering in pain.

"I'm a fucking killer. I've always known it. I've thought about it since I was a kid. Dreamed about it. Drew about it. But I learned to control myself. I kept people away. I never let anybody get too close. Until *you.*"

Knight's eyes snapped open, and although they were glistening with unshed tears, they were positively murderous.

"You make me fucking *weak.*" Knight jerked me up by my crushed fingers and grabbed me by my biceps, squeezing them tighter than he probably realized.

"The thought of him pointing that fucking shotgun at you…" Knight shook me. "I want to kill him again for that!"

"Shhhhhh…" I whispered again, lifting my crushed fingers in an attempt to touch him. With my biceps pinned to my sides, the best I could do was touch his forearms. Knight rejected my comfort, shoving me backward the moment I made contact.

I grabbed the stair railing to stay upright, then instinctively began rubbing my arms with my hands, trying to coax the blood back into them.

"Why the fuck are you still here, Punk? I told you, I destroy everything! Fucking look at you!" Knight shoved a bloody finger in my direction again as his rabid eyes darted up and down the length of my body. "You were a kid! A freckle-faced fucking kid! And I took your innocence, burned it to the ground, and pissed on the fucking ashes. I shoved needles through your body. I fucked you. I cut you. I branded you with my name. And now I made you a fucking accomplice to murder!"

"Manslaughter," I blurted out, still rubbing my arms. "If it wasn't premeditated I think they just call it manslaughter."

"Why the *fuck* are you so calm?!" Knight screamed. "What is wrong with you?! You should be running for the fucking hills right now!" Knight pointed in the direction of the street behind us for emphasis.

"What do you want me to do?! Call the cops? Turn you in? That's not gonna bring him back, Knight. That's not gonna fix what happened. It's only gonna ruin more lives—yours and mine." Now I was the one pointing fingers.

"I know you think the worst of yourself," I continued, "but you're not some mindless killer. You saved my life back there, because you love me. So, no, I'm not running from you. I love y—"

Before I could continue my monologue about how we were in this shit together, the blood-soaked skinhead before me took two giant steps up the stairs, gripped the railing on either side of my body, and screamed into my face, "I WAS THE REASON YOUR LIFE NEEDED SAVING IN THE FIRST PLACE, YOU STUPID BITCH!"

I recoiled, and Knight brought his fists to either side of his head, wincing at his outburst. I wanted to slap him. Shove him. Scream at him. Not for yelling at me, but for beating up the man I loved from the inside out.

"Get the fuck away from me," Knight said more quietly, his eyes screwed shut, fists boring into his head.

"I'm not going anywhere without you." My words came out with more attitude than I intended.

Knight's eyes flew open and he grabbed me by my biceps again. Turning me to face the bottom of the stairs, Knight gave me a shove, causing me to stumble down the first few steps until I caught the railing and steadied myself at the bottom.

"GO!"

I turned and looked up at the seething, broken, bloody monster looming over me at the top of the stairs. I should have been afraid of him. He'd bruised the shit out of my arms—even through my puffy jacket—and might have fractured a finger or two, but I didn't care. The man I loved was coming unglued before my eyes and all I wanted to do was put him back together.

"Knight," I said quietly. "Don't do this. Please. You're beating yourself up. I get it, but don't push me away. I can help you." I could feel him shutting me out. Walling me off. "You...you need me."

With my words the old Knight came crashing back. Not the Knight I'd grown to love. Not the fuzzy-headed boy who wrote me love letters and drew me pictures and whose heartbeat always synchronized with mine whenever we were close. No, this was the version I met on the first day of school. Cold. Calculating. Staring down at his victim and considering his next strike.

Devoid of emotion, Knight announced, "You're right. I *need* you to get the fuck away from me."

"Knight, stop it."

"I wish I'd never met you."

"Knight."

"All of this shit happened because of you. You make me fuck-ing weak…" Knight's eyes roamed over my body, scowling at my appearance, pausing at my arms, which were undoubtedly smeared with blood from where he'd grabbed me. When he finally locked eyes with me again I grimaced, bracing myself for his final blow. "…And I make you way too fucking hard."

With that, Knight turned and headed inside. The sound of the heavy metal fire escape door slamming shut rattled in my ears for minutes before I actually registered that he was gone, and that I was all alone, in an alleyway, at God only knows what time, in downtown Atlanta.

I should have been upset about almost being killed twice in one night, or remorseful about the man who'd lost his life because of me, but what made me crumple and clutch myself and weep like a wet rag being wrung out was the fact that my first boyfriend, my first *love*, had just broken up with me.

When my sobs eventually subsided, I realized that my purse and all my stuff were still locked inside Knight's truck. I probably could have walked to the gas station and borrowed the phone—called Juliet or August or even my fucking mom—but I physically couldn't leave. I was tethered to the man on the other side of that door, and the invisible cord that linked us was stretched as far as it would go. I had no choice but to sit on the stairs, pull my arms and legs inside of Knight's jacket for warmth, and wait for him to come out.

When I woke up, I was disoriented. Wherever I was, it was not where I'd fallen asleep. I was warmer. My cheek was stuck to vinyl. And there were illuminated digital numbers above my head.

The break room.

I leapt up in a panic and tore through the shop looking for Knight, hoping I'd find him asleep in his tattoo chair or smoking out on the fire escape, but he was gone. The only sign that he'd been there at all was a pile of stuff on the floor by the back door. I flipped on the light in the hallway and I saw my backpack, my overnight bag, a stack of cash sitting on top of my purse, and a note scrawled on the back of a blank Terminus City Tattoo receipt that read:

GET THE FUCK OUT

That invisible cord that wouldn't let me leave earlier? Evidently Knight had chopped that fucker in half while I was sleeping.

Chapter 32

Knight ripped himself out of my life just as forcefully as he had pushed his way in. He stopped returning my calls. He stopped coming by his locker. He stopped smoking at the church between classes. And we didn't even have the same lunch period that semester.

He disappeared so entirely that for the first few days I thought he must have been arrested for manslaughter. I scoured the internet, my parents' newspapers, and the evening news shows but the only information I found said that a local junkyard owner had been killed in a "senseless act of violence" and that there were no leads. The police had set up an anonymous tip line in case anyone would like to come forward with information, but I knew they wouldn't be getting any calls. The only people who had any information about what happened were me, a dog, and a ghost. And none of us was talking.

Once I realized that Knight hadn't been arrested, I figured out that the only way to see him was to bolt out the door the second the dismissal bell rang and sprint to the back of the parking lot where his truck was parked. But seeing him was literally about all that I accomplished. Knight would walk right past me, climb into his truck, and drive away. Leaving me a shattered mess in his rear-view mirror.

I refused to give up though. I knew Knight loved me. I knew whatever he was doing he was doing to protect me. And I knew he was destroying himself from the inside out. I just had to show him that I was capable of loving him through it. That I was strong enough to handle him at his worst. He may have been able to push everyone else on the fucking planet away, but I wasn't everyone else. I was motherfucking Brooke Bradley. I was the bitch who jumped on her parents' bed until it broke because they wouldn't buy her a trampoline. I got what I fucking wanted. And I wanted Knight to let me love him again.

After a few weeks of crying myself to sleep every night, leaving notes in Knight's locker, calling Terminus City when I knew he'd be at work, and trying to beat him to his truck just so he could breeze past me like I wasn't there, I decided to up the ante. I was going to Peg's motherfucking house.

I felt like an asshole for doing it, but I asked August if I could ride the bus home with him. He and I wound up with the same lunch period again that semester, and we were the two saddest sacks of shit you'd ever seen. Although having me all to himself seemed to cheer August up a little bit, his black flop of hair and chipped black nail polish were still the perfect complement to my mood.

I swore I'd never hang out at his trailer ever again, but he did live pretty close to Peg...and a certain skinhead I was stalking. August agreed to let me ride home with him, but I could tell it hurt his feelings. I didn't mean to use him, but I know that's how it probably felt.

Goddamn it.

I hugged August hard once we got off the bus and thanked him profusely before stomping off in the direction of Peg's house. I cut through the woods between August's trailer park and Peg's neighborhood to shorten the trip, the tall pines casting a chilly, ominous blanket over an otherwise beautiful early-April afternoon.

I emerged from the woods in the cul-de-sac at the end of Peg's street. My backpack weighed me down, but in a good way. It felt like armor. And as I cast my eyes up the street at Knight's monolithic white monster truck, I knew I was going to need it.

I made my way up Peg's rickety front stairs and felt the blood drain from my extremities with every step. When I reached the top I could no longer feel my feet, nor my finger as it pressed the shiny new doorbell that Knight must have installed since the last time I'd been there. My empty stomach churned out a batch of fresh acid as I waited for the door to open.

When it did, the blood drained out of my face as well. The person who answered was not Knight. And it was not Peg.

It was Angel fucking Alvarez.

She didn't smile. She didn't invite me in. She raised her eyebrows, cocked her head to one side and said, "What the fuck do you want, bitch?"

What the fuck do I want?

"Um...I just want to talk to Knight," I replied, not masking my confusion in the slightest.

"Well, he don't wanna talk to you." Angel looked me up and down, her nose wrinkled in disgust.

"I just...we just need to talk about some stuff. Angel, please." I felt so ridiculous asking this person who didn't even know Knight, who had no idea what we'd been through, if I could come in and talk to my own fucking boyfriend. I wanted to shove her out of the way and find him myself. Honestly, I wanted to claw her eyes out and rip her two-tone hair out by the roots, but Angel was built like a brick shithouse and would have torn my ass limb from limb.

"I don't give a fuck what you need. Knight don't fucking love you no more, and he don't want yo ass here." Angel puffed up her ample bosom, draped in a low-cut L.A. Lakers jersey, and put her hands on her enviously full hips. "Now either you gon' leave, or I'ma make yo skinny ass leave."

I blinked at her in disbelief. Was he fucking Angel now? It had only been a few weeks. What the fuck had I missed?

"Angel, I don't know what you think—"

"Bye, bitch," Angel said, just before she slammed the door in my face.

While I might not have had much luck interacting with Knight—at school or anywhere else—Angel was suddenly more than happy to engage me. As were her hood rat friends. She and a handful of other baggy-jeans-and-big-hoop-earrings-wearing scrappers started waiting for me at my locker in the morning and between classes. They heckled me in the hallway and postured like they wanted to fight. Angel would say adorable things like, "Knight told me you can't suck cock for shit," and her friends would chime in with, "Angel might be pregnant."

I felt betrayed. I felt attacked. I felt unsafe and alone and heart-broken and borderline suicidal, but above all, I felt so fucking confused. This was the girl who said her brother and her friends would beat Knight's ass for bothering me. This was the girl whose brother's friend got the shit beat out of *him* against the side of her apartment by *Knight*. This was the girl whose brother might kill him if I quit paying Tony every month to keep his mouth shut. What the fuck had I missed? Suddenly they were in love? Knight went from trying to protect me from these people to serving me up on a fucking platter?

It didn't make any fucking sense, but my brain was also not

really functioning properly considering that it had been fueled exclusively by fear and grief for weeks. Not food. Or sleep. Or education. Those were luxuries of the past.

All I had left was August, the occasional hallway or phone conversation with Juliet, fading memories of a relationship that may have only existed in my head, and a fading tattoo on the inside of my ring finger.

Chapter 33

With Knight being out of the picture, Juliet's boyfriend extorting me for money, and August's house being off-limits, I was fresh out of options for after-school transportation. Which was actually totally fucking fine with me. I didn't want to talk to anyone anyway. I didn't want to laugh and drink cheap beer and watch daytime talk shows. All of that shit seemed so trivial now. Sitting on a curb for two hours every day studying and writing poems that no one would ever read sounded fanfuckingtastic.

Of course, it was April, which meant that I actually spent most of my after-school wait time huddled in the B hall doorway trying to stay out of the rain. I could have waited in the front office, but fuck if I was about to hang out in the same space as all of the school administrators smelling like cigarette smoke. I'd rather get drenched.

On one particularly monsoonish day, I was leaning up against the wall just inside the B hall doorway, reading *A Clockwork Orange*—which I'd convinced my Language Arts teacher was a perfectly appropriate piece of British literature for my book report—when one of the double doors burst open and almost squished me against the brick wall I was leaning up against. Luckily, my steel-covered toes took the brunt of the force rather than my face, but I still screamed and dropped my book like a little bitch.

The person who'd opened the door spun around, and immediately took what was left of my breath away. It was a boy. A cute boy. A really fucking cute boy with short black hair that was a little bit spiky on top. He was wearing a Nine Inch Nails T-shirt, black Dickies with a chain wallet, and black Converse. His eyes were open wide, in shock over almost crushing someone, and I could see that they were green, like mine. They also looked like they might be rimmed in eyeliner, like mine.

He was slender and stylish and beautiful and edgy and I wanted to be him and bang him all at once.

"Holy shit! I'm so sorry!" the green-eyed boy said, bending over to pick up my sopping wet paperback. Standing back up, he handed it to me, touching my outstretched hand as he asked, "Are you okay? I didn't even see you back there."

I didn't know if it was the jolt of being touched by a stranger or the embarrassment of almost being crushed by a door, but my face heated and my words faltered. I just stared into those big, pretty, green and black eyes and felt as if I were looking into a mirror. They were warm and familiar. Not icy. Not undead. They were very much alive, and they were blinking at me in concern.

Fucking speak, BB!

"I'm fine," I sputtered as I accepted the wet rag that used to be my book. "Thanks."

He smiled at my words, and my knees went a little weak. "Why are you thanking me? I almost killed you."

"I don't know," I laughed. "For this?" I held up the mushy book, which dripped down my hand and into the sleeve of my thermal undershirt.

The green-eyed boy raised one eyebrow in amusement. "You're thanking me for ruining your book?"

"No." I smirked. "I'm thanking you for picking up the book you ruined."

"How about you thank me after I replace it for you?" he said with a playful smile. "I think I have that book at home."

"Are you inviting me over?" I asked, batting eyelashes that, for the first time in a long time, hadn't had all the mascara cried off of them yet.

"I was going to say I could bring it to you tomorrow, but I like your idea better."

Oh my God!

My cheeks were on fire. I was making such an ass of myself.

"You can just bring it tomorrow," I backpedaled. "That's fine. I'm waiting on my ride, anyway."

"When is your ride coming?" he asked.

"Four thirty," I said.

He laughed and the sound made my insides squirm. "That's over an hour from now! Come on. Let's go."

"I don't even know your name," I teased. "You know, *stranger danger?*"

The hottie extended his hand in an exaggerated show of formality and said, "I'm Trevor. Trevor Walcott."

I straightened my back and choked down my giggles as I accepted his smooth, perfect hand. "Pleased to meet you, Trevor. I'm BB."

"I know who you are," Trevor said, not letting go.

I chased Trevor through the rain to a little black two-door Honda Civic in the student parking lot. He opened the door for me and knocked a bunch of empty drink cups and cigarette packs onto the floor so that I could sit down.

Such a boy.

On the way to his house Trevor told me that he'd just moved to Georgia from Detroit a few weeks ago. He said our school was really different from his old one. It was about three times bigger, and he'd had to stay for detention that afternoon for being late, which nobody gave a shit about at his old school.

As we pulled up to his house, a cute little blue-gray ranch in a neighborhood full of modest little ranches, Trevor explained that the house belonged to his mom's friend and they were just staying with her until they got settled. The way he shifted in his seat and cleared his throat when he said the word "friend" made me think that maybe his mom and her "friend" might be more than just friends.

What Trevor didn't tell me was where his dad was and why he and his mom moved across the country at the end of the school year. I got the feeling that Trevor had secrets. And I wanted him to tell me *all* of them. I could have propped my chin on my hands and listened to him talk for days. He was so pretty—almost feminine, especially with those eyes—but he carried himself with the masculine confidence of a star quarterback.

Trevor let us into the house and was greeted by a woman's voice coming from a back bedroom.

"My mom, um, hurt her foot, so . . . she has to stay in bed," he explained as he led me down a short hallway.

Okaaaay.

Trevor's room was a little messy, like his car, and had been decorated with a few Nine Inch Nails, Tool, and *The Crow* posters. He walked in and dropped his backpack on the floor, then made his way over to a bookshelf in the far corner of the room, next to his unmade bed. When he turned around Trevor was holding a much drier copy of *A Clockwork Orange*.

My face lit up. "Oh my God! You do have it!"

Trevor smiled back, all warm green and smoky black. "You know what's weird? I don't even know why I have it. I just noticed it when we moved."

"Must be destiny," I teased, moving a pile of dirty black clothes from his bed to his dresser so that I could have a seat. They smelled like boy. Not cologne. Not vegan deodorant. Not dryer sheets. Just maleness. I liked it.

"Must be," Trevor said, sitting down next to me and handing me the book. Our eyes locked, and I felt something very different than I was used to. Relief. When Knight looked at me it was like staring into the sun glinting off of an iceberg. Too bright. Too cold. Too clear and hard. These eyes were as easy to look at as my own. They were warm and friendly, rimmed in thick black lashes that I was close enough to tell were not accentuated by eyeliner—they were just that thick.

And they held secrets, just like mine.

Despite my interest in this mystery boy, I was still acutely aware that I was sitting on a bed with a guy I'd just met that hour, and there wasn't even a TV in the room. Just us, a book, and a bed.

Time to go.

I asked Trevor to drop me off at my mom's school, and we smoked and talked about music and movies on the way there. It was just like hanging out with Lance or Colton or August, only I actually liked Trevor's taste in music. It was a little dark, a little industrial, but it was way better than the sounds of people just screaming and breaking shit.

When Trevor pulled up in front of Peach State Elementary School I leaned over the gear shift and hugged him goodbye. I couldn't help it. He'd been the only bright spot in what would go down in history as the worst month of my life. I didn't even know if I'd ever see him again.

"*Now* you can thank me," Trevor said into my ear, competing with the sound of the rain pelting the car.

I smiled as I squeezed his neck. "Thanks for the book...and the ride."

I gathered my stuff up slowly, hoping he'd ask me for my number, something, anything, before I disappeared into the downpour.

"Hey, BB?"

My head snapped up way too fast. "Yeah?"

Trevor draped his arm over the back of his seat as he turned toward me. "You think you're gonna need a ride again tomorrow?"

Chapter 34

The next day I didn't think about Knight that much. I rolled my eyes and held up my middle finger when Angel's friend Tina called me a whore. I dragged Juliet's pregnant ass out to the church parking lot so that I could talk to her about Trevor while I smoked and paced. And I even made August laugh at lunch by doing an impersonation of Edward Furlong doing an impersonation of Eddie Vedder.

I kind of, almost, felt like myself again.

When the dismissal bell rang I didn't sprint out to the parking lot to torture myself by watching Knight and Angel leave together. I sprinted to the bathroom to check my makeup before dashing down B hall and out the double doors where destiny had dumped a cute green-eyed boy in my lap the day before. Even though I got there in record time, Trevor was already waiting for me.

And he was wearing a "Kiss Me Kiss Me Kiss Me" T-shirt.

Fuck me.

I walked up and said, "I'm gonna need that shirt, like right now. Give it."

Trevor smiled. "You're a Cure fan, too?"

"Oh honey, I'm *the* Cure fan. Hand it over." I flicked my fingertips at him, demanding the shirt off his back.

"You first," he said, calling my bluff.

I looked down at my shirt. I couldn't ever find band T-shirts in my size, so I'd bought a bunch of children's size large T-shirts and ironed band logos onto them. The one I was wearing had the Anthrax symbol on it, and the edges were starting to peel from my mom putting it in the dryer.

"Uh, I'm pretty sure you couldn't get one arm into this thing."

"Suit yourself," Trevor said with a shrug. He held out his arm for me to take, and I instantly became aware of our surroundings. If Knight saw me holding another guy's arm he would flip the fuck out.

Or would he? I mean, he didn't seem to give a shit about being seen with Angel. Or about how I felt about it.

You know what? Fuck it.

I linked arms with Trevor and walked toward his little black car, not a care in the goddamn world.

Trevor drove me to my mom's school, but instead of having him drop me off in front, I had him pull around to the parking lot by the playground. He sat on a bench with me while I waited for my mom to get off work.

"When do you get your license?" Trevor asked. I couldn't help but pick up on a twinge of uneasiness in his voice, like he was hoping I'd say never.

"My birthday is June second, so...like five or six weeks? I can't fucking wait."

"Do you know how to drive?"

I blinked at him.

"Um...well...I have my learner's permit...and my mom lets me drive us home whenever she's has too many margaritas at El Burro...and I haven't killed us yet."

"Oh shit," Trevor laughed. "Do me a favor and warn me whenever you're gonna be on the road, okay?"

I covered my face with my hands. "How did this happen?! Trevor! I don't know how to driiiive!"

"Come on." He stood up and held out his hand. "Let's go ruin my clutch."

I peeked at him from between my fingers and asked, "What's a clutch?"

Trevor was so sweet and patient while I spent the next hour and a half barking his tires and stalling out in the Peach State Elementary School parking lot. I'd never driven a stick shift before. That shit was harder than it looked. I'd finally gotten the hang of accelerating out of a rolling stop by the time my mom was ready to go, but dead stops were an entirely different story.

"I think we better practice some more tomorrow, for the sake of mankind," Trevor teased as I hugged him goodbye.

The next few days went the same way. Trevor let me practice driving his car while I waited for my mom to get off work. Evidently, driving around aimlessly with someone is a great way to get to know them. Trevor told me that his dad was the one who bought him the car and taught him how to drive a stick shift. His dad had said that it was important because once you know how a manual transmission works you can drive anything. His parents had recently gotten divorced—that's why his mom moved down here and his dad and older sister had stayed behind in Detroit. I could tell that Trevor missed them, even though he admitted that his dad had "anger issues."

I could relate. I knew all about loving a man with "anger issues."

By the end of the week I had gotten to where I could drive from Peach State High to Peach State Elementary all by myself without stalling out once. And I had gotten closer to the boy who, without even knowing it, was helping me find my way back to myself.

April melted into May, and the sunny days began to outnumber the rainy ones. Trevor and I didn't hang out at his house much. I got the sense that he liked being at his house about as much as I liked being at mine, so we mostly spent our afternoons sitting on the swings in the back of the wooded elementary school playground, smoking and talking.

One day Trevor sat in his usual swing, but as I walked past to take my spot next to him he grabbed my hips and pulled me into his lap. His arms around my waist made everything inside of me come back to life. I had missed being held so much. I leaned my head back on his shoulder and walked my toes back and forth across the ground beneath us as we swung gently. Trevor rubbed his cheek against my fuzzy shaved head and squeezed me tighter.

I wanted to kiss him. I wanted to thank him for being there, for bringing me back from the abyss. I stood up and turned around. Holding onto the chains of the swing for support, I placed my shins on either side of Trevor's hips and straddled him. He wrapped his arms around my back, smiled at me with those warm green eyes, and kissed me first. It was a lingering peck, no tongue, and it was the sweetest thing I'd ever experienced.

When I opened my eyes, I noticed that Trevor seemed on edge. He glanced to the left and right of us quickly before sliding his self-confident smile back into place and meeting my gaze.

"What's wrong?" I asked. "Are you afraid a teacher is going to see us?"

"Sorry, I just..." Trevor took a deep breath before continuing. "I met Knight today."

All the blood drained out of my face. Knight. *The* Knight. *My* Knight.

"Oh shit. Are you okay? Trevor, what did he do to you?" My eyes searched his face for any signs of injury. "I should have warned you about him—I'm so sorry—I honestly didn't think he'd care. He's seeing somebody else now."

That was the first time I had said those words out loud, and they reopened all the cracks in my heart that Trevor had just begun to glue back together.

He's seeing somebody else now. Somebody with tits. He doesn't love you anymore.

Trevor met my stare and said, "Oh, he cares."

"What did he do? Trevor, tell me."

"Don't worry about it," he said, plastering his charming smile back on. It did little to hide the fear in his earthy eyes though.

"Did he hurt you?"

"Nah. He just wanted to flex his muscles. Make sure I knew whose girl you were."

"I'm nobody's fucking girl," I spat.

How dare he? How motherfucking dare he! He's sticking his dick in Angel Alvarez and he has the balls to tell Trevor that I'm his girl?

Trevor swallowed and said, "BB, are you guys still…'cause if so, I'll back off. Just say the word."

"No! We're not anything! He's fucking psychotic, Trevor. Stay away from him, okay? I'm serious."

He'll kill you. I've seen him do it.

"So you guys aren't together?"

"No! Fuck no!"

"So I can do this again?" Trevor said, pressing his perfect lips to mine in another incredibly sweet closed-mouth kiss.

"Mmm hmm," I hummed against his lips, letting their warmth melt away some of my fear. Pulling away slightly, I added, "But maybe not at school, okay?"

"Okay," he repeated, kissing me again. "Only at school."

I smacked him on the chest, but Trevor only tightened his arms around my waist and kissed me deeper. His tongue slid across and twirled around mine as if we had all the time in the world. As if there wasn't a motherfucking target on his back. Knight only had three weeks left until graduation, so he probably wouldn't pick a fight at school, but if he saw Trevor off campus...I shuddered and opened my eyes mid-kiss, just to make sure there weren't cross-hairs on his forehead.

When Trevor's hands moved to my hips and his teeth tugged at my bottom lip, my worries scattered like dandelion petals in the warm spring breeze. I lost myself in the moment, allowing this beautiful, mysterious boy to temporarily distract me from my pain. It was selfish, putting him at risk like that. Trevor didn't know what he was getting himself into, but I did. I knew what Knight was capable of. I knew how easily he snapped. But in that moment, I needed Trevor's mouth on my mouth more than I needed all my tomorrows.

Or his.

Chapter 35

It doesn't even look like a knight anymore, I thought to myself, rubbing my tattoo in the middle of Language Arts class. The black silhouette had faded to a medium gray color, and the edges were beginning to disappear. I'd done some research and found out that tattoos on the palms of your hands and insides of your fingers aren't permanent. In fact, some only last a few months. That must have been why Knight put it there instead of the outside of my finger, like I'd wanted. That motherfucker knew it wouldn't last.

Just like he knew *we* wouldn't last.

The varsity football player who sat next to me and shamelessly cheated off all my tests leaned over and said, "You got some ink, Punk?"

Knight took weight training class with most of the football team, so my nickname had spread throughout the jock community. I think it was just easier for them to remember. *The chick with the shaved head = Punk. Got it.*

I held out my hand for him to see and whispered, "I used to."

The jock—I think his name was Jason—furrowed his thick brow trying to decipher the image. "What was it? A butterfly?"

I recoiled in horror and whispered back, "Fuck no! It was a knight."

"Oh. Oh! Like *Knight*! I get it."

Ding-ding-ding. Congratulations, dumbass.

I turned my hand back over and faced the front of the classroom, pretending to give a shit about Oxford commas, when the meathead leaned over again and asked, this time at least attempting to whisper, "Lemme ask you a question. Can he still…get it up?"

What?

I snapped my head around and narrowed my eyes at him. "What the fuck is that supposed to mean?"

Jason the Jock held up his hands and said, "No offense. I was just curious. With the amount of 'roids in that dude's system, I just figured his nuts would be shriveled up like raisins by now."

"'Roids? You mean, like steroids?"

The meathead chuckled and said, "Hell yeah. Don't tell me you didn't know. Your boyfriend is on the same shit as the pros. Hell, half the football team is. I thought about taking 'em too, but my sack is just too pretty to risk."

He may have said more, but I don't remember. I was too busy trying to see through my blinding anger. Steroids. Knight was taking motherfucking steroids. It made perfect sense—the violence, the rages, the hair-trigger temper, the muscles on top of muscles— but after the way he'd freaked out about me doing drugs? After confiding in me about his mom's drug abuse, his history of violence, he goes and starts taking *drugs* that make him *more violent*?

Was he on them when he almost choked Tony to death?

Was he on them when he beat Lance's face in?

Was he on them when he almost broke my fingers and shoved me down the fire escape stairs?

Was he on them when he killed a man and then blamed it on me for making him "weak"?

The dismissal bell hadn't rung yet, but I packed up my shit and walked out anyway. No more hiding. No more avoiding. No more fear. All I had pumping through my veins was blinding, deafening *fuck you* as I stomped down D hall to Knight's fourth-period classroom.

Chapter 36

When the dismissal bell rang, I was standing outside Knight's classroom, my chest tight, my skin crawling. I dropped my purse and backpack to the floor next to me to free myself up in case I needed to flee or fight.

No, not in case. *When.*

As soon as Knight crossed the threshold his zombie eyes locked onto mine and pure, unbridled malice shot out of them like poison daggers. He was so much bigger than I'd remembered. It had been weeks since I'd seen him up close, and the change in his appearance was glaring. His neck was just a series of cascading bulges leading to his shoulders, and the sleeves of his T-shirt had actually ripped to accommodate his swollen biceps. Johnny Football Team was right—Knight was on some serious fucking steroids.

The sight of him still knocked the wind out of me. I had expected to feel angry. I hadn't expected for my heart to implode in my chest all over again. My brain knew that I should hate him. That he was a piece-of-shit hypocrite who just wanted to torture me and make me bleed. But my hands didn't get the memo. They longed to touch his fuzzy head. My legs itched to wrap around his waist again. And my heart begged to be pressed against his just one more time.

Before I could catch my breath and attack, Knight beat me to it. Within seconds, he was towering over me screaming, "Did you fuck him? Did you? Did you suck his pretty little cock, Punk?"

Oh, hell no.

That was it. Knight's noxious rage cloud enveloped me, mixed with my own, and created something even more potent and destructive in me than I ever knew was possible. I was absolutely mad. Possessed.

I shoved Knight's chest as hard as I could, moving him a full foot away from me, and screamed back, "ME?! What about you and Angel?!"

"What about me and Angel?!"

A crowd of students began to form, a safe distance away, while the teachers all ducked back into their classrooms and shut their doors.

"Um, I'm pretty sure you're fucking her, that's what. Trevor only started giving me rides so that I wouldn't have to stand in the rain. *You*, on the other hand, are probably giving Angel a *ride* every night!" I jammed my finger in his rock-hard chest and tried to sound confident, but my hands were shaking so violently I probably looked like I was having a petit mal seizure.

Knight laughed, loudly, maniacally, then said in a sarcastic tone I'd never heard him use before, "Yeah, Punk. I'm fucking Angel. In fact, I usually fuck her doggie-style so that I can wrap all that long blonde hair around my fist and give it to her *hard*."

Angry tears blurred my vision as my hands clenched into balls by my side. I thought I knew agony. I had no idea. Knight's words impaled me. Gutted me. I could almost hear the sound of my heart seeping through my wounds and landing on the speckled tile floor with a wet smack. Everyone's eyes were on the flopping, gasping organ at my feet, but no one came to my aid. They just stood and waited for the death blow.

Along with my heart, my will to survive must have leaked out too. I was sick of being tortured. Sick of being afraid. And sick of biting my fucking tongue. If Knight was going to slay me where I stood, I'd at least get a few jabs in first.

"Oh really?" I spat. "I'm surprised you can even get it up with the amount of steroids pumping through your system."

Boom. Secret's out, motherfucker.

The shock on Knight's face fueled me. I'd wounded him, and I wanted to twist the knife before he got a chance to recover.

"Look at you, Knight—taking drugs that make you mean, sleeping with trash, hurting the only person who cares about you— your mom would be *so* proud."

Suddenly a hand was around my throat, my back was against the lockers, and my toes were barely touching the floor. I struggled to breathe, to get my eyes to focus on the monster in front of me, to make my arms beat against him. I struggled to process his words.

"Say it again! Say that shit again!" he screamed in my face.

My mind flashed back to the first time I ever saw Knight, screaming those same words to a scared little skater boy in the church parking lot.

I tried to bring myself back to the present, to fight, to claw, to kick, but my arms were too heavy. My legs were like lead. My eyelids wouldn't open anymore, and then, for a brief moment, it all went away. Stars danced around me as I floated, suspended in blissful nothingness.

From somewhere far away I heard the sound of a door slam, and it pulled me from the quiet twinkly place. I realized, slowly, that I was lying on the cold tile floor. With my eyes still closed I tried to reconnect with my body.

What hurts? Everything.

I opened my eyes to find dozens of shoes gathered around, all pointing in my direction.

A pair of gentle hands wrapped around my arms and sat me upright. My head felt like it was about to explode. Or already had. My throat hurt when I swallowed. And breathed. My tailbone was sore when I sat on it. And my elbow protested being touched. August's face swam into focus before me. He was crouched on the floor, touching my neck, softly probing. There was a deep crease in his brow, and his mouth was set in a hard line. August was angry. I'd never seen him angry before.

"August?" I choked out, my voice not sounding like my own.

August pressed his forehead to mine and took a deep breath.

Then he kissed me, right between the eyes.

"No!" I screamed, shoving him backward.

Oh, August! No, no, no! Knight will kill you!

I immediately came to my senses and scanned the faces of the kids in the hallway to see if there were any defectors in the crowd who might tell Knight what had just happened. The crowd dissipated quickly, pretending like they weren't fucking salivating over the whole goddamned spectacle, and I looked at my dearest friend with tears in my eyes.

"I'm so sorry," I whispered. "I'm so, so sorry."

August reached for my hand, cooing, "Hey, don't apolo—"

But I snatched my hand away and scooted backward across the floor. "Stay away from me! Stay away from me, August. I'm serious." I held my hands up and looked around again, paranoid that Knight was going to emerge from the shadows any second.

August looked about as heartbroken as I felt. "BB. You don't mean—"

"Go away. Please! Just go!"

The look of confusion and hurt on his face was like a self-inflicted stab to the gut. I didn't know what made me want to cry more—knowing that August was in pain, or knowing that I had to stay in pain. I wanted nothing more than to let August comfort me and put me back together, but for his own safety I had to reject his affection. Knight had even taken that away from me.

I hid the bruises on my neck with my jacket when my mom picked me up, but I couldn't hide the rivers of mascara streaming down my cheeks. I told her Knight and I had gotten into a fight. That he had screamed at me in the hallway while everyone watched. I told her that his new girlfriend and her friends had been tormenting me at school. I cried and shook and hyperventilated and cradled my aching elbow the entire way home.

My mom just rubbed my thigh and shushed me like a baby and told me I could stay home for the rest of the week. Told me to stay away from "that asshole." When we walked inside she took me upstairs, gave me a Xanax, wiped the makeup off my face with a hot washcloth, and tucked me into bed. She kissed me on the same spot that August had kissed, and within minutes I was blessedly tranquilized.

I woke up hours later to the sound of my cell phone ringing. It was Trevor. He'd just heard what had happened. He wanted to know if I was okay. He was sorry he didn't come look for me when I didn't meet him outside. He said he'd called a few times, but I never answered, so he left. He felt like shit about it. He asked if there was anything he could do. But we both knew there wasn't.

No one could help me.

Trevor told me his mom was letting him have a graduation party on Friday. I'd been such a self-absorbed asshole I didn't even realize he was graduating. He asked me if I wanted to come.

"Are you kidding?" I asked, incredulous. "After what happened today? Aren't you afraid to be seen with me?"

"Well, I was thinking that maybe we could just keep it friendly at the party, but then, after everybody leaves, if you want, maybe you could spend the night?"

I knew if I showed up at that party there was a good chance that I'd be delivering hell right to Trevor's front door, but my need to feel Trevor's hands on me again—to escape into the sweet oblivion he was offering—was stronger than my need for self-preservation. I'd rather die trying to feel better than live in misery.

"Okay," I said.

"Okay? You'll come?"

I laughed at the enthusiasm in Trevor's voice, then immediately winced in pain. "Okay," I said, tenderly rubbing my neck. "I'll come."

Chapter 37

I didn't leave the house for three days. My mom called the school and told them I was sick, and I told my work the same story. It wasn't a lie. I *was* sick—sick and fucking tired. I mostly stayed in my room—smoking, writing poetry, and either destroying or hiding every shred of evidence I could find that Ronald McKnight had ever existed.

My dad made me lunch every day, which I barely touched, but it forced me to at least come downstairs. My dad didn't really know what to say about the whole boy situation, so he basically filled the silence by telling me about all the awful things that were happening in other parts of the world. In a twisted way, it cheered me up. I mean, things really could have been a lot worse. I could have lost my entire family to genocide.

That Friday I spent most of the day primping for Trevor's party. I wanted to look like a girl for a change, to remind him what his boy parts were for. I shaved my whole body, buzzed my hair shorter, trimmed my bangs, and bleached my strawberry hair blonde. While I waited for the bleach to develop I must have weighed myself at least three times.

Ninety-five pounds. Not bad.

Once my hair was done, I applied concealer to the greenish bruises on my neck and at least fourteen coats of black liquid eyeliner and mascara to my well-rested eyes. I considered wearing the only skirt I owned—the plaid wraparound that fastened with safety pins—but I just...couldn't. The last time I'd worn that thing I ended up losing my virginity to a zombie-eyed boy in a torrent of pain and blood and honey. I didn't want those memories haunting me tonight. I wanted to make new ones. So I grabbed my skintight fuzzy tiger-striped stretch pants instead—they made my ass look good—and pulled a lacy black camisole over my bright red Wonderbra. I finished the look off with some bright red lipstick and matching nail polish. I never wore lipstick, so to me that was about as girlie as it got.

I'd told my mom that I was still going to spend the night at Juliet's house, *like I did every Friday* (wink, wink), and said that Juliet and Tony were going to come pick me up after school. But it wasn't Tony's Corvette waiting for me in the driveway at three o'clock. It was Trevor's little black Civic.

As soon as I saw him pull into our long, wooded driveway I ran downstairs and poked my head into the living room to give my dad an obligatory wave goodbye. He was playing guitar with his headphones on, but paused long enough to wave me over for a hug. I squeezed him quickly, then flew out the front door and into Trevor's idling Honda.

"Go, go, go!" I said as I slammed the door shut behind me. I didn't think my dad would get up and check to see whose car I was getting into, but I didn't want to press my luck either.

Trevor did as I said, backing down my skinny driveway at top speed before flipping the little coupe around and taking off down the street. I watched the front windows of my house for any signs of movement until the woods swallowed them up. Then I relaxed into my seat.

Turning to face Trevor, I finally said, "Hey."

"Hey," he said back, casting me a quick glance and a smile. "You doing okay?"

"Yeah," I said, not wanting to talk about it. "I missed you."

Trevor stopped at a red light and turned toward me. "I missed you, too." Tucking one of my longer side pieces of hair behind my ear, he said, "I like your hair. It's lighter."

"Thanks."

"I like your lipstick too. It's gonna look good smeared all over my face in a minute."

"Oh shit." I blushed. "I didn't even think about that. I knew there was a reason why I never wear this stuff."

Trevor smirked at me as the light turned green. "Maybe it'll make me look like Robert Smith."

"Ooh, maybe I should stock up then."

When we got to Trevor's house we spent the first hour just rolling around and making out on his bed. He discovered my nipple piercings (I'd put the winged barbells back in. The hearts just depressed me.) and acted like it was the sexiest thing he'd ever seen.

Three days away from my problems and three full nights of sleep (thanks to the Xanax my mom was probably crushing into my Diet Cokes) had me feeling better, but Trevor Walcott telling me my nipple piercings were sexy had me ready to fucking party.

The keg arrived just as I was considering taking Trevor's pants off. He had the guy set it up on the front porch, and Trevor took the invoice to the master bedroom for his mom to sign.

Fucking weird.

People started trickling in around six, and almost everyone brought party favors. Pizza or booze or weed or pills. One guy walked in carrying a blonde blow-up doll under his arm.

It really is just like on TV, I thought.

Trevor didn't know most of the people there, but he didn't care. He just smoked whatever was passed to him, kept his red Solo cup full, and mingled. I'd never seen somebody so cool and confident in a crowd full of strangers before. I, on the other hand, was ready for everyone to get the fuck out so that we could finish what we'd started in his bedroom.

I wandered outside to smoke and get some air when I noticed August standing in the driveway by himself. I watched him as I refilled my cup at the keg. He looked terrible. He'd lost a ton of weight but hadn't gotten any new clothes, so everything just hung off of him. He swayed on his feet—as if he were already sloppy drunk—and puffed on a cigarette that had at least an inch of ash hanging off the end. And even in the darkness I could see that he'd let his chestnut brown roots grow out longer than ever.

I hadn't spoken to August since I'd flipped out and pushed him away from me at school earlier that week. I didn't know what to say, but I figured it would come to me once I got over there.

I didn't get over there though.

Just as I stepped off the porch Trevor came bursting through the front door and announced, "There she is!"

I turned around at the sound of his voice and was immediately scooped off my feet by a very happy Trevor Walcott.

"I missed you," he mumbled into my neck before putting me back down.

I smiled up at him and said, "I missed you, too." Then, pulling on the back of his neck so that he would lower his ear to my mouth, I drunk-whispered, "I can't wait for you to kick all these fuckers out."

Trevor immediately stood back up and yelled, "Everybody! Get the fuck out!"

The crowd outside laughed and cheered, then resumed their rowdy side conversations.

Trevor bent back down and whispered, "I think you're gonna have to do it. Nobody fucking listens to me around here."

I cracked up. Oh my God, it felt good. I hadn't laughed in days—probably since the last time I'd hung out with Trevor. As my giggling subsided, I noticed August walking past us and into the house. I made a mental note to go in and talk to him—just as soon as I smoked the cigarette I'd come outside for.

I stuck the Camel Light into my mouth, and then I heard it.

At first I thought it was just in my head, but as the rumble grew louder and those headlights rounded the corner onto Trevor's street, I knew. Ronald McKnight—'roided-up archfiend from hell—was coming for me, and all I could do was stand trapped inside my paralyzed body and silently scream at myself to run.

Trevor, oblivious to my impending doom, lit the cigarette hanging out of my slack-jawed mouth, then slapped at all of his pockets, muttering something about losing his pack. He went back inside the house to find it, leaving me all alone. As usual.

Maybe he won't kill me in front of all these witnesses, I thought. *Maybe he'll just almost kill me. Maybe he'll just almost kill me . . .*

As Knight's monster truck screeched into Trevor's teenager-filled cul-de-sac, my heart slammed itself against my rib cage as if it were trying to escape.

Stay here and die if you want, it said, *but I'm getting the fuck out!*

But it wasn't Knight who leaped from the roaring monstrosity before it had even come to a complete stop. It was Angel. And she was running straight for me, screaming obscenities and flailing her arms like a wild, flaming banshee.

As she approached, my mind oscillated between fear over my imminent death and confusion about why the hell Angel would want to jump *me* when *she* was the one fucking *my* boyfriend.

While my mind spun, trying to connect whatever dots I had obviously missed, my body braced for impact. Angel's red eyes and bared teeth closed in on me, but just as she was about to attack, she disappeared. I looked down to find her body on the ground at my feet, then watched in disbelief as it rose before my eyes and began moving backward—shrieking, kicking, and thrashing in midair. It was as if someone had pressed the Rewind button on my worst nightmare.

I just stood there and stared in a stunned stupor. As I squinted into the darkness, the silhouette of a monster finally came into view. The creature was wearing a black hoodie and was shoving Angel's writhing body back into the truck with the force of a thousand men.

As they peeled away, it slowly dawned on me that I was not going to die. I blinked and looked around, realizing that everyone had come outside, including Trevor, who had been watching the spectacle from the safety of the front porch.

He hadn't tried to protect me.

He left me out there to die.

Trevor didn't fucking care about me. He was just like everybody else—too chickenshit to stand up to Knight, but too voyeuristic to look away.

Everybody except for August, who was nowhere to be seen.

I picked my cup up off the driveway—I didn't even remember dropping it—and pushed my way through the crowd over to the keg. Trevor reached for my arm as I passed him, but I snatched it away.

"Are you okay?"

I ignored him. I wasn't giving those fuckers two shows in one night. I was going to get wasted, and I was going to bed.

"BB, come here." A hand pulled on my still-sore elbow from behind.

"What?" I snapped over my shoulder.

"Talk to me."

I huffed and threw my empty cup to the ground—that time on purpose—and let Trevor pull me into the house, down a hallway, and into a tiny bathroom. We didn't do much talking, though. We mostly tore each other's clothes off.

I was pissed off—at him, at Angel, at Knight, at the whole fucking world—but when I was in Trevor's arms I at least felt better than when I wasn't. So I assumed that getting into his pants would make it all just go away.

I unfastened Trevor's belt and fly, desperate to lose myself in him, and discovered, much to my surprise, that he wasn't even hard. Not even a tiny little bit.

Trevor blew out a breath and tilted his head back in frustration. "Goddamn Lithium."

I looked up at him with my eyebrows pulled together. "You took Lithium tonight?" Even I knew that wasn't a party drug.

"No, I *take* Lithium," he said, zipping his pants back up. "For depression. And cutting."

"Jesus. You cut yourself?"

"Not since I started on the Lithium, but…it has side effects. Especially when I drink."

I should have felt bad for the guy, but I didn't. I couldn't. I had come there looking for comfort and sweet fuck all, but instead all I found was a houseful of pussies who wouldn't stand up for me, and one in particular who couldn't even *get it up* for me.

I was done. I waited until Trevor disappeared into the crowd of delinquents in his living room, then I grabbed my shit and walked to Juliet's house. It was at least two miles away, but I let my utter, soul-crushing disappointment in the human race fuel me.

When I got to her house it was well after midnight, so I used the key under the planter to let myself in. I tiptoed to Juliet's room, pulled off my boots, and crawled into bed with what felt like my last remaining friend.

The next morning Juliet seemed happy to see me. While I got ready for work I told her everything that had happened the night before, and she told me that things hadn't been going that great with Tony, either. The more she tried to talk to him about getting his shit together for the sake of the baby, the more he seemed to be hiding things from her. Just the night before Tony had left with Carlos Alvarez and, obviously, hadn't come home yet.

Man, I felt like an asshole. I thought I had problems. Juliet had just turned sixteen and she was about to have a fucking baby with a gang-affiliated drug dealer. How was that for perspective?

Juliet drove me to work in Tony's Corvette. Her belly barely fit behind the wheel. She drove like a paranoid grandma, but when Madonna's "Holiday" came on the radio we cranked that shit up and sang at the top of our lungs, and—for one fleeting moment—allowed ourselves to act our age.

I hugged Juliet *and* her big belly when she dropped me off in front of Pier 1 Imports and told her that I loved her. I don't know why. I just felt like she needed to hear it. As she pulled away, I could have sworn I heard the sound of Knight's engine roaring in the distance. I froze like a deer in headlights—listening, looking—but the sound got farther away instead of closer.

Oh, thank God.

I blew out a breath and headed into work, eager to focus on something meaningless for a change.

Chapter 38

After a few hours at work, I ducked outside for a smoke break and saw that I had six missed calls and three voicemails, all from Trevor. *Jesus.* I listened to the voicemails right away, expecting to hear, "*Where did you go last night? I was worried sick. Blah, blah, blah,*" but instead Trevor was asking about August. He wanted to know if I'd heard from him, if I knew where he was.

In his last voicemail Trevor simply said, "Call me."

I called him back with a boulder in the pit of my stomach. Trevor answered on the first ring.

"BB?"

"Sorry I'm just now calling you back. I'm at w—"

"Did you hear about August?" he interrupted.

"Um, no. What about August?" I asked, the boulder in my stomach turning into bile.

"Shit. BB ... August is dead."

BB.

August.

Dead.

"What?" I heard myself ask.

"I'm so sorry. I know he was your friend. I guess at some point last night he left the party, and he...he killed himself."

"How?" I needed more information. Nothing was making any sense.

"He jumped off the water tower. The cops found his body this morning."

The world was spinning out from under me. "Can I come over?"

"I, um, I don't think that's such a good idea." Trevor's voice sounded distant and shaky.

Oh no. No, no, no.

"Trevor, did Knight come back last night? After I left?"

Trevor was quiet for a long time and then finally said, "I just... we just can't, okay?"

"What did he do to you? Trevor, tell me what happened!"

Silence.

"Trevor?!"

"He didn't do anything, okay? It's just that...he will. He saw you at my house, BB. He knows where I live now. If we keep seeing each other...I mean, what do you want me to do? I can't fight that guy."

I couldn't believe my fucking ears. Every word out of Trevor's mouth was like a fresh knife to the gut.

"So let me get this straight," I seethed. "You basically called to tell me that my childhood best friend is dead, and, *oh by the way*, you're breaking up with me because you're too chickenshit to stand up to my ex-boyfriend. Does that about sum it up? Anything else you want to throw on the pile?"

"I'm sorry," Trevor said. "For what it's worth, I really am sorry. But, before you hang up on me, there is one more thing I have to tell you."

"Jesus fucking Christ. Just say it!"

"August left you a note."

Chapter 39

I offered to sign my entire paycheck over to my coworker if she'd let me borrow her car. She was a single mom with a pile of medical bills from a sick kid, so I knew she needed the money. I told her I'd bring it back in a few hours, but she said she didn't need it until she got off work that night. I thanked her profusely as she handed me the keys to her piece-of-shit Pontiac Grand Prix.

"Do you even have your license, honey?" Lisa asked, looking at me over the top of her crooked glasses.

"Of course," I lied. "Thank you so much, Lisa."

"Don't thank me, thank God. I was just praying to Him this mornin' to help me pay my light bill, and this money's done answered my prayer. Lord, thank you, Jesus!"

Lisa pulled me in for a hug. "You be careful, sugar."

I thanked her again and dashed out to her car. I went to look for the clutch, but realized that Lisa's car was an automatic.

Lord, thank you, Jesus.

I drove straight to Trevor's house, my last few moments with

August playing over and over in slow motion in my head. Me not talking to him at the party. Me pushing him away at school. Me *not* asking why he'd lost so much weight. Me *not* riding the bus home with him anymore.

By the time I got to Trevor's house I was racked with guilt and fighting to hold back my tears. I didn't want to cry yet. I didn't want to accept it.

I pulled up to his mailbox and parked. Trevor told me he'd just leave the note in there. Motherfucker was too much of a pussy to even talk to me face-to-face.

Inside the metal box I found a folded-up piece of paper taped to a folded-up piece of clothing. I pulled off the note and spread the soft black cotton out on Lisa's passenger seat. It was Trevor's Kiss Me Kiss Me Kiss Me T-shirt.

The lump in my throat swelled.

I looked at the folded paper in my hand and noticed a note written in not-August's handwriting on the outside.

Dear BB—
I found this note in the kitchen this morning while I was cleaning up from the party. My mom called the cops and they found August's body pretty quickly. I tried to save the original note for you, but the cops needed it for evidence. That's why this one is in my handwriting.

For what it's worth, I really am sorry. About everything.

Trevor

PS—I won't tell anybody what it says. I promise.

I stared at the folded paper in my hands, hoping that it would magically open by itself. I couldn't make my hands work. They weren't ready to show me what was inside. Reading it would make it real, and I didn't want it to be real. It couldn't be real.

Instead my hands reached of their own accord, shifted the car into drive, and grasped the steering wheel.

I drove straight to the water tower. I can't remember if I stopped at a single stop sign or traffic light. I don't even know how Lisa's old Grand Prix made it up the hill. All I know was that one minute I was in Trevor's driveway and the next I was staring out a dirty windshield at a yellow strip of tape that was shouting POLICE LINE: DO NOT CROSS at me in all capital letters.

The foggy mist of denial cleared away, revealing a simmering volcano of anger underneath. That tape enraged me. It told me what I didn't want to know, and it did it by screaming it directly into my face. Why did they have to make the police tape so aggressive? Didn't they realize that somebody's baby boy just died? Somebody's oldest friend? Why couldn't the tape be a somber shade of gray and just say WE'RE SO SORRY FOR YOUR LOSS on it?

And where the fuck were all the teddy bears?! There was a fucking protocol! A kid from your school dies, you go to the site of the event, bring some friends to cry on, maybe pass out some candles with those little paper wax-catching things on the bottom, sing "Kumbaya," and LEAVE A FUCKING TEDDY BEAR ON

THE GROUND. Where were all the weepy teens? Where was the Channel Five news team? Where were August's teddy bears? August deserved fucking teddy bears!

All there was on the top of that hill was a patina-green water tower, that bitchy fucking police tape blocking my path, and what I'm sure was probably a huge red stain on the brown Georgia clay behind it. Oh, and a folded-up piece of paper with not-August's handwriting on it smashed between my hand and the steering wheel.

I rolled the driver's side window down before I read it. I don't know why. Maybe to help me breathe.

Dear BB,

You're the only person who ever really cared about me, so I had to at least tell you goodbye. I don't want you to be sad, but I can't do this anymore. Every morning when I wake up I wish that I hadn't. Everything hurts, all the time, and I just want it to stop.

I always thought that one day you and I would end up together. I loved you, BB. You were my best friend. But I realized a few months ago that I wasn't in love with you. Because I'm gay. I didn't tell anyone because I didn't want it to be true. I fell for a boy who broke the parts of me that weren't already broken. He used me up until there was nothing left. Nothing but the pain.

I see you wasting away. You're killing yourself over a guy too. You just don't realize it yet. But you're stronger than me. You'll be happy again, like you were before. When I saw you laughing with Trevor tonight I knew that you were going to be OK. That's all I wanted to see. I couldn't leave without making sure that you were going to be OK.

Thank you for seeing me when no one else did. If you ever feel like no one sees you, I'll be there. I'll see you, I promise. I just won't be hurting anymore.

Your friend forever,
August

I don't even know if I read the last few lines correctly—they were so blurry through my tears. I clutched the paper and tried to process what I'd just read. August thought I was going to be okay?

What the fuck about my life was okay? How was I supposed to be okay when he was gone? I read the note three, five, fifteen times, then I ripped it into little pieces and screamed into the humid afternoon stillness.

I got out of the car and slammed the door, glaring at that fucking police tape. Grabbing a sturdy-looking stick off the ground, I took the sharp end and stabbed and gouged and mutilated the hard Georgia clay right in front of that callous yellow strip of pain until my muscles ached and my anger gave way to sorrow.

I sprinkled the scraps of August's letter inside the hole, covered it back over with dirt, and used my stick to carve a heart with our initials in it on top of the mound. When I was done, I sat on the ground next to my friend's buried confession—probably twenty feet away from where he left his body when he decided he couldn't drag it around any longer—and said the only prayer I knew.

Our Father who art in heaven, hallowed be thy name.
Thy kingdom come. Thy will be done on Earth as it is in heaven.
Give us this day our daily bread, and forgive us our trespasses
As we forgive those who trespass against us.
Lead us not into temptation, but deliver us from evil.
Amen.

Chapter 40

I sat in the Grand Prix and stared at my phone. I needed to tell somebody about August, but who? Lance and Colton were his friends, but I didn't even have their numbers. I didn't even really know where Lance was. Juliet was the only person I could think of who might care, so I took a deep breath and hit the *Send* button.

Juliet answered, but before I could even tell her what happened she started flipping out about Tony. She said she went home and took a nap after she dropped me off and when she woke up his car was gone. He must have come home and left again without even telling her where he was going. And the sonofabitch still wasn't answering her calls.

I wanted to be there for her, but it was kind of hard to give a fuck about her loser boyfriend when I was staring at the place where my friend had just taken his own life.

"Did he say where he and Carlos were going last night?" I asked, trying with all my might to care. To be a better friend to her than I had been lately.

"All he said before he left the house was, 'It's payday, baby.' Whatever the fuck that means."

Payday.

Tony's words rang out in my ears. *From now on, the fifteenth's gon' be* my *payday...You forget about good ol' Tony when you cash that check, and I'ma forget we had this conversation.*

"Juliet, what is today's date?"

"The sixteenth. Why? Are you even listening?"

The sixteenth.

"Um, I'm sorry. I just...August killed himself last night."

I don't remember the rest of the conversation.

I'd missed payday.

I had to warn Knight.

I hated that I still felt responsible for protecting him—for saving him from himself—even after everything he'd put me through. I hated that I wasn't strong enough to walk away from him, the way he'd been able to walk away from me. I hated that no matter how long it had been since I'd seen him or how badly he'd hurt me, I still had to fight the urge to run into his arms and stroke his fuzzy head and try to make him smile *that* smile whenever I saw him.

I called Knight's number with trembling fingers—the number he had programmed into my phone the day he made Tony want to kill him in the first place. It went straight to voicemail. I left a message letting him know that Tony and Carlos might be after him and to please let me know that he was safe.

Maybe he's not picking up because he thinks I'm going to scream at him about what happened last night.

Or maybe he's not picking up because he's too busy fucking Angel doggie-style.

Or maybe he's at work.

That had to be it. Knight always worked on Saturdays. I cranked up the Grand Prix and careened back down the hill and onto the highway and into the city.

When I pulled into the parking lot behind Terminus City Tattoo I immediately noticed a complete and utter lack of monster trucks. I glanced at the clock in the dashboard. 4:42. Knight should have been there.

I walked through the alleyway, past the dumpster that Knight had dented with a bloody baseball bat, past the fire escape where he told me he wanted to marry me, and around to the front of the building—where people who *aren't* girlfriends of the artists should probably enter—passing half a dozen empty bowls along my way.

Empty bowls.

The place was slammed. There was a body in every tattoo chair, at least that I could see from the front reception area, and several folks were sitting in the waiting area flipping through flash art albums. I couldn't see Knight's station though. It was hidden from view by the wall that divided the reception area from the main studio.

I thought my heart was going to pound its way out of my chest.

What if he's here?

Oh God, what if he's not here?

I swallowed hard and ran my sweating palms over my jeans.

"We don't take fake IDs here, little girl." The voice coming from behind the front counter sounded feminine, but it came out of a broad, masculine-looking human with tattoos all over his Bic-bald head.

That must be Bobby.

"Um, hi. I'm a friend of Knight's—I mean, Ronald's—is he... working today?"

Bobby scowled and said, "Fuck no. That piece of shit no-call-no-showed on me. If you hear from him, you tell that asshole I'm docking his pay for all the time I spent rescheduling his clients."

I had to read Bobby's lips. Everything after the word *no* had been drowned out by the sound of blood thrumming in my ears. Knight wasn't there. He hadn't even called. I missed payday and now Knight and Tony were both missing.

I nodded at the person making the words that I could no longer hear and slowly backed away until my hand found the door handle. As soon as the warm, stagnant, almost-summer air hit my lungs, I bolted. I ran around the side of the building to the entrance of the parking lot, but my legs didn't stop.

They carried me past the parking lot, away from the shops and bars, and into the wooded surrounding neighborhood, full of crumbling bungalows and old Victorians. When my lungs began to burn from trying to extract oxygen from that viscous air, I slowed to a walk, but I still couldn't fight the force propelling me forward.

I'm sure I looked like any other teenaged junkie on the streets of Little Five Points. Pale. Emaciated. Running from something too painful to face. Chasing something too painful to give up.

Then, just as suddenly as I'd started running, I stopped. When I looked up I realized that I was standing at the entrance of the path that led to the junkyard fence. My feet had carried me back to the scene of the crime.

How fucking cliché.

Emotionally drained, physically exhausted, and excruciatingly hungry, I slumped against a tree next to the fence and thought about the night that everything went to shit.

Maybe this is karma, I thought. *Maybe the universe is taking away the people I love to punish me for what happened here.*

I deserved it. I had been more concerned about my boyfriend breaking up with me than I had been about the innocent man whose brains had been splattered all over the ground on the other side of that fence. I was more devastated about August taking his own life than I was about the one Knight had taken just a few feet away from where I stood. I was the only person who could have brought his killer to justice, but I'd let him go free without a second thought. The guilt I felt over not feeling guilty enough gnawed away at my empty stomach.

My mind conjured image after image from that night like some kind of macabre slide show. The fence, the dog, the Cadillac, the baseball bat, the man, the shotgun, the sounds, oh God, *the sounds*, the running, the running, the running, the alley, the blood.

Struggling to stay in the present, I shook my head and tried to find something to focus on, something real. My eyes drifted over to where the Cadillac had been. The one we thrashed. The one we cuddled on. The one I hid behind while Knight killed its owner. It wasn't there.

My surprise over the Cadillac's disappearance lasted only a second or two before being replaced with cold, paralyzing dread when I realized what had been parked in its place.

No. Fuck no. That's impossible.

I stared at my phone, clutched in hands that I didn't even know were shaking, and waited for my brain to access the instructions for how to make a call. When I finally figured it out, the sound of Juliet's voice on the other end felt like a lifeline, tethering me to reality.

"Have you heard from Tony yet?" I blurted out.

"No."

Juliet's tone was a lot less pissed off and a lot more concerned than it had been earlier. She began spiraling about *What if something happened to him?* and *What if he got hurt?* and *The baby is due any day now*, but I wasn't listening. How could I access my ears when I wasn't even in my body? My consciousness was sitting on a tree branch overhead, staring down at a faded red blood stain marking Knight's first kill and a faded red 1980 Corvette, possibly marking his second.

"BB?"

. . .

"BB!"

"What? I'm sorry. I..."

"What if he got in a car accident?!"

"I...I don't know. I don't know what's going on. Can I come over?"

"Yes. Please. Now. All I've been doing is calling Tony's phone nonstop."

I told her I'd be there soon and robotically ended the call, never once taking my eyes off the faded red Corvette on the other side of the fence. As I stood there—unmoving, unfeeling, unblinking, unbelieving—I heard something melodic in the distance struggling to cut through the thick mid-May air.

It was the sound of a phone ringing, no louder than a whisper, and it was coming from *inside* Tony's car.

Chapter 41

I ran. As fast as my empty stomach, lack of sleep, and steel covered toes would carry me, I ran. I found my way back to the parking lot using the route Knight and I had taken so many weeks ago, and once I was safely inside Lisa's Grand Prix I slammed the door, gripped the steering wheel with both hands, and screamed.

When I stopped screaming the passenger door opened and someone got in. I blinked and tried to swallow down my panic as a thousand long black braids—and one very big belly—filled the passenger seat.

Juliet? How the fu—

I looked around and noticed that I wasn't in the parking lot anymore. I was idling in Juliet's driveway. The confusion I felt was the same as when I'd taken crank or acid or ecstasy—like time and space just suddenly decided they weren't going to play by their old rules anymore. I could blink and lose an hour or I could have an entire conversation in a minute. But I wasn't on drugs.

So this is what a mental breakdown feels like, I thought. *Interesting.*

I looked at my friend through eyes that felt like they belonged to someone else. Like I was in that movie *Being John Malkovich,* and I was inside a stranger's body, observing her life with detached curiosity.

Oh look. That must be BB's best friend. Hmm...She looks really pregnant. I wonder why she's wearing a bathrobe. And crying. Maybe because there's blood on the bathrobe. She's looking at BB, and her mouth is moving. She must be telling her about the blood. She seems scared. Now she's twisting her face up and breathing hard like somebody just stomped on her foot. BB should take her to the hospital. I wonder if I can make BB's body do that.

The interior of the car might as well have been the cockpit of an alien spaceship. *Okay, let's see...that's a steering wheel. And BB's hands are on it. Good. Those are the pedals down there, and that stick thingie—that needs to move, I think. BB, if you can hear me, move the stick thing down to the* R. *You did it! Now put your foot on the other pedal and press gently. Good girl!*

While I managed to get Lisa's car to Juliet's house practically by teleportation, the trip to the hospital felt like it took two weeks. I was trying to drive a body and car at the same time—neither of which were very user friendly—while somewhere in the back of my mind I tried and failed to process the situation in my passenger seat.

There was a girl there. Making loud noises. She was hurting. Yes. She needed help. I would get her help. I would make BB's body make the car go to the place where she would get help.

"Just turn in here!"

Words. I heard her words.

I looked at Juliet as she pointed out the windshield, and my hands naturally turned the steering wheel in that direction. I looked back at my hands in disbelief. They were working on their own again!

I pulled Lisa's car into the first empty parking spot I saw, and smiled when my hands automatically put the stick thingie into the *P* position and shut off the ignition.

My passenger door opened, but Juliet didn't get out. She had her feet on the pavement, but she was still sitting, grasping the door opening and doing that breathing thing she did when she was hurting.

I got out of the car and ran over to her. The bright red spot on her white robe had gotten bigger, but that didn't bother me. The face she was making bothered me. I didn't like to see her in pain.

Juliet held her hand out for me to help her up. "I can walk. The contractions aren't that close together yet. I might be able to make it inside before the next one."

The people inside asked her a lot of questions. They called her mom at work. They called Tony, who, of course, didn't answer. They put Juliet in a gown, in a bed, in a room. They hooked her up to machines and computers and said, "Not yet," when she asked for something to make the pain go away.

Then they left us alone.

And I could see that Juliet was leaving too. Going where I was. Going somewhere that hurt less.

Our bodies were in that room, but our selves were locked out. Looking in through the window.

I didn't want Juliet to be alone. I thought about August. When he was hurting at Trevor's party—I wasn't there for him. I left him alone. Maybe if I hadn't been so selfish—so absorbed in my own feelings and my own drama—he would still be alive.

He.

Alive.

The baby!

My consciousness slammed back into my body and I looked at Juliet, who was cringing and clutching the sides of the bed in the throes of another contraction. I wrapped my hand around hers and shushed her and used my other hand to push the wet hair off her sweaty face, like my mom would have done.

"Something's wrong, BB! There's not supposed to be this much blood! Why won't anyone tell me what's going on? Why won't they give me an epidural yet? Where is the doctor?"

I leaned over the bed railing and moved my hands to her tight swollen belly. I stared at it, concentrating on the little boy inside who needed to come out. Then I did the only thing I could think of—what my mom used to do to calm me down when I was little—I sang "Hey Jude" by the Beatles, softly.

When the song was over, Juliet's hands appeared next to mine on her belly. I looked up at her and saw an unfamiliar wisdom looking back at me. Something ancient was stirring. Women had been doing this since the dawn of time—since before there were Lamaze classes and *What to Expect* books—and we could do it too.

"BB, I want to push."

The ancient voice inside me shouted *No!*

"Not yet," I said, gripping her hand and pushing the call button on the bed rail at the same time. A woman's voice answered through the adjacent speaker, asking how she could help us. No sooner had I uttered the words "She wants to push" than a nurse appeared between Juliet's legs and told her she still had two more centimeters to go.

"If you push now," she explained, "you could damage the baby's head. I'm going to send the anesthesiologist up to give you that epidural now. That should help reduce your urge to push while you finish dilating."

Fifteen minutes later Juliet was completely numb from the waist down and smiling like a drunkard when her mom walked in. I was hoping for Tony, but I'd take what I could get.

Juliet's mom was a moody bitch who was known to slap her kids across the face whenever they mouthed off to her (which was pretty often in Juliet's case), but she and I got along fine. I think she thought I was a good influence on her daughter, and maybe I was, hard as that was to believe. After all, Juliet was the one who introduced *me* to cigarettes, booze, boys, and now...to babies.

When the nurse came back a little while later, she stuck her entire fist inside of my friend and announced that she was ready to start pushing. Since Juliet couldn't feel her legs, the nurse instructed Mrs. Iha and me to each hoist up one of Juliet's thighs and keep them pulled apart to help her push.

From that vantage point I. Could. See. Everything.

It was horrifying. The body fluids. The smells. The tearing. The agonizing, never-ending cycle of pushing and breathing and chewing on ice chips.

Just when I was beginning to think it would never end, the doctor—an older man with white hair and a face that suggested he had better things to do—took out what looked like a pair of pruning shears and fucking CUT A SLIT in Juliet's already ravaged vagina. Out popped her blue and purple baby boy one push later, and while the nurses cleaned him up, Dr. Disinterested stitched her back up with a needle and thread.

Fuck. All. This.

Nope. Nay. Never.

Not my vagina.

Not on my watch.

Because of the bleeding and the baby's distress, the nurses said they would have to run some tests on him before they could hand him over. As soon as they left Juliet fell asleep from sheer exhaustion, and her mom excused herself to go make some phone calls.

Once again, it was just me and Jules in that little room, but everything had changed. She looked so different. Older. Sweatier. Wiser. Wearier. Juliet had turned into a mom before my very eyes.

"Excuse me." One of the nurses poked her head back into the room. "Oh, she's sleeping. You don't happen to know the baby's name, do you? I need to write it on his bracelet and paperwork."

Shit.

"Juliet," I whispered, gently shaking her awake. "Juliet, they need a name for the baby." Her face fell before she'd even opened her eyes, and her chin began to wobble.

"Tony," she whispered, looking absolutely heartbroken.

"You want to name the baby Tony?" I asked, forcing back my own tears.

Oh, God. Tony.

"We were going to name him Anthony Junior—but now..." Her eyes, filled with tears, looked to mine. "He didn't come, BB. He didn't even come. How could he? He missed it! I can't name the baby after him! He didn't even come!"

But I knew the truth. I knew that Tony didn't show up because something bad had happened. Something really, really bad. And now Juliet's baby didn't have a name, and might not even have a father. And it was all my fault.

"I'll name him for you." I didn't know what I was saying. I just needed to fix something for her. Anything. "I'm really good with names! I can do it!"

Juliet wiped her eyes with the edge of the bed sheet and nodded, too angry and heartbroken and traumatized and drugged up to do anything else. "As long as you don't name him after some *asshole*, then go for it."

The nurse who had asked about the baby's name opened the door the rest of the way and pushed in a rolling bassinet. "Take your time with the name, ma'am. We don't technically need it until you discharge. He had a rough start, but his vitals are all within normal limits now."

She reached in and handed Juliet a little man. He was wrapped tightly in a white blanket with blue stripes and had a head full of black hair.

She told us his length and weight, time of birth, et cetera, et cetera, but I was too focused on the little face peeking out from inside that blanket to pay attention. He was awake. And he was looking at his mama.

I didn't know newborn babies could be so alert. I didn't even know they could open their eyes. I thought they were like puppies, all mushy and blind. But not this one. He was so tiny. And beautiful. And when the nurse handed him to my friend, and I saw her face change from devastated to elated, I knew that that little boy was going to turn out to be the best thing that ever happened to her.

Juliet finally had someone who would love her the right way— unconditionally and for the rest of his life.

And that's when the name came to me.

"How about Romeo?"

"Romeo?" Juliet looked down at the handsome baby in her arms and smiled. "Romeo Jude." She snaked one arm around my waist and rested her head on my hip, while we both gazed down at little Romeo Jude Iha. "It's perfect."

I squeezed her back, but the lump in my throat was threatening to choke me. No, it was choking me. I couldn't breathe. The room started to tilt on its axis, and I could feel the walls starting to close in on me.

Oh no. Not here. Not now.

"I'm, just, I'm gonna go to the bathroom..." I remember releasing Juliet and turning to walk toward the bathroom, but the tunnel vision narrowed to blackness before I could get there.

When I woke up I was in Juliet's bed. Or at least what I thought was her bed. I sat up and looked around in confusion. Where was Juliet? Where was the baby? Why was I still there if they were gone? Was the baby okay?

I threw the covers off and went to leave, but a sharp pain in the crook of my arm prevented me from getting very far. I looked down to find an IV line sticking out of my elbow and a hospital gown covering my body.

"What the—"

A hand touched my back just as a voice began to speak from somewhere behind me, "Shh…lie back down, baby. You need to rest a little bit longer."

The voice belonged to my mother. I snapped my head over to the other side of the bed where my mom was sitting in a chair smiling at me anxiously.

"What happened?"

"A nurse called me and said you fainted and hit your head. I came up here as fast as I could. They let me into your room, but I haven't gotten to talk to anyone yet. Did you fall at work? How did you get here, honey?"

Work! Shit! I still needed to return Lisa's car.

I groaned.

"I left work early. I was here with Juliet and her mom… because—"

A nurse whom I hadn't met yet burst into the room wearing light blue scrubs and a scowl. She looked older than my mom—her short hair was mostly gray—and she spoke to her as if she were sitting in the principal's office, not a hospital room. No pleasantries. No nothing.

"Your daughter is suffering from complications of anorexia nervosa, Mrs. Bradley. She weighs ninety-one pounds, which is roughly thirty pounds underweight for her height. As a result, her blood pressure and body temperature are dangerously low. We strongly encourage you to schedule an appointment with our nutritionist and behavioral health specialist before you leave. Brooke is severely malnourished and dehydrated and will not be discharged until she has had enough fluids to urinate."

Who the fuck did that lady think she was? She didn't know me.

She couldn't just come in there and say some upsetting shit like that to my mom. I stared back at Nurse Bitchface, but she acted like I wasn't even there. She was too busy looking at my mom as if she were the scum of the earth, and I didn't fucking appreciate it.

I turned to look at the other side of the bed, where my mom was sitting. Her brow was furrowed and her mouth was slightly agape.

"I'm not anorexic," I declared, turning back to Nurse B. "I eat. I eat every day."

Well, maybe not every *day, but...*

Nurse Bitchface turned her judgmental attention to me and said, "Miss Bradley," hissing on the *S* sound to emphasize that I was still a child. "Anorexia is when someone intentionally maintains an underweight state. Unless you have a terminal illness or a tapeworm, which you do not have, intentional caloric restriction is the only way to maintain a weight this far below normal." She stared at me, daring me to argue with her again.

"Anorexic?" My mom tried the word out and—from the look on her face—decided she didn't like the way it tasted.

"*Mrs.* Bradley, please remove all bathroom scales from your home and have Brooke keep a food diary. Her nutritionist will need to see it. Please buzz the nurses' station when Brooke has urinated, and be sure to schedule those appointments before you leave."

Nurse Bitchface left, and the room was suddenly way too quiet.

I didn't want their "help." I didn't want to go to the behavioral whatever or the goddamn nutritionist. I had finally gotten rid of my gut and I was *not* growing that shit back. They couldn't make me. My body looked like an alien's before—all belly and no breasts. I wasn't going back to that.

I needed to change the subject before my mom made me talk about it. Although the silence in the room told me that she didn't exactly want to talk about it, either.

"What I was going to tell you, before," I said, "is that Juliet is here. I left work early because Juliet was having a baby. A little boy. She let me name him Romeo. And his middle name is Jude, like the Beatles song…"

I was rambling—anything to keep from addressing the emaciated elephant in the room.

"I saw the whole thing, Mom. It was horrible. I had to hold her leg up while she pushed, and there was so much blood. And the sac—whatever the baby was in—looked like a mushy brain when it came out and it was, like, the size of another baby. It was so gross. I am *never* having kids!"

My mom gladly went along with my grossly obvious avoidance tactic and even laughed at my dramatics. That's just one of the innumerable things I love about that woman—when presented with the option to laugh or cry, my mom will choose laughter ninety-nine times out of a hundred.

"If I had seen something like that when I was your age you probably wouldn't be here right now," she said with a knowing smile. "There's no better birth control than seeing what happens when you don't use it."

My mom climbed up onto the bed next to me—which was probably against protocol—wrapped her arm around me, and coaxed my head onto her shoulder. I hadn't realized how much I'd missed her.

After a minute or two she asked me how Juliet was doing. I told her that she was going to be okay, but she was really upset because her boyfriend didn't come to the hospital. What I didn't tell her was that her boyfriend didn't show up because his body might or might not be locked inside the trunk of his Corvette in a junkyard in downtown Atlanta.

My mom sighed and shook her head. "Some men are just assholes, honey. When your Nana went into labor she had to take a cab to the hospital and deliver your daddy by herself because Pop was fall-down drunk at a party and wouldn't leave."

I'd heard that story before, from my father. I thought about his poor mom, delivering her first child all alone, with no family nearby and with no idea what to expect. It made my heart ache for her. At least Juliet had had her mom and me. I wasn't the father of her baby, but I probably did a better job comforting her than fucking Tony would have.

My mom squeezed my arm and said, "Your daddy may not be good for much, but I will say that when I went into labor that man stayed right by my side the entire time. He let me squeeze his hand while I pushed, and he even cut the umbilical cord to help bring you into this world. And do you know what he did when he saw you for the first time?"

"He cried, didn't he?"

My mom laughed. "Your daddy cried like a baby and sang you a Jimi Hendrix song through his tears. It was the sweetest thing I've ever seen. I didn't think I'd ever get a chance to hold you."

My eyes filled and overflowed onto my mom's navy-blue and white tie-dyed T-shirt. August's face appeared in my mind. He'd always reminded me of my dad. Sweet and sensitive and so, so sad. August would have shown up at the hospital for me, whether it was his baby or not.

"It's not fair."

I didn't realize I'd said those words out loud until my mom stroked her thumb across the back of my hand and asked, "What's not fair, baby?"

I looked up and saw her face change as she registered my heartbreak.

"August killed himself last night."

My mom squeezed me tighter. "Oh, God. I'm so sorry, honey. He was such a nice boy."

"He was *so* nice! It isn't fair!"

My mom shushed me and played with my hair while I cried, and when that didn't work to dam up my tears, *she sang.*

My mom was a simple woman. She loved her man, no matter how neurotic and anxious and obsessive-compulsive and reclusive he'd turned out to be. She loved her baby, no matter how she dressed or who she fucked or how much she cursed or what trouble she got into. She loved her plants, her pets, her weed, and her wine. She loved the Beatles. And when she prayed, she prayed to a woman, not a man.

But as gentle and loving and accepting as my mother was, she was also the strongest person I'd ever known. Strong enough to cradle her skinny, broken baby girl with a smile, sing her a song about taking something sad and making it better, and put her back together again.

Chapter 42

When my mom went to fill out my discharge papers, I quickly called Lisa at work to let her know that I was in the hospital. She, of course, told me not to worry about the car. She and her boyfriend would come up there later and get it. I blew out a sigh of relief. My mom was cool and all, but I still didn't want to have to explain why I was in the possession of a Pontiac Grand Prix when I didn't even have my license yet.

Before she hung up, Lisa made sure that I knew that she was "prayin' for me." There seemed to be a lot of that going around.

My mom hit up the Taco Bell drive-through on our way home and ordered half the menu. I ate until I wanted to throw up, but I didn't, for a change. After dinner, I kissed my mom, hugged my oblivious dad, went to bed, and didn't get up until dinner the following night. After which, I went right back to sleep.

On Monday morning, I woke up in a panic. Looking at the clock on my nightstand to see what time it was, I realized there was a handwritten note blocking the digital numbers from my view.

I called the school and told them you were still sick.

Rest up.

Love,
Mom

God, I loved that woman.

I sat up, feeling reborn. Like it had all just been a bad dream. Out there in the woods, with my sweet, easygoing parents, I was separated from the real world. Sheltered. And safe.

I took a long, hot shower, and for once, I didn't fantasize about Lance or cry about Knight. I didn't worry about Tony or mourn over August. I simply delighted in the feeling of hot water coursing over my body.

Not everyone has this, I thought. *I'm so lucky.*

I ate a massive bowl of cereal, and it was as if I were tasting all of the flavors for the first time. I noticed the sounds of birds singing outside while I put on my makeup. And when my dad drove me to work that afternoon, the colors outside my window seemed brighter somehow.

Maybe August was right, I thought. *Maybe I am going to be okay.*

I threw myself into my job. I made a pyramid out of martini glasses so tall that I had to stand on top of a bar stool to finish it. I turned the labels of every single candle so that they were fronted and perfectly aligned. I arranged the throw pillows in the pillow wall by color *and* texture *and* size. And at the end of the day, I dusted off my pants, helped my manager lock up, and inhaled the thick, humid spring air outside as if it were a Caribbean breeze.

Then I choked back vomit when my eyes landed on Knight,

leaning against the grille of his truck in the back of the employee parking lot.

My renewed optimism leaked out through my pores in a cold sweat, forming puddles of what could have been inside my boots.

I could almost feel his hands around my neck again, taking me to the place where it doesn't hurt anymore. To the place where August went. It felt better there than here, where my fingers ached from the absence of his fuzzy blond buzzcut. Where my chest echoed hollow heartbeats that went unanswered. Where the fading tattoo on my finger hurt worse than the needle that had put it there.

I wasn't afraid that Knight would hurt me again. I was afraid that he would leave me whole.

My manager looked at me, then at the skinhead lurking at the edge of the employee-only parking lot, then back at me.

Leaning toward me, she lowered her voice and asked, "You okay, BB?"

Unable to tear my eyes away from the specter in front of me, I muttered, "Yeah. It looks like I don't need a ride after all. I'll see you tomorrow, okay?"

She hesitated, so I forced myself to turn and face her. Faking a smile, I said, "Thanks anyway, Lakshmi."

"Okay, hun. If you're sure. See you tomorrow."

She cast one last suspicious glance at Knight, then hopped into her modest sub-compact and left me there. Alone. In the back parking lot. With the thing that went bump in the night.

Those cold, dead eyes were back, only the monster they belonged to was twice as big as the one I used to fear. He looked like Bruce Banner halfway through his Incredible Hulk transformation. Sleeves torn, muscles literally bulging off of other muscles. And his neck had all but disappeared.

That's his armor, a voice inside me whispered.

And suddenly I saw him, clear as day. Knight was wearing layer upon layer of armor. It was as if every time something had gotten past his defenses, Knight thickened the wall between Ronald and the outside world. His attitude, his aggression, his steel-toed boots, his skinhead wardrobe, his shaved head, the tattoo of a giant shield on his back, his knife, his bat, his room full of guns, his monster truck, his muscles, on top of muscles, on top of muscles—every layer probably had a story behind it. Some trauma, some catastrophic disappointment that he swore he would never let happen again.

Judging by the amount of muscle mass he had put on in two short months, what he went through in the junkyard—and after—must have taken more of a toll on him than I'd realized.

I flashed back to his drawings, hanging on my mother's classroom bulletin board next to mine. Knights and weapons and blood and dragons. Ronald had finally become a knight, but he was slaying all the wrong dragons.

I felt my body begin moving toward him as if pulled by a magnet. I struggled to resist, to think of a way to escape, to swallow, to breathe, to stop my traitorous feet from delivering me to my doom, but I was helpless.

Stopping just beyond arm's reach, I took a deep breath and readied myself for whatever fresh hell awaited me.

Knight's nostrils flared as he inhaled through his nose. His jaw was clenched shut, so I knew whatever he had to say was going to be painful. He was already shutting down, and we hadn't even spoken yet. I usually tried to make him laugh whenever that happened, but I wanted to live in that silence a little bit longer. It was safer in the silence.

Knight looked away and took a few deep breaths through his nose, then swallowed hard. Looking back at me, he forced out the words "Are you okay?"

I didn't know how to answer that. I thought I was okay, or at least getting there, but the pain radiating off of Knight had blanketed my shimmering, iridescent soul in a shroud of gray.

"I've been better," was all I could think of to say.

He inhaled again, deeply, searching for more words. Or maybe he had the words, and he was searching for courage to say them.

Gripping the chrome bumper on either side of his thighs, Knight finally said, "I saw you."

"I know. I saw you too. And I saw your fucking girl—"

"No," he interrupted. "*Here.* I saw you here. Getting out of *his* car." Knight's jaw flexed and his eyes blazed with something that made my blood run cold.

"Knight—"

"I saw you! Right fucking here!" Knight pointed down at the poorly lit pavement beneath our feet. "Getting out of *his* fucking car!"

"Knight—"

"What did I say? What did I fucking say?! I told that motherfucker if he ever gave you a ride again I was gonna kill him! Didn't I?!"

Oh my God. He did hurt Tony.

"Knight." I put my hands in the air the way one would after being cornered by a rabid dog. "I swear to God—I haven't been in a car with Tony since you said that. I haven't even seen Tony."

"Bullshit!" Knight slammed his hand down on the hood of his truck. "Don't fucking lie to me! Tony dropped you off, right here, the morning after your little fucking boyfriend's party!"

The combination of Knight's irrational anger and his mention of Trevor's party had my hands balled into fists at my sides and my eyes temporarily blinded by a bright bloody shade of red. It was as if the word *party* was a psychological trip wire that set off a bomb inside of me that I hadn't even known was there.

Kaboom!

"FUCK YOU!" I screamed, my voice taking on a shrill vibrato that bounced off the back of the store and signaled that my ass was about to come unhinged. "How the *fuck* are you going to come here and act jealous about somebody *driving* me to work after you *drove* that whore to my friend's party so that she could jump me?! Did you have so much fun choking me out in front of half the school that you decided to let your girlfriend have a crack at it, too?!"

I was shaking. All I wanted was for the full moon overhead to give me claws and fangs and the ability to rip his hulking body to shreds like an animal. How fucking *dare* he come there and act jealous. Try to justify whatever he did to Tony when he's out fucking someone else and rubbing it in my face.

I wanted him to die. No, more than that. I wanted to kill him. Knight's bloodlust must have been contagious, because I was feeling absolutely murderous.

"I didn't fucking bring her there to jump you! I'm the one who pulled her off you, remember?"

"No, you fucking didn't! The curb saved my ass, not you! And if you didn't bring her there to jump me, then why the fuck *did* you bring her there? Just to show off your pretty blonde meth head with the big tits? Well, I hope you're using protection, because—"

Knight grabbed me by the wrist and pulled me into his body, wrapping an arm around my neck and a thick hand around my mouth. "Shut the fuck up, Punk!"

I grabbed his hand, but instead of pulling it away from my mouth I pushed it farther in. Then I bit down as hard as I could. The coppery taste of blood hit my tongue just as Knight yelled, "Fuck!" and shoved me away.

He examined his hand quickly, then leveled me with those laser scope eyes.

Adrenaline was pumping through my veins at the speed of light.

I threw my purse on the ground and raised both of my tiny fists, praying that motherfucker would come at me. I was done freezing in the face of fear. I was fucking fighting. I'd never known fury until I met Knight. Or cruelty. Or vengeance. But since meeting him I'd gotten a fucking crash course in all three. And I was a quick study.

Knight stalked toward me, then grabbed my biceps and crushed his forehead into mine before I could even react.

I saw stars and winced in pain as Knight continued pressing his forehead into mine. I had to push back with all my strength just to keep my head upright.

"Now you fucking listen to *me*," he hissed. "You don't know shit, BB. You don't know a motherfucking thing."

"I know you killed Tony," I growled.

Let's do this. I'm ready.

Knight quickly glanced around the parking lot, making sure we didn't have an audience, then growled back, "Get in the truck."

"I'm not going anywhere with you."

Knight's face morphed into something lethal. Eyes narrowed to slits. A pulsing vein bulged between them as his lip curled into a sneer.

"Get in the *fucking* truck."

I jerked against him suddenly, trying to catch him off guard and break free from his grasp, but it was pointless. Before a scream could even escape my lips, Knight had my jaw clamped shut with one hand, and my arms pinned to my sides with the other. I tried to kick free, but Knight dragged my flailing ninety-one-pound body over to the driver's side door as if I were nothing more than a child having a temper tantrum.

Which I was.

As soon as Knight shoved me in I scrambled for the passenger side door, hoping I could yank it open and scurry out before he caught me. The moment my fingertips touched the cool metal of the door handle, a vise clamped down on my ankle and yanked me backward.

Fuck!

I kicked Knight's hand off my leg with one heavy steel-toed boot while struggling to find a place to grip for leverage. Knight responded by wrapping one arm around both of my ankles and hog tying them together with his driver's side seatbelt. Frustrated tears seared my eyes as I shrieked and struggled for my life in vain, hitting and scratching at any exposed flesh my hands could find.

Knight straddled my legs and captured my hands mid-strike. Yanking them above my head, he bound my wrists together with the passenger seatbelt, wrapping them until there was absolutely no slack left. Or hope of escape.

I bucked under him and yanked on my restraints as hard as I could, but that only tightened them more. I had to stop struggling to keep from cutting off my circulation entirely, and the defeat broke me. I rolled onto my side, my arms twisted above my head, buried my face in the cracked vinyl upholstery, and sobbed.

A tidal wave of thoughts flooded my mind, all competing to be my last. Thoughts of Juliet and Romeo. Regrets about not telling anyone where I'd seen Tony's car. Regrets about not turning Knight in to the police when I had the chance. Thoughts of August. Would I get to see him again, in the starry place? Thoughts of Lance and his adorable pick-up lines, and Colton, and even Trevor, smiling at me with red lipstick smeared across his beautiful face.

But mostly, I thought about my parents. How sorry I was that they might never get to see me graduate, or walk down the aisle, or have a baby of my own. How badly I'd fucked up. How much I loved them. How lucky I was to have two people in my life who loved me unconditionally when most of my friends didn't even have one. How much I wished that I had told them that.

Knight suddenly punched the back of his seat, sending shock waves rippling through the cab of the truck, and screamed, "Will you fucking listen to me *now*?"

I quieted my sobs to whimpers and hid the exposed part of my face behind my shoulder, trying to protect myself from whatever emotional or physical lashing Knight was about to deliver.

"Look at me."

Fuck no.

"Open your motherfucking eyes or I swear to God I will pry them open myself."

I complied, just barely, and winced up into the face of the man who would decide my fate.

"Good. Now I'm going to talk, and you're going to fucking listen. Do you understand?"

I nodded once, slightly, and held my breath.

"First of all, I'm not fucking Angel."

"Bullshit," I spat.

Knight clamped his hand down over my mouth again and yelled, "Stop fucking talking! Just listen to me, goddamn it! Blink once if you fucking understand."

Blink.

"I'm. Not. Fucking. Angel."

I narrowed my eyes at him and refused to blink, even though they burned from my running mascara.

"When we broke up she just started following me around, like a lost fucking puppy. I knew she didn't want me. She just wanted me to protect her from her brother's fucking crew. She said they never left her alone and she didn't feel safe at home, so I let her hang out at Peg's house to get away from that shit. That's all. Blink if you're fucking listening."

Another one of his fucking strays. I used to be one of his strays too.

"Blink!" he yelled.

Blink.

"But when I saw how jealous it made you to see us together I let it go too far. I just wanted you to hate me so that you would stop ripping my fucking heart out every day with your big sad eyes at my truck. That shit killed me, Punk. It fucking destroyed me. When Angel started riding home with me you stopped coming around as much. That was all I wanted—to be able to get through the day without having to see you fucking cry. Blink."

As I blinked, a mascara-filled tear rolled down my cheek, right on cue.

"I didn't bring her to your little boyfriend's party to fight you, okay? I didn't even know you were gonna be there. Angel called me screaming and crying from a gas station that night saying that she was running away. I fucking left work to go pick her ass up, and that's where she told me to take her. Now blink."

Bitch.

"Blink, goddamn it!"

Blink.

"When I pulled up and saw that fucking pretty boy hanging all over you I couldn't even see straight. I wanted to make him bite the curb so that I could smash every one of his perfect little teeth out with one boot to the back of his head. I told that motherfucker what would happen if he put his hands on my girl again."

Jesus Christ.

"Then I saw Angel running toward you, and I . . . I lost my fucking mind. I was so mad I blacked out, Punk. That's never happened before. I don't know what I did or where I took her, but when I woke up, I was in my truck, over there"—Knight gestured out the window above my head at an adjacent parking lot—"and Angel's hair was all over my seat."

Knight looked back down at me with a ravine of remorse cutting across his brow. "Blink. Please."

I blinked.

"I decided to just wait there until you came to work. I wanted to see that piece of shit pretty boy drop you off with my own two eyes. I wanted to know if you had spent the night with him, like you used to with me. If you were fucking him. But it wasn't him, *was it*?" Knight's voice rumbled with malice.

I pulled at my restraints and mumbled something indecipherable into his palm. Knight released his grip on my mouth and sat back on his haunches, allowing me to finally speak. The full moon's glow and a distant streetlight illuminated his tortured face.

My jaw was sore from being clamped shut for so long. I opened it slowly, testing it, before I said, "I didn't fuck Trevor. Or Tony. They were just friends, Knight. Am I not allowed to have friends?"

"There's no such thing, Punk."

"No such thing as friends? How can you say that? You used to be my friend."

"I wasn't your friend. I was a guy who wanted to fuck you. Same as Trevor."

"August was my friend."

"August is dead."

"Lance was my friend."

"Because he's a fucking homo."

"Why do you keep saying that?"

"Because he likes to suck dick."

Fuck you, Knight.

"*Tony* was my friend." I let the implication hang in the air.

"I didn't fucking kill him." Knight's scowling face did little to hide the hurt radiating out those crystal-clear irises. He was telling the truth. I was the only person Knight had let see what was underneath his armor, and even I had assumed the worst of him. No, I'd *expected* it.

I sputtered and rambled, trying to explain my reasoning. "I'm sorry, I shouldn't have assumed...It's just...I never told you, but I've been paying Tony to keep the Kings off your back—"

"You've been *what*?" Knight interrupted.

"I was just trying to protect you! Tony said if I missed a payment the deal was off, and I missed my payment on Friday so I thought he was coming after you with Carlos's crew. I tried to warn you, but you weren't answering your phone and you didn't show up at work and then I wandered over to the junkyard and that's when I saw Tony's car, right where...you know..."

"So you assumed I killed him? Did you not read the fucking signs, Punk? The county took over that property and turned it into a police impound lot. If Tony's car was there it's because his dumb fucking ass got arrested."

Oh, thank God.

"But, if he's in jail, then why hasn't he called Juliet to let her know? It's been two days. She was so upset she went into fucking labor!"

"That's not my problem. My problem is that a man goes missing and you automatically assume I fucking killed him."

"Knight, I'm sorr—"

"Don't fucking apologize. You were right. I *do* want to kill Tony—more now than ever. I wanted to kill Trevor with my bare hands in the middle of the fucking street just for lighting your cigarette. I wanted to kill Angel, and for all I know I may have fucking done it. You know what I am. You know it'll happen again. That's why I came to see you tonight."

I wanted to argue with him—to tell him he was wrong, that he wasn't a monster—but we were done lying to each other.

"I came to tell you bye, Punk. I enlisted in the Marines. I'm shipping out on Thursday, right after graduation."

All I heard was *goodbye*, *Marines*, and *after graduation*.

I couldn't speak. And I obviously couldn't move my arms or legs. I just had to lie there and absorb the full force of his words.

"After I put my hands on you last week, I wanted to fucking die. That night I drank an entire fifth of whiskey, drove into the woods, and spent the night with a loaded shotgun pressed under my chin. But I couldn't pull the fucking trigger. I wanted to, so bad, but I got too much fight left in me to take my own life."

Knight stared out the windshield at the back of the building. The moonlight cast severe shadows on his severe face. "That's *all* I got left in me. I can't run from who I am anymore. I'm a killer, just like my grandfather. The only difference is that he killed for his country, to protect the people he loved. I think that's what I'm supposed to do too."

I managed to push a few tiny, squeaky speech sounds past the suffocating lump in my throat. "Where? Where are you going?"

"Basic training in North Carolina, then Iraq. I want to get as far away from you as I can."

His painful words rained down on me like punches, and I had no way to defend myself.

"Why?" I cried. "Why do you have to send yourself into a war zone? Why do you have to get away from me? Why can't we just be together, like we were before?"

"Because look at you!" Knight yelled, jerking the bottom of my T-shirt all the way up to my chin. He wrapped both of his thick hands around my rib cage and squeezed, his fingers digging into the valleys between each bone. "Because you're fucking dying, and I'm the one killing you!"

His chin began to quiver, and angry tears glistened, unshed in his mist-colored eyes. I wanted so badly to reassure him that I was fine. That if he stayed we'd live happily ever after. I'd go to college, and he'd open a tattoo parlor, and we'd have a little boy and name him Diesel or Axel and he'd be smart like me and strong like his daddy, but I couldn't. Because it wasn't true.

The truth was that Knight had already hurt me worse than any human being ever had or ever would, and I knew that when the going got tough, he'd do it again. He'd push me away. Torture me to make me hate him. Convince me that he really was the monster he wanted everyone to believe. But even knowing what he was capable of, and how bleak our future together would be, it still didn't stop a fresh stream of black tears from running down my cheeks.

"Knight," I whispered. "Untie me. Please?"

Knight released my exposed ribs and unwound the nylon straps from my wrists and ankles. As soon as my arms were free I spread them wide and said, "Come here."

I'd never seen a soul so broken. Knight's glistening eyes and pained expression weren't Knight's at all. They were Ronald's—the freckle-faced boy with the soft, fuzzy head who loved animals and drawing and always did his chores. I cradled him to my concave breast, and shushed him like his mama never did.

Shh-shh-shh-shh-shhhhhhhh . . .

While I rubbed Knight's broad, rippled back with one hand, I raked my fingertips over *Ronald's* velveteen head with the other. While the arms of a bulletproof man wrapped around my body, pulling me to him, the soul of a boy shuddered softly in my embrace. Because of Knight, Ronald had to go away. He didn't want to leave. He wanted to stay there and let me love him.

I wanted that too.

I pulled his frowning face to mine and kissed him for the first time in what felt like centuries. His lips felt like home. His cinnamon musk smelled like heaven. And in my mind, I was transported to an itchy brown couch in my ex-boyfriend's living room where, together, Ronald and I taught Knight about love.

Ronald may have been the one kissing me, but it was Knight who shoved my pants down around my ankles and entered me in one desperate thrust. Followed by another. And another. I wasn't ready for him. It was too much, too fast. And he knew it. It was as if Knight was taking control back from Ronald. Ronald may have wanted a sweet goodbye, but Knight would rather burn what we had to the ground.

I wrapped my hands around his hipbones and pushed against him to keep his next thrust from entering as deeply. Then I looked up, into his conflicted eyes, and said, "Hey, Ronald."

His body stilled. His breathing stopped. And the voice of the boy whose drawings hung next to mine all those years ago answered back.

"Hey, Brooke."

Smiling, I said, "Guess what?"

Knight's brow furrowed in confusion, but Ronald knew what game I was playing. "What?" he asked.

"I love you."

Smiling back, Ronald said, "I love you, too, Punk."

I sat up and kissed him, guiding him backward until I was able to straddle him, my jeans still bunched around the tops of my boots. In that position, neither Knight nor Ronald was in control. I was. And I wanted to love them both. One last time.

We came together—all three of us—and for one generous moment, time stopped. We stayed like that—joined in every way, foreheads mashed together, heartbeats synchronized—and just breathed, until the silence was broken by the sound of my phone ringing from somewhere outside the truck.

"My mom's probably wondering where I am," I whispered, the imminence of our goodbye starting to sink in.

"What are you gonna tell her?"

"I'll just tell her that I ran into a friend," I said.

"You're not my fucking friend, Punk. You're my everything. You will always be my everything. I just hope you can find somebody better than me to be yours."

Chapter 43

That was the last time I saw Knight before he left for basic training. The next day I went to school for the first time in a week, actually hoping to see him, but he wasn't there. Angel wasn't either, and I wondered if she was okay.

Juliet was at home with Romeo. I'd called her after Knight dropped me off the night before and suggested that she call the county jail to look for Tony. And that's exactly where she found him—alive and well.

Juliet found out that Tony had been arrested for selling crank to a narc, but they'd been able to connect him with a whole lot of other drug sales—including one to August Embry that they were trying to use as evidence that he contributed to the death of a minor. Tony was being held without bail and was facing major jail time. He hadn't called Juliet to tell her because he'd left his phone in his car when he got arrested and his dumb ass didn't have a single phone number memorized. Classic fucking Tony.

On Wednesday, I took my final exams. I'd missed the entire week of review leading up to them, and was in no frame of mind for a cram session, so I just used the copy machine at work to shrink all my study guides to the size of large note cards. I stashed them under my thighs while I took my tests. Any time I got to something I didn't know I'd spread my legs a little bit and look down. Worked like a charm. My 4.0 GPA was safe.

Thursday was the last day of school. I only went so that I could pick up my report card and proof of attendance. You had to have both to get your driver's license, and my sixteenth birthday was less than two weeks away.

I also went because graduation was that afternoon.

I sat by myself in the bleachers, baking in the late-May sun and rubbing the tattoo that was now almost completely gone. I wondered what Lance was up to. I missed him. The sting of that unrequited love suddenly felt like a fun little distraction compared to the agony of true love lost.

All my other friends were gone, dead, or at home with babies. But Lance, he was still a big fat question mark. Was he still in Las Vegas? Were he and Colton in school? Did I have enough money for bus fare to go live with them?

I hadn't heard from either one of them since they'd moved. They didn't even come in town for August's viewing—not that anyone else did, either. And not that there was anything to view. August's "service" consisted of a half-dozen lawn chairs clustered in the overgrown weeds next to his mama's trailer, filled with the asses of a few aunts and uncles who were drinking Natural Ice out of the can and arguing about NASCAR.

August had been right.

Nobody fucking cared.

I scanned the sea of graduates down below—looking for one in particular—but I knew without even straining my eyes that he wasn't there. I could feel it. Or rather, I couldn't feel it. There was no sizzle in the air. No waft of cinnamon on the breeze. Only the heavy humid summer heat, smothering me.

I needed shade, a cigarette, and a good cry. I slunk off through the parking lot, through the woods, and didn't stop until I felt the familiar crunch of gravel under my feet. I dug a Camel Light out of my purse and lit it, inhaling a little deeper than usual. When I exhaled and looked up, what I saw startled the cigarette right out of my hand. Its red-hot tip burned through my flesh on its way to the ground.

The entire side of the church bore the black silhouette of a knight on horseback, identical to the tattoo that had once been on the inside of my left ring finger. Black spray-paint cans littered the ground. I didn't even bother to look for him—I knew he was long gone.

I sat on the railroad ties on the edge of the parking lot and stared at the image, trying to determine whether or not I was hallucinating. Although I felt much saner than I had the day I took Juliet to the hospital, I still had moments every day where I wondered if I was *right* yet. If time was racing for everyone, or just me. If watching myself from above and feeling like an amateur puppeteer was normal, or if that was my own special brand of psychosis.

I was definitely having one of those *Am I still crazy?* moments, because not only was the image of my tattoo spray painted across the side of the church, but there also appeared to be a steady stream of smoke drifting out of a broken window just beside it.

I hope it's real, I thought, picking my still-lit cigarette out of the gravel.

When the temperature began to rise, I decided I wasn't crazy. And when the sad old building began to creak and moan as its insides burned, it spoke to my soul.

I feel you, old girl. It'll all be over soon. Just let it happen.

A rustling in the woods near the back of the church caught my attention. I looked over, expecting to see another bored graduation attendee sneaking away for a smoke, but it wasn't.

It was Lance Motherfucking Hightower.

Goddamn it. Now I know I'm hallucinating.

I would have been elated to see him, had it been the real him, but I was pretty sure this version was just the product of my stress-scorched synapses misfiring. Something about him was off. Different. I didn't trust this apparition.

For one, he was wearing normal clothes. No, not normal. Fancy. He looked like he'd just stepped out of *GQ* magazine. The dyed part of his Mohawk had been cut off—leaving him with a shorter, perfectly coiffed, dark brown 'do—and on his head were a pair of expensive-looking sunglasses. Lance was still wearing all black, but his slacks and T-shirt were crisp and looked like they'd been tailor-made for him. But the biggest change was the pair of leather sandals on his feet where his boots should have been.

He looked like Lance's stylish evil twin.

Whoever or whatever it was, it kept coming toward me, so I stood up and met it halfway—with arms outstretched, just in case it really was my long-lost love.

When Lance noticed me, he smiled and said, "Hey, girl!" before accepting my hug, but his embrace was quick and cold.

I answered back automatically, "What's up?" but Lance didn't have a pick-up line for me this time. He was more interested in checking out the source of the smoke. Lance took a few steps past me to look at the situation, then stopped and lit a cigarette of his own.

Gesturing to the burning building beside us, Lance asked, "You do that, you bad girl?"

I shook my head. "I just got here. I was at the graduation ceremony and got bored. When did you get back? God, I haven't seen you in forever."

"Oh, I don't know. A while ago." Lance's voice had a tinge of sass to it, as if he were intentionally being coy with me.

"Really? Why haven't I seen you at school?"

"I'm taking online classes."

Oh, right. Because Peach State High probably expelled you for drug possession.

"That's cool," I said, trying to mask the hurt in my voice. All that time that I'd been out there smoking by myself after Knight and I broke up and Lance had been just a few hundred feet away. Why hadn't he come out to see me?

"How was Las Vegas?" I asked. "Did you make it to Colton's dad's house? Dude, please tell me that he used to be in Whitesnake."

Lance took another drag from his cigarette, then held it away from his fancy clothes as he exhaled.

"It was fun, but there was some...*drama*, so I came back after a few weeks."

Everything about him was different. His mannerisms, even the way he talked. He sounded so...

No way.

Had Knight been right all along? I scanned my memory for any missed signs. I mean, Lance's voice was always kind of...effeminate, for someone so big and rough-looking, but he kissed me! Why would he do that if he was gay?

Then, I thought about August. He had kissed me, and he turned out to be gay. Hell, he talked about getting married and having kids with me.

August.

Lance.

Oh, my fucking God.

The words, "Lance, were you and August seeing each other?" exploded from my mouth like a gunshot.

Lance snorted as he took another drag. Even the way he held his cigarette was different. Pinky up, like a teacup. "I guess you could call it that."

"What did *you* call it?" I snapped, my hands beginning to shake.

This? This was the motherfucker who hurt my August? Made him hate himself? Made him leave me?

I couldn't believe it. But there he was. Outing himself to me in a pair of two-hundred-dollar Armani flip-flops.

"I didn't call it anything," Lance said, rolling his eyes.

"What is *that* supposed to mean?" I seethed.

"It was supposed to just be fun. Jesus." Lance blew a delicate little stream of smoke out and said, "These cherry boys are so much fucking work. You take somebody's V-card and suddenly they want to fly to Vermont and get married."

Boys?

"Lance, did you cheat on him? Is that why he…was so upset?"

Is that why he threw himself off a fucking water tower?

Lance let out an exasperated sigh and put his free hand on his hip. "God*damn*. I just came out here to see what was on fire. I didn't know I was going to get the third degree."

Always so clever.

Annoyed with me and choosing his next words carefully, Lance said, "You can't cheat on someone you're just fucking, B. But speaking of cheating, you might want to sit down because I've got some news for you, Little Miss Perfect."

I stared at him defiantly, but my gut was churning with anticipation.

"Your angry little boy toy Knight cheated on you too."

What?

"With who?"

"With *me*."

I burst out laughing. I couldn't help it. Everything was so tense that Lance's little joke caught me off guard. Knight was the straightest person I'd ever met.

"I'm serious as a heart attack, honey. Knight fucked around with me while you guys were together."

He *seemed* serious, but it made no sense. "You're so full of shit. Have you even met Knight?"

Lance took another dramatic drag from his cigarette and said in a matter-of-fact tone, "It's always the biggest homophobes who turn out to be gay."

Knight isn't a homophobe, I thought. *He just hates you.*

After everything that had happened I didn't know who the fuck to believe anymore, but my gut told me it wasn't this person. In the six months since I'd last seen him *this* person had changed his entire wardrobe, his personality, his sexual orientation, and had driven my sad, sweet August to suicide. This person was a fucking stranger.

"When did this happen?" I asked, challenging him.

"The day before I left for Vegas. I sucked him off in his truck between classes."

Holy shit. I saw them walking through the parking lot together that day. I remember thinking that was super weird. And then Knight was in such a shitty mood after school, and...

"He attacked you that afternoon," I said.

"Yeah, *and* he fucking narced on me the next day." Lance flicked his cigarette in the direction of the burning building. "Knight just wanted me out of the picture so that he wouldn't have to face the fact that he's gay."

"Bullshit," I spat. A crash sounded next to us as flames ate away at the broken window frame. "Knight and I had sex, Lance. Like, crazy, amazing sex. All the time. How would he be able to do that *with a girl* if he were gay?"

Lance looked me up and down and smirked. "I hate to be the one to say this to you, B, but...look at yourself. You're basically a super-fucking-hot boy with a vagina. You're like, every gay man's gateway drug."

I couldn't tell if the intense heat I was feeling was from the church, which was now completely engulfed in flames to my right, or from the shame and embarrassment that I'm sure were turning my face a nice rosy shade of *fuck you*.

Another crash sounded next to us, and this time I looked. The image of Knight's burning artwork in my periphery emboldened me, and I shoved Lance backward with both hands. I shouted over the fire, over the cheering families and friends at the stadium on the other side of the woods, and over the sound of my own run-away heartbeat, "Do you want to know *why* my body looks like a boy's, Lance? It's because of YOU!"

I shoved him again, causing him to take a step backward, but he didn't seem threatened. He simply smirked at me in response.

"It's because I've been trying to lose weight since the moment I first saw YOU!"

Shove.

"And the longer you led me on, the harder I worked to be pretty for YOU. Skinny for YOU."

Shove.

"I started wearing studs and patches and punk rock T-shirts, for YOU."

Shove.

"Do you like these boots? I saved up for an entire summer to buy them so that I could impress YOU when I came back to school."

Shove.

"I shaved my fucking head, for YOU."

Shove.

"So if I look like a little boy, it's only because deep down I must have known that that's what YOU really wanted."

I gave Lance one last shove, the hardest one yet. That cruel side-ways smile still played on his lips as he went to humor me with another step backward. Only this time there was nowhere for his foot to go. He had backed up all the way to the edge of the gravel parking lot without either one of us realizing it. The bottom of his sandal got caught in the railroad ties as the rest of him kept traveling backward.

I watched in slow motion as Lance's big body went down, turning and extending one hand to brace for impact at the last minute.

Then I heard a snap.

And a scream.

Lance rolled onto his side in a bed of pine needles, grunting and shrieking and cradling his left arm to his chest. It didn't look right. A huge lump was jutting out of his skin, just above his elbow, and the rest of his arm below that was bent at an unnatural angle.

"You fucking bitch!" he cried. "You broke my arm!"

I stood over him as he writhed—one foot on either side of his beautiful Armani-swathed body—knelt down, and pointed the butt of my cigarette in his face. "I used to think Knight was a monster, but I was wrong." I flicked the cigarette behind me—adding it to the pile of burning, forgotten things in my past—and jabbed my index finger into his chest.

"It was YOU. The whole fucking time. You're the monster."

Through the sounds of the crackling fire, the crowd, and the cries, I somehow registered the wail of sirens in the distance. Glancing over my shoulder at the empty street beyond, I caught a glimpse of the blazing hole in the side of the church where Knight's image stood minutes earlier. It was gone. Just like my tattoo. Just like *him*.

I looked down at the crumpled vulnerable boy on the ground before me, curled into the fetal position and whimpering like a little bitch. Then, I flashed back to the first time I ever laid eyes on Knight, right there in that very parking lot. As I recalled, he was standing over another crying, sniveling little shit who liked to run his mouth.

You know what? Maybe that fucker did have it coming...And maybe this one does too.

And with that thought, I pulled my ten-pound steel- and leather-covered foot back as far as I could, and kicked Lance Hightower directly in the lower back, a few inches away from his spine, right in the motherfucking kidney.

Then, I ran like hell.

Chapter 44

Staying off the main roads, I cut through Lance's neighborhood and made a beeline straight for the highway. I only stopped once, to wait for the light to change so that I could cross the four-lane highway that bisected our town. By then I was too tired to keep running anyway. On the other side of the highway I walked through the parking lot of a strip mall shopping center, an apartment complex, and a used car lot before making my way back into the woods.

And up the steep hill.

To the place where I drank my first sip of whiskey and lost my first friend.

Pouring sweat and gasping for air by the time I reached the top, I was simply too tired to consider what I might see up there. I guess, if I had thought about it, I would have expected it to look the way I'd left it—insensitive yellow police tape, maybe a heart on the ground with our initials in it, and not much else—but what I saw took my breath away. What little breath I had left after that climb.

Teddy bears—dozens of them—littered the ground. All colors

and sizes. White wooden crosses jutted out of the hard clay, dripping with silk flowers. Framed photos of August were propped up against tree trunks—some included images of kids I knew, draping their arms around him and smiling for the camera. And tiny white candles—their paper skirts soiled—peeked out from under a thin layer of fresh pine needles.

All the anger and exhaustion I carried with me up that hill drifted away like a balloon on the breeze, and for the first time in almost a week, I smiled. Tears pricked my eyes as a bubbly feeling spread through my body and out of my mouth. Laughter so loud that it chased the birds from their nests erupted from me, and I watched in wonder as the flock took to the sky through the opening in the canopy surrounding the water tower. They were so beautiful. Fast and graceful and free.

As I squinted into the white-hot midday sky, an even whiter thing caught my eye. It floated down to earth and landed gracefully at my feet. It was a feather. Long and full. *An angel feather*, I thought. I didn't even believe in angels, but I knew. August was there, just like he said he would be.

I picked up the feather and kissed it, blinking back bittersweet tears as I whispered, "Look at all your teddy bears," into its downy tufts.

Ducking under the yellow barricade, I walked over to the front side of the tower, to the spot where the clearing was. Stroking the underside of my chin with the feather, I remembered the conversation I'd had with Knight there months before. How his truck and pockets held so many World War II mementos from his grandfather. Maybe joining the Marines would be good for him after all. Give him a sense of purpose. A more productive outlet for of all his rage. I hoped so.

I thought about what Lance said too, about him and Knight.

Maybe he just made the whole thing up to deflect from the fact that I knew about August. Or maybe he was jealous that I'd been giving my undivided attention to someone else when it had belonged to him for so many years. But as I gazed out at the column of smoke rising from the spot where Knight and I first met, I realized that it didn't matter. What we'd shared had been real.

Knight had allowed himself to be vulnerable with me. Only me. He'd let me in, shown me everything that was broken, and then watched helplessly as I tinkered around, not fixing much of anything. He'd come to me broken, and he'd left me broken, and I vowed, right then and there, that it would never happen again.

For the first time in my life, I felt like I had a purpose.

I was going to become a psychologist.

I was already on my way to an early graduation, but I hadn't been pushing for it too hard because I didn't want to leave all my friends. Well, I didn't have that problem anymore. All my friends were ghosts. Even the ones who were still alive. Not a single one of them would be back at Peach State High School the next year. And that's when I decided—neither would I.

A small smile tugged at my lips as I stared down at the smoking crater below—the place where so many bad things had happened—and a lightness filled me.

"I'm never going back there," I whispered into my feather.

I was free.

With my grades, I could enroll in community college for my junior year instead of attending a regular high school, and, if I busted my ass, I could skip my senior year altogether. By the time I turned seventeen, I could enroll at a major university with a few college credits already under my belt.

I relaxed.

I lit a cigarette.

I stroked the underside of my chin with my angel feather.

And together, August and I watched our old life burn.

All my friends may have been ghosts, but me?

I felt more alive than ever.

EPILOGUE

I didn't think it would ever happen, but that summer I finally fucking turned sixteen. I didn't have enough money to buy a car yet, but my mom agreed to loan me what I needed to make it work. I was a muscle car girl on a Ford Escort budget, but I managed to find a '93 Mustang hatchback with a five-liter engine and, much to my dismay, a stick shift transmission for pretty cheap. It wasn't exactly vintage, but at least I wouldn't have to rely on a boy for rides ever again.

All I'd wanted for my birthday that year was every Mustang accessory ever made. I got a pony key chain and pony-embroidered floor mats and little pony mud flaps and a shiny pony license plate cover. But the coup de grace was the brand-new set of alloy five-spoke pony wheels that my parents gave me to replace the piece of shit plastic hubcaps the car had come with.

Evidently, A&J Auto Body was the cheapest shop in town—and for good reason. The place was grimy as hell and appeared to have been decorated by a blind person in the 1970s. A squat, furry, troll-like man who looked like he had a dark brown toupee stuffed in the collar of his shirt greeted me with a grunt, then took my keys and left me standing at the front desk.

Not knowing where to go, I wandered through a door to what I assumed would be a nicotine-colored waiting area but instead found myself in the main garage. I normally would have just turned around and gone back in, but the car on the lift closest to me refused to let me leave.

It was love at first sight—a late '60s Mustang fastback body style, matte black paint job, matte black rims, blacked-out windows, and a massive open-air scoop on the hood. It looked like something straight out of *Mad Max*.

"Can I help you with somethin'?"

I turned and met the amused stare of a broad-shouldered, baby-faced, blue-eyed mechanic. His dirty-blond hair was pushed back in a messy pompadour. His forearms were covered in hot-rod tattoos. His pouty bottom lip was pierced. And his name was embroidered on the A&J Auto Body shirt hugging his hard chest.

Hellooo, Harley.

"Sorry," I sputtered. "I know I'm probably not supposed to be back here, but I..." I looked back up at the beast on the lift, and a deep longing seized my chest. "I can't leave her."

Harley—if that was even his real name—chuckled and said, "So, you like the ladies, huh?"

"What? No!" I snapped.

"Good." The mechanic smiled, and the twinkle in his mischievous blue eyes reminded me just how much I liked boys.

Trying to bring the subject back to cars and away from my sexual orientation, I looked around the garage and pointed to my faded black hatchback on the farthest lift. "I drive the baby version of this."

Harley glanced over at my most prized possession and nodded in approval. "Five-oh, huh? Not bad. Manual or automatic?"

"Manual," I groaned.

"No shit? Your boyfriend teach you how to drive that thing?"

"No," I said, letting my mouth hang open in pretend offense.

"Ah." Harley nodded. "You met him after you got the car."

"I don't have a boyfriend," I said, rolling my eyes.

God, he was cute. The guy had a face like James Dean and a body like Dean Cain. And that accent. In the South, southern accents are a dime a dozen, but Harley's was just subtle enough to be cute. Cute, cute, cute.

Harley smirked at me and asked, "Your old man must be a car guy then, huh?"

"You got me." I smiled. "I've been hoarding all his old *Muscle Car* magazines since I was a kid. I used to cut out all the Mustang pictures and tape them to my bedroom walls, but the tape fucked up the Sheetrock, so my mom bought one of those clear plastic shower curtains with the photo pockets and—"

Harley held up a hand to silence me. "I'm gonna have to stop you right there," he interjected, " 'cause right now all I can picture is you in the shower, and I'm pretty sure I'm not gonna be able to process another word you say."

Oh my God!

I could feel the prickly heat of a blush creeping up my neck. I bit the insides of my cheeks to keep my face from splitting open into a blotchy, big-toothed grin caused by his sexy little comment. This guy, Harley, had to be in his early twenties, he was fiiiine as hell, and he was flirting with me.

Having no idea how to respond to that, I tried again to change the subject. "So, what do you drive?"

"Hmm…" Harley tilted his head and smirked. "Why don't you take a guess?"

Oh, we're playing games now. Okay…

I tapped my lips with my fingertips and eyed him, thinking hard.

"You strike me as a…Volkswagen Beetle kinda guy."

Harley almost laughed, then quickly scowled, trying to look offended.

"No? Oh, I got it. PT Cruiser."

Harley pursed his ample lips, fighting back a grin.

"Wood-paneled Pinto?"

That one had him wrinkling his nose in genuine horror.

"Oh, I know! It's a trick question! You drive a Vespa!"

Snort.

I was running out of ideas, so I looked around the shop and spotted a '64 Impala lowrider. "Ooh! I found it. Right there," I said, pointing to the hooptie. "The gold rims were a nice touch. I bet you even put hydraulics on it, didn't you?"

Harley finally let out the laugh he'd been biting back. It was deep and raspy and made my insides tingle.

"You're getting warmer," he said. "It's actually on hydraulics right now." Harley lifted an oil-smudged finger and pointed to the matte black sex machine above my head.

"No!" I screamed and smacked him in the chest with the back of my hand. "No fucking way!"

"Yep. That's my old lady." Harley beamed.

"Oh my God! That's yours? Yours? Like you own it? And you get to drive it? Holy shit! What year is it? A '69? What engine does it have? Is it all original?"

Harley cocked his head to one side and said, "You said you're a muscle car girl—you tell me."

"Oh, shit." I rubbed my hands together, accepting his challenge. "Let's see…if it's a '69, which I think it is, then it could be a GT, a Mach One, or a Boss. Or an E, but those are super rare. The GTs had different hood scoops than this one, and I'm pretty sure the Mach Ones had cable and pin tie-downs. So, this has got to be a Boss, right? But is it a Boss 302 or a Boss 429? Ugh!"

Harley let out a low whistle and clapped his oil- and tattoo-covered hands together a few times. "Damn, girl. If you weren't so young, I'd ask you to marry me."

I laughed on the outside, but on the inside I was doing fucking round-off back handsprings. The owner of that car, and that face, and that body, and those tattoos was flirting with me!

Unable to filter my big fucking mouth, I said, "You know, sixteen-year-olds can get married in the state of Georgia as long as they have a note from their parents."

Harley laughed and said, "Well, hell. I guess I'd better scrounge up a ring quick 'cause I'm not lettin' you get away."

My stomach did a double salto with a full twist and stuck the fucking landing.

I decided to change the subject from our impending engagement back to the car, if only to help me regain my composure.

"So, is it a 302 or a 429?" I asked, nudging my head toward the matte black orgasm on wheels above us.

"Guess you're just gonna have to wait to find out."

"Ah, man!" I whined. "Wait until when?"

"Tonight." Harley grinned at me like the devil himself, about to convert another sinner. "I'm taking you to the track, lady."

Knight, Harley, and BB's story
continues in *Speed*.
Available now.

PLAYLIST

The following playlist includes most of the '90s punk/alternative songs mentioned in this book, as well as several modern-day tracks that I listened to while writing it. I am grateful to all of these brilliant artists. Their blood, sweat, and tears provided me with hours of "Knightspiration." You can stream the playlist for free on Spotify here:

https://open.spotify.com/user/bbeaston/playlist/3dStteQk
F2a995rMa7r1fg

"Be Alone" by Paramore
"Blood in the Cut" by K. Flay
"Calling All" by Phantogram
"Can't Sleep" by K. Flay
"Catch" by The Cure
"Cities in Dust" by Siouxsie and the Banshees
"Daddy Issues" by The Neighbourhood
"Die, Die My Darling" by Misfits
"Ego" by The Sounds
"Fade Into You" by Mazzy Star
"Fire Escape" by Andrew McMahon in the Wilderness
"Genghis Khan" by Mike Snow
"Gold" by Kiiara
"Joga" by Björk

"Mr. Jones" by Counting Crows

"Mr. Self Destruct" by Nine Inch Nails

"Rise Above" by Black Flag

"Sheena Is a Punk Rocker" by Ramones

"Skinhead on the MBTA" by Dropkick Murphys

"Sound System" by Operation Ivy

"Strange Girl" by The Airborne Toxic Event

"Stubborn Love" by The Lumineers

"The Cops" by K. Flay

"You Don't Get Me High Anymore" by Phantogram

ACKNOWLEDGMENTS

This book almost killed me. I didn't sleep. I didn't eat. I didn't bathe. I didn't leave the house, and I considered taking up smoking again because my characters just made it seem so damn cool. I ate angst for breakfast, lust for lunch, and depravity for dinner—interspersed with chai tea and red wine. I became a zombie-eyed freak myself, for a time, and these are the people who loved me through it.

Ken—This year was probably harder on you than anyone. I quit my good-paying job as a school psychologist—the job you supported me through seven years of college to do—to stay home with the kids and write romance novels about you and my ex-boyfriends. You weren't happy about that, obviously. You made spreadsheets, lots of them. You refused to read my books. (Thank God.) But you still came with me to every single author event. You analyzed my sales and tracked my budget. And you helped out with the kids when I was too sleep-deprived to remember how pants work. You are the true definition of a life partner. No, I take that back. *Life partner* implies one life. You, sir, are my soul mate. Thank you for letting me have this.

Knight—Writing this book felt like exhuming a body. It was arduous work, it happened under the cover of nightfall, and there were ghosts involved. I could feel yours cheering me on like a drill sergeant and filling my head with crazy, violent thoughts. I hope I did you justice. And I hope that, wherever you are, you've found peace.

Mom—If I ever killed somebody, I'm pretty sure you would help me bury the body, but only after tripping over a rock and dropping your side of the cadaver in a puddle and laughing your ass off for fifteen minutes about it while I dug the hole all by myself. You are unconditional love personified. You support me without question and without fail. You never take life too seriously. You never ask for thanks or recognition. You are the kind of mom I aspire to be.

Ken's Mom—Mrs. Easton, thank you so for stepping up to watch my children while I gallivanted all over the country promoting books that you are never, ever, *ever* allowed to read. I love you.

My Editor, Ellie McLove—Thank you, from the bottom of my heart, for always squeezing me in at a moment's notice, working with any deadline I threw at you, being available at *literally* all hours of the night to answer my questions, and for supporting my Shia LaBeouf meme habit. You are a magical unicorn, and you spoil me rotten.

My Formatter, Jovana Shirley—You knock it out of the park every time, lady. Your professionalism and attention to detail are unparalleled. Thank you for being on my team.

My Agents, Flavia, Meire, and Maria at Bookcase Literary Agency—I know it's not easy to sell books that don't fit into one category. Thank you for embracing my strange, genre-bending style and finding homes for these stories on bookshelves all over the world.

My Talent Manager, Larry Robins—You have been my champion since the very beginning. Thank you for arguing with me when I told you, "It's a book, not a movie." I hope you prove me wrong.

My Beta and Proof Readers (April, Bex, Chante, Jamie, Kellie, Mary, Meg, Leigh, Sunny, and, of course, Sara Snow)—

You guys: Hey! We heard you wrote another book! We want to read it right now and find all your typos for free!

Me: Uh...okay?

You girls are my bottom bitches. The fact that anybody cares about Knight's story will never cease to amaze me, nor will the fact that you ladies continue to support me so rabidly. I have the best friends in the world. I love you!

Colleen Hoover—Thank you for not judging me even a little bit when I showed up at your fancy book signing still drunk from the night before and wearing a two-person Christmas sweater with only one person in it. Thank you also for inspiring me every day, to be my silly self, to dream big, to give back, to support others, and to always be bold and brave. You are beautiful, lady.

Ace Gray—Or should I say, Ace Cray? It's a good thing you and I live on opposite sides of the country because the two of us together is a recipe for facial tattoos, amateur porn, and liver transplants. Thank you for being my biggest cheerleader and the bearer of my name. Ken could learn a thing or two from you.

KinkyGirlsBookObsessions (Kellie, Chante, Jen, and Andrea)—Y'all a bunch of pimps and hustlers and I think we should buy a mansion and live together forever. I love you!

My Author Friends and Muses (Brittainy C. Cherry, Tillie Cole, Claire Contreras, Jay Crownover, Mary Elizabeth, Tarryn Fisher, T.M. Frazier, Ace Gray, Staci Hart, Helena Hunting, Colleen Hoover, Charleigh Rose, Kennedy Ryan, Jamie Shaw, Kandi Steiner, L.J. Shen, K. Webster, and many more)—In a society that teaches us to compete, compete, compete, you ladies chose to share instead. You shared with me your time, your advice, your encouragement, your resources, and often, your platforms, to help me succeed in an oversaturated market where so very few do. Thank you for letting this pink-haired, foul-mouthed new kid sit with you.

The Readers, Bloggers, and Bookstagrammers of #TeamBB— Thank you for the gorgeous teasers, the comments and shares, the reviews that never fail to make me cry, the thoughtful gifts, and the relentless, rabid support you've showered me with over the years. You overwhelm me with your love, and I hope when you come see me at an event or interact with me online that you feel it returned tenfold.

A few exceptional #TeamBB teaser makers whom I would like to thank personally for their help promoting *Skin* are (in alphabetical order by first name) Amber Cooper, Amada Söderlund, Amanda Young, BexLovesBooks, Cassandra Magnussen, Crystal Blanton, Danielle Robbins, Dyllan Erikson, Emma Healy, Innergoddess Booklover, Jen Wachowski, Kellie Richardson, Kristi Webster, Lisa Marie Soares, Lisa Mondragon, Lisa Reads, Liz Milner, Lyndsey Aaron, Mabkenyie Bibliophile, Maria Blalock, Meg Tracy, Mia's Book Blog, Simmy Owens, Sonal Dutt, Sonya Paul, Sunny Borek, and Susan Rees. I cherish your art, your passion, and your friendship.

ABOUT THE AUTHOR

BB Easton lives in the suburbs of Atlanta, Georgia, with her long-suffering husband, Ken, and two adorable children. She recently quit her job as a school psychologist to write books about her punk rock past and deviant sexual history full-time. Ken is suuuper excited about that.

BB's memoir, *Sex/Life: 44 Chapters About 4 Men*, and the spin-off Sex/Life novels are the inspiration for Netflix's steamy, female-centered dramedy series of the same name.

The Rain Trilogy is her first work of fiction. Or at least, that's what she thought when she wrote it in 2019. Then 2020 hit and all of her dystopian plot points started coming true. If you need her, she'll be busy writing a feel-good utopian rom-com to see if that fixes everything.

You can find her procrastinating at all of the following places:

Email: authorbbeaston@gmail.com
Website: www.authorbbeaston.com
Facebook: www.facebook.com/bbeaston
Instagram: www.instagram.com/author.bb.easton
Twitter: www.twitter.com/bb_easton
Pinterest: www.pinterest.com/artbyeaston
Goodreads: https://goo.gl/4hiwiR

BookBub: https://www.bookbub.com/authors/bb-easton
Spotify: https://open.spotify.com/user/bbeaston
Etsy: www.etsy.com/shop/artbyeaston
#TeamBBFacebookgroup: www.facebook.com/groups/BBEaston
And giving away a free e-book from one of her author friends each month in her newsletter: www.artbyeaston.com/subscribe.